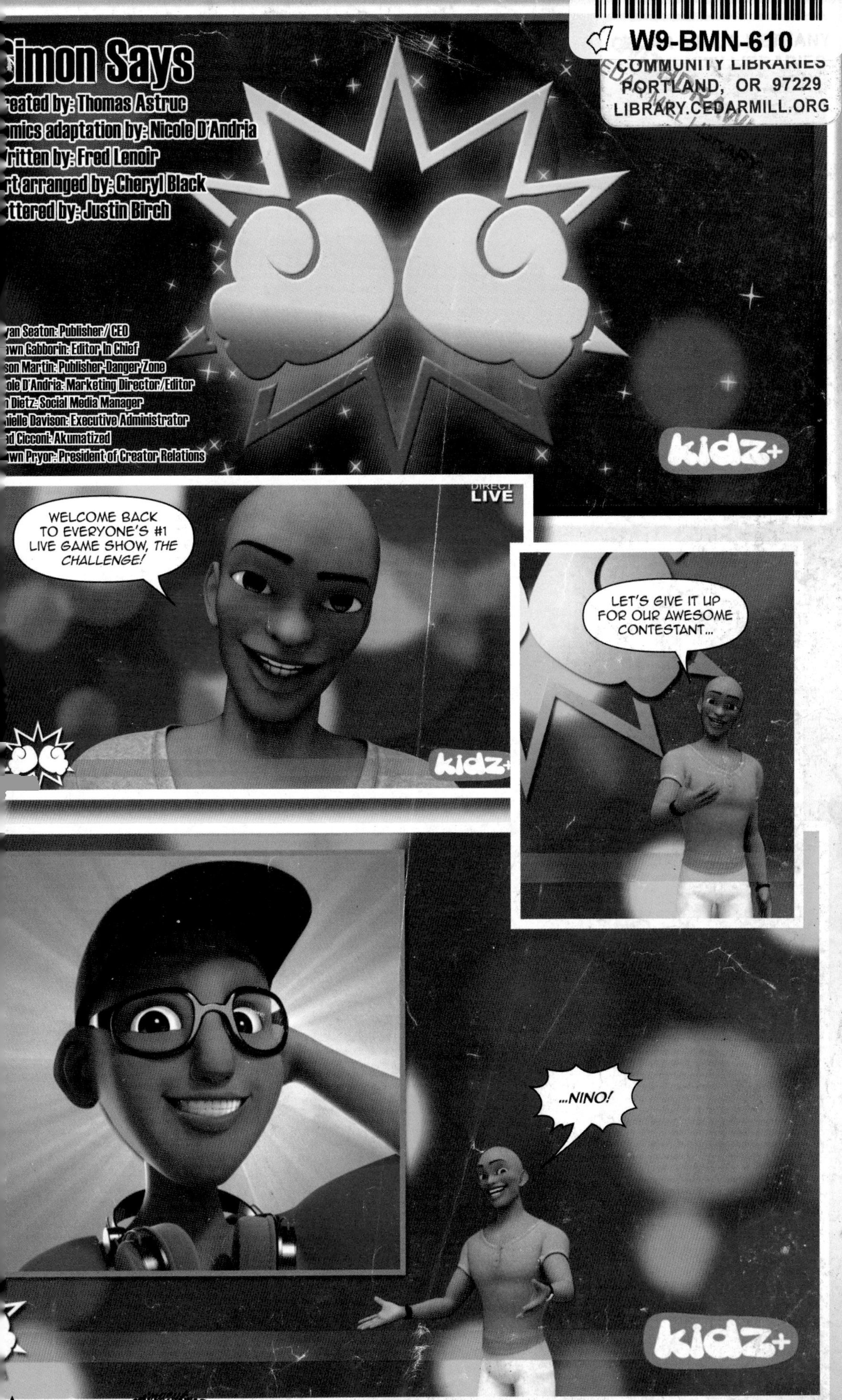
Simon Says
reated by: Thomas Astruc
omics adaptation by: Nicole D'Andria
ritten by: Fred Lenoir
rt arranged by: Cheryl Black
ttered by: Justin Birch
yan Seaton: Publisher / CEO
awn Gabborin: Editor In Chief
son Martin: Publisher-Danger Zone
ole D'Andria: Marketing Director/Editor
n Dietz: Social Media Manager
nielle Davison: Executive Administrator
ad Cicconi: Akumatized
wn Pryor: President of Creator Relations
kidz+
DIRECT
LIVE
WELCOME BACK TO EVERYONE'S #1 LIVE GAME SHOW, THE CHALLENGE!
kidz+
LET'S GIVE IT UP FOR OUR AWESOME CONTESTANT...
...NINO!
kidz+

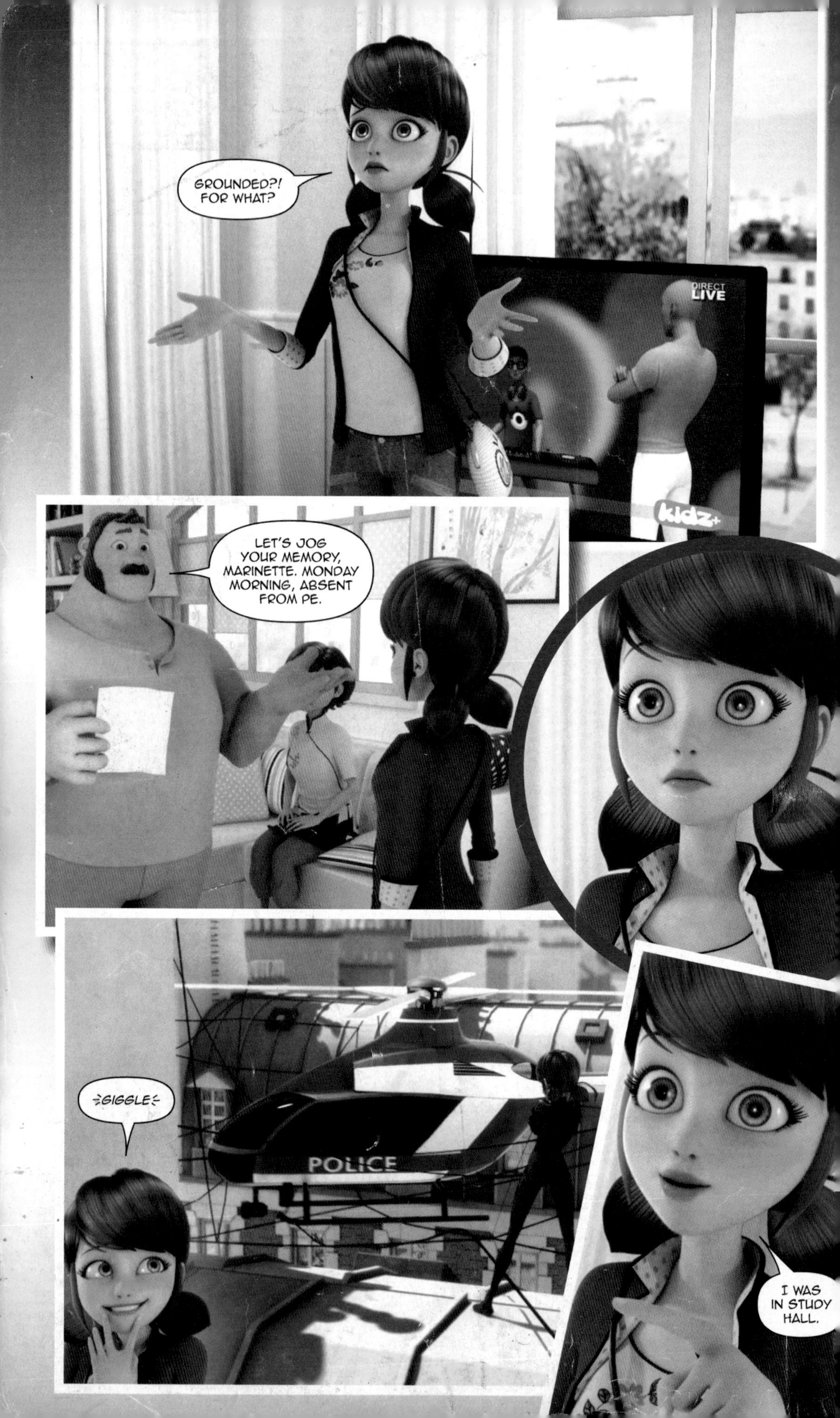
GROUNDED?! FOR WHAT?
DIRECT LIVE
kidz+
LET'S JOG YOUR MEMORY, MARINETTE. MONDAY MORNING, ABSENT FROM PE.
POLICE
GIGGLE
I WAS IN STUDY HALL.

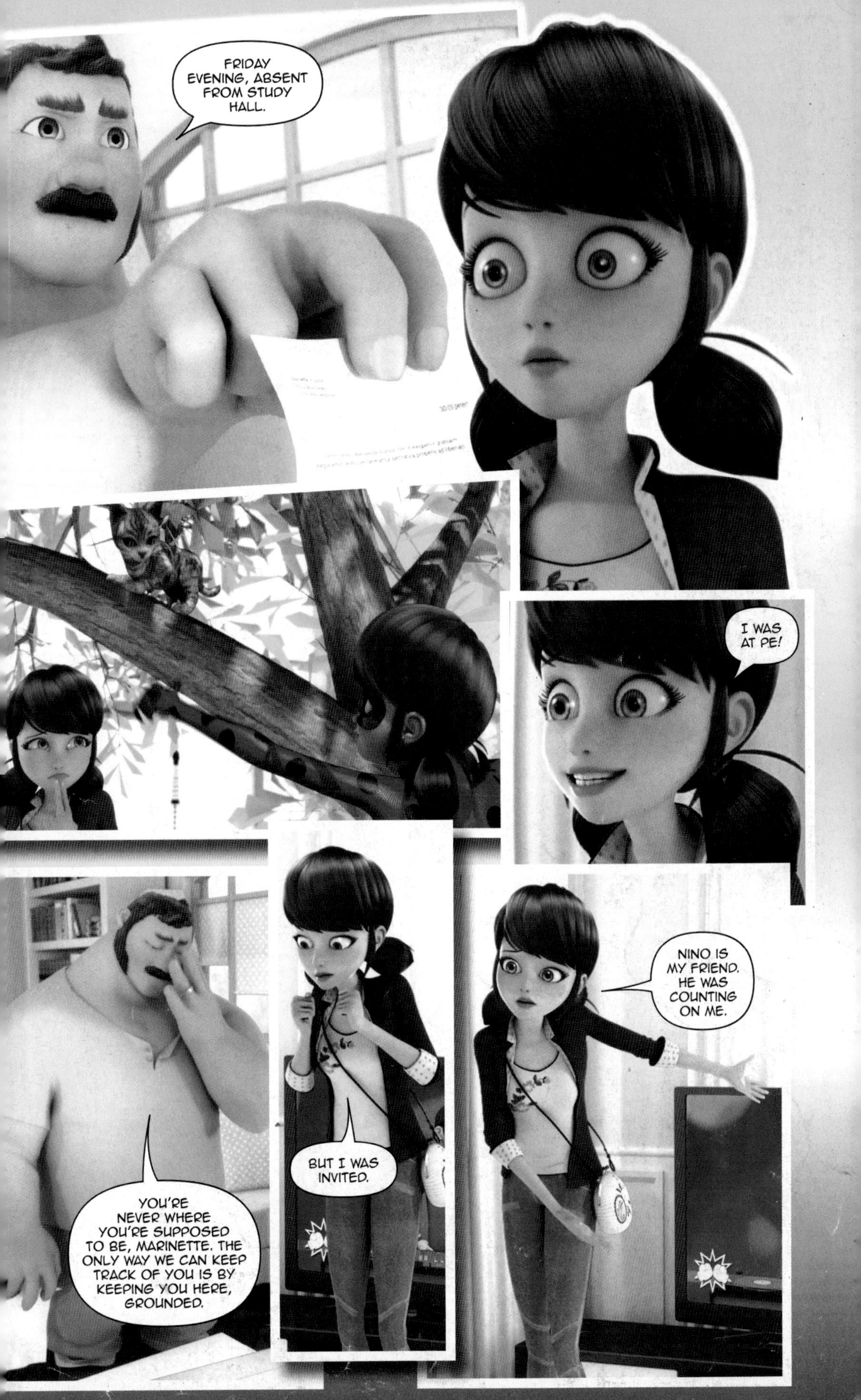
FRIDAY EVENING, ABSENT FROM STUDY HALL.
I WAS AT PE!
YOU'RE NEVER WHERE YOU'RE SUPPOSED TO BE, MARINETTE. THE ONLY WAY WE CAN KEEP TRACK OF YOU IS BY KEEPING YOU HERE, GROUNDED.
BUT I WAS INVITED.
NINO IS MY FRIEND. HE WAS COUNTING ON ME.

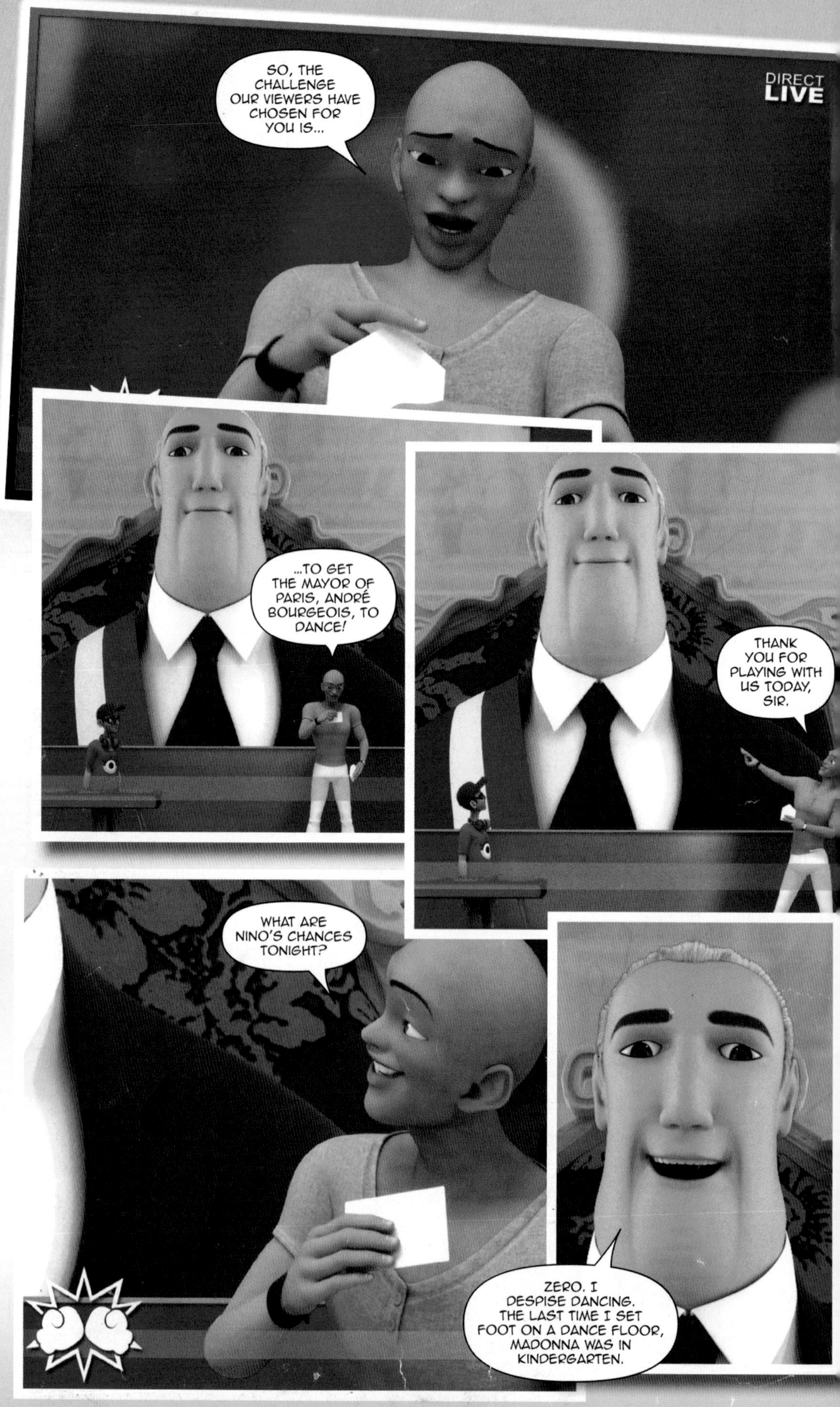

SO, THE CHALLENGE OUR VIEWERS HAVE CHOSEN FOR YOU IS...
DIRECT LIVE
...TO GET THE MAYOR OF PARIS, ANDRÉ BOURGEOIS, TO DANCE!
THANK YOU FOR PLAYING WITH US TODAY, SIR.
WHAT ARE NINO'S CHANCES TONIGHT?
ZERO. I DESPISE DANCING. THE LAST TIME I SET FOOT ON A DANCE FLOOR, MADONNA WAS IN KINDERGARTEN.

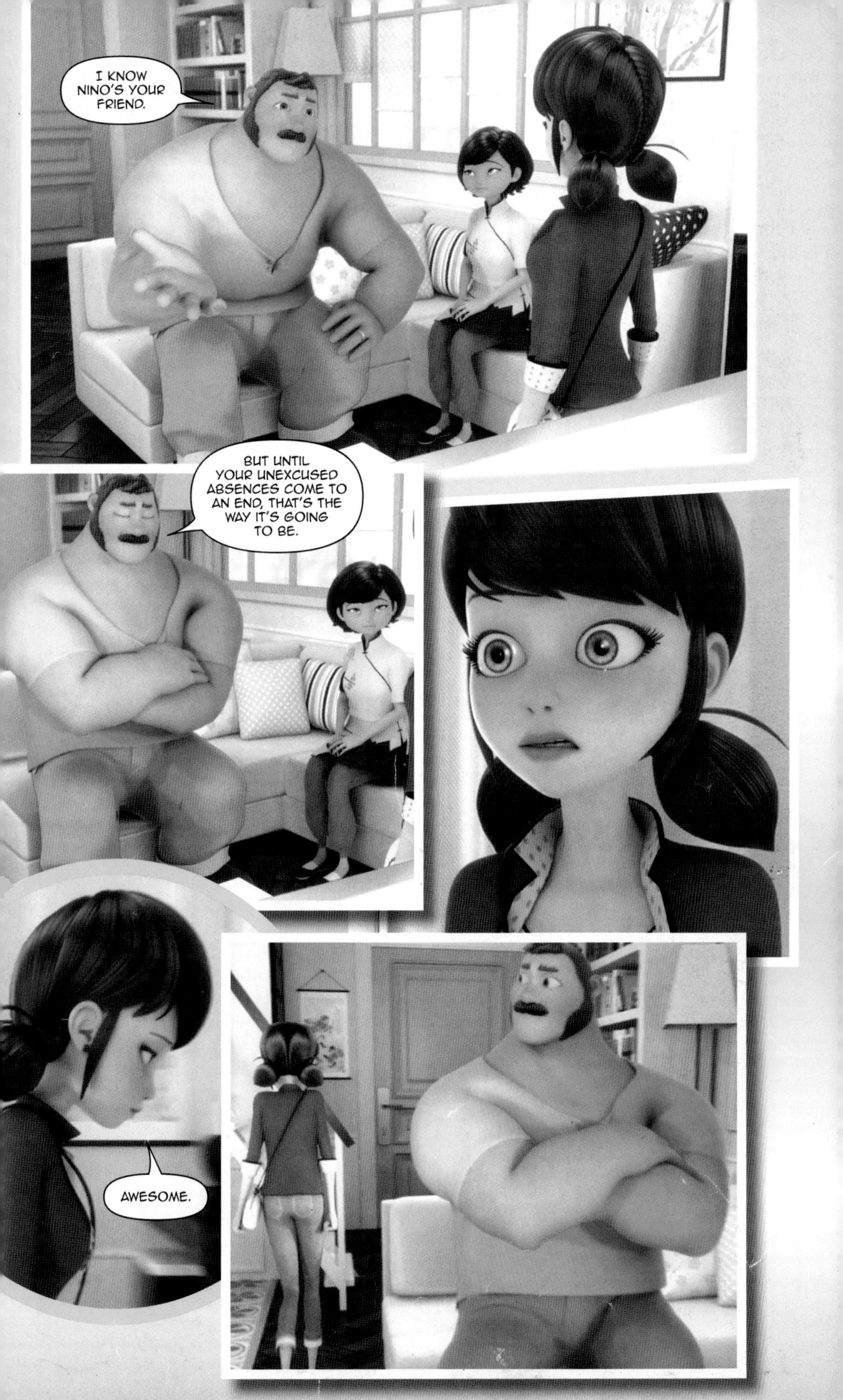
I KNOW NINO'S YOUR FRIEND.
BUT UNTIL YOUR UNEXCUSED ABSENCES COME TO AN END, THAT'S THE WAY IT'S GOING TO BE.
AWESOME.

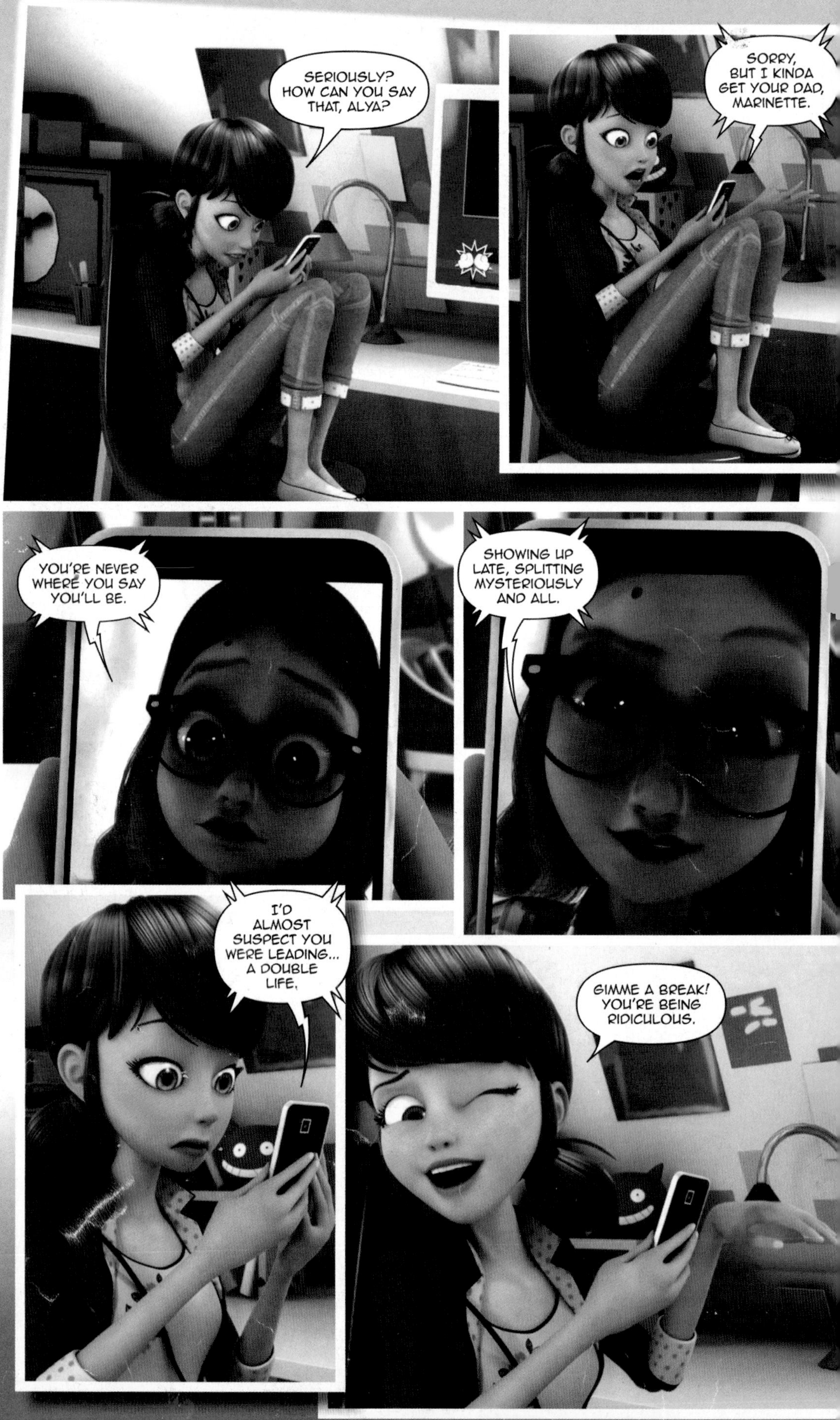
SERIOUSLY? HOW CAN YOU SAY THAT, ALYA?
SORRY, BUT I KINDA GET YOUR DAD, MARINETTE.
YOU'RE NEVER WHERE YOU SAY YOU'LL BE.
SHOWING UP LATE, SPLITTING MYSTERIOUSLY AND ALL.
I'D ALMOST SUSPECT YOU WERE LEADING... A DOUBLE LIFE.
GIMME A BREAK! YOU'RE BEING RIDICULOUS.

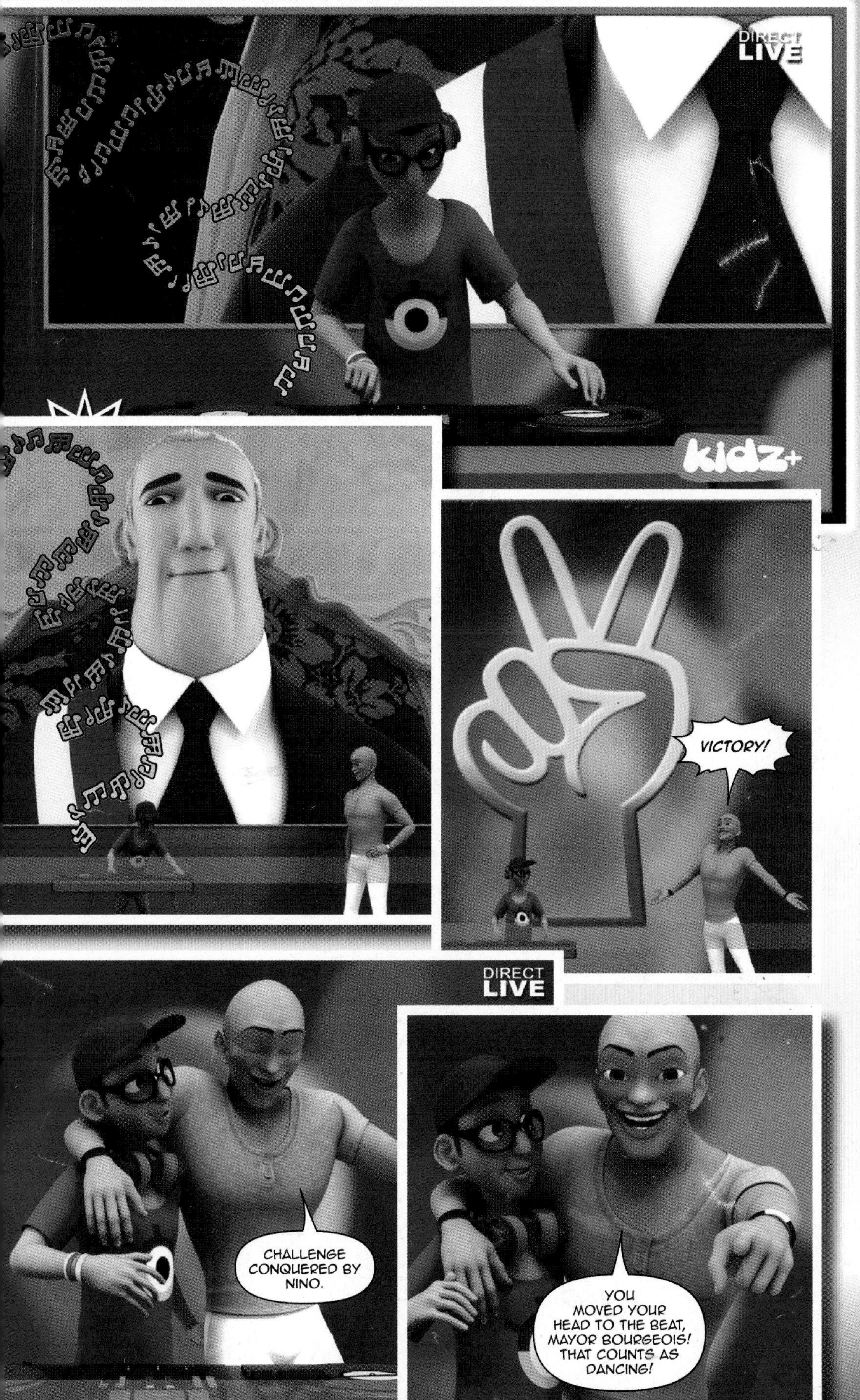
DIRECT LIVE
kidz+
VICTORY!
DIRECT LIVE
CHALLENGE CONQUERED BY NINO.
YOU MOVED YOUR HEAD TO THE BEAT, MAYOR BOURGEOIS! THAT COUNTS AS DANCING!

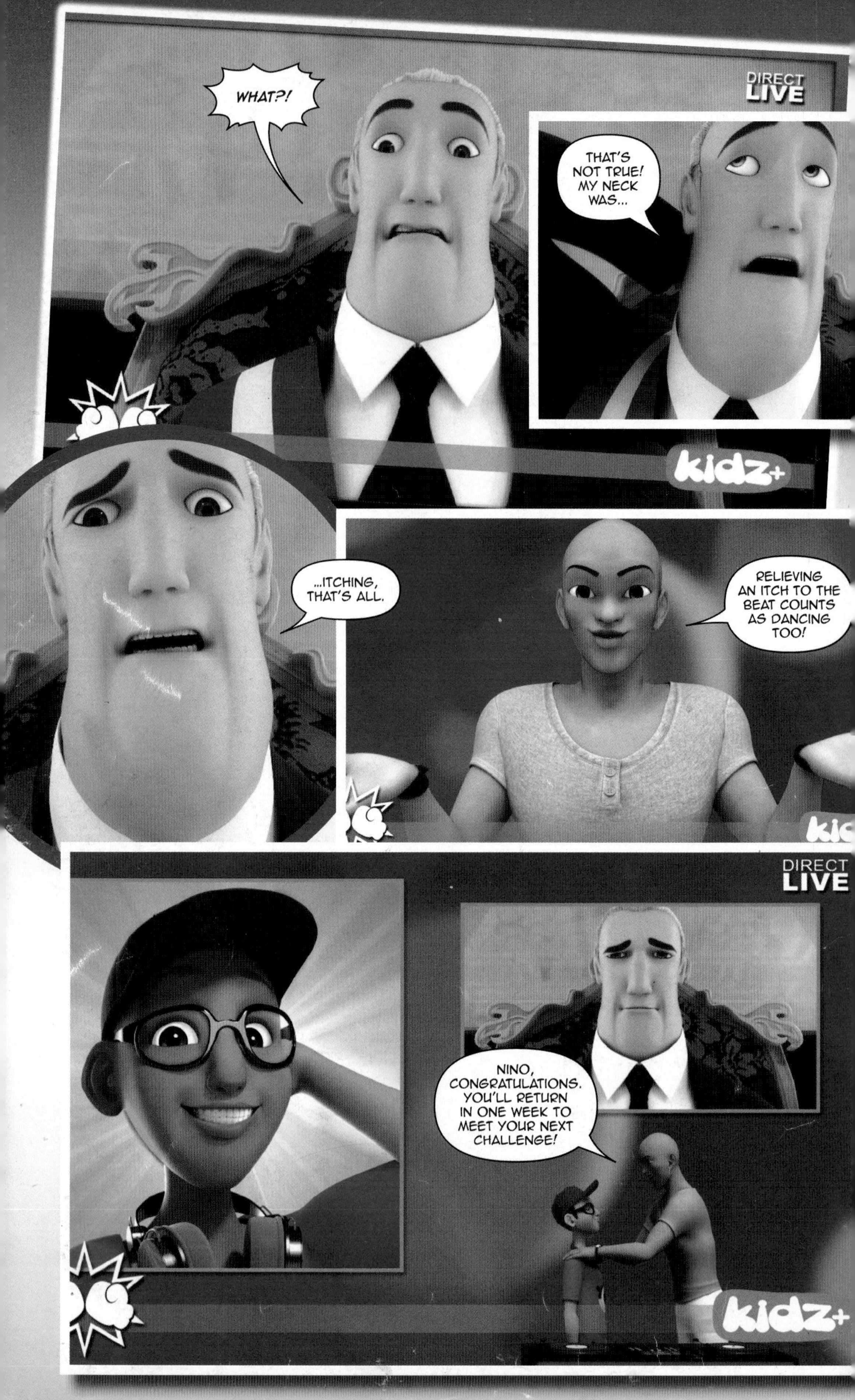

WHAT?!
DIRECT LIVE
THAT'S NOT TRUE! MY NECK WAS...
kidz+
...ITCHING, THAT'S ALL.
RELIEVING AN ITCH TO THE BEAT COUNTS AS DANCING TOO!
DIRECT LIVE
NINO, CONGRATULATIONS. YOU'LL RETURN IN ONE WEEK TO MEET YOUR NEXT CHALLENGE!
kidz+

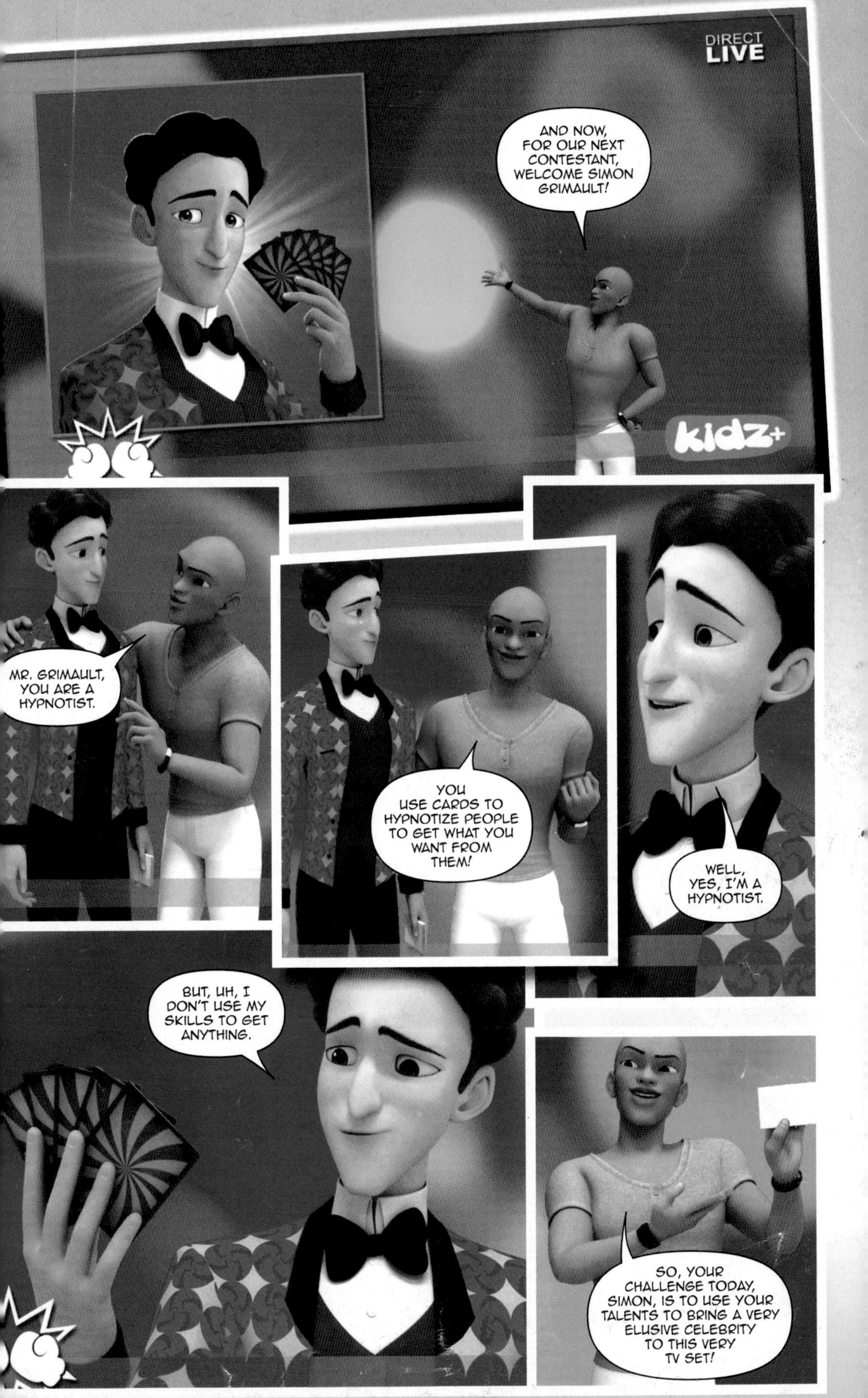
DIRECT
LIVE
AND NOW, FOR OUR NEXT CONTESTANT, WELCOME SIMON GRIMAULT!
kidz+
MR. GRIMAULT, YOU ARE A HYPNOTIST.
YOU USE CARDS TO HYPNOTIZE PEOPLE TO GET WHAT YOU WANT FROM THEM!
WELL, YES, I'M A HYPNOTIST.
BUT, UH, I DON'T USE MY SKILLS TO GET ANYTHING.
SO, YOUR CHALLENGE TODAY, SIMON, IS TO USE YOUR TALENTS TO BRING A VERY ELUSIVE CELEBRITY TO THIS VERY TV SET!

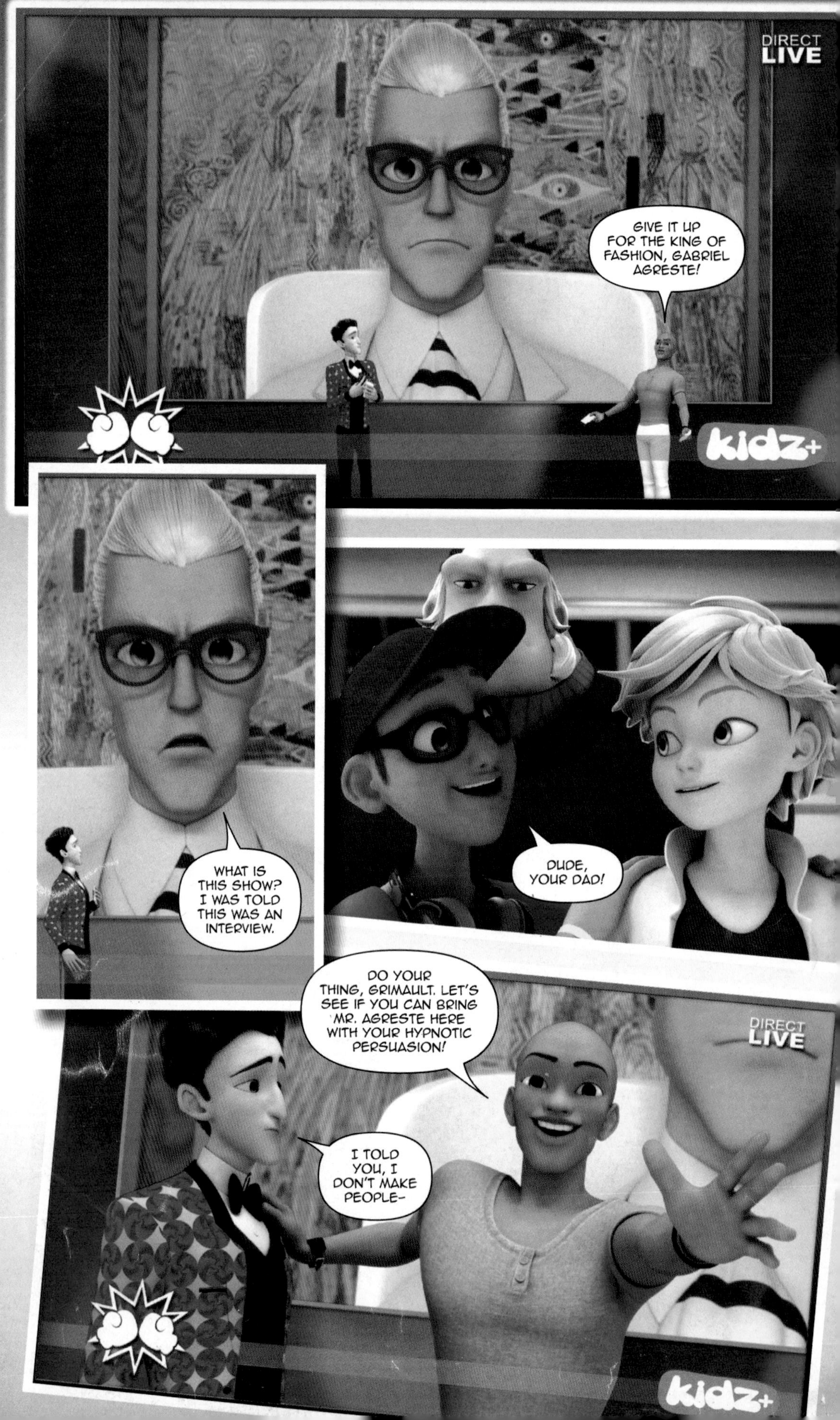
DIRECT LIVE
GIVE IT UP FOR THE KING OF FASHION, GABRIEL AGRESTE!
kidz+
WHAT IS THIS SHOW? I WAS TOLD THIS WAS AN INTERVIEW.
DUDE, YOUR DAD!
DO YOUR THING, GRIMAULT. LET'S SEE IF YOU CAN BRING MR. AGRESTE HERE WITH YOUR HYPNOTIC PERSUASION!
DIRECT LIVE
I TOLD YOU, I DON'T MAKE PEOPLE-
kidz+

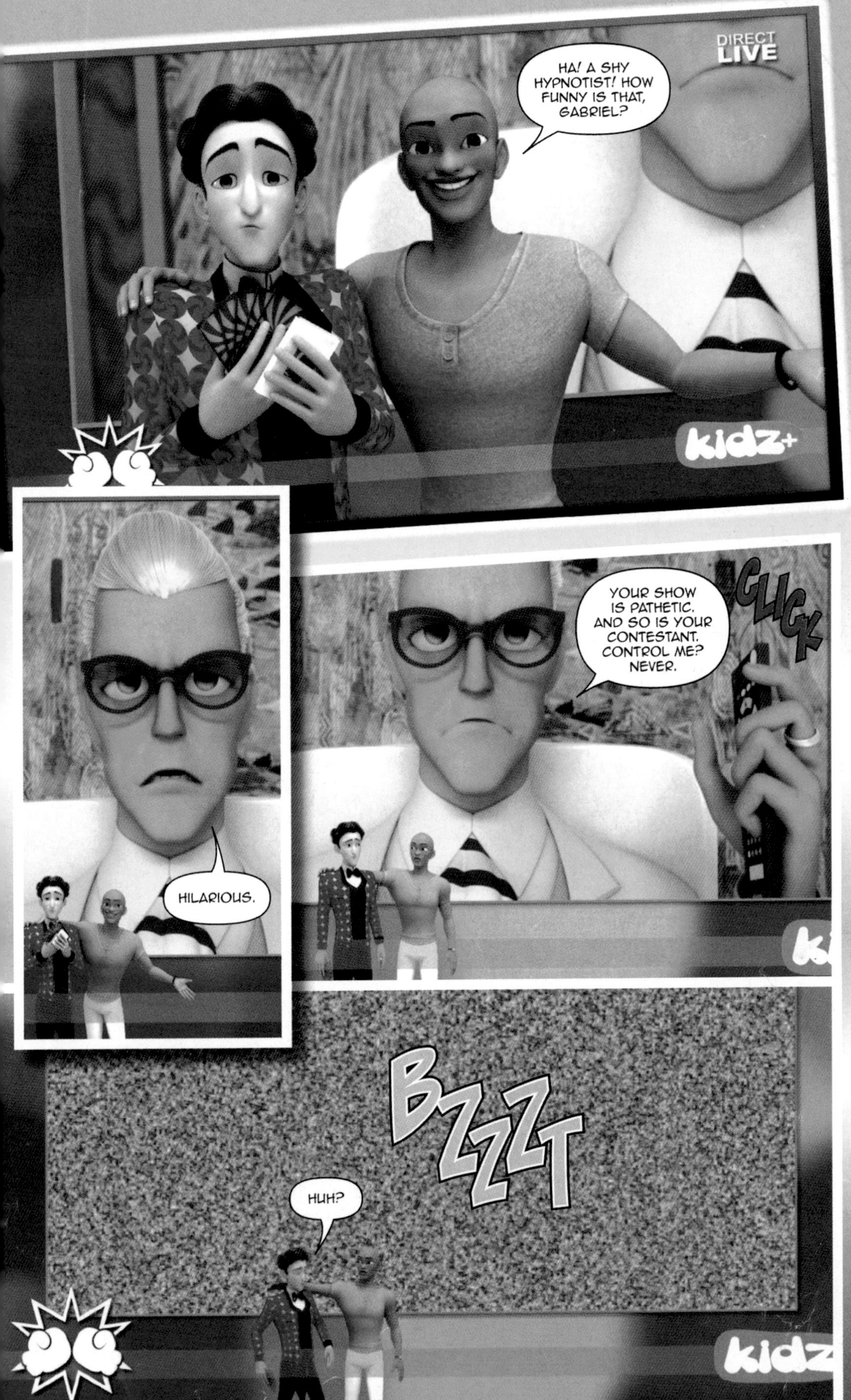
DIRECT
LIVE
HA! A SHY HYPNOTIST! HOW FUNNY IS THAT, GABRIEL?
kidz+
HILARIOUS.
YOUR SHOW IS PATHETIC. AND SO IS YOUR CONTESTANT. CONTROL ME? NEVER.
CLICK
BZZZT
HUH?
kidz

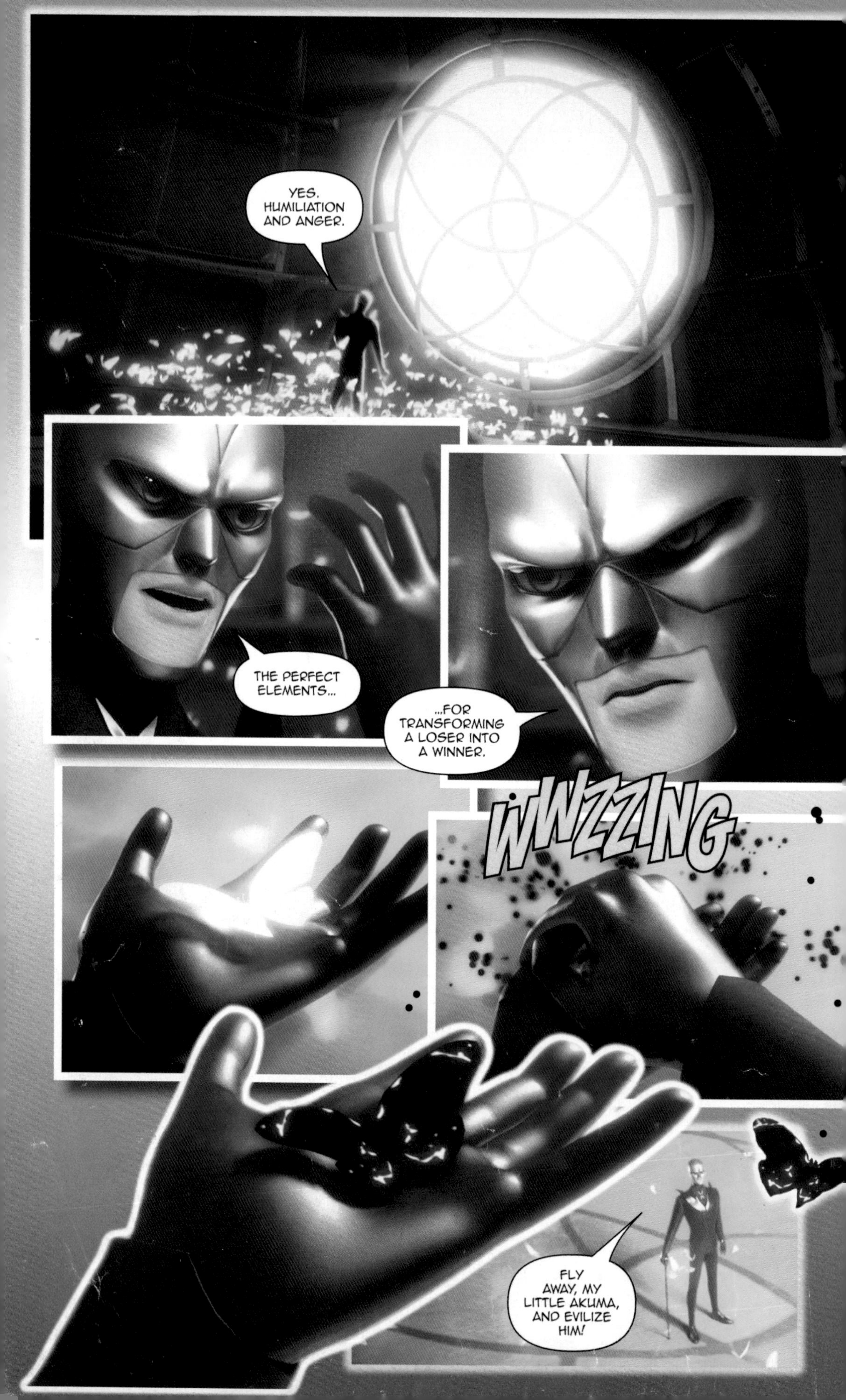
YES. HUMILIATION AND ANGER.
THE PERFECT ELEMENTS...
...FOR TRANSFORMING A LOSER INTO A WINNER.
WWZZING
FLY AWAY, MY LITTLE AKUMA, AND EVILIZE HIM!

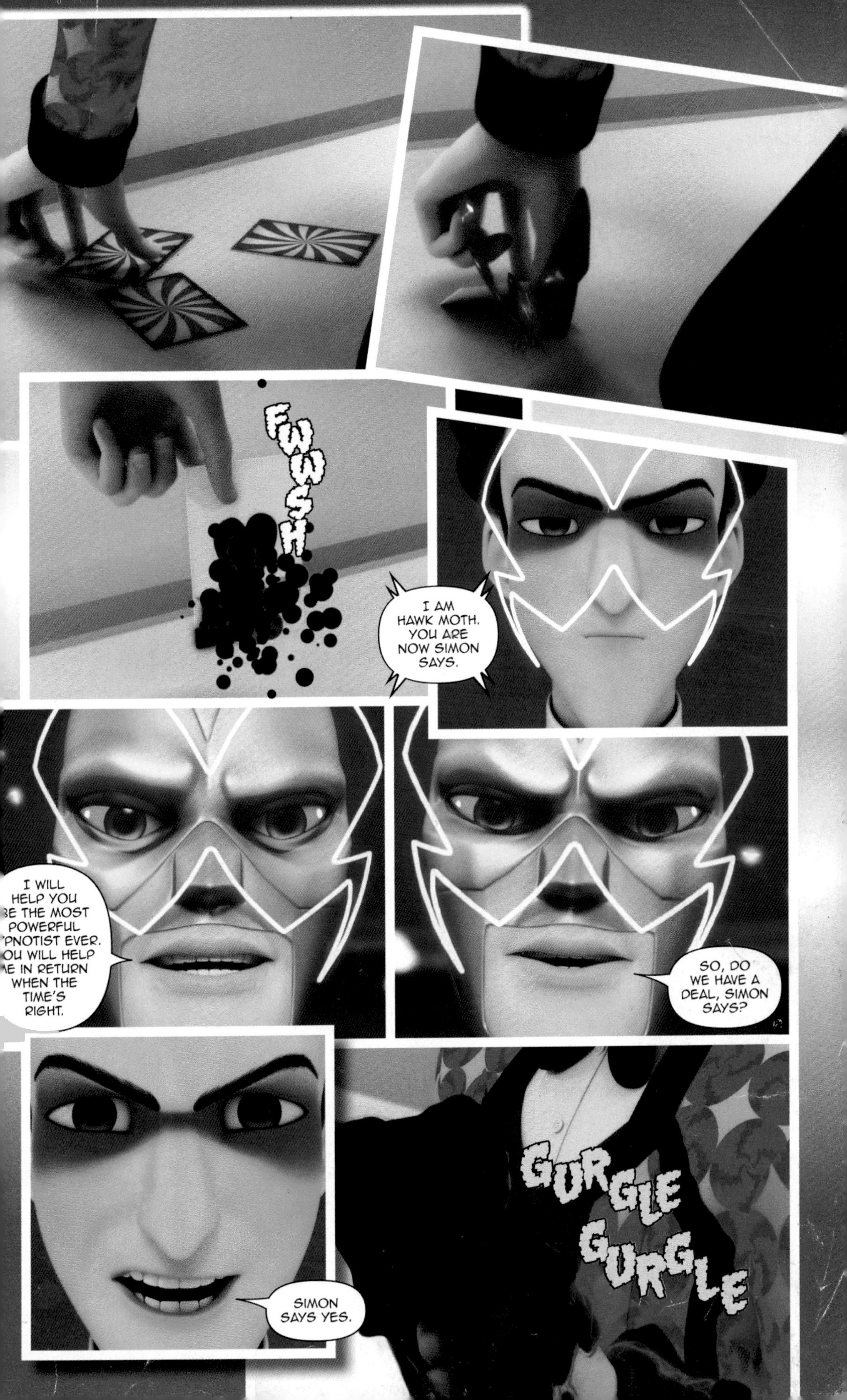

FWWSH
I AM HAWK MOTH. YOU ARE NOW SIMON SAYS.
I WILL HELP YOU BE THE MOST POWERFUL HYPNOTIST EVER. YOU WILL HELP ME IN RETURN WHEN THE TIME'S RIGHT.
SO, DO WE HAVE A DEAL, SIMON SAYS?
SIMON SAYS YES.
GURGLE GURGLE

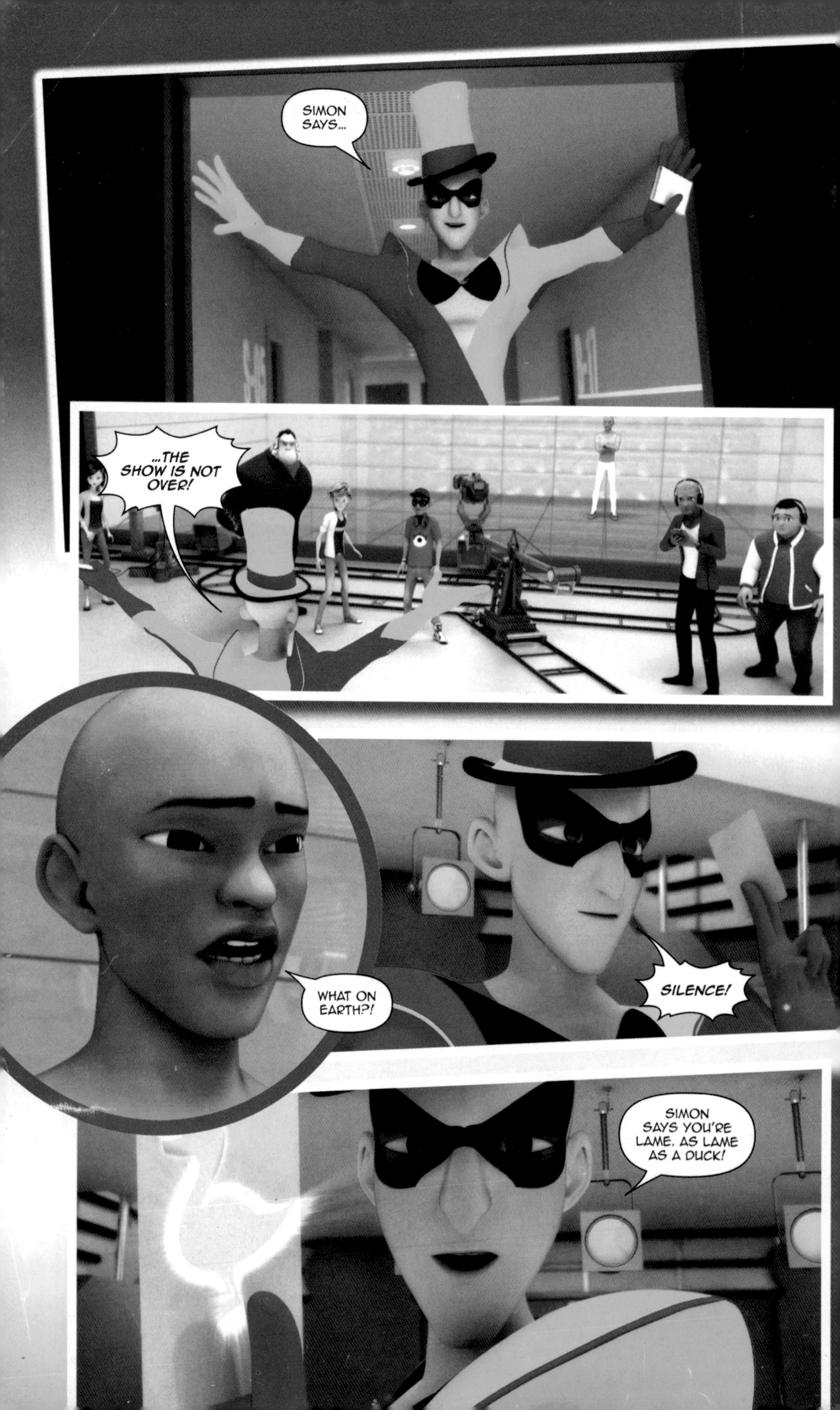

SIMON SAYS...
...THE SHOW IS NOT OVER!
WHAT ON EARTH?!
SILENCE!
SIMON SAYS YOU'RE LAME. AS LAME AS A DUCK!

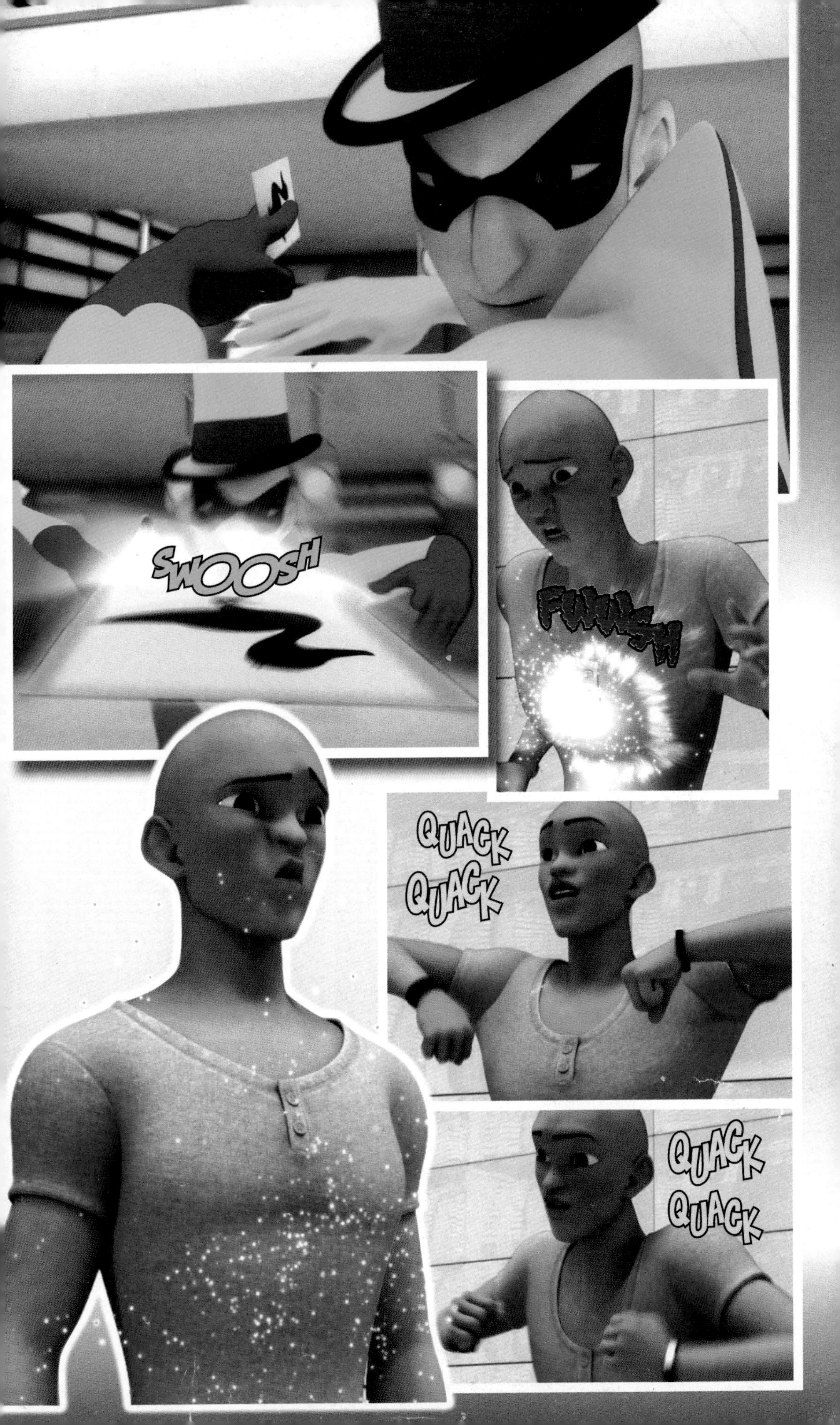
SWOOSH
FWUSH
QUACK
QUACK
QUACK
QUACK

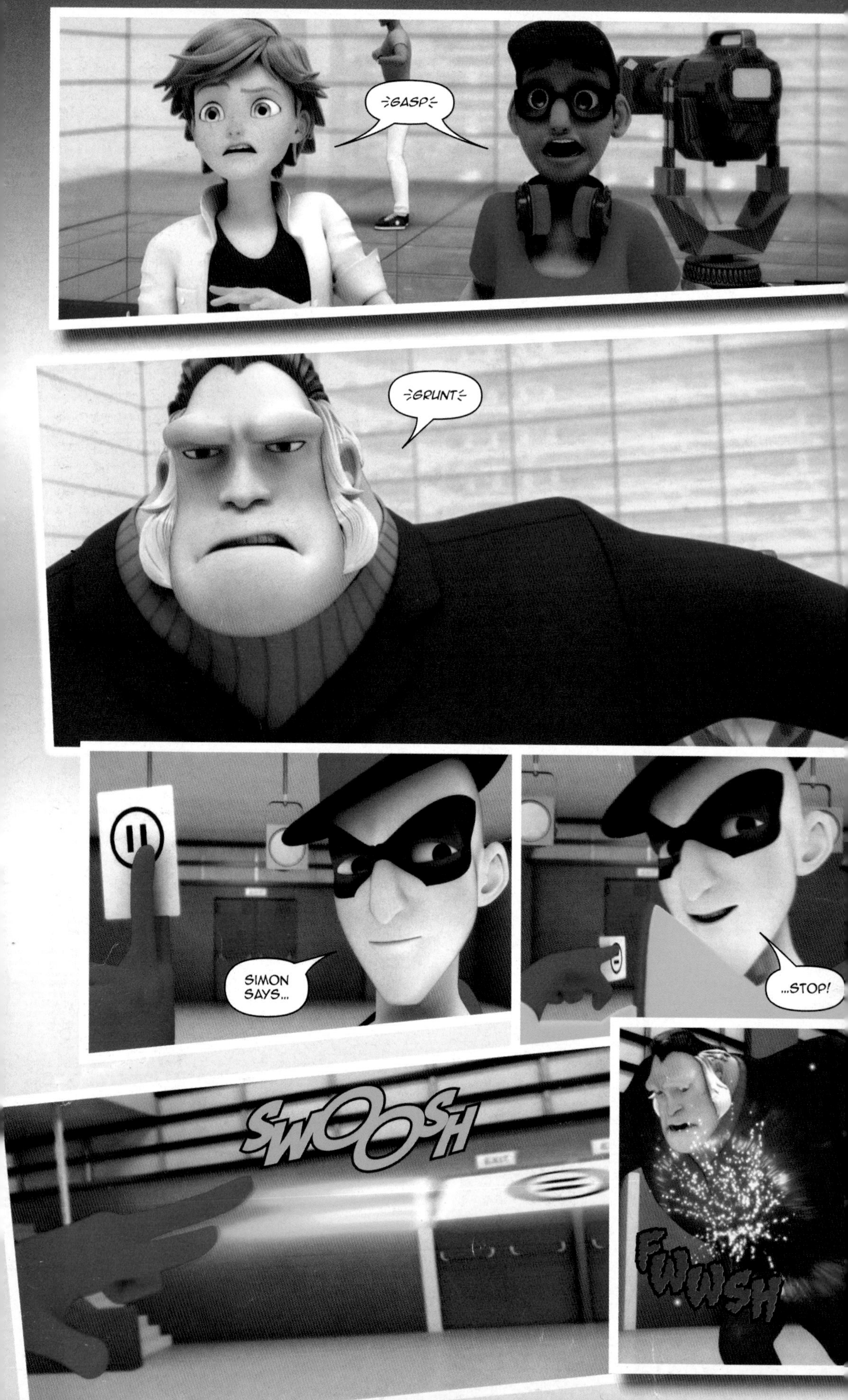

GASP
GRUNT
SIMON SAYS...
...STOP!
SWOOSH
FWWSH

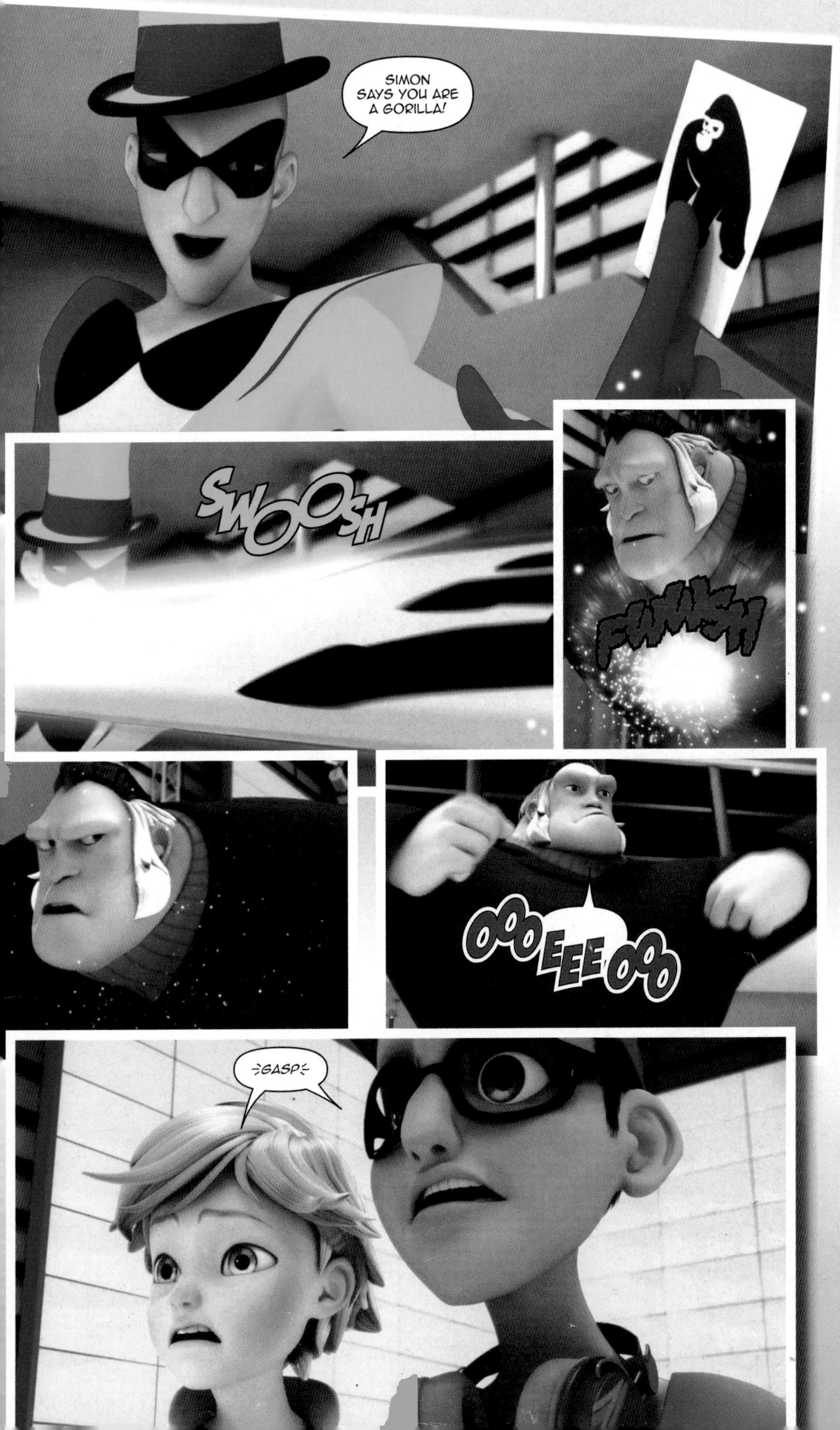
SIMON SAYS YOU ARE A GORILLA!
SWOOSH
FWASH
OOOEEEOOO
GASP

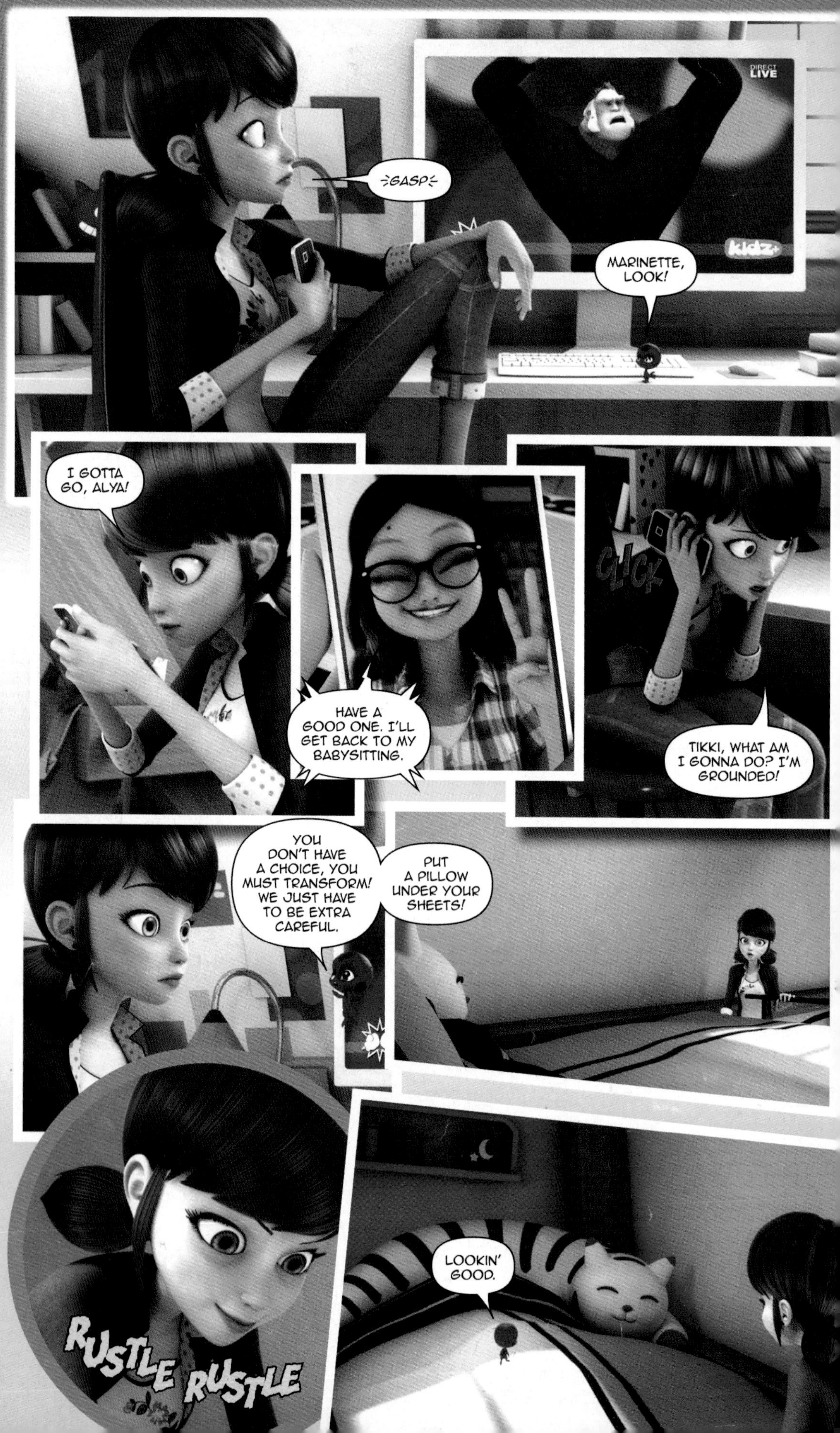

GASP
LIVE
MARINETTE, LOOK!
I GOTTA GO, ALYA!
HAVE A GOOD ONE. I'LL GET BACK TO MY BABYSITTING.
CLICK
TIKKI, WHAT AM I GONNA DO? I'M GROUNDED!
YOU DON'T HAVE A CHOICE, YOU MUST TRANSFORM! WE JUST HAVE TO BE EXTRA CAREFUL.
PUT A PILLOW UNDER YOUR SHEETS!
RUSTLE RUSTLE
LOOKIN' GOOD.

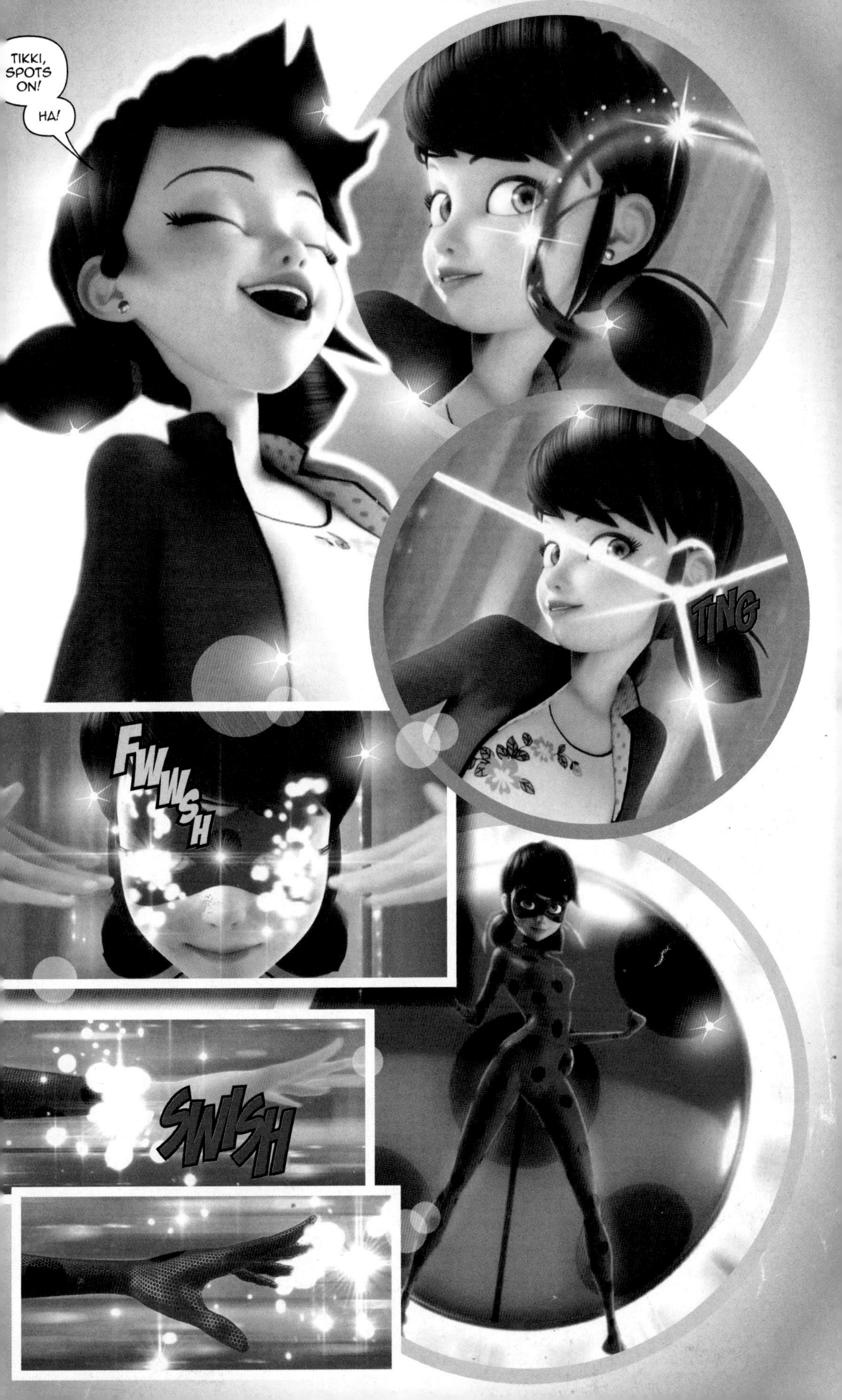
TIKKI, SPOTS ON!
HA!
TING
FWWSH
SWISH

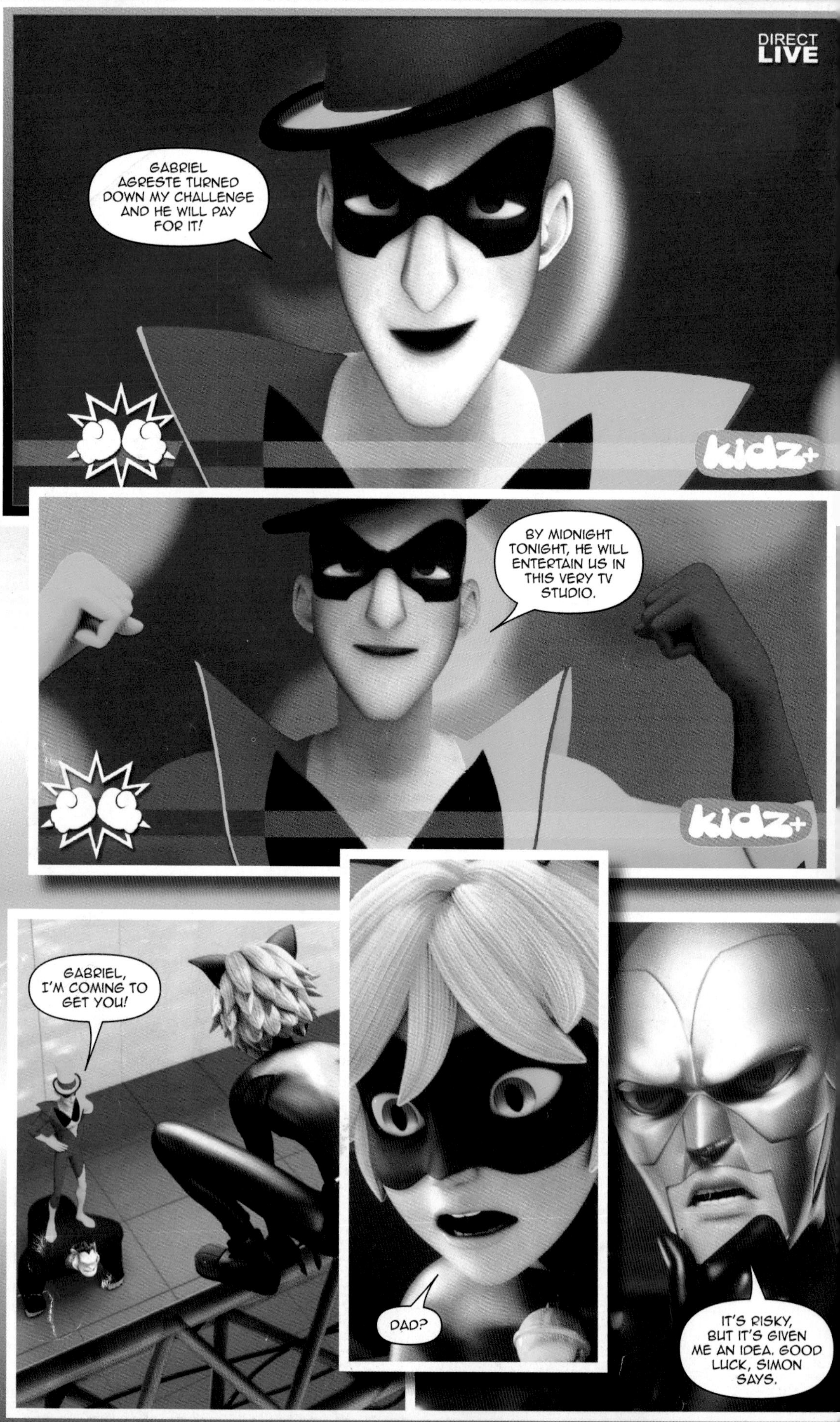
DIRECT
LIVE
GABRIEL AGRESTE TURNED DOWN MY CHALLENGE AND HE WILL PAY FOR IT!
kidz+
BY MIDNIGHT TONIGHT, HE WILL ENTERTAIN US IN THIS VERY TV STUDIO.
kidz+
GABRIEL, I'M COMING TO GET YOU!
DAD?
IT'S RISKY, BUT IT'S GIVEN ME AN IDEA. GOOD LUCK, SIMON SAYS.

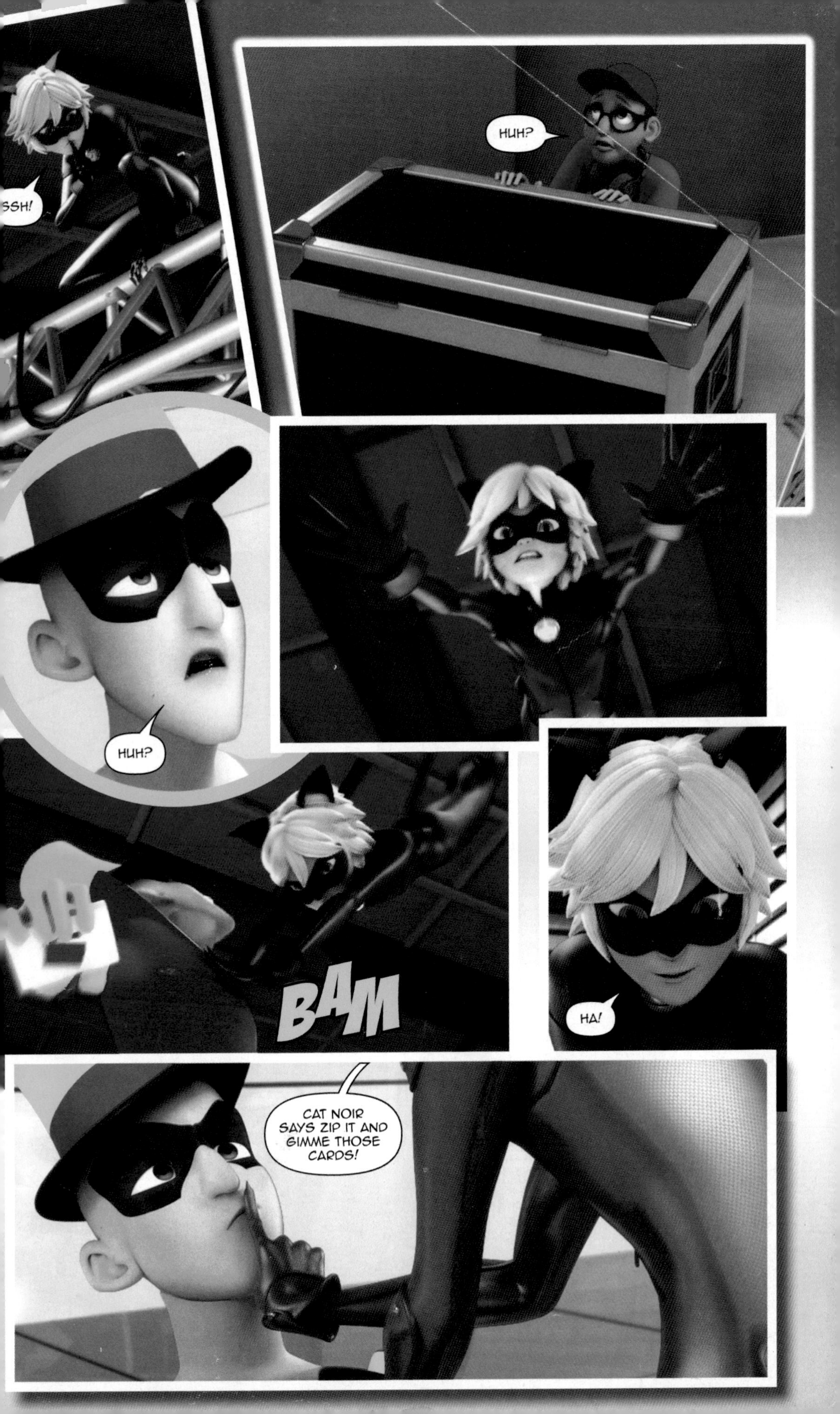
SSH!
HUH?
HUH?
BAM
HA!
CAT NOIR SAYS ZIP IT AND GIMME THOSE CARDS!

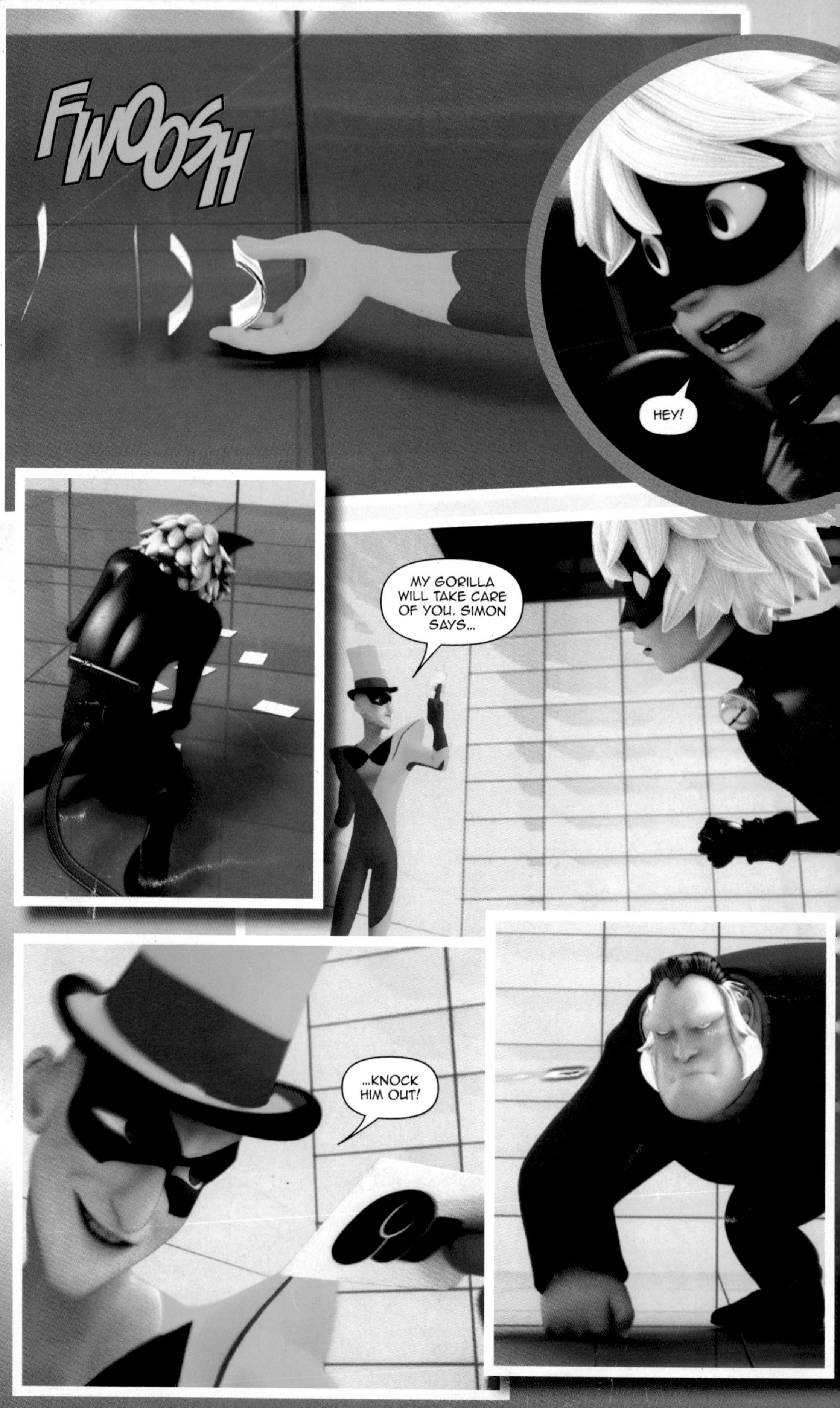
FWOOSH
HEY!
MY GORILLA WILL TAKE CARE OF YOU. SIMON SAYS...
...KNOCK HIM OUT!

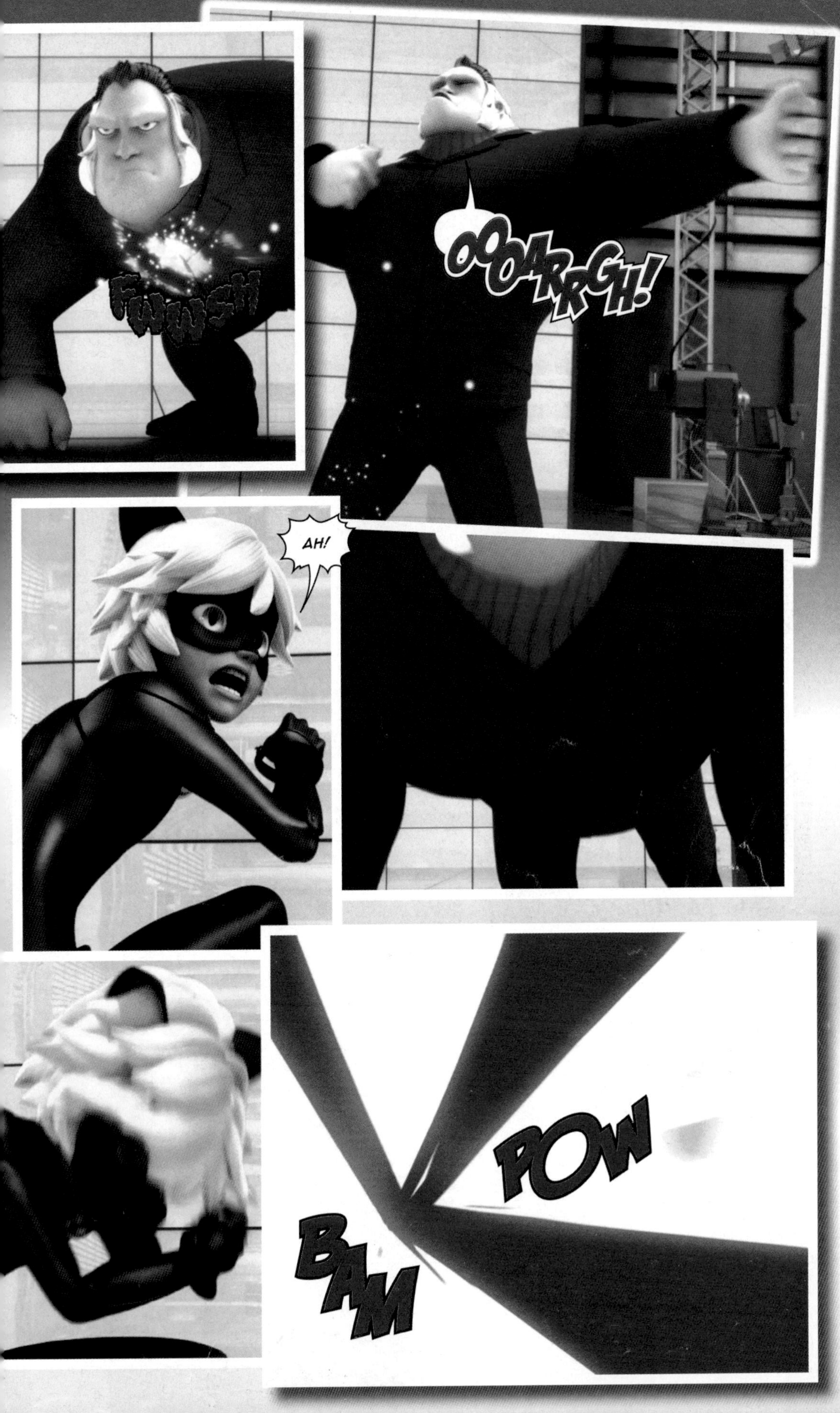
FWWSH
OOOARRGH!
AH!
POW
BAM

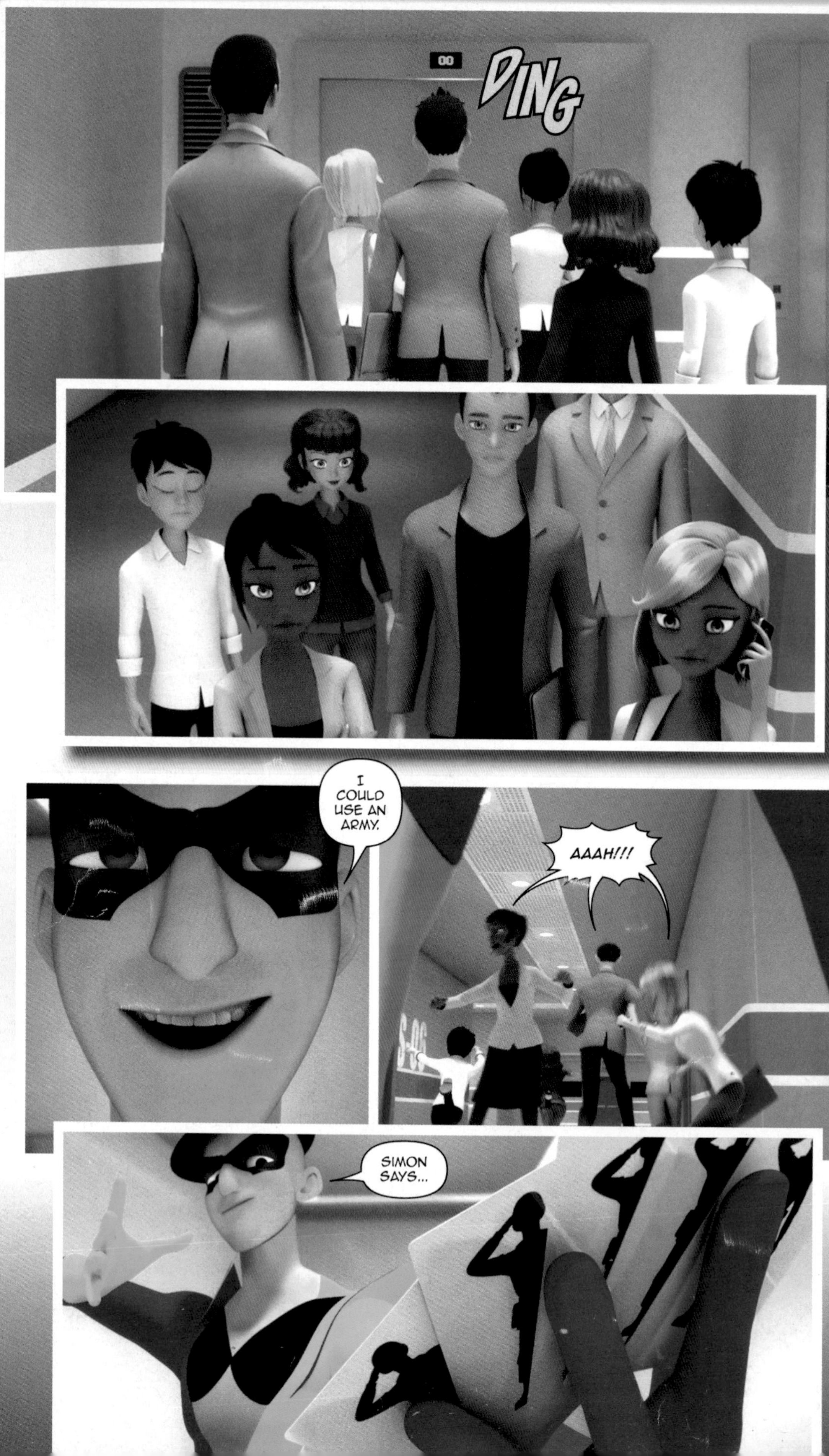
DING
I COULD USE AN ARMY.
AAAH!!!
SIMON SAYS...

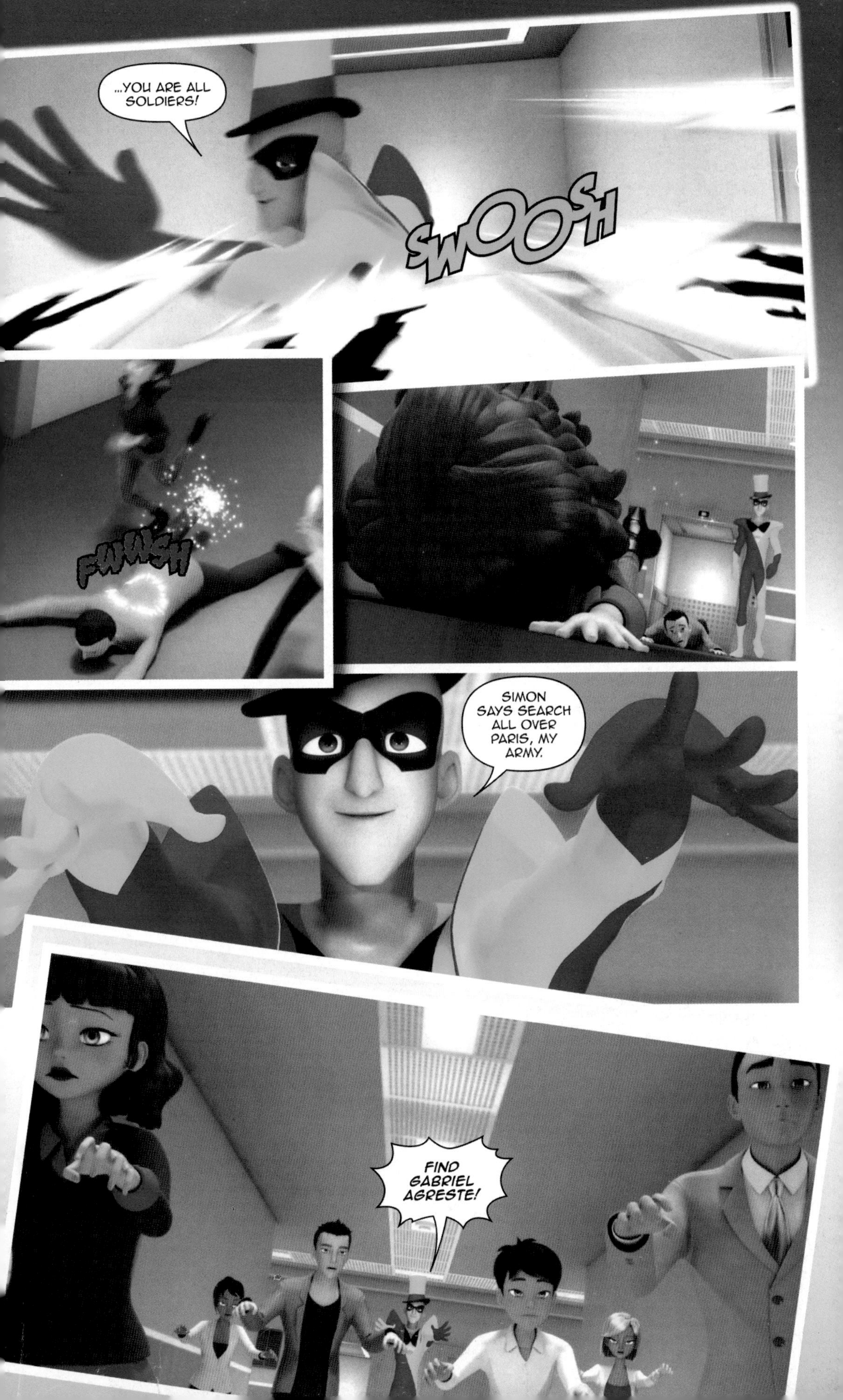
...YOU ARE ALL SOLDIERS!
SWOOSH
FWUSH
SIMON SAYS SEARCH ALL OVER PARIS, MY ARMY.
FIND GABRIEL AGRESTE!

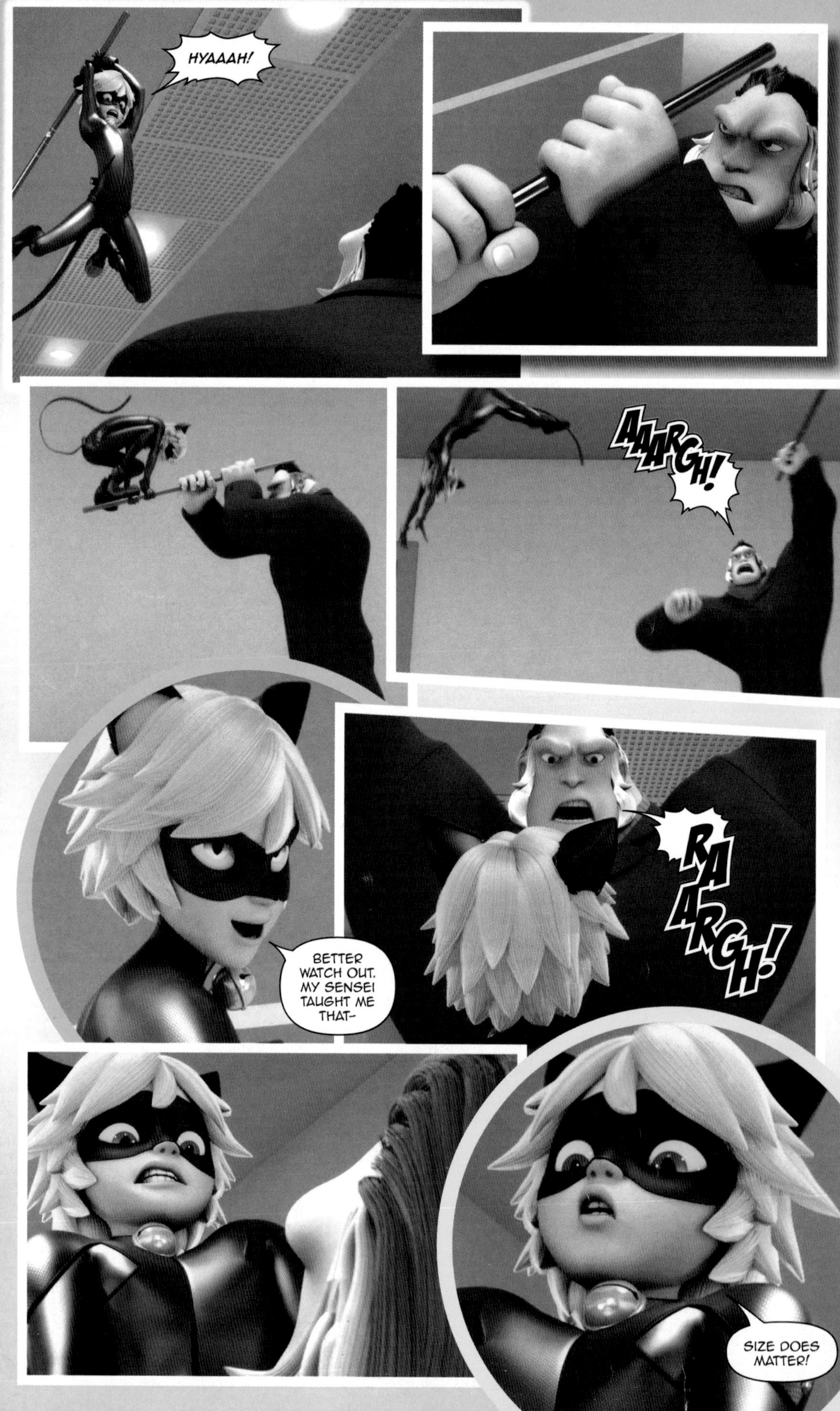
HYAAAH!
AAAARGH!
BETTER WATCH OUT. MY SENSEI TAUGHT ME THAT-
RAAARGH!
SIZE DOES MATTER!

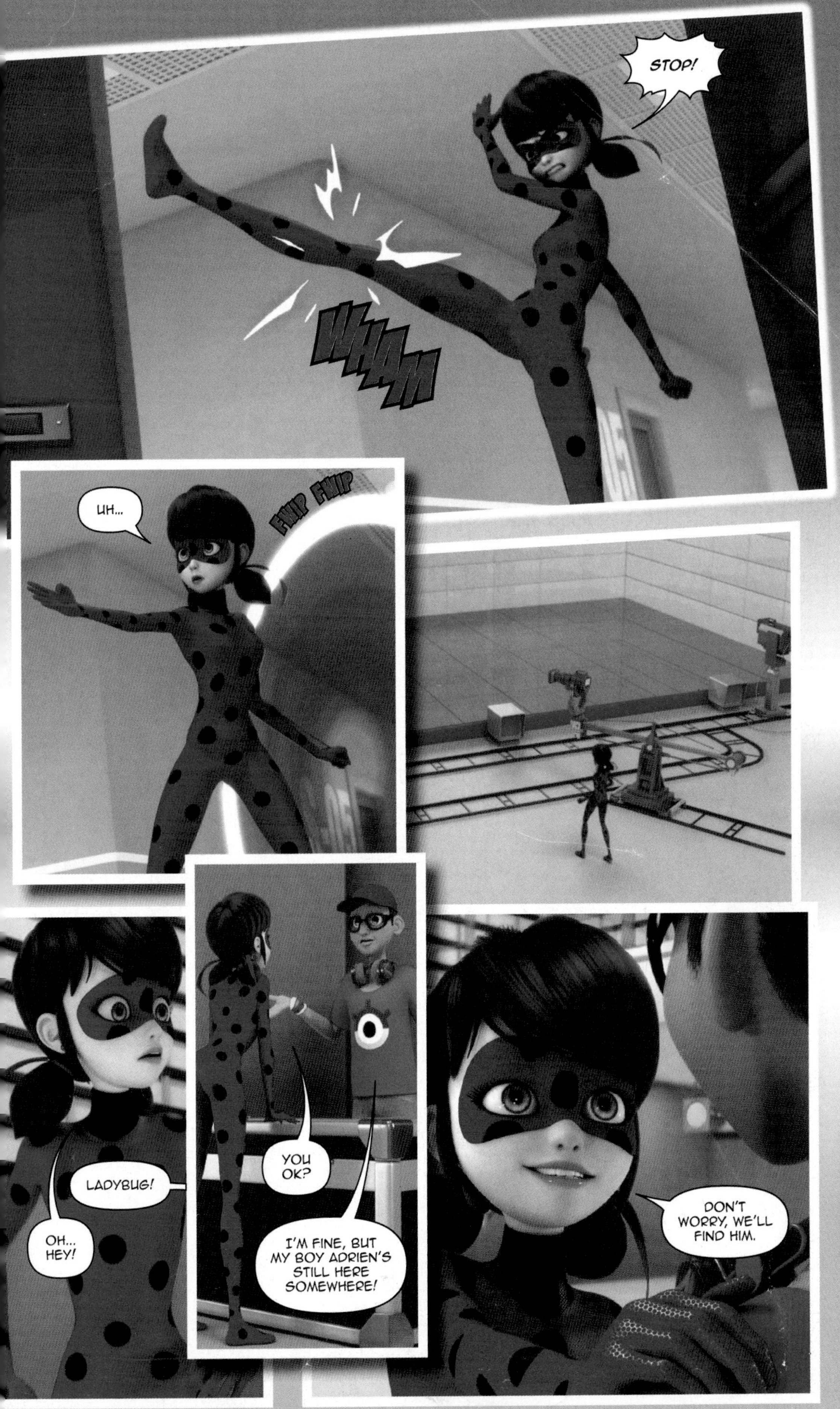
STOP!
WHAM
UH...
FWIP FWIP
LADYBUG!
OH... HEY!
YOU OK?
I'M FINE, BUT MY BOY ADRIEN'S STILL HERE SOMEWHERE!
DON'T WORRY, WE'LL FIND HIM.

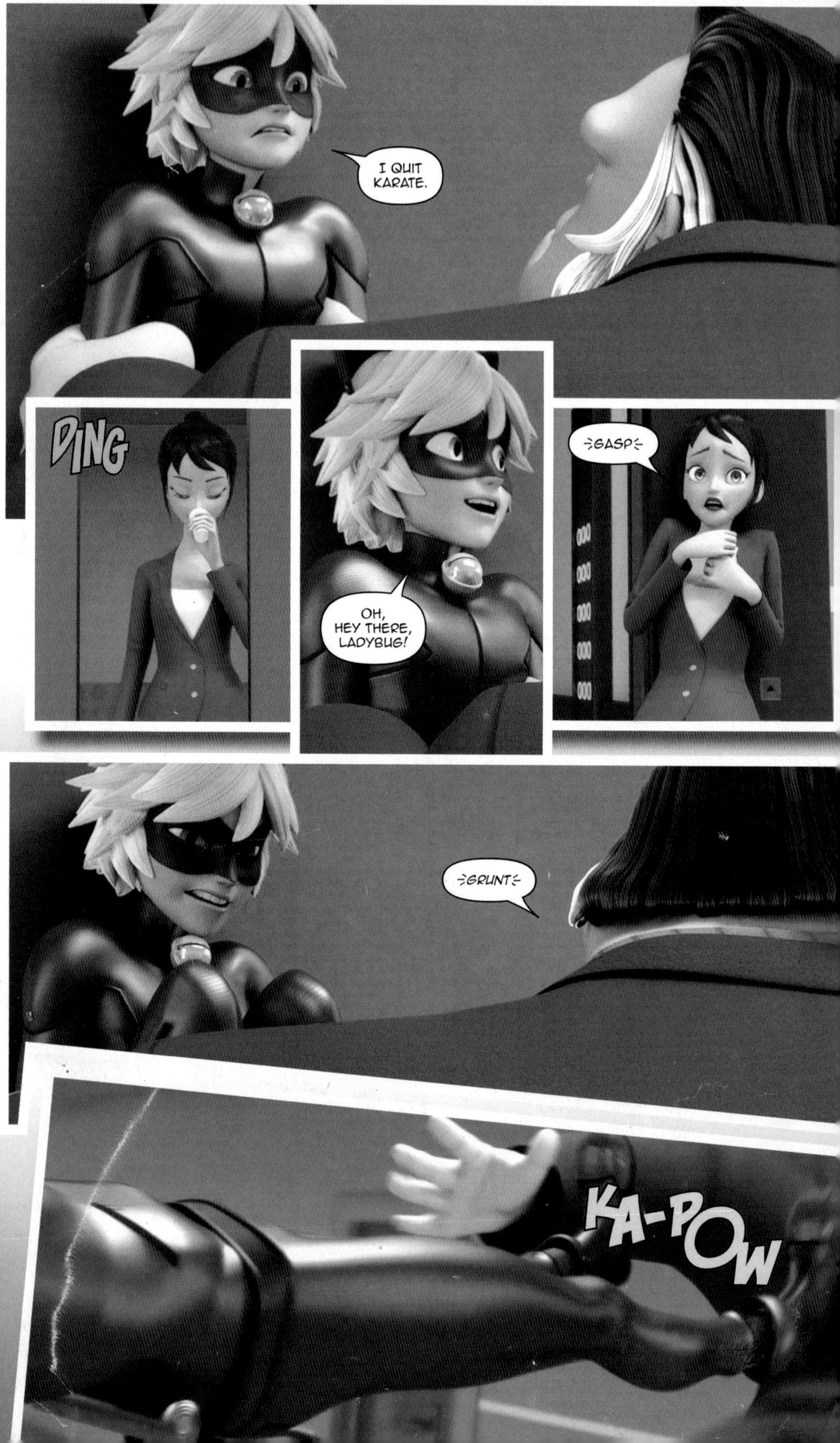
I QUIT KARATE.
DING
OH, HEY THERE, LADYBUG!
GASP
GRUNT
KA-POW

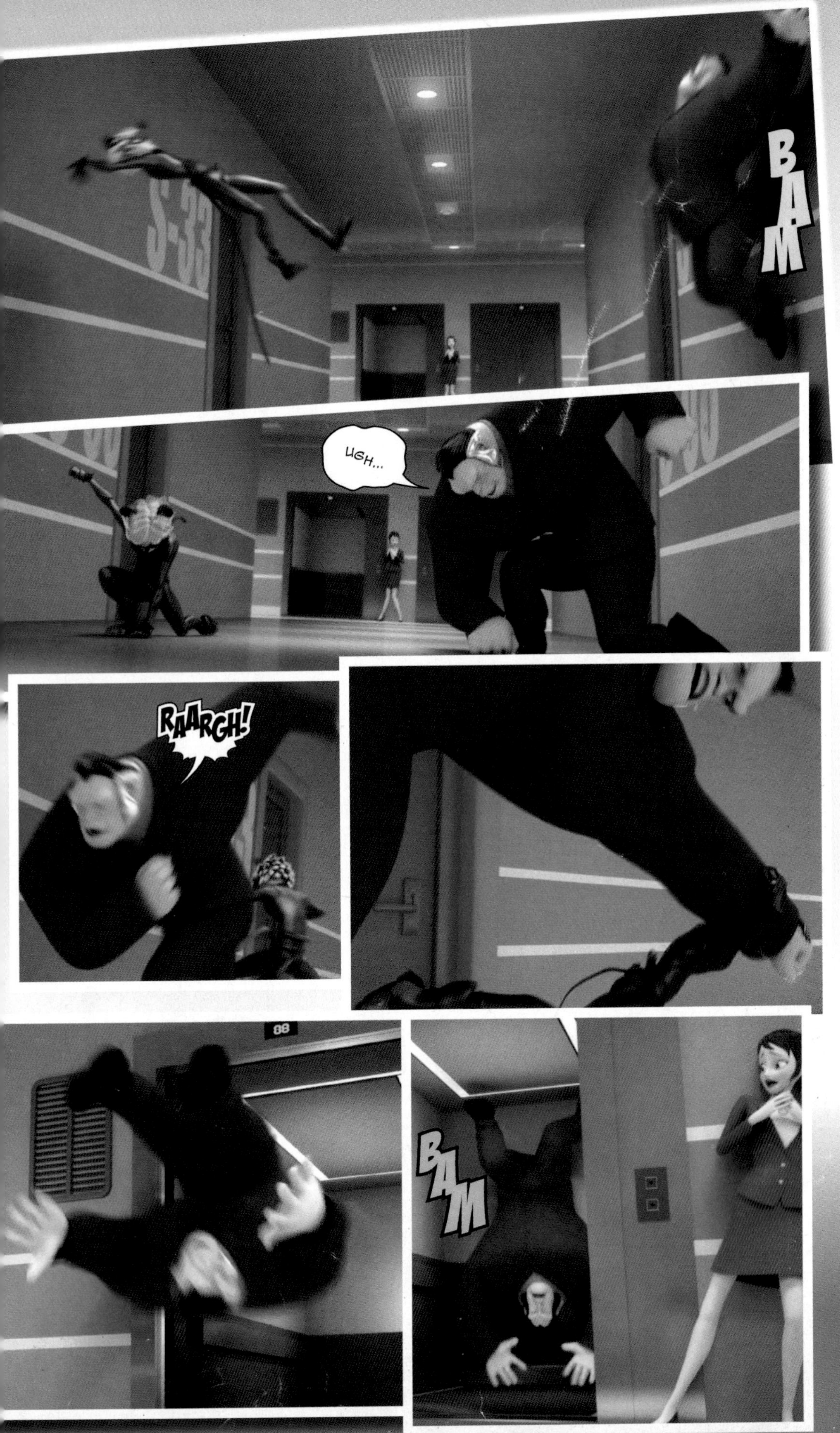
BAM
UGH...
RAARGH!
BAM

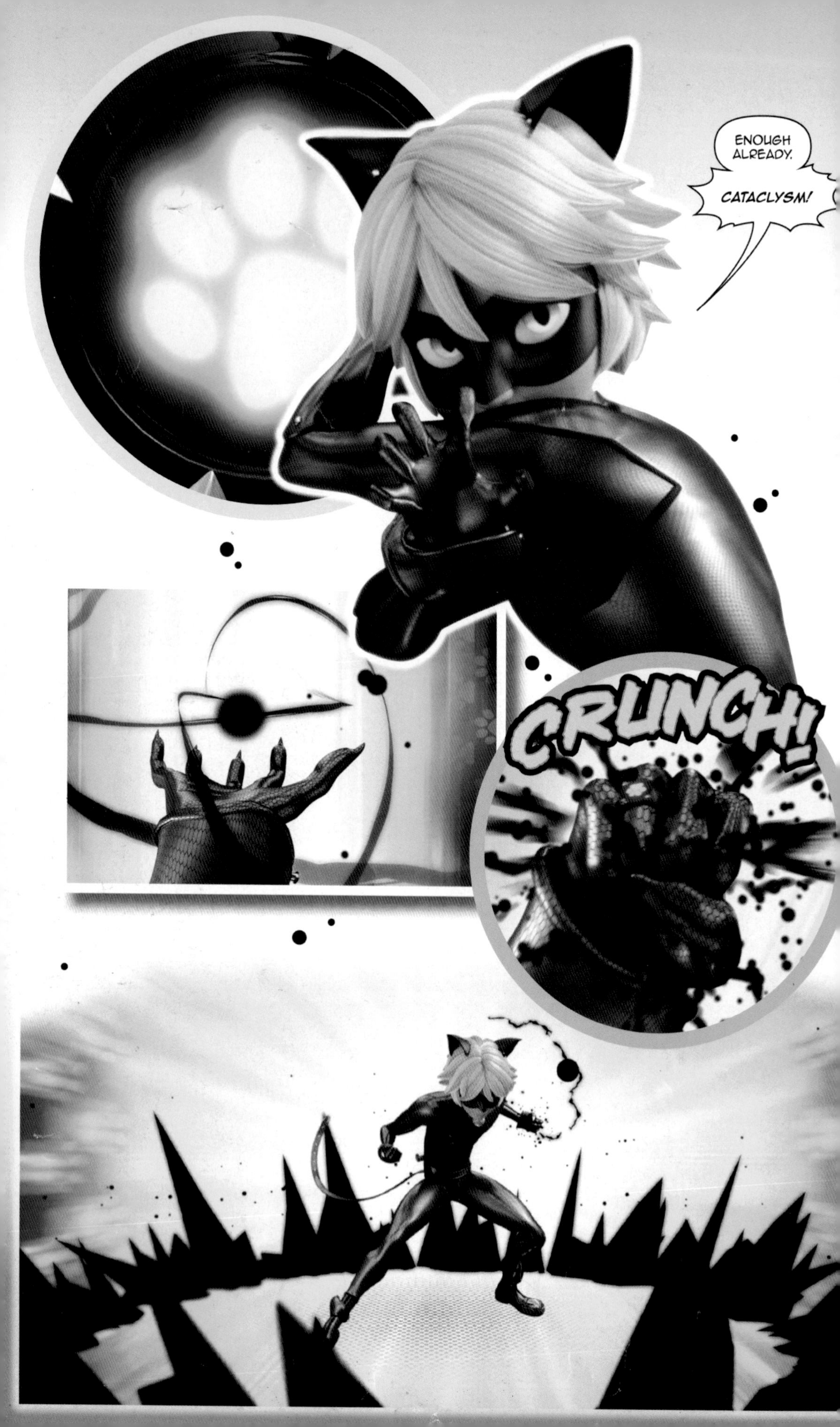
ENOUGH ALREADY.
CATACLYSM!
CRUNCH!

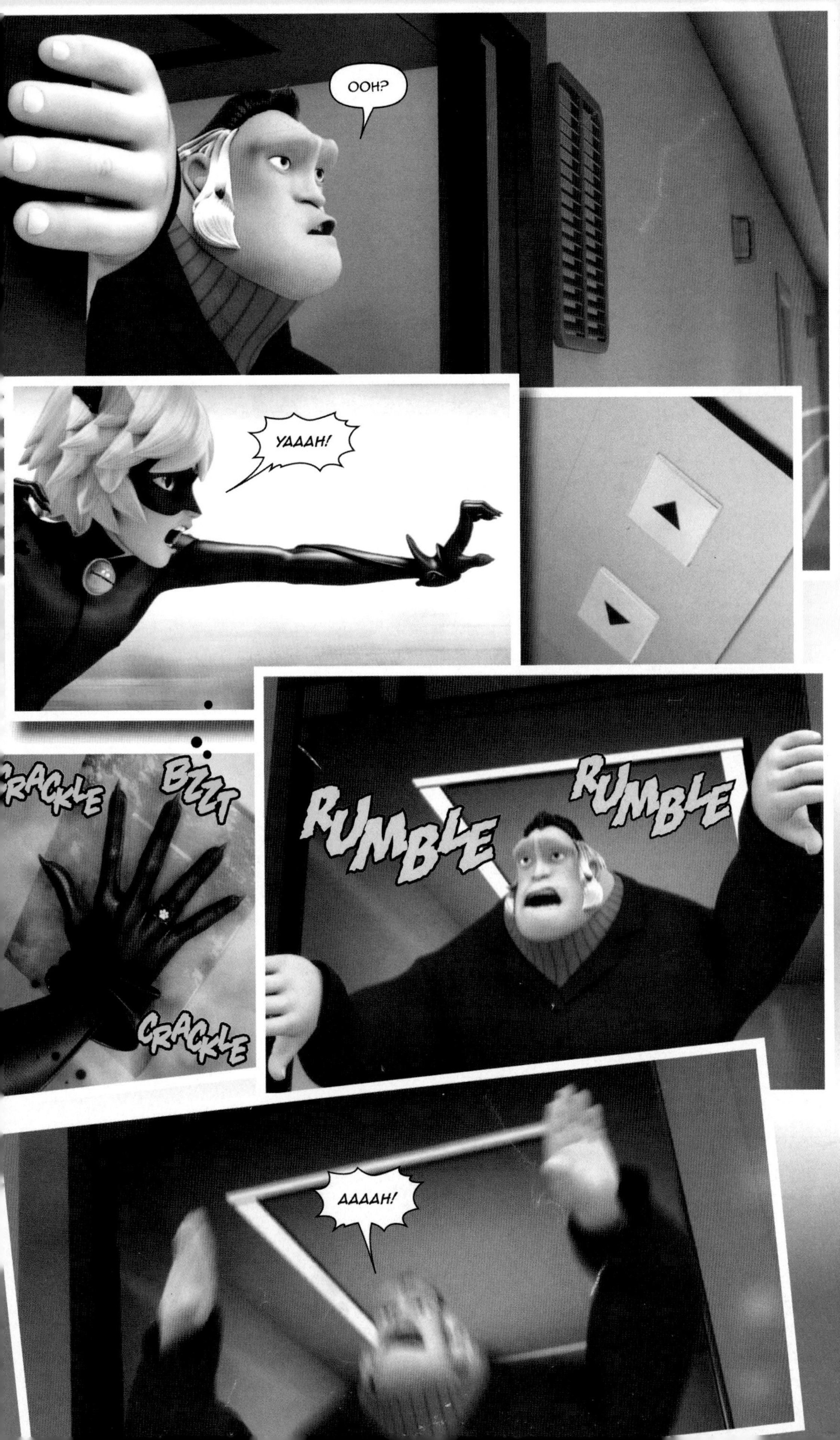
OOH?
YAAAH!
CRACKLE
BZZZT
CRACKLE
RUMBLE
RUMBLE
AAAAH!

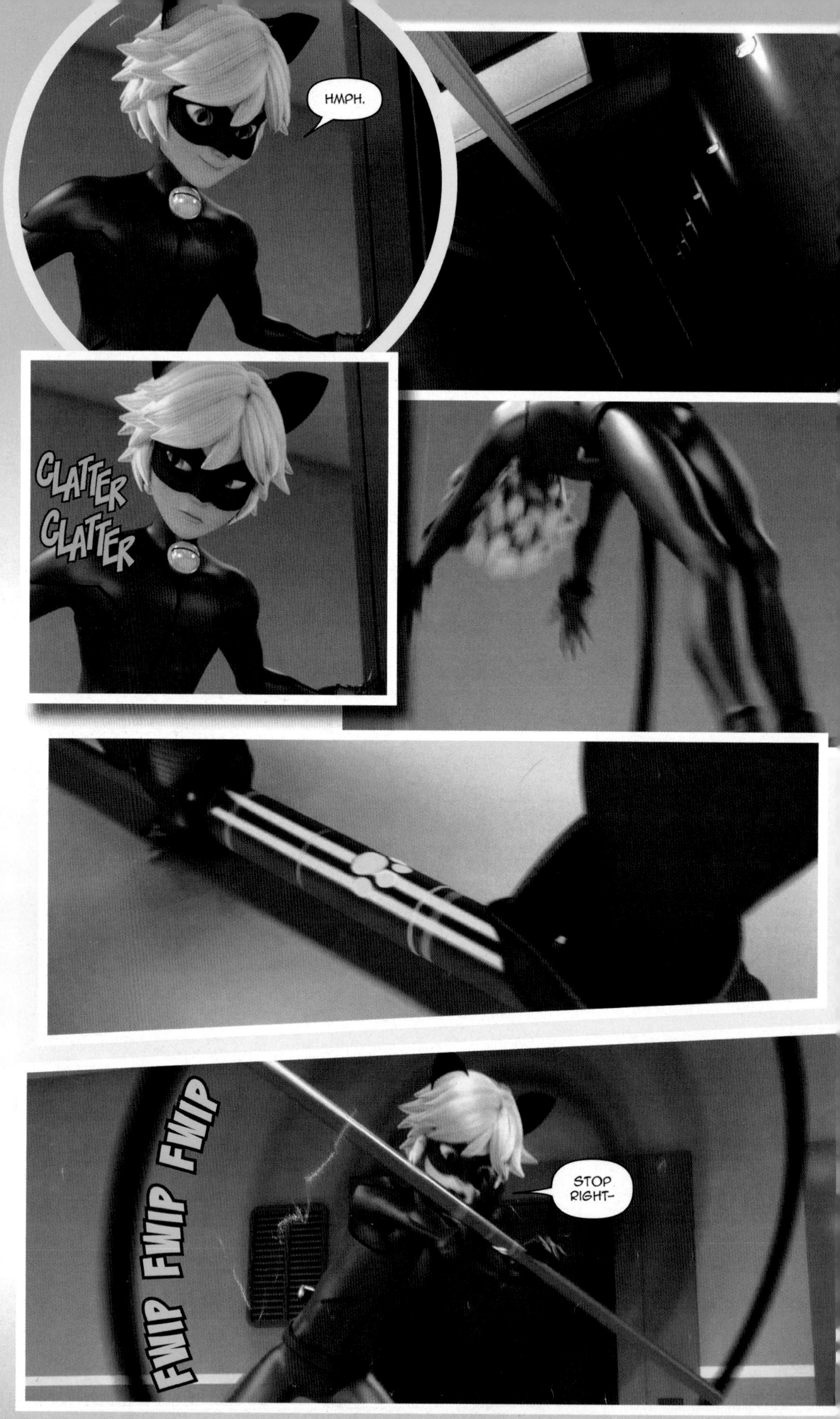

HMPH.
CLATTER
CLATTER
STOP RIGHT-
FWIP FWIP FWIP

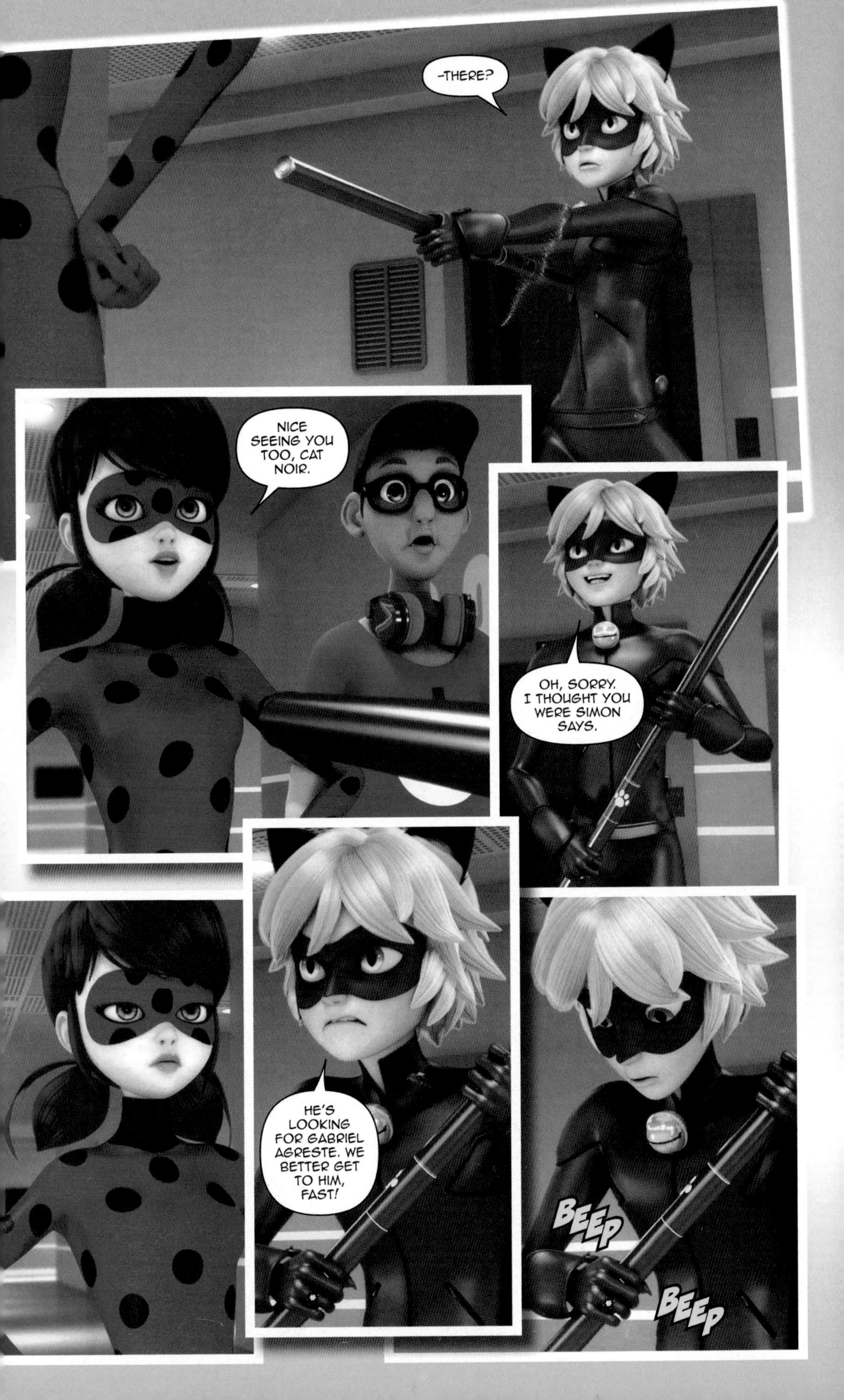
-THERE?
NICE SEEING YOU TOO, CAT NOIR.
OH, SORRY. I THOUGHT YOU WERE SIMON SAYS.
HE'S LOOKING FOR GABRIEL AGRESTE. WE BETTER GET TO HIM, FAST!
BEEP
BEEP

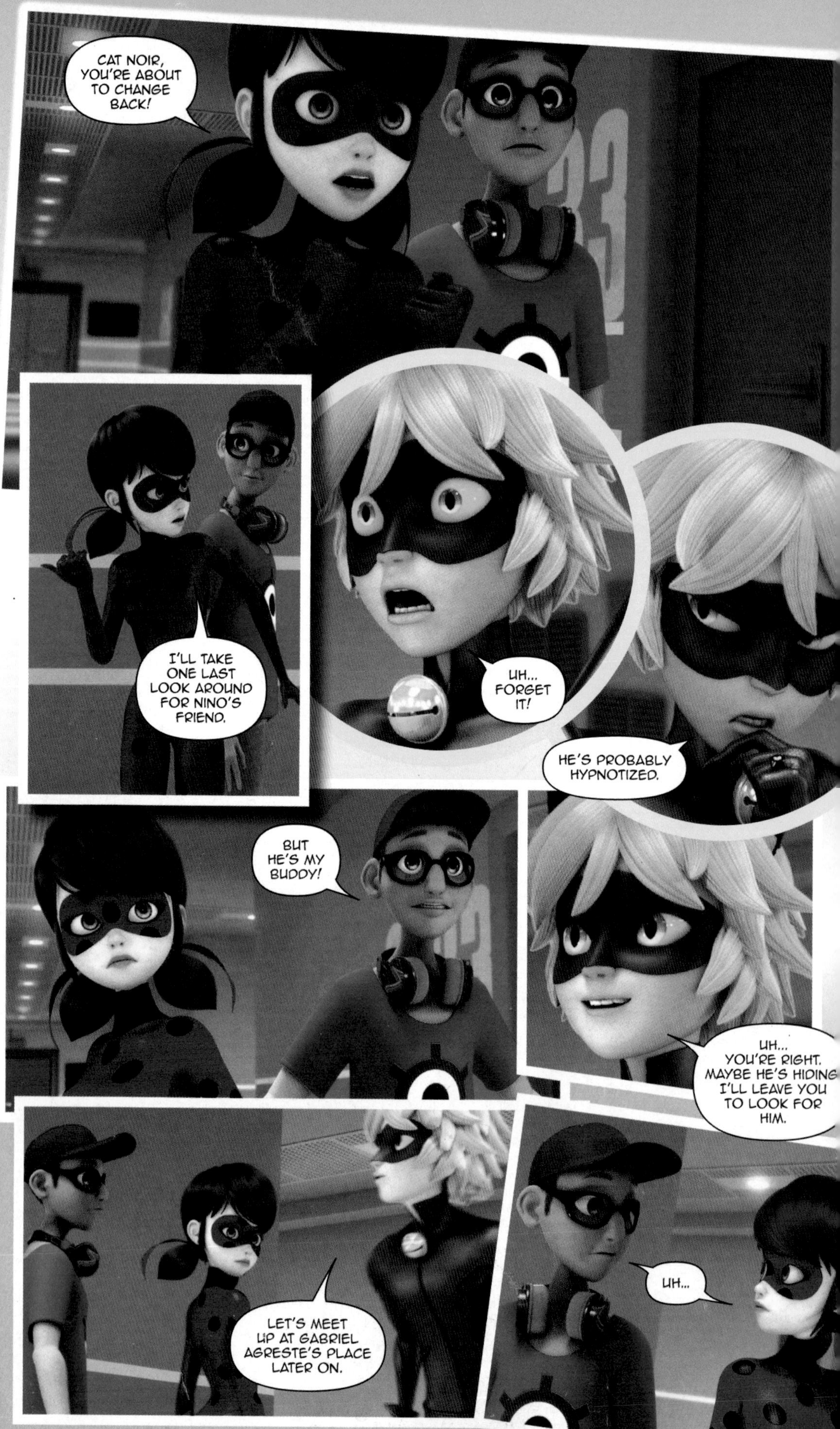
CAT NOIR, YOU'RE ABOUT TO CHANGE BACK!
I'LL TAKE ONE LAST LOOK AROUND FOR NINO'S FRIEND.
UH... FORGET IT!
HE'S PROBABLY HYPNOTIZED.
BUT HE'S MY BUDDY!
UH... YOU'RE RIGHT. MAYBE HE'S HIDING I'LL LEAVE YOU TO LOOK FOR HIM.
LET'S MEET UP AT GABRIEL AGRESTE'S PLACE LATER ON.
UH...

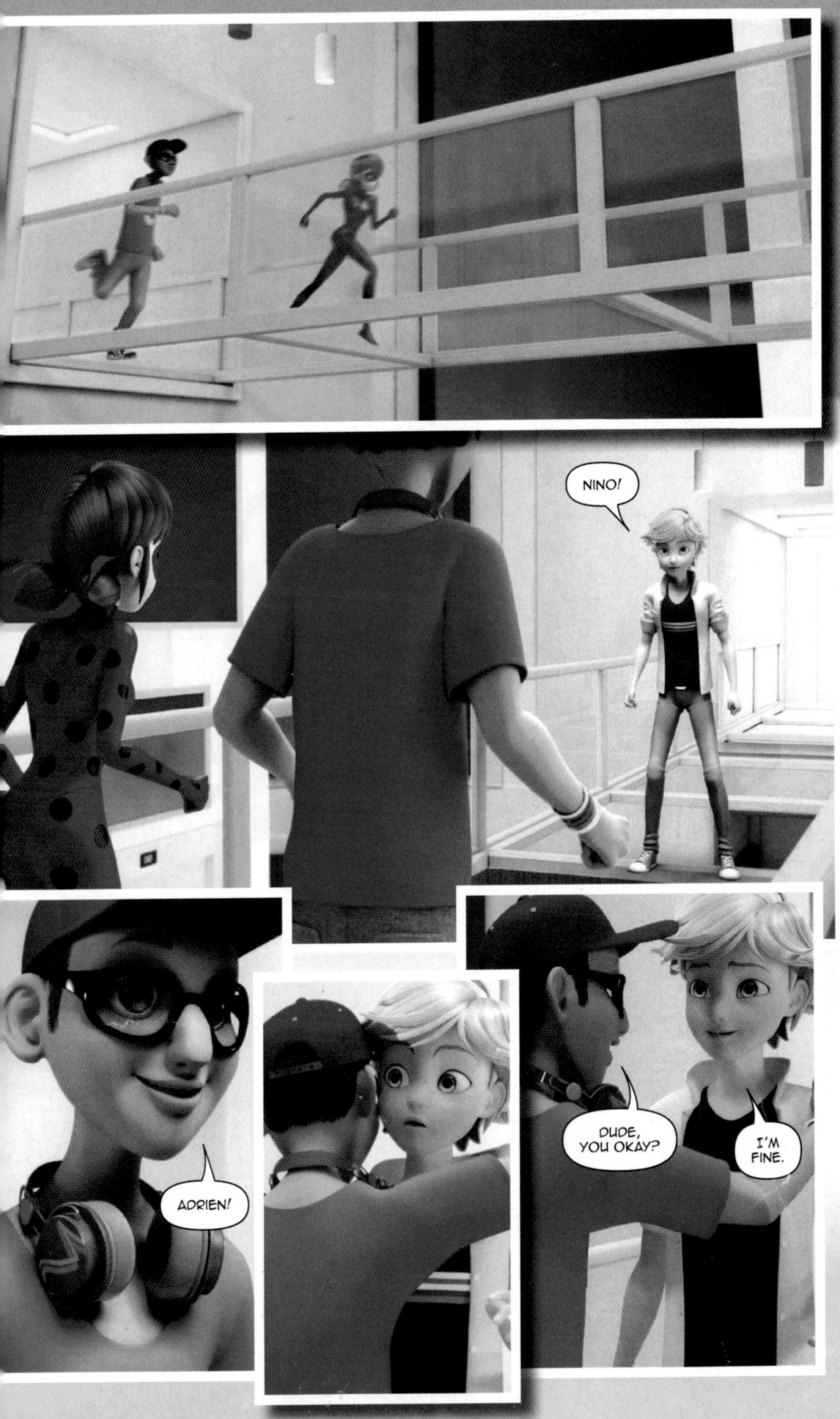
NINO!
ADRIEN!
DUDE, YOU OKAY?
I'M FINE.

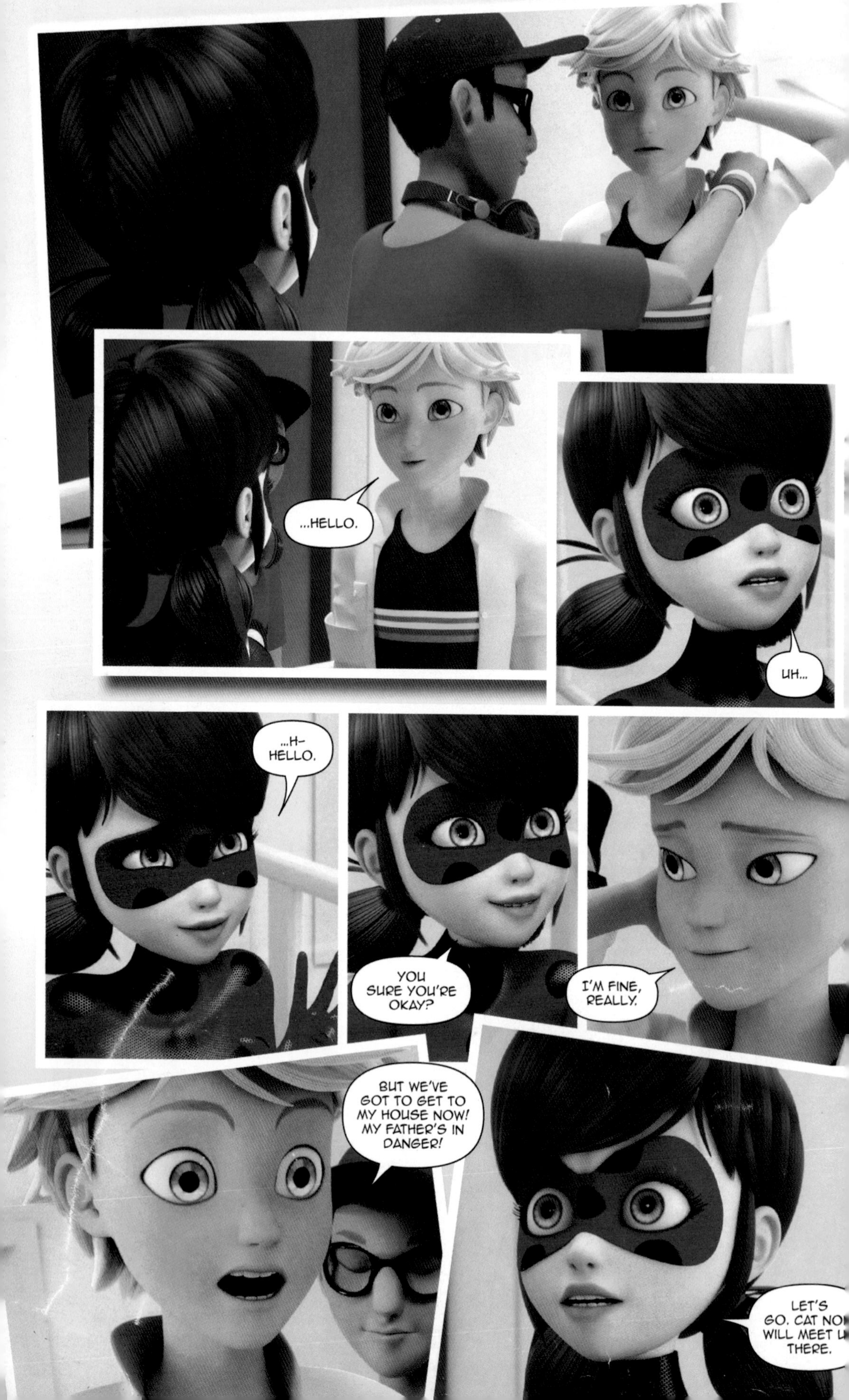
...HELLO.
UH...
...H-
HELLO.
YOU
SURE YOU'RE
OKAY?
I'M FINE,
REALLY.
BUT WE'VE
GOT TO GET TO
MY HOUSE NOW!
MY FATHER'S IN
DANGER!
LET'S
GO. CAT NO
WILL MEET U
THERE.

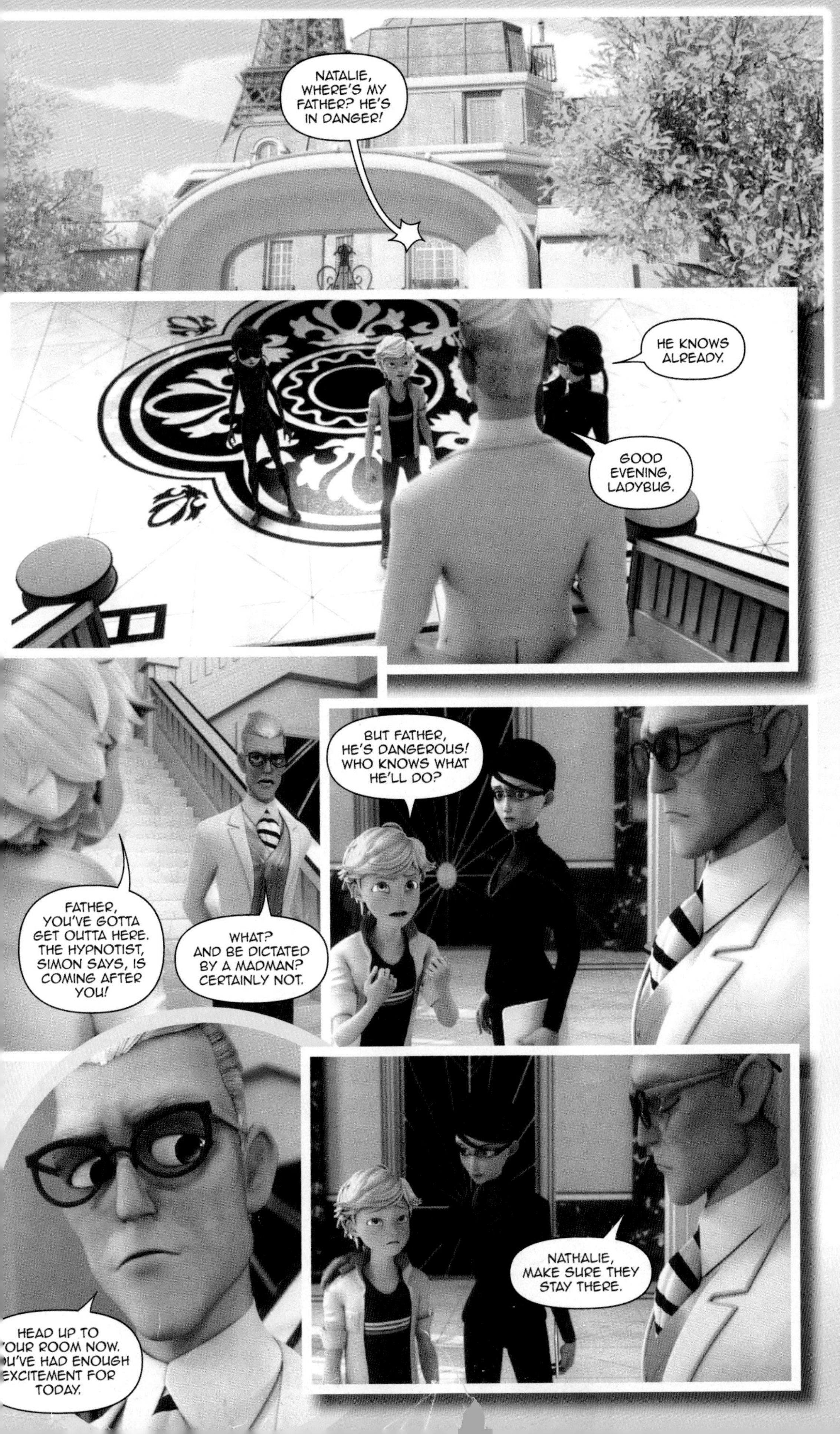
NATALIE, WHERE'S MY FATHER? HE'S IN DANGER!
HE KNOWS ALREADY.
GOOD EVENING, LADYBUG.
FATHER, YOU'VE GOTTA GET OUTTA HERE. THE HYPNOTIST, SIMON SAYS, IS COMING AFTER YOU!
WHAT? AND BE DICTATED BY A MADMAN? CERTAINLY NOT.
BUT FATHER, HE'S DANGEROUS! WHO KNOWS WHAT HE'LL DO?
HEAD UP TO OUR ROOM NOW. OU'VE HAD ENOUGH EXCITEMENT FOR TODAY.
NATHALIE, MAKE SURE THEY STAY THERE.

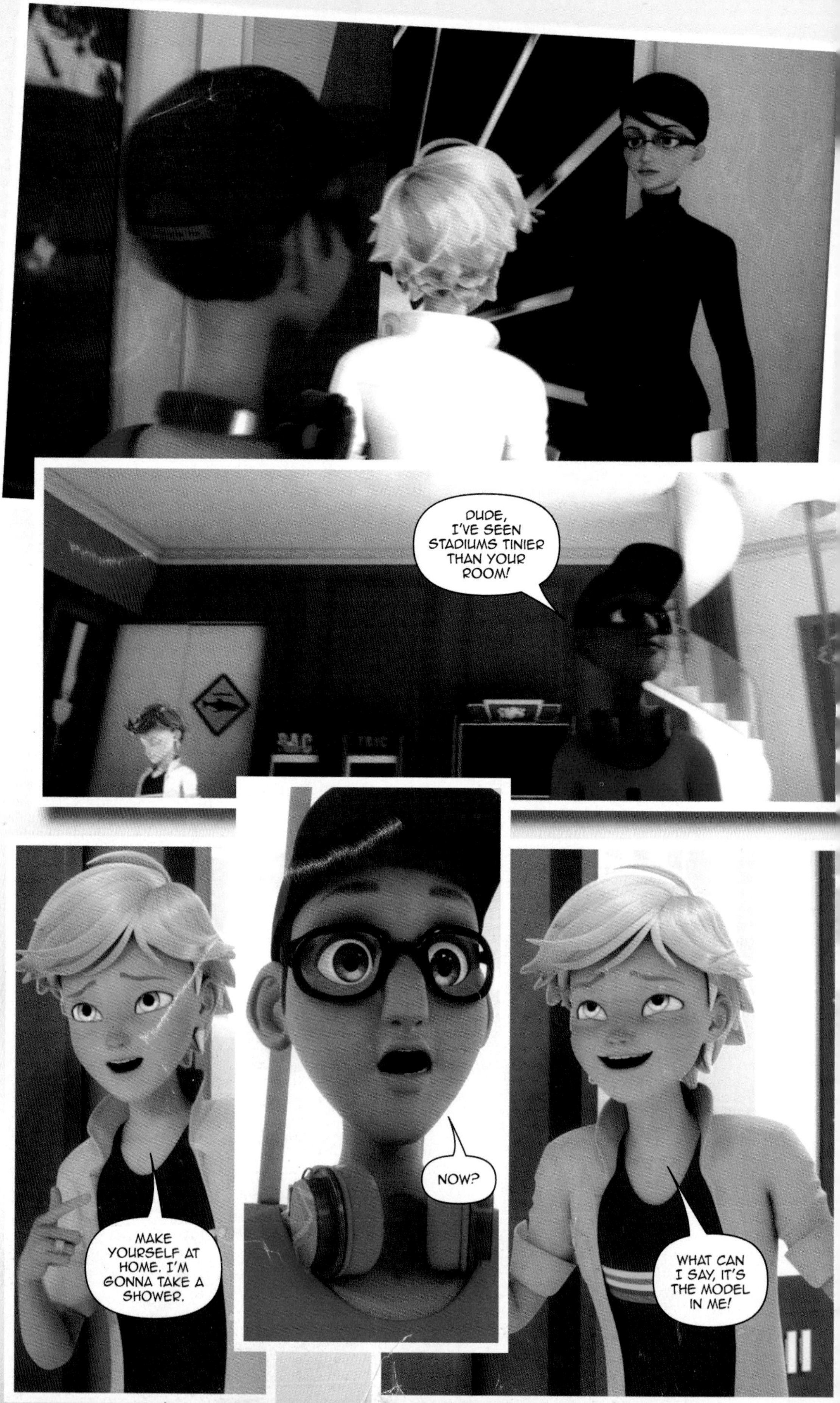
DUDE, I'VE SEEN STADIUMS TINIER THAN YOUR ROOM!
MAKE YOURSELF AT HOME. I'M GONNA TAKE A SHOWER.
NOW?
WHAT CAN I SAY, IT'S THE MODEL IN ME!

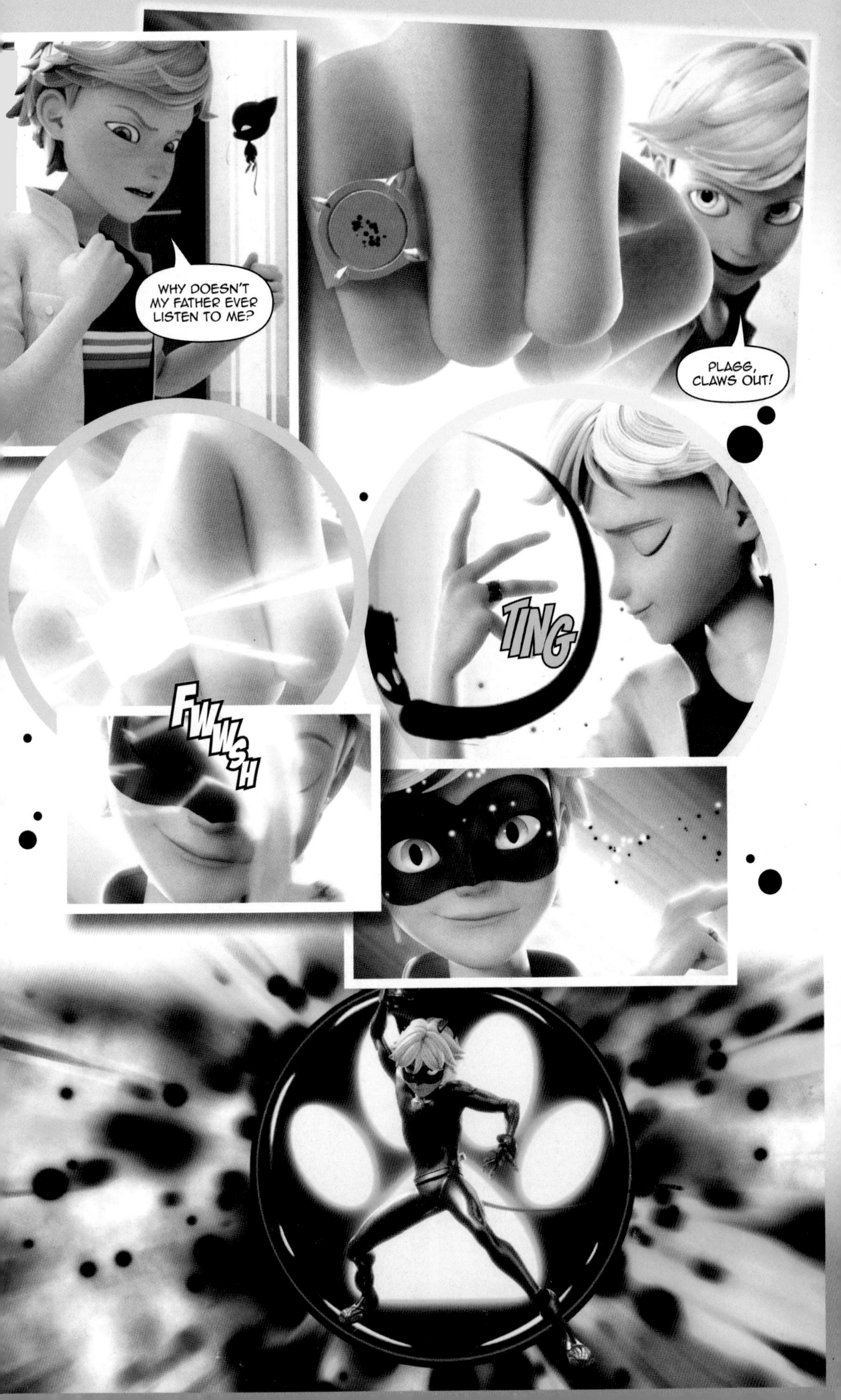

WHY DOESN'T MY FATHER EVER LISTEN TO ME?
PLAGG, CLAWS OUT!
TING
FWWSH

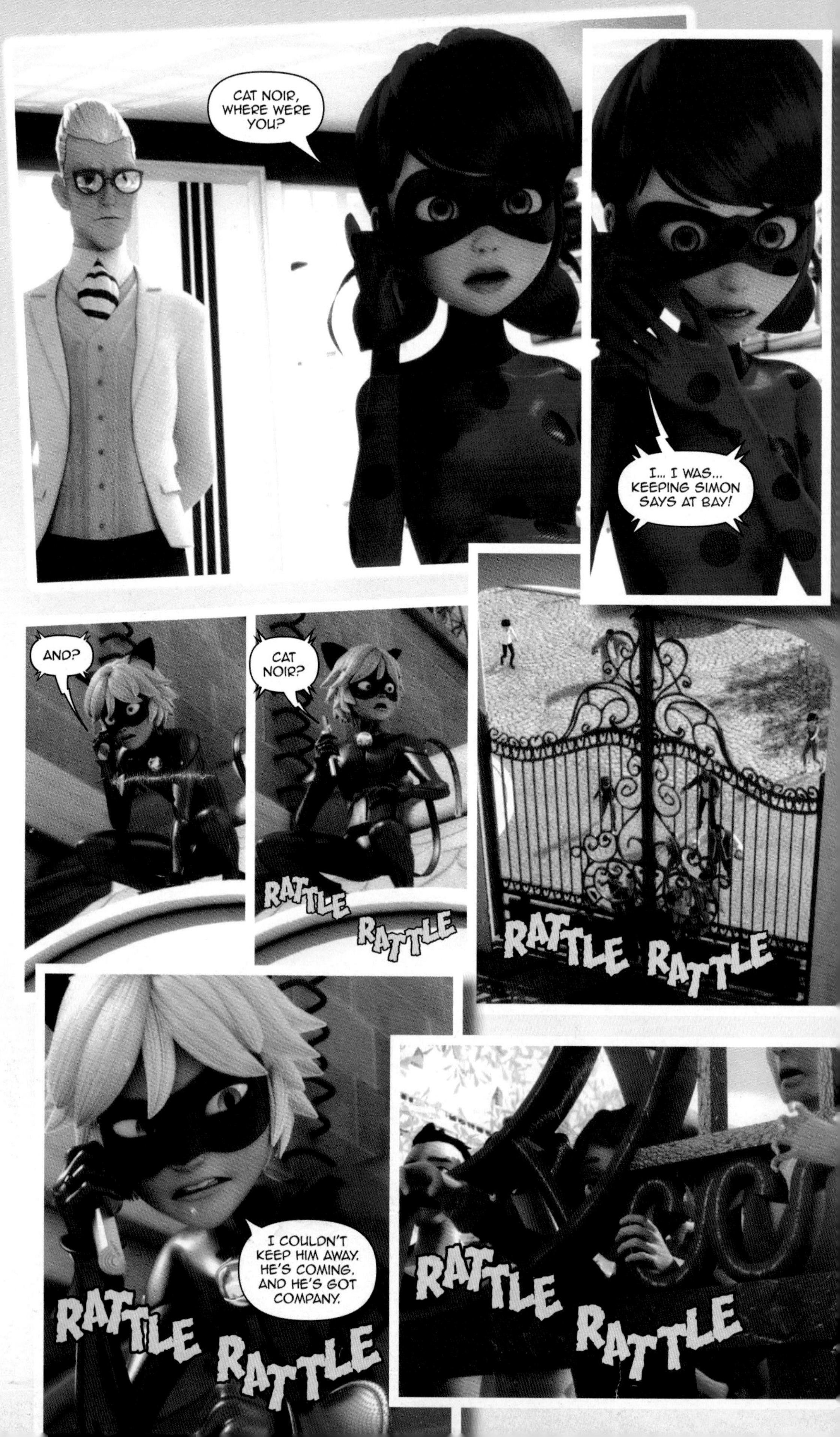

CAT NOIR, WHERE WERE YOU?
I... I WAS... KEEPING SIMON SAYS AT BAY!
AND?
CAT NOIR?
RATTLE
RATTLE
RATTLE RATTLE
I COULDN'T KEEP HIM AWAY. HE'S COMING. AND HE'S GOT COMPANY.
RATTLE
RATTLE
RATTLE
RATTLE

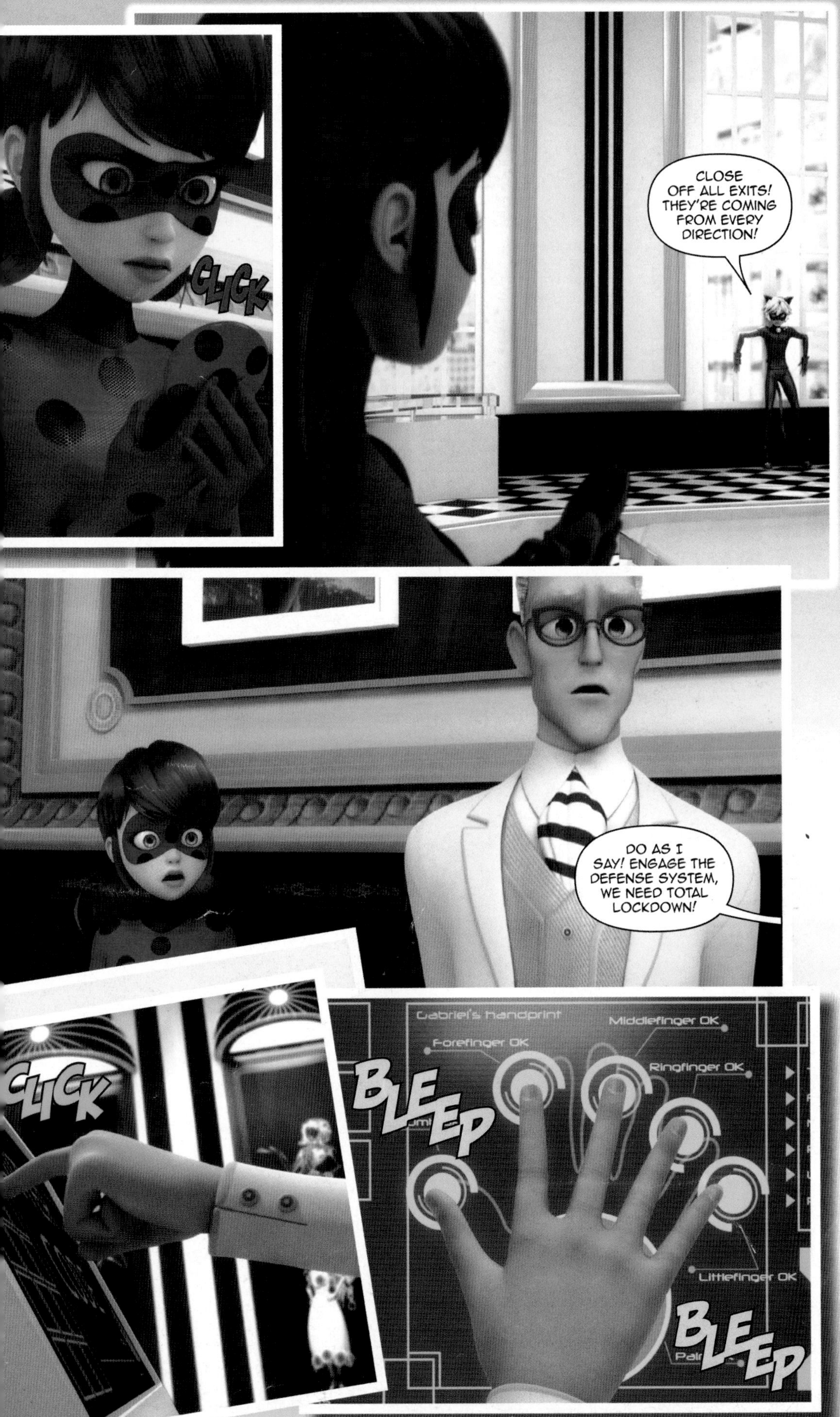
CLICK
CLOSE OFF ALL EXITS! THEY'RE COMING FROM EVERY DIRECTION!
DO AS I SAY! ENGAGE THE DEFENSE SYSTEM, WE NEED TOTAL LOCKDOWN!
CLICK
Gabriel's handprint
Forefinger OK
Middlefinger OK
Ringfinger OK
Littlefinger OK
BLEEP
BLEEP

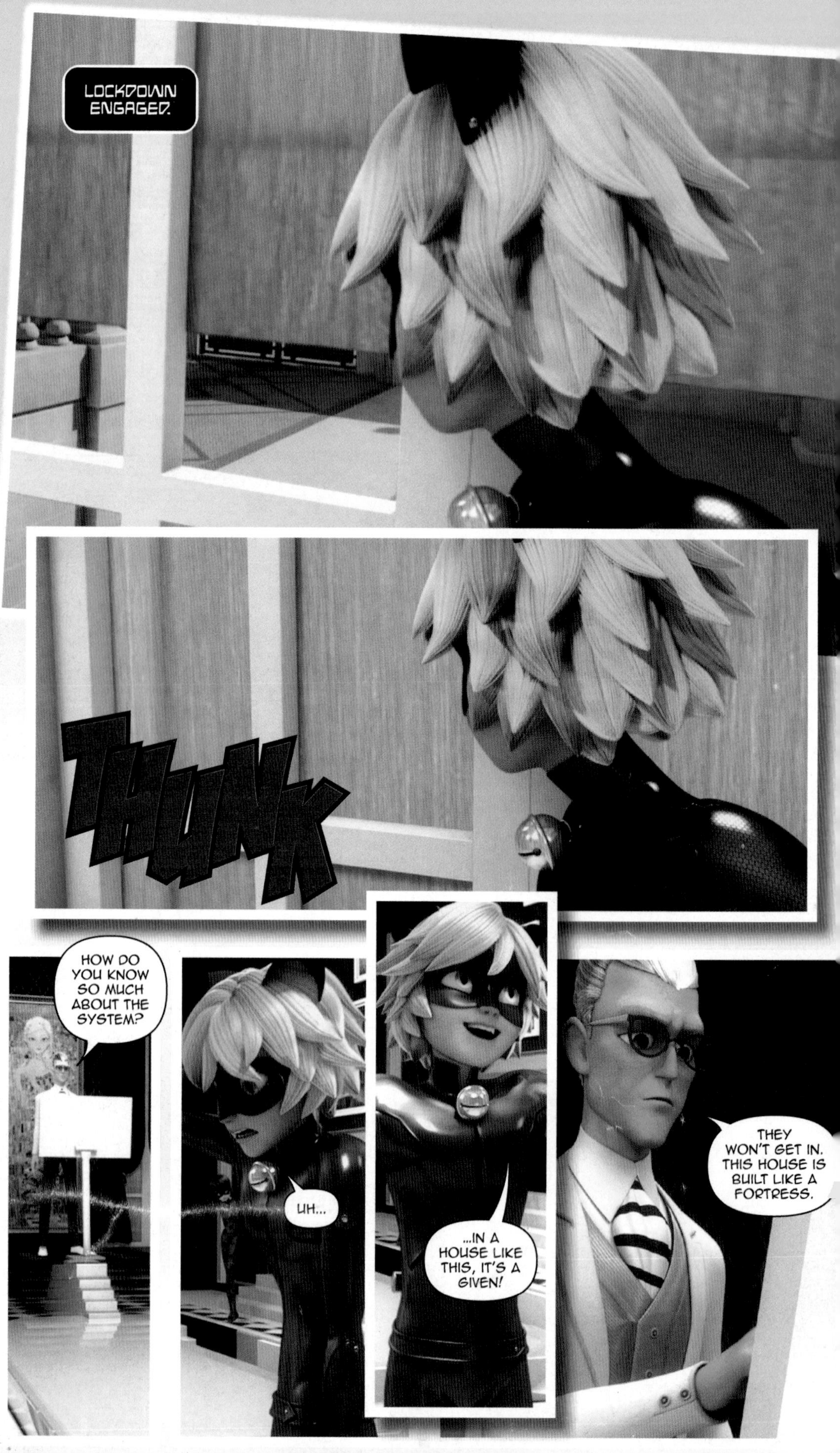

LOCKDOWN ENGAGED.
THUNK
HOW DO YOU KNOW SO MUCH ABOUT THE SYSTEM?
UH...
...IN A HOUSE LIKE THIS, IT'S A GIVEN!
THEY WON'T GET IN. THIS HOUSE IS BUILT LIKE A FORTRESS.

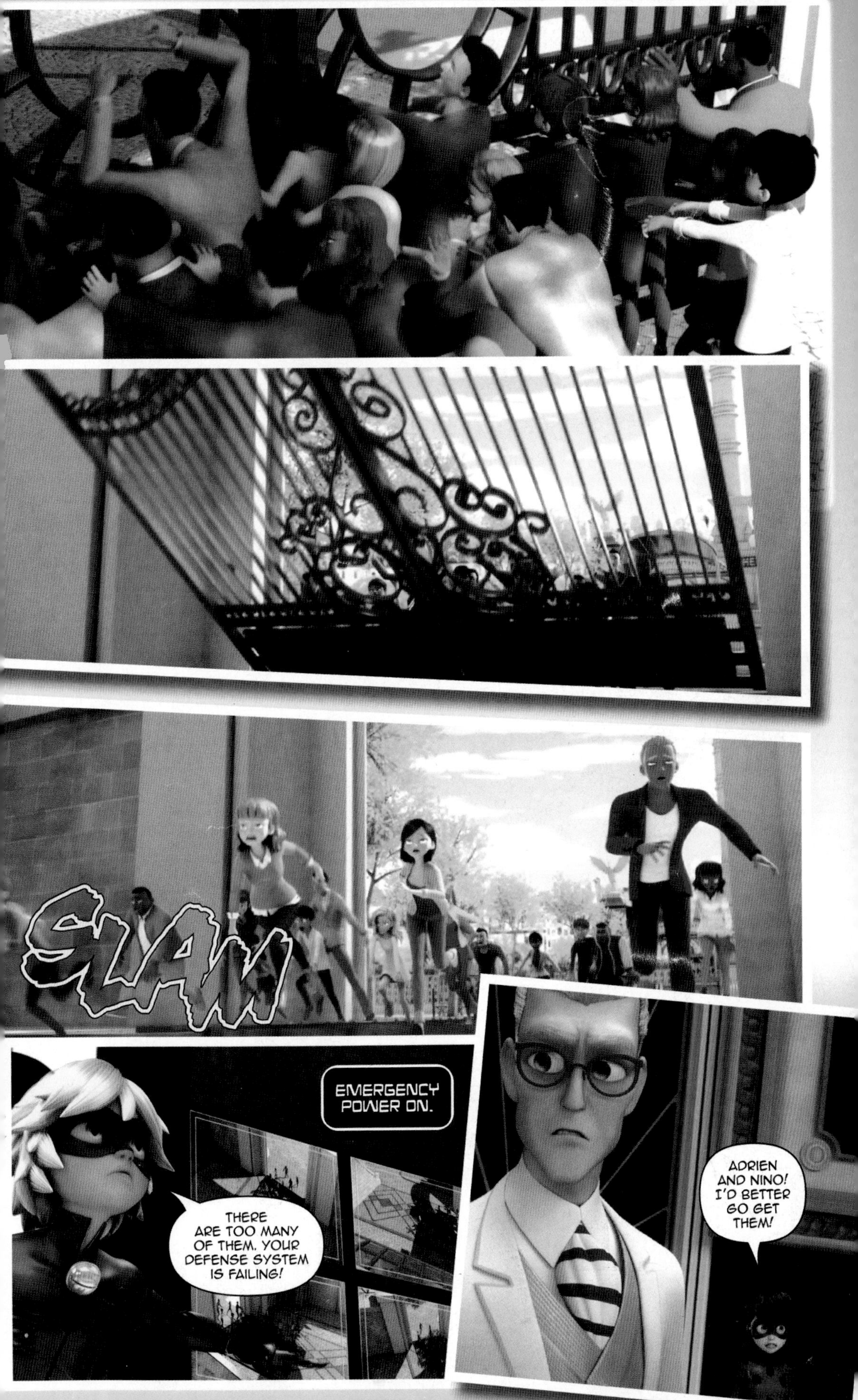
SLAM
EMERGENCY POWER ON.
THERE ARE TOO MANY OF THEM. YOUR DEFENSE SYSTEM IS FAILING!
ADRIEN AND NINO! I'D BETTER GO GET THEM!

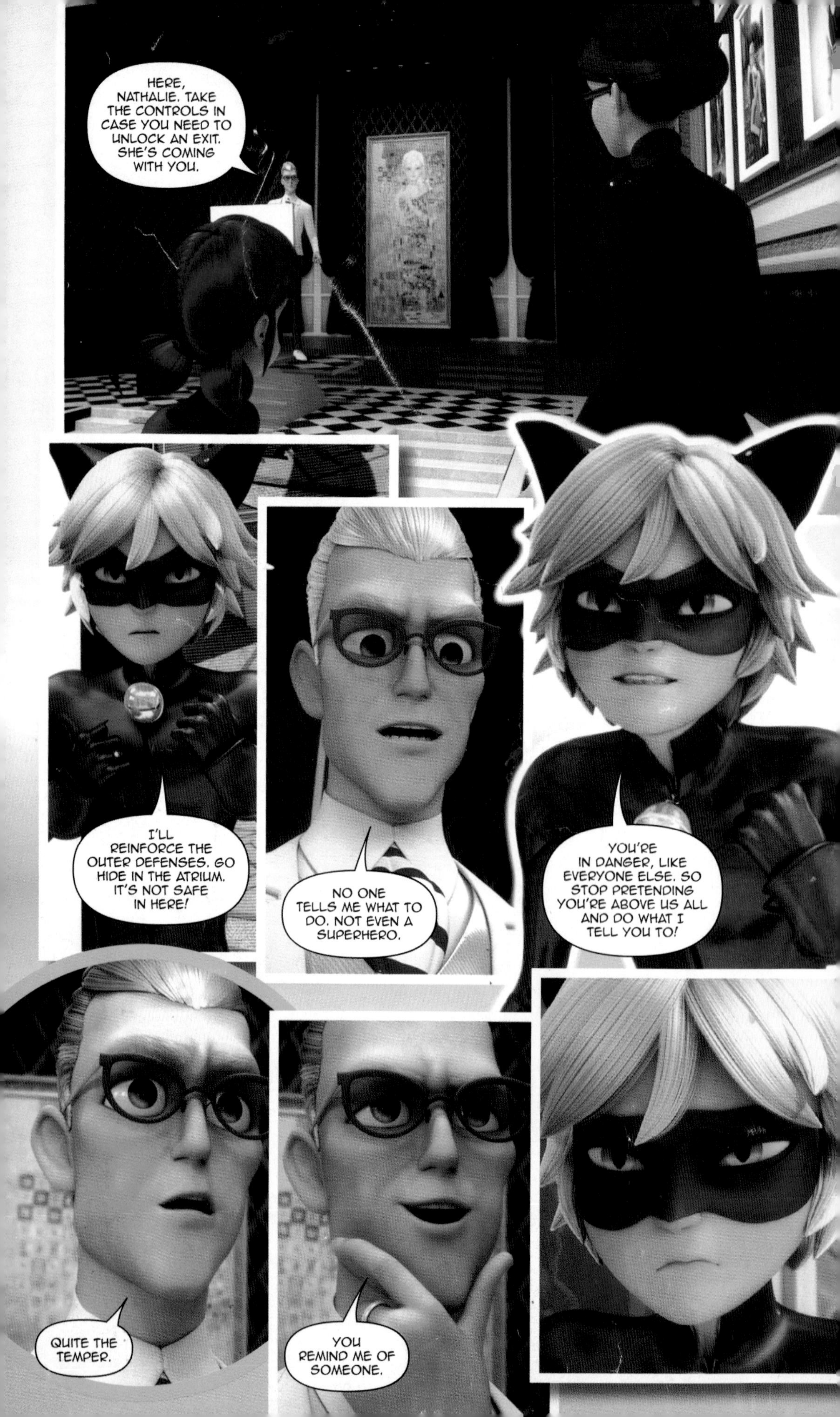
HERE, NATHALIE. TAKE THE CONTROLS IN CASE YOU NEED TO UNLOCK AN EXIT. SHE'S COMING WITH YOU.
I'LL REINFORCE THE OUTER DEFENSES. GO HIDE IN THE ATRIUM. IT'S NOT SAFE IN HERE!
NO ONE TELLS ME WHAT TO DO. NOT EVEN A SUPERHERO.
YOU'RE IN DANGER, LIKE EVERYONE ELSE. SO STOP PRETENDING YOU'RE ABOVE US ALL AND DO WHAT I TELL YOU TO!
QUITE THE TEMPER.
YOU REMIND ME OF SOMEONE.

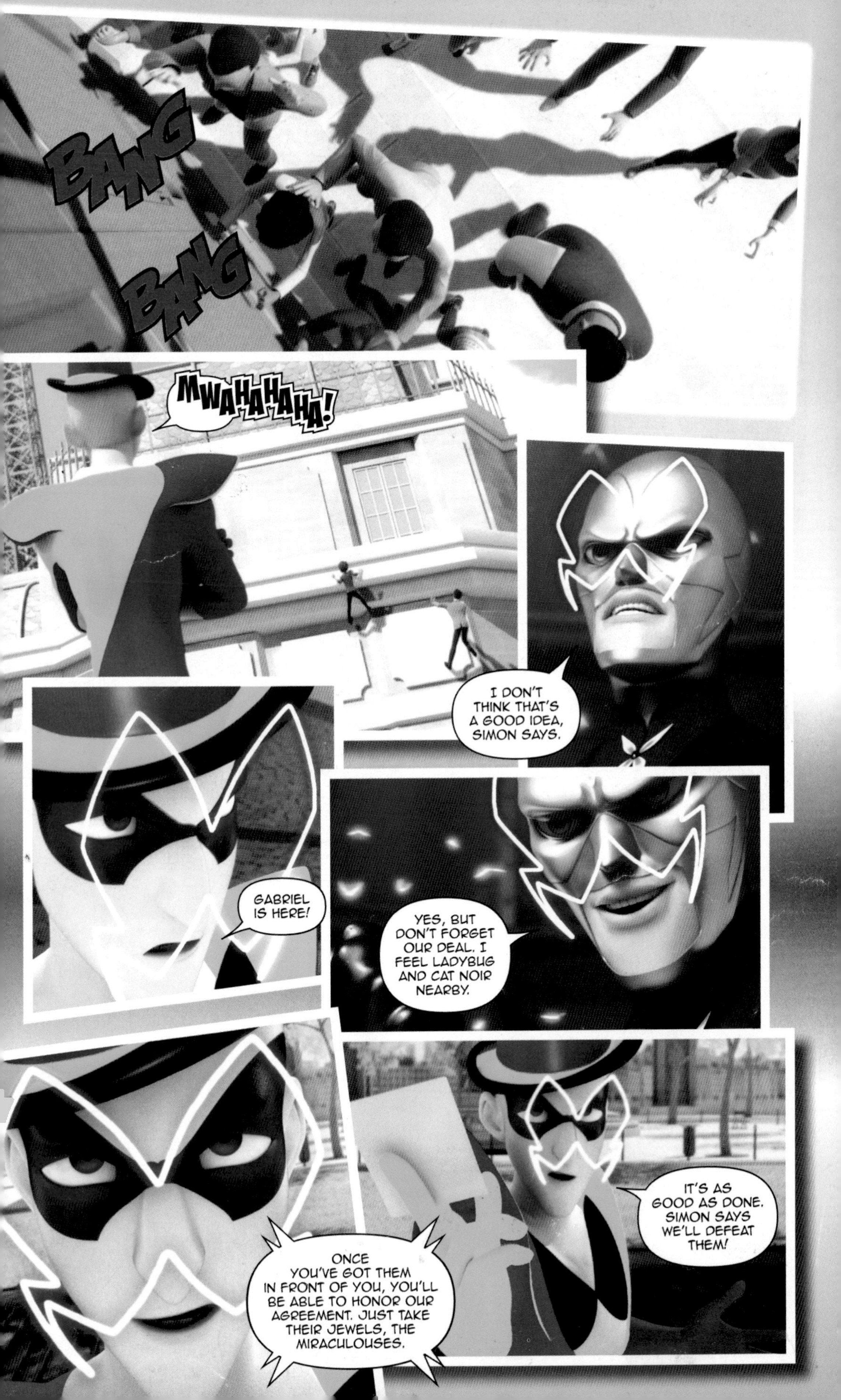
BANG
BANG
MWAHAHAHA!
I DON'T THINK THAT'S A GOOD IDEA, SIMON SAYS.
GABRIEL IS HERE!
YES, BUT DON'T FORGET OUR DEAL. I FEEL LADYBUG AND CAT NOIR NEARBY.
ONCE YOU'VE GOT THEM IN FRONT OF YOU, YOU'LL BE ABLE TO HONOR OUR AGREEMENT. JUST TAKE THEIR JEWELS, THE MIRACULOUSES.
IT'S AS GOOD AS DONE. SIMON SAYS WE'LL DEFEAT THEM!

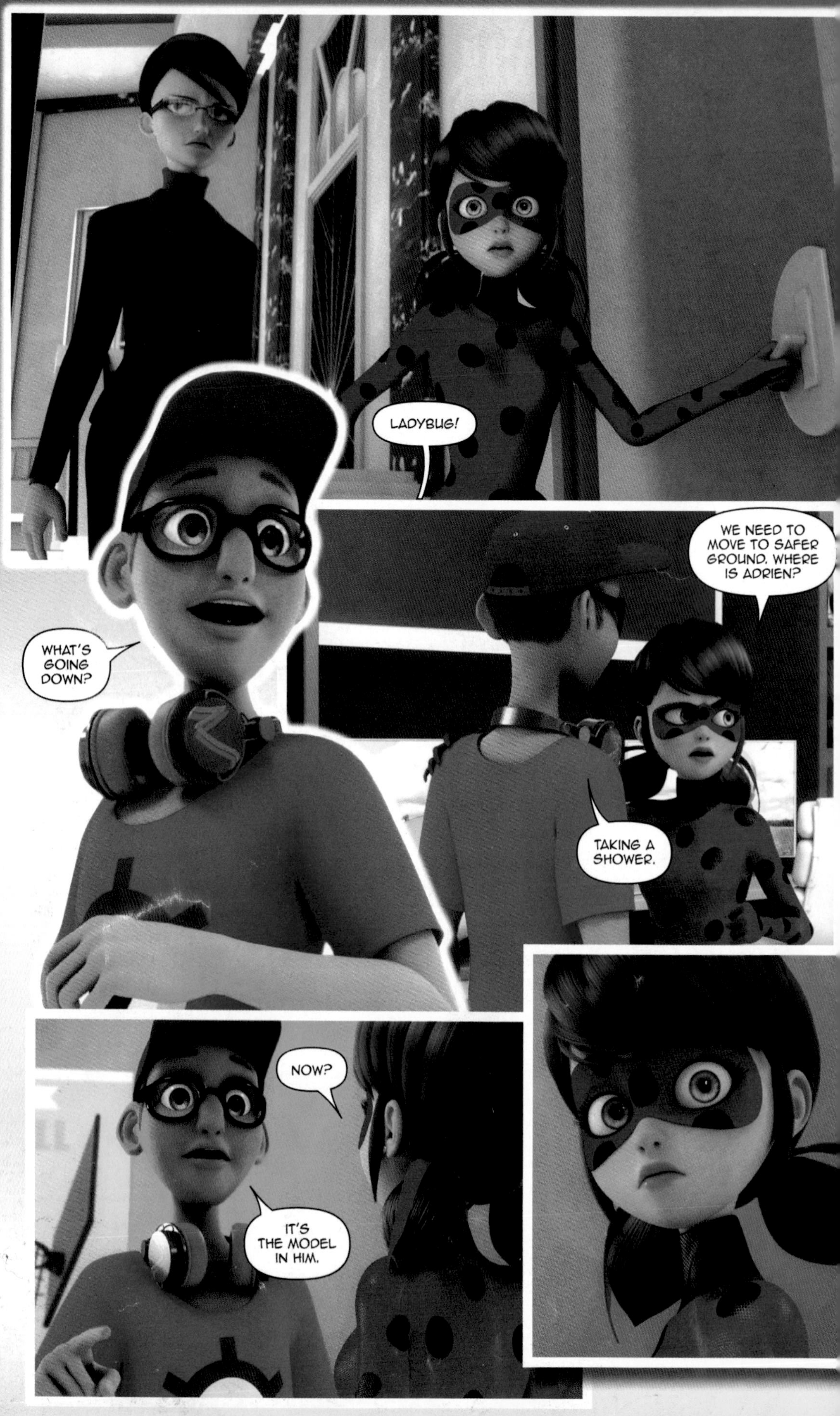
LADYBUG!
WHAT'S GOING DOWN?
WE NEED TO MOVE TO SAFER GROUND. WHERE IS ADRIEN?
TAKING A SHOWER.
NOW?
IT'S THE MODEL IN HIM.

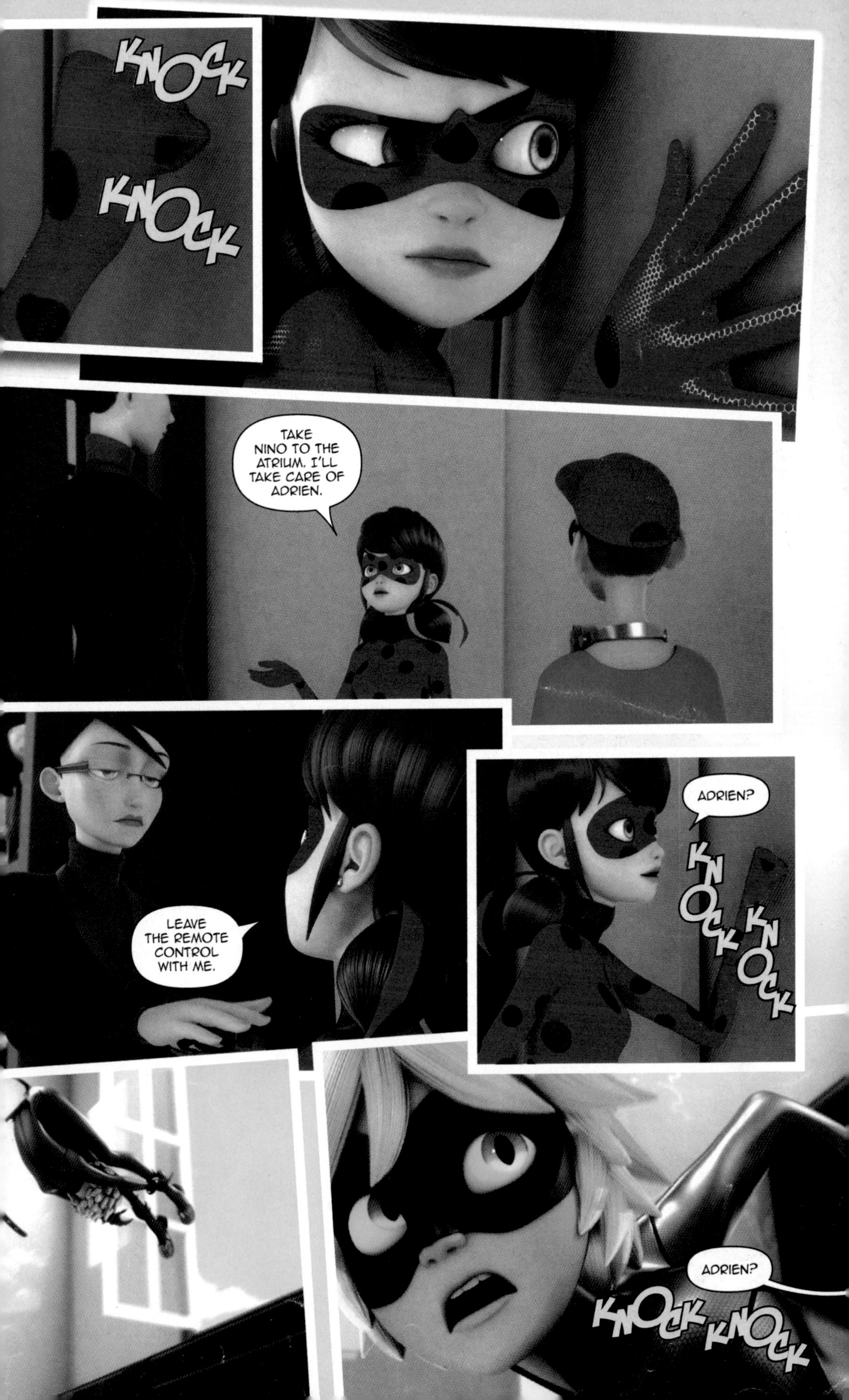
KNOCK
KNOCK
TAKE NINO TO THE ATRIUM. I'LL TAKE CARE OF ADRIEN.
LEAVE THE REMOTE CONTROL WITH ME.
ADRIEN?
KNOCK KNOCK
ADRIEN?
KNOCK KNOCK

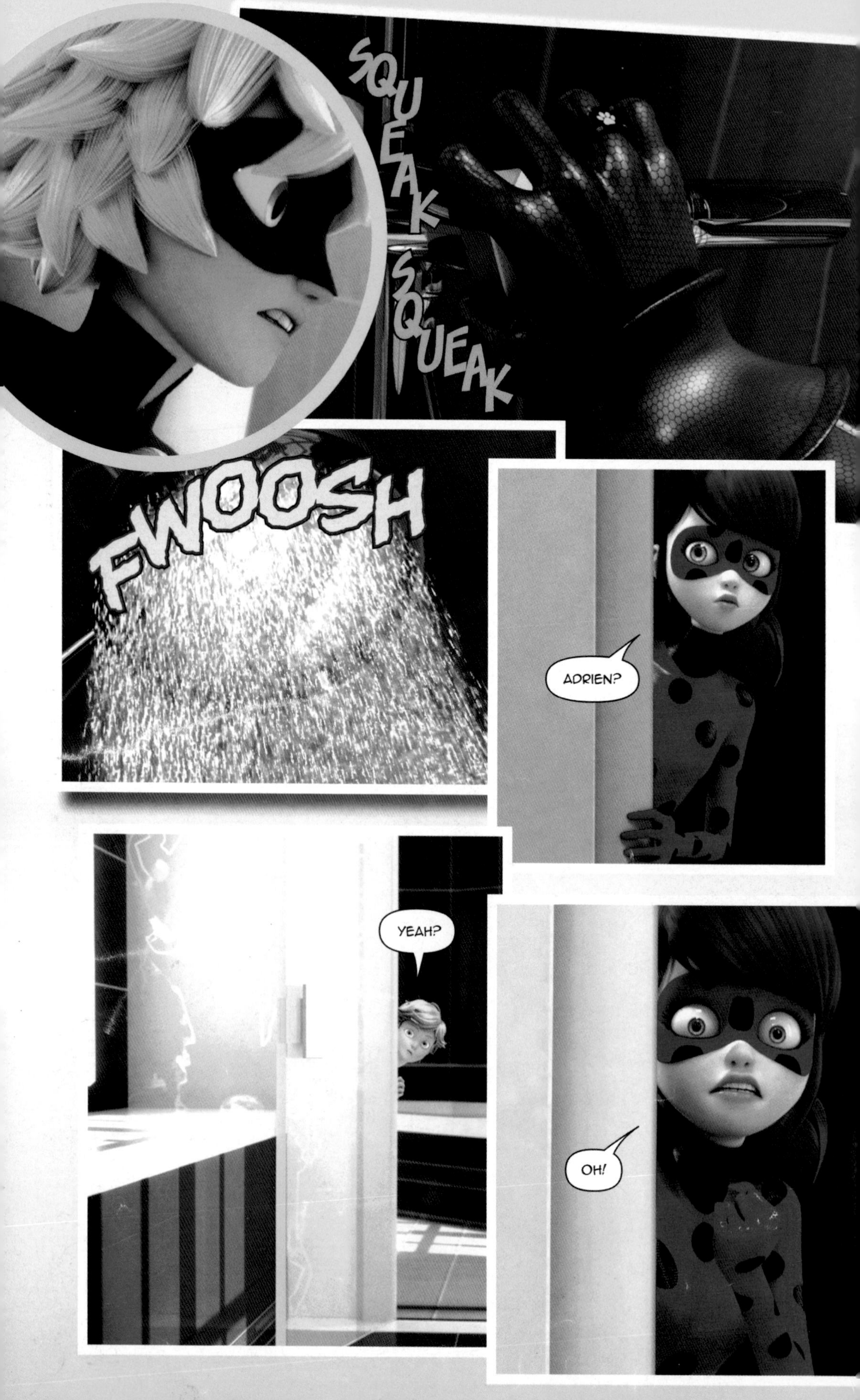
SQUEAK
SQUEAK
FWOOSH
ADRIEN?
YEAH?
OH!

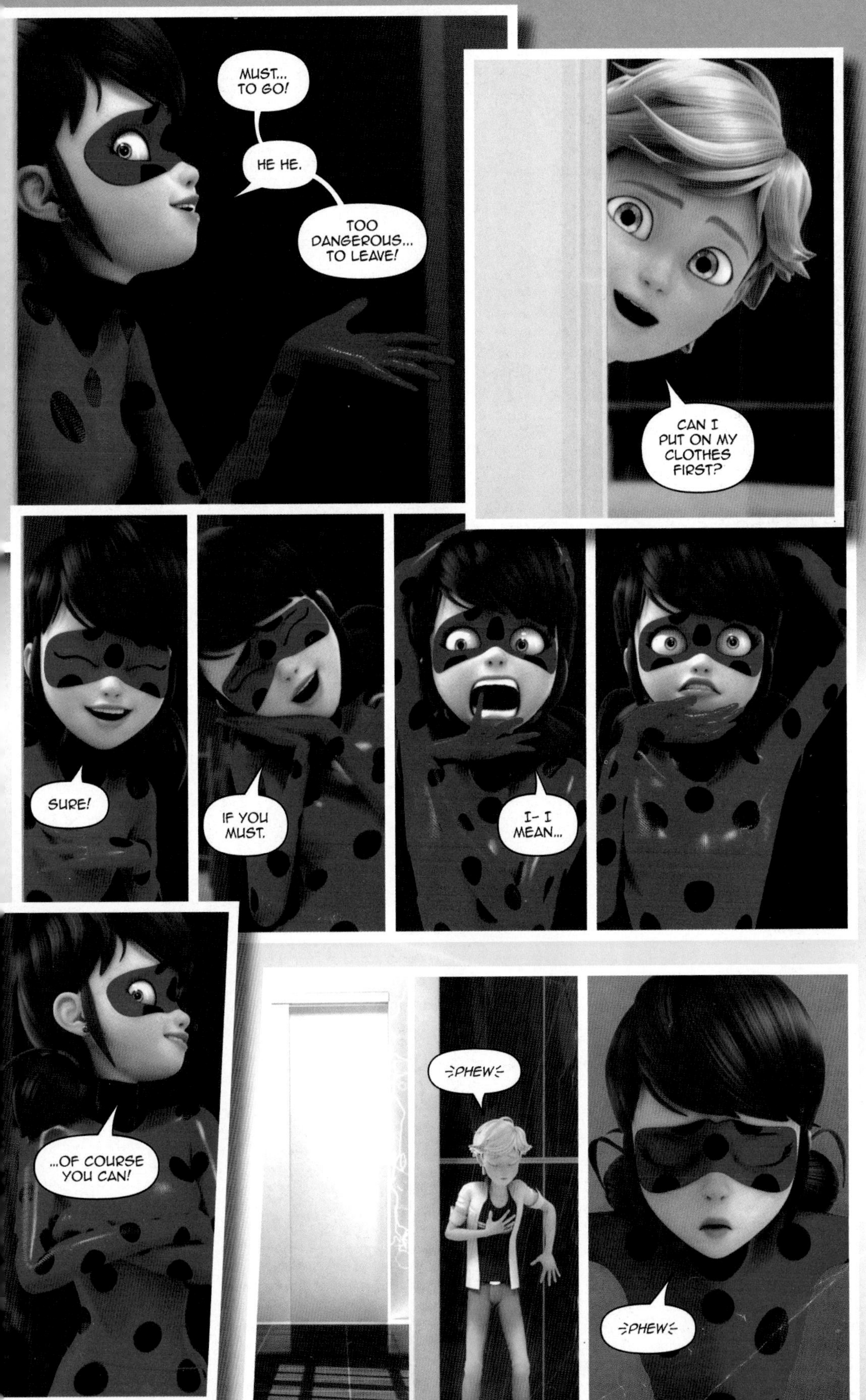
MUST... TO GO!
HE HE.
TOO DANGEROUS... TO LEAVE!
CAN I PUT ON MY CLOTHES FIRST?
SURE!
IF YOU MUST.
I- I MEAN...
...OF COURSE YOU CAN!
PHEW
PHEW

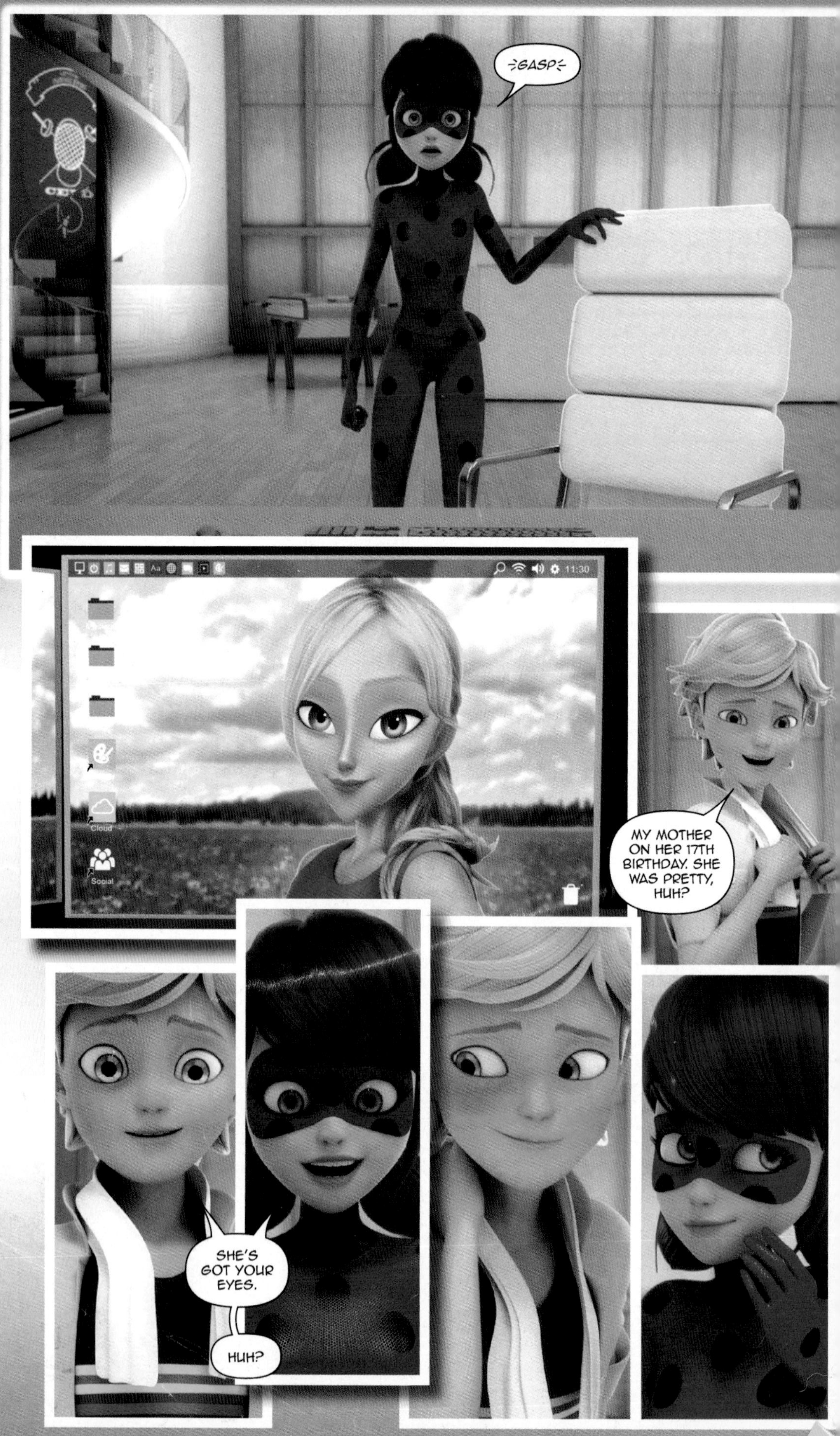
GASP
MY MOTHER ON HER 17TH BIRTHDAY. SHE WAS PRETTY, HUH?
SHE'S GOT YOUR EYES.
HUH?

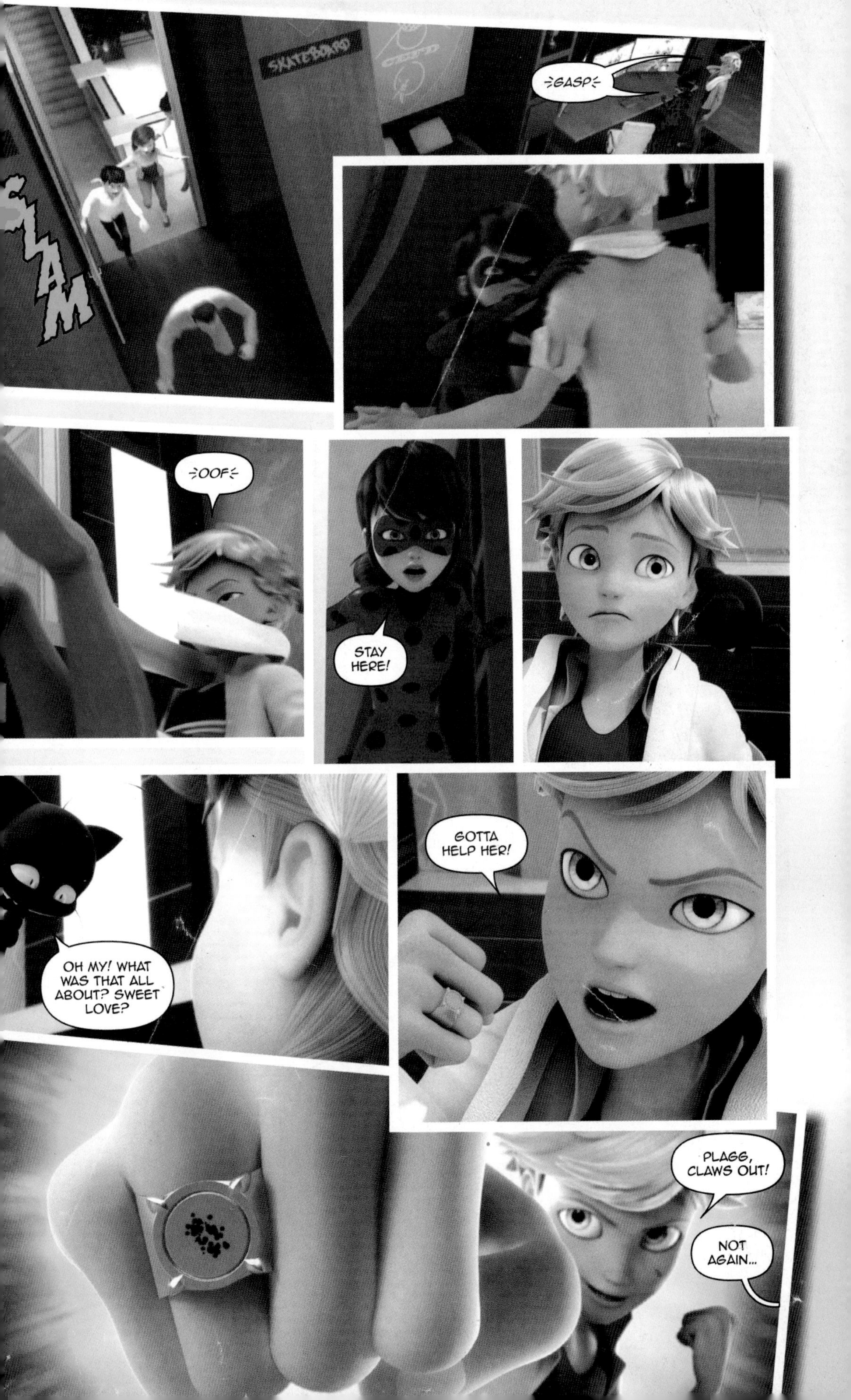
SLAM
GASP
OOF
STAY HERE!
GOTTA HELP HER!
OH MY! WHAT WAS THAT ALL ABOUT? SWEET LOVE?
PLAGG, CLAWS OUT!
NOT AGAIN...

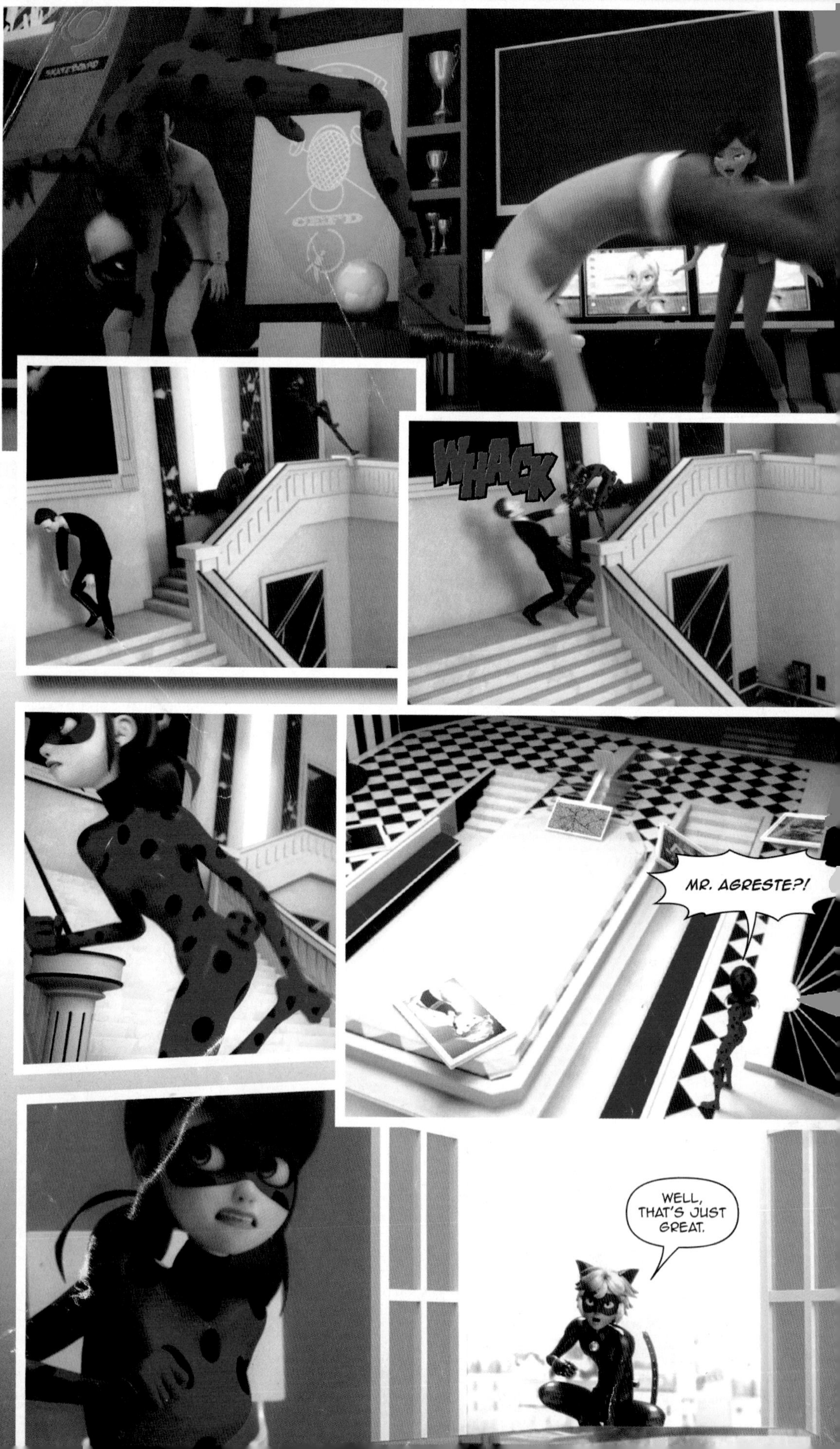
WHACK
MR. AGRESTE?!
WELL, THAT'S JUST GREAT.

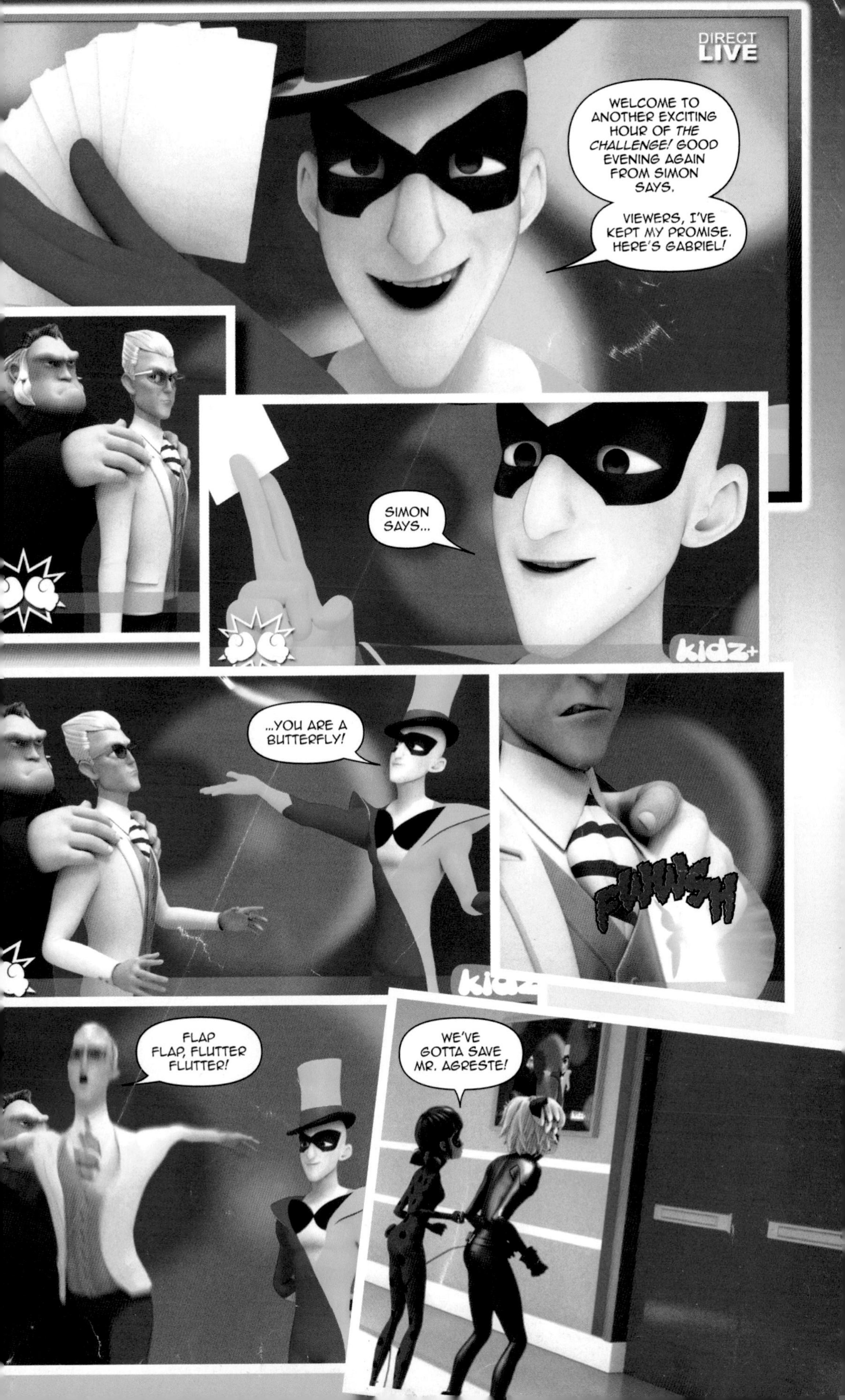
DIRECT LIVE
WELCOME TO ANOTHER EXCITING HOUR OF THE CHALLENGE! GOOD EVENING AGAIN FROM SIMON SAYS.
VIEWERS, I'VE KEPT MY PROMISE. HERE'S GABRIEL!
SIMON SAYS...
kidz+
...YOU ARE A BUTTERFLY!
FWWISH
FLAP FLAP, FLUTTER FLUTTER!
WE'VE GOTTA SAVE MR. AGRESTE!

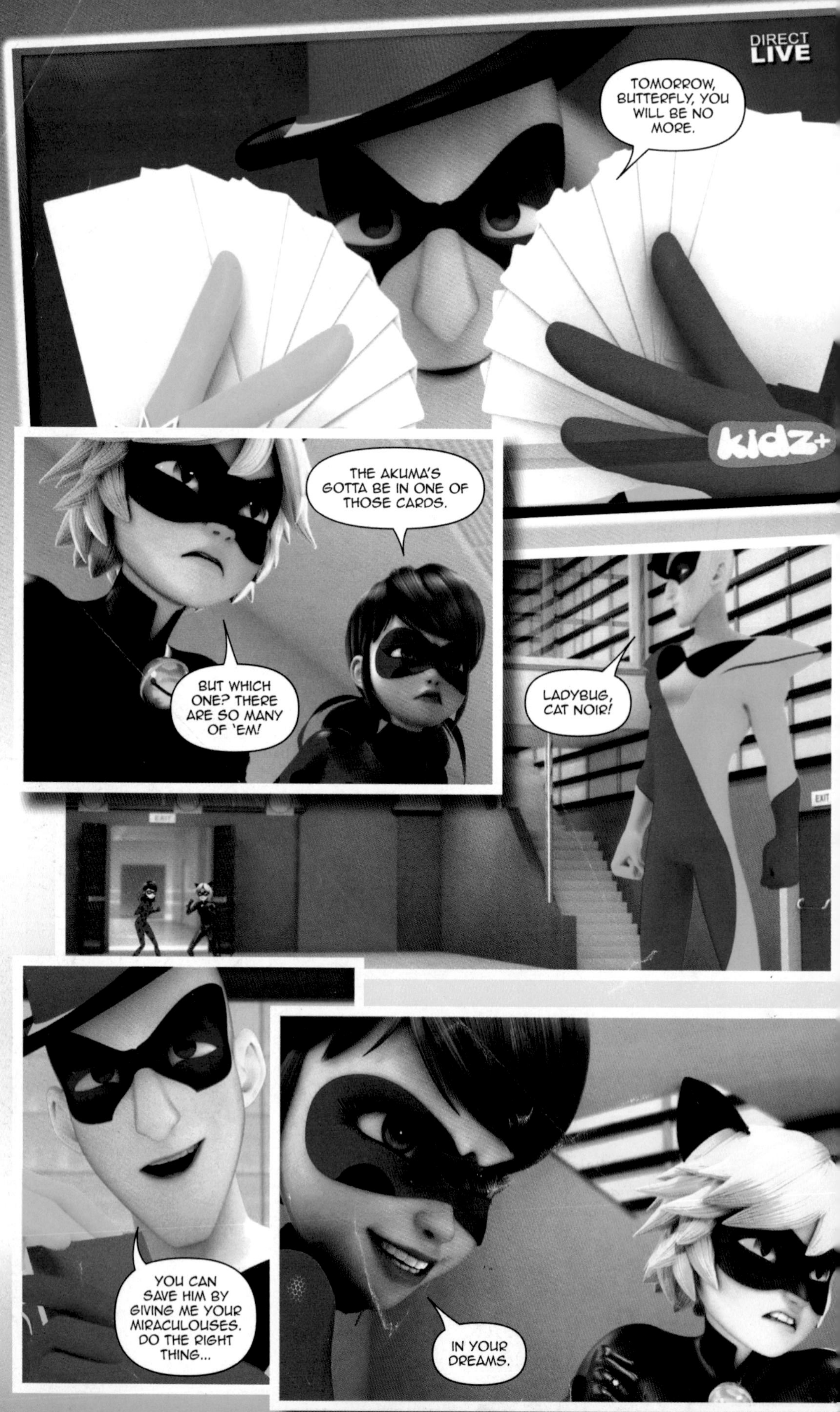
DIRECT
LIVE
TOMORROW, BUTTERFLY, YOU WILL BE NO MORE.
kidz+
THE AKUMA'S GOTTA BE IN ONE OF THOSE CARDS.
BUT WHICH ONE? THERE ARE SO MANY OF 'EM!
LADYBUG, CAT NOIR!
YOU CAN SAVE HIM BY GIVING ME YOUR MIRACULOUSES. DO THE RIGHT THING...
IN YOUR DREAMS.

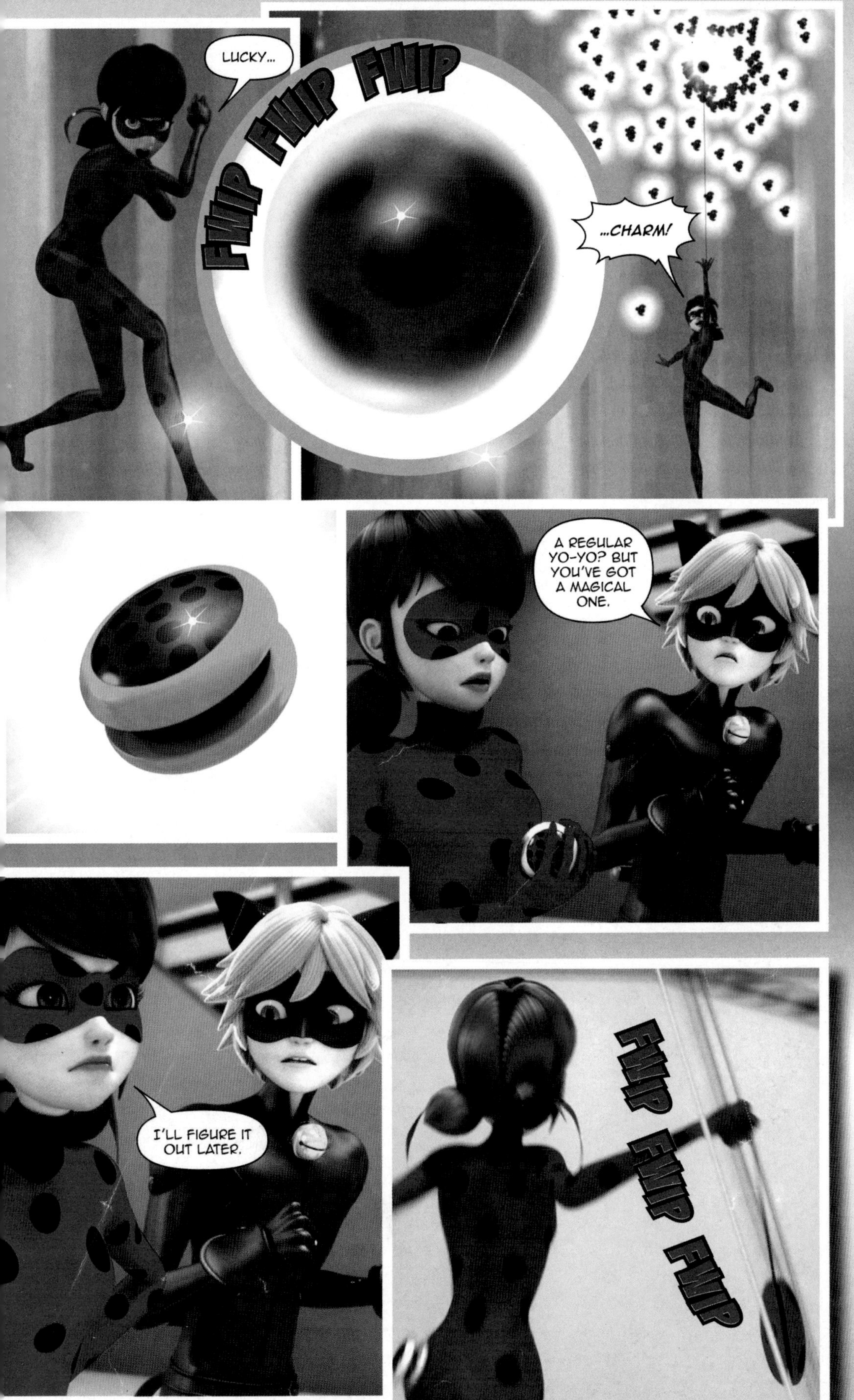
LUCKY...
FWIP FWIP FWIP
...CHARM!
A REGULAR YO-YO? BUT YOU'VE GOT A MAGICAL ONE.
I'LL FIGURE IT OUT LATER.
FWIP FWIP FWIP

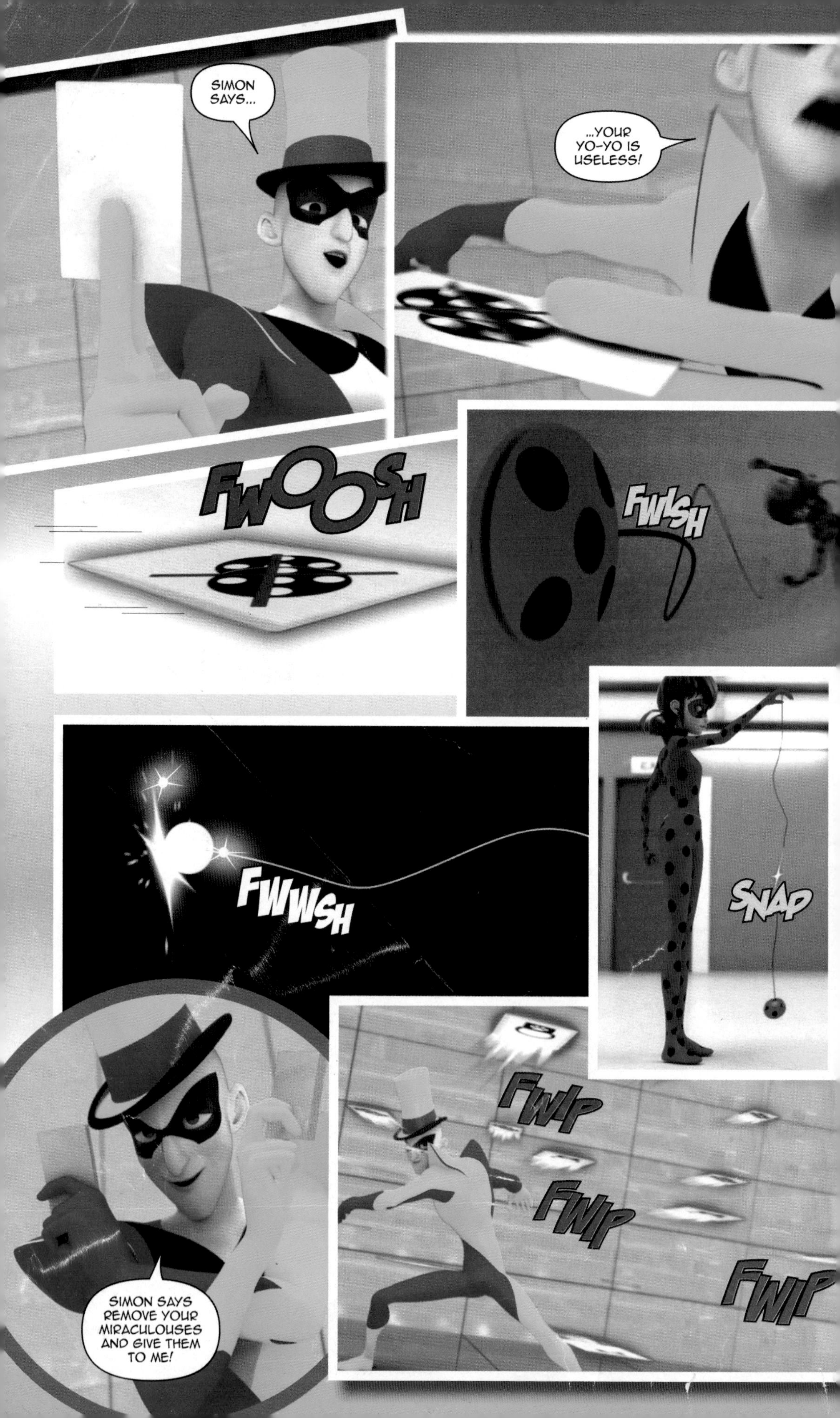
SIMON SAYS...
...YOUR YO-YO IS USELESS!
FWOOSH
FWISH
FWWSH
SNAP
SIMON SAYS REMOVE YOUR MIRACULOUSES AND GIVE THEM TO ME!
FWIP
FWIP
FWIP

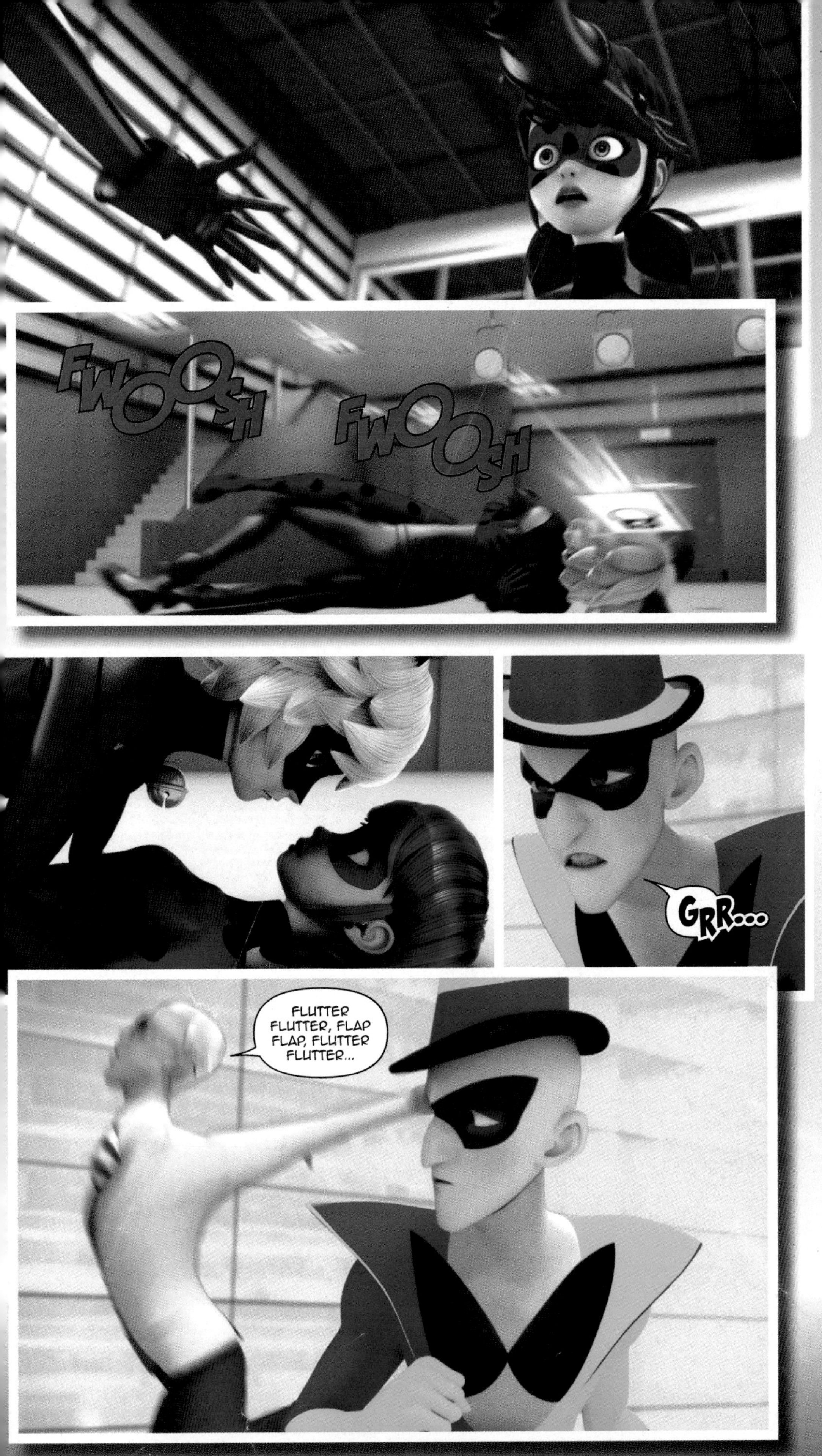
FWOOSH
FWOOSH
GRR...
FLUTTER FLUTTER, FLAP FLAP, FLUTTER FLUTTER...

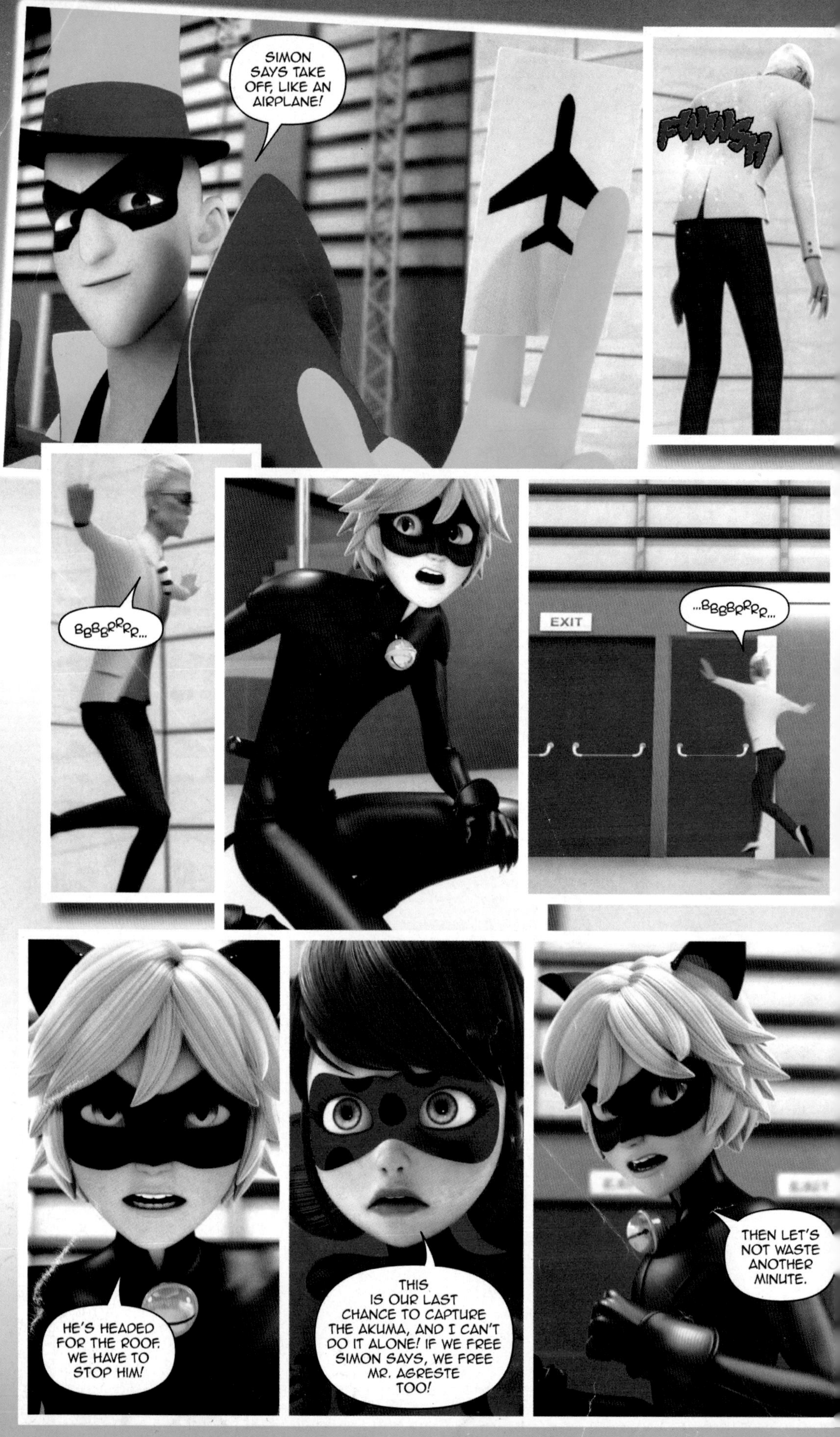
SIMON SAYS TAKE OFF, LIKE AN AIRPLANE!
FWISH
BBBBRRRR...
...BBBBRRRR...
EXIT
HE'S HEADED FOR THE ROOF. WE HAVE TO STOP HIM!
THIS IS OUR LAST CHANCE TO CAPTURE THE AKUMA, AND I CAN'T DO IT ALONE! IF WE FREE SIMON SAYS, WE FREE MR. AGRESTE TOO!
THEN LET'S NOT WASTE ANOTHER MINUTE.

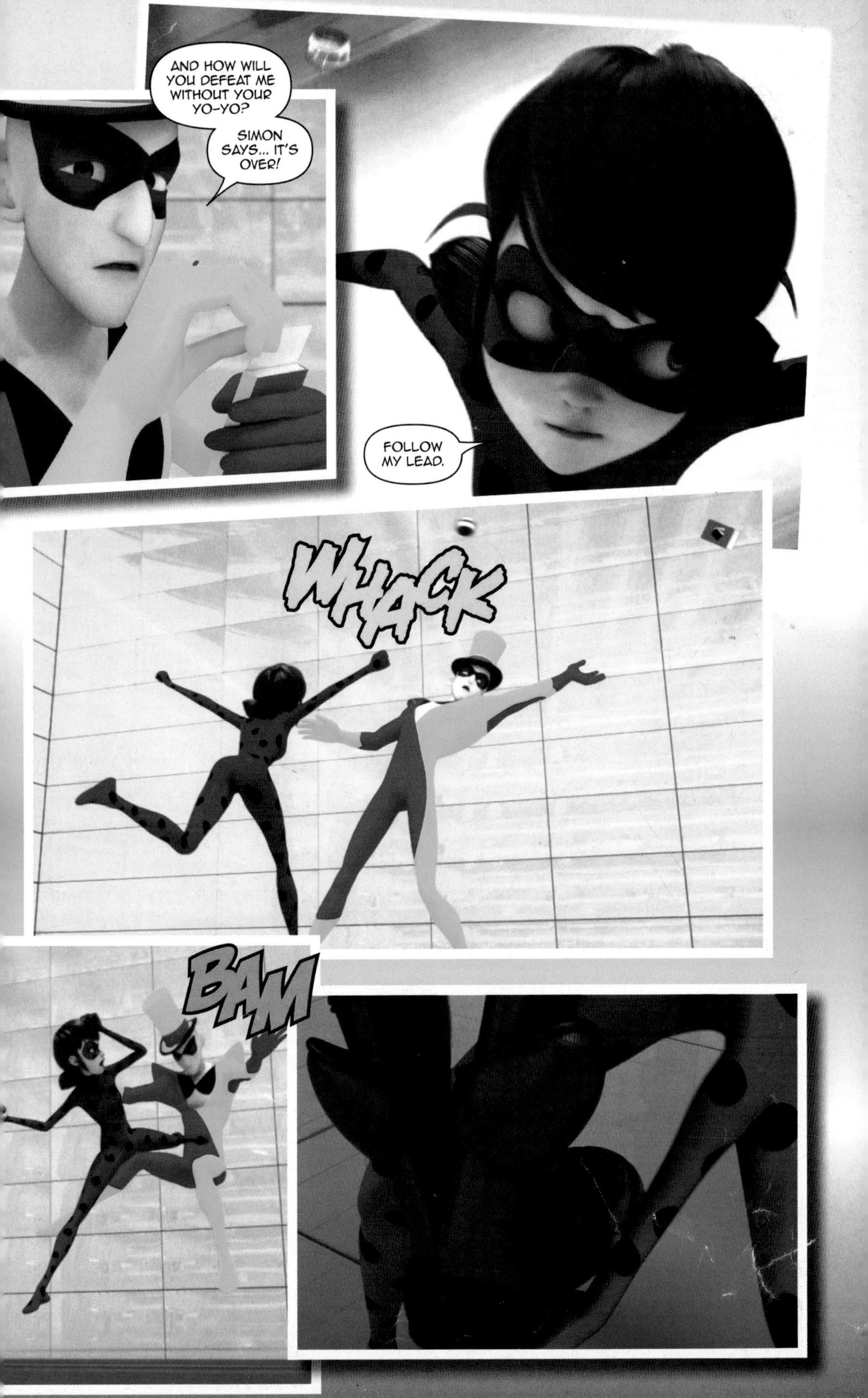
AND HOW WILL YOU DEFEAT ME WITHOUT YOUR YO-YO?
SIMON SAYS... IT'S OVER!
FOLLOW MY LEAD.
WHACK
BAM

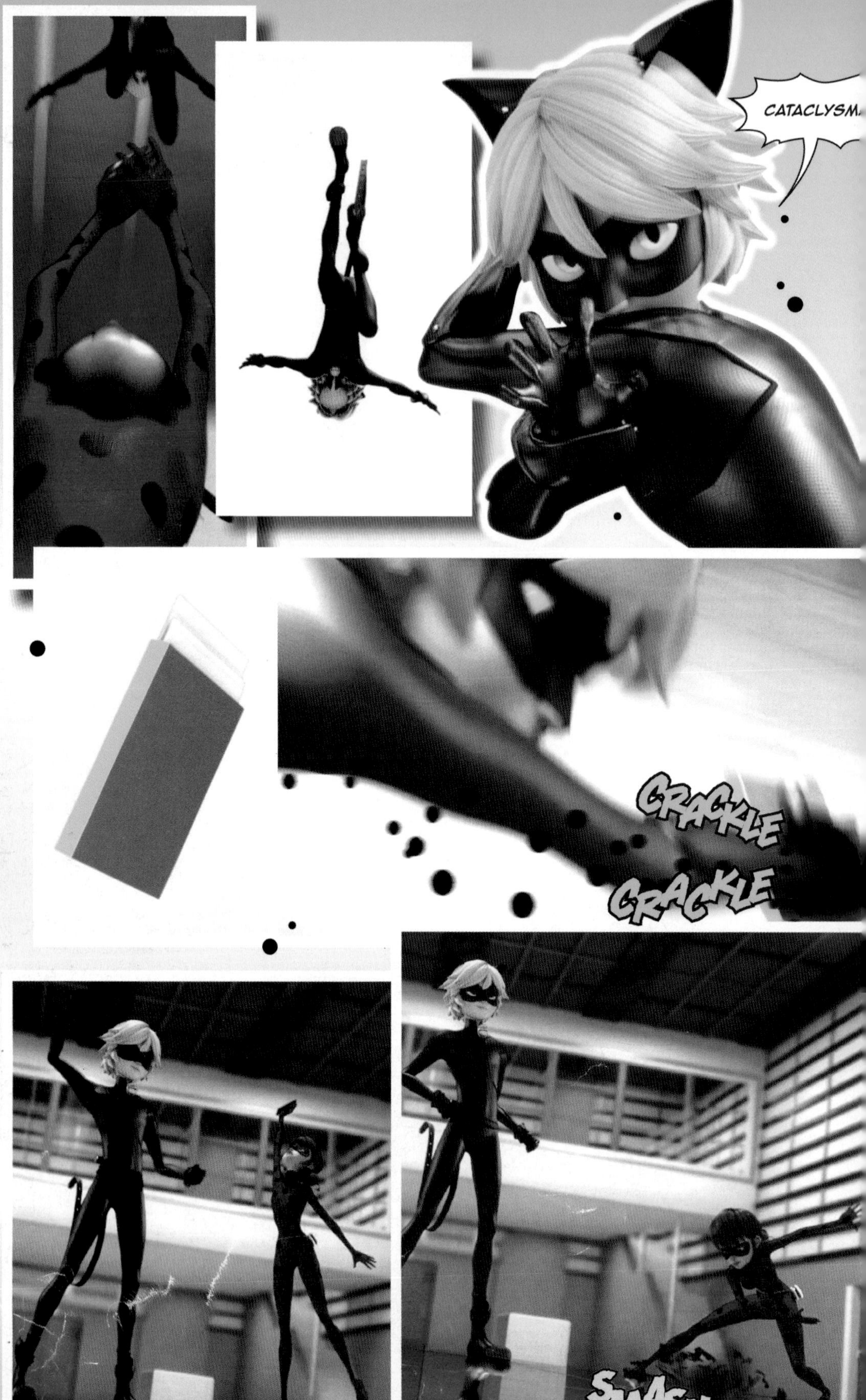
CATACLYSM
CRACKLE
CRACKLE
SMASH

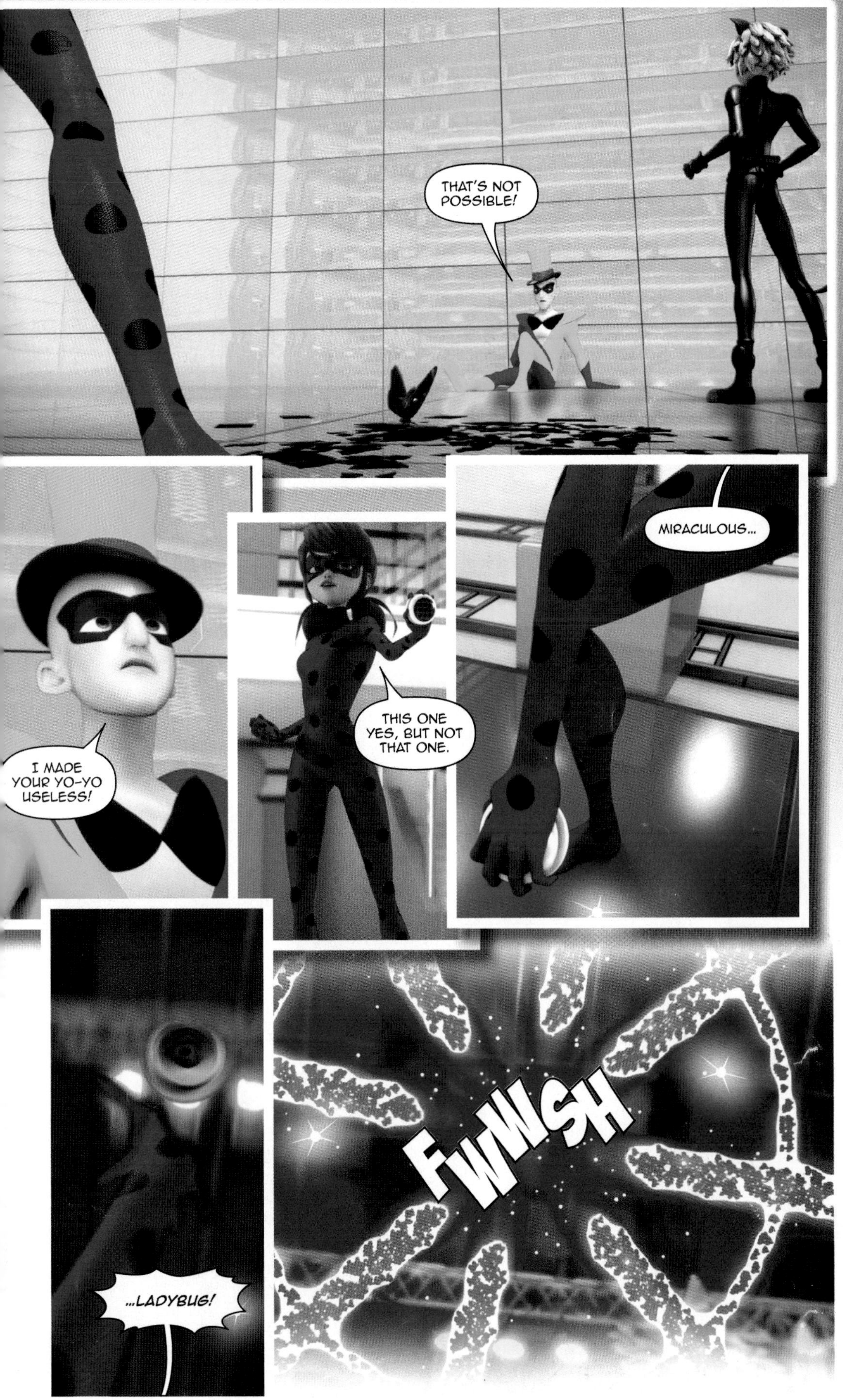
THAT'S NOT POSSIBLE!
I MADE YOUR YO-YO USELESS!
THIS ONE YES, BUT NOT THAT ONE.
MIRACULOUS...
...LADYBUG!
FWWSH

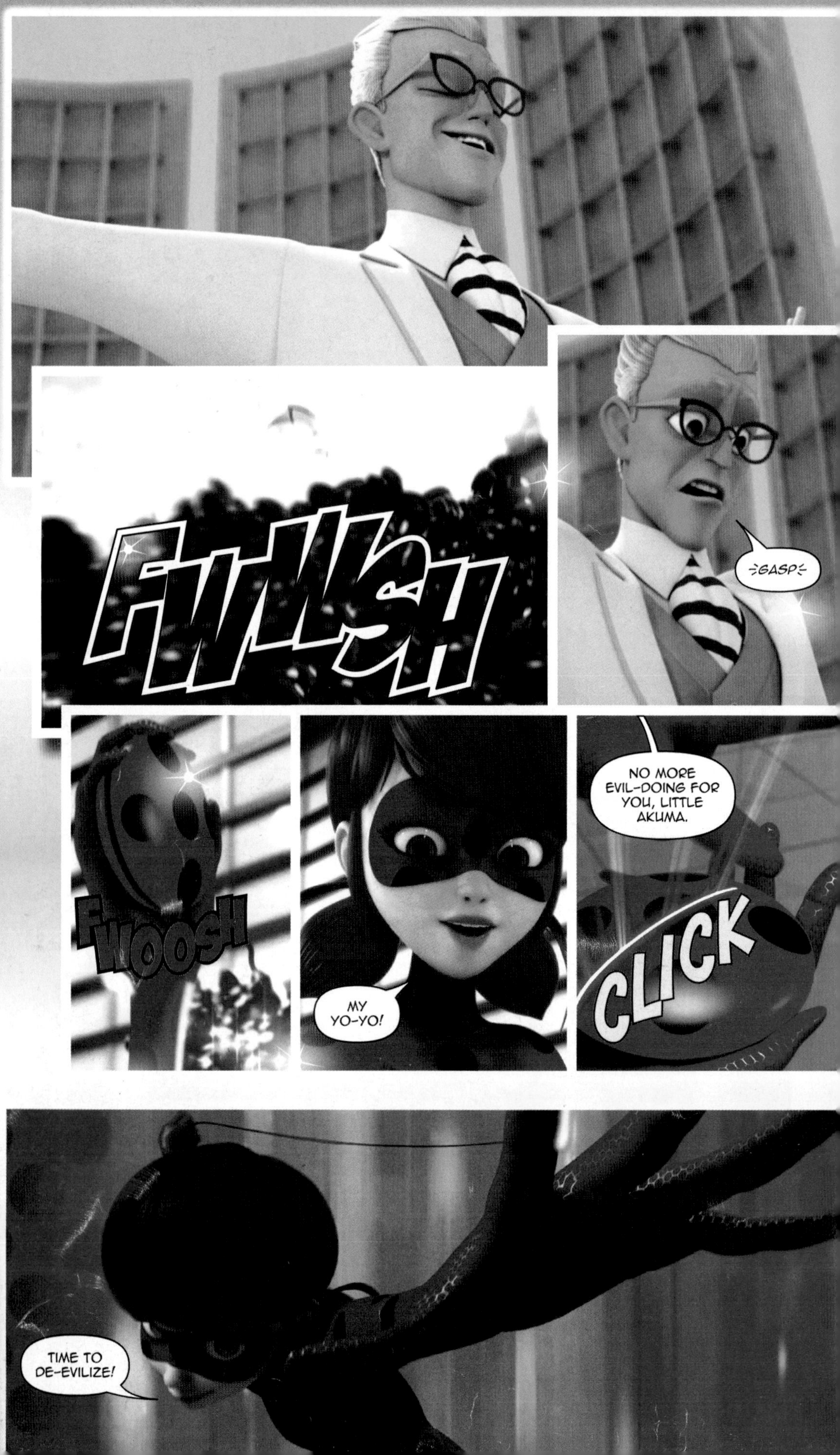
FWUSH
GASP
FWOOSH
MY YO-YO!
NO MORE EVIL-DOING FOR YOU, LITTLE AKUMA.
CLICK
TIME TO DE-EVILIZE!

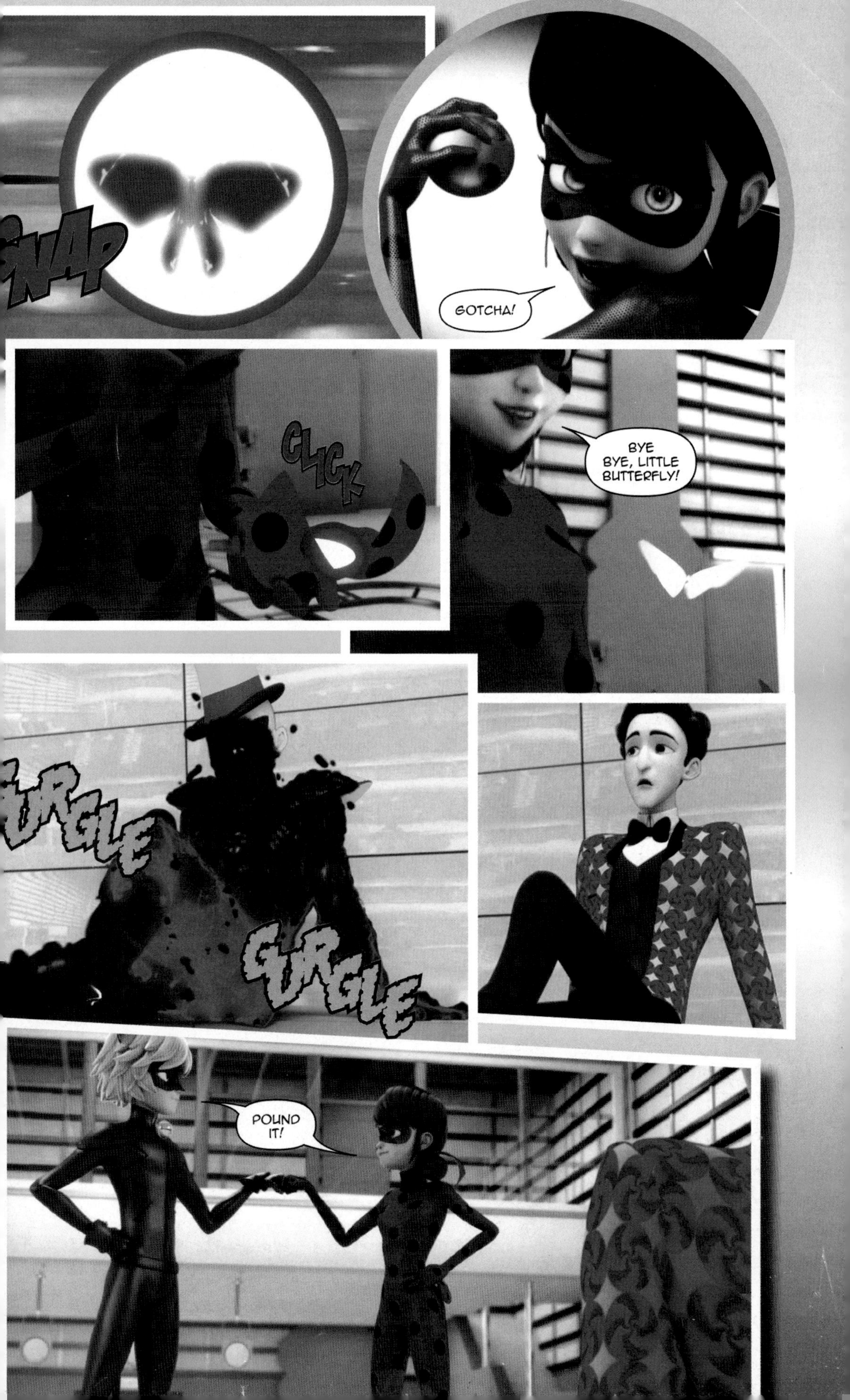
SNAP
GOTCHA!
CLICK
BYE BYE, LITTLE BUTTERFLY!
GURGLE
GURGLE
POUND IT!

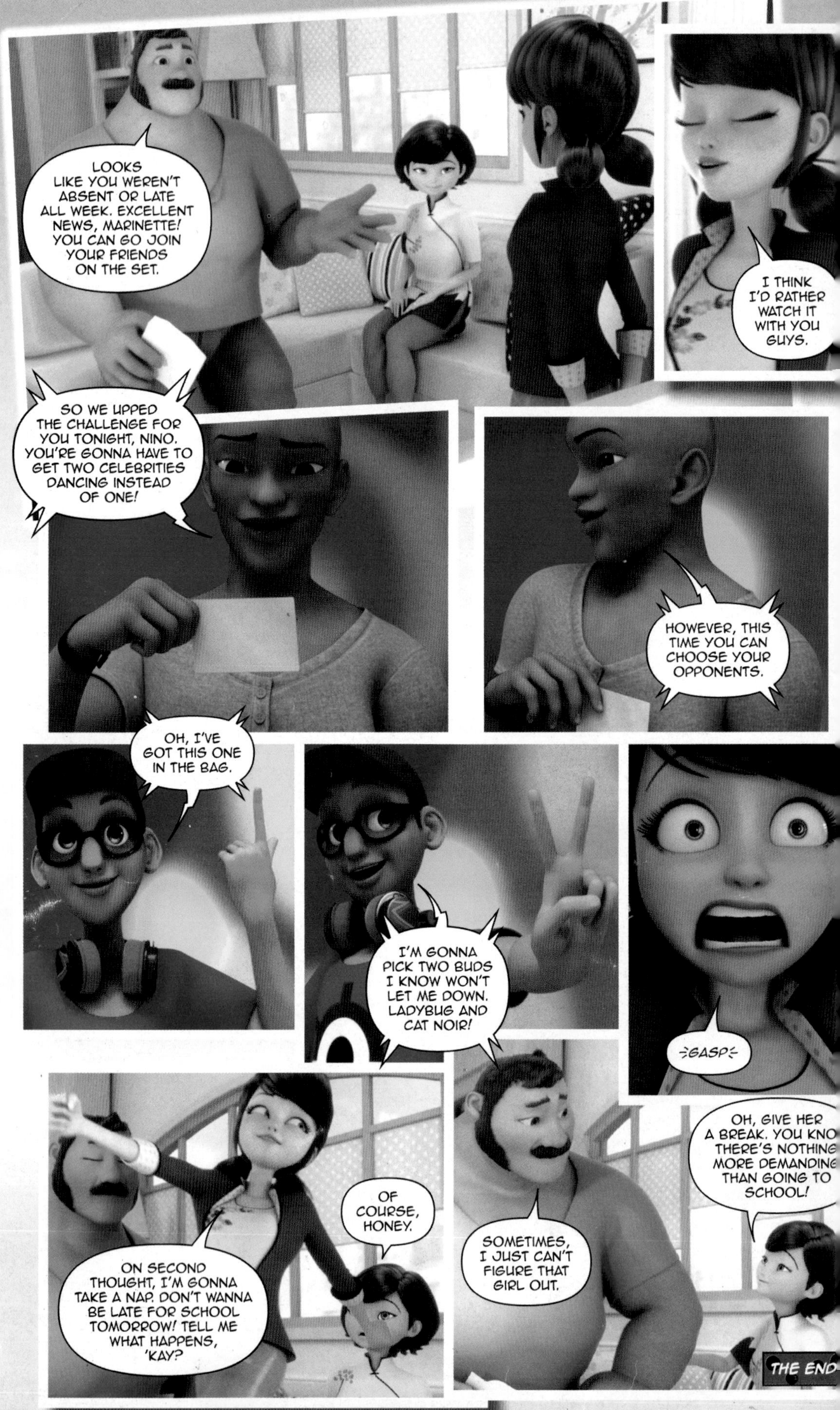
LOOKS LIKE YOU WEREN'T ABSENT OR LATE ALL WEEK. EXCELLENT NEWS, MARINETTE! YOU CAN GO JOIN YOUR FRIENDS ON THE SET.
I THINK I'D RATHER WATCH IT WITH YOU GUYS.
SO WE UPPED THE CHALLENGE FOR YOU TONIGHT, NINO. YOU'RE GONNA HAVE TO GET TWO CELEBRITIES DANCING INSTEAD OF ONE!
HOWEVER, THIS TIME YOU CAN CHOOSE YOUR OPPONENTS.
OH, I'VE GOT THIS ONE IN THE BAG.
I'M GONNA PICK TWO BUDS I KNOW WON'T LET ME DOWN. LADYBUG AND CAT NOIR!
GASP
ON SECOND THOUGHT, I'M GONNA TAKE A NAP. DON'T WANNA BE LATE FOR SCHOOL TOMORROW! TELL ME WHAT HAPPENS, 'KAY?
OF COURSE, HONEY.
SOMETIMES, I JUST CAN'T FIGURE THAT GIRL OUT.
OH, GIVE HER A BREAK. YOU KNO THERE'S NOTHING MORE DEMANDING THAN GOING TO SCHOOL!
THE END

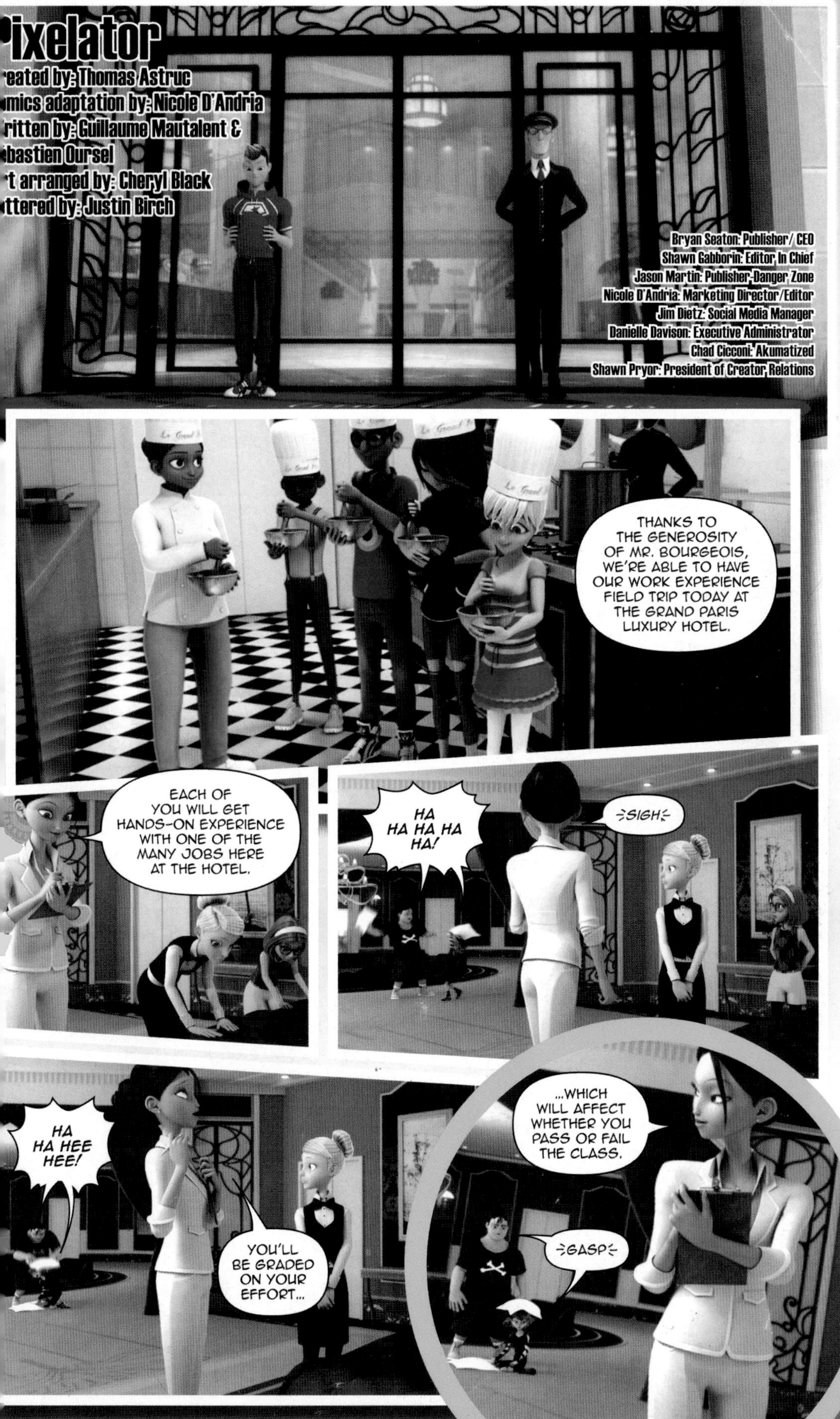

ixelator
eated by: Thomas Astruc
mics adaptation by: Nicole D'Andria
ritten by: Guillaume Mautalent &
bastien Oursel
t arranged by: Cheryl Black
ttered by: Justin Birch
Bryan Seaton: Publisher/ CEO
Shawn Gabborin: Editor In Chief
Jason Martin: Publisher-Danger Zone
Nicole D'Andria: Marketing Director/Editor
Jim Dietz: Social Media Manager
Danielle Davison: Executive Administrator
Chad Cicconi: Akumatized
Shawn Pryor: President of Creator Relations
THANKS TO THE GENEROSITY OF MR. BOURGEOIS, WE'RE ABLE TO HAVE OUR WORK EXPERIENCE FIELD TRIP TODAY AT THE GRAND PARIS LUXURY HOTEL.
EACH OF YOU WILL GET HANDS-ON EXPERIENCE WITH ONE OF THE MANY JOBS HERE AT THE HOTEL.
HA HA HA HA HA!
SIGH
HA HA HEE HEE!
YOU'LL BE GRADED ON YOUR EFFORT...
...WHICH WILL AFFECT WHETHER YOU PASS OR FAIL THE CLASS.
GASP

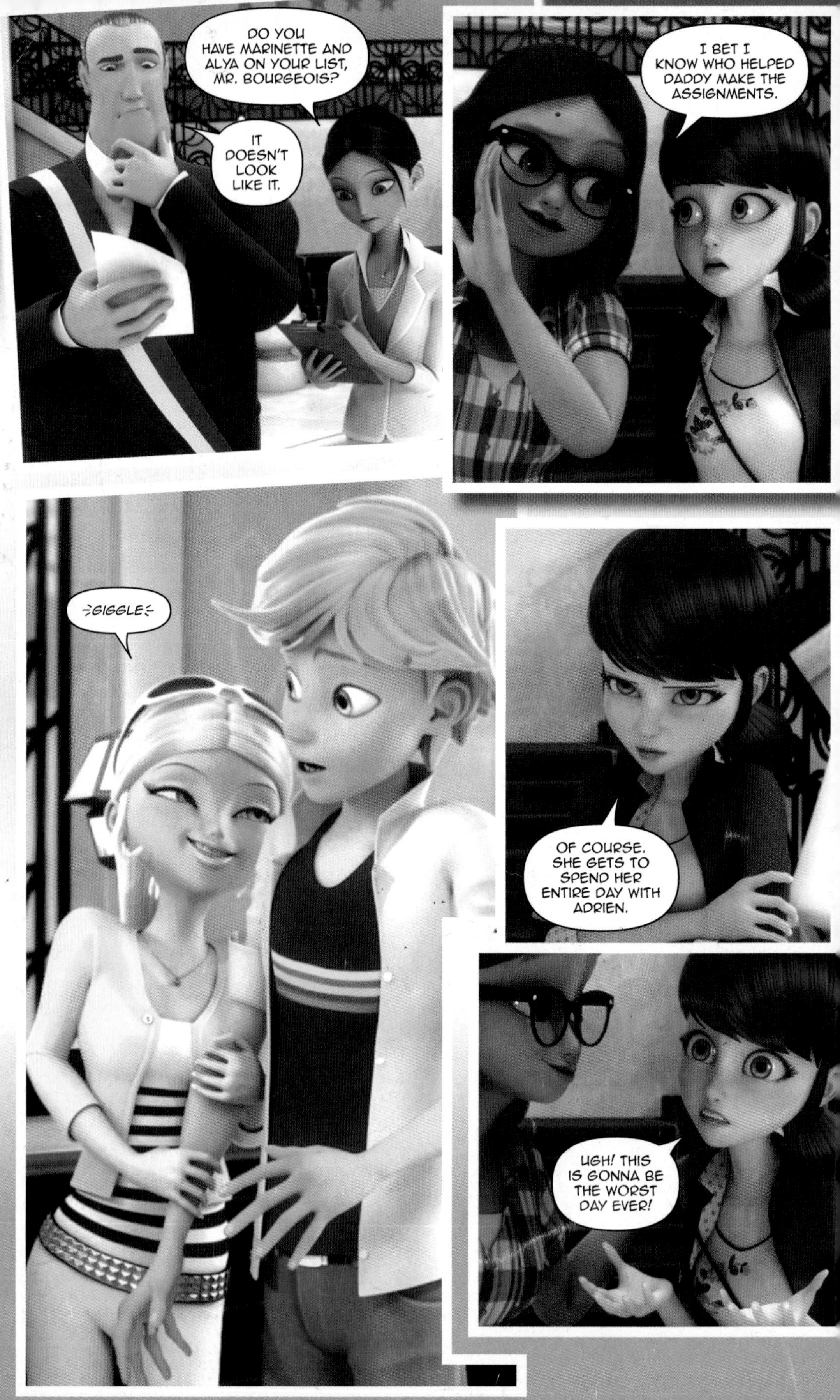
DO YOU HAVE MARINETTE AND ALYA ON YOUR LIST, MR. BOURGEOIS?
IT DOESN'T LOOK LIKE IT.
I BET I KNOW WHO HELPED DADDY MAKE THE ASSIGNMENTS.
GIGGLE
OF COURSE. SHE GETS TO SPEND HER ENTIRE DAY WITH ADRIEN.
UGH! THIS IS GONNA BE THE WORST DAY EVER!

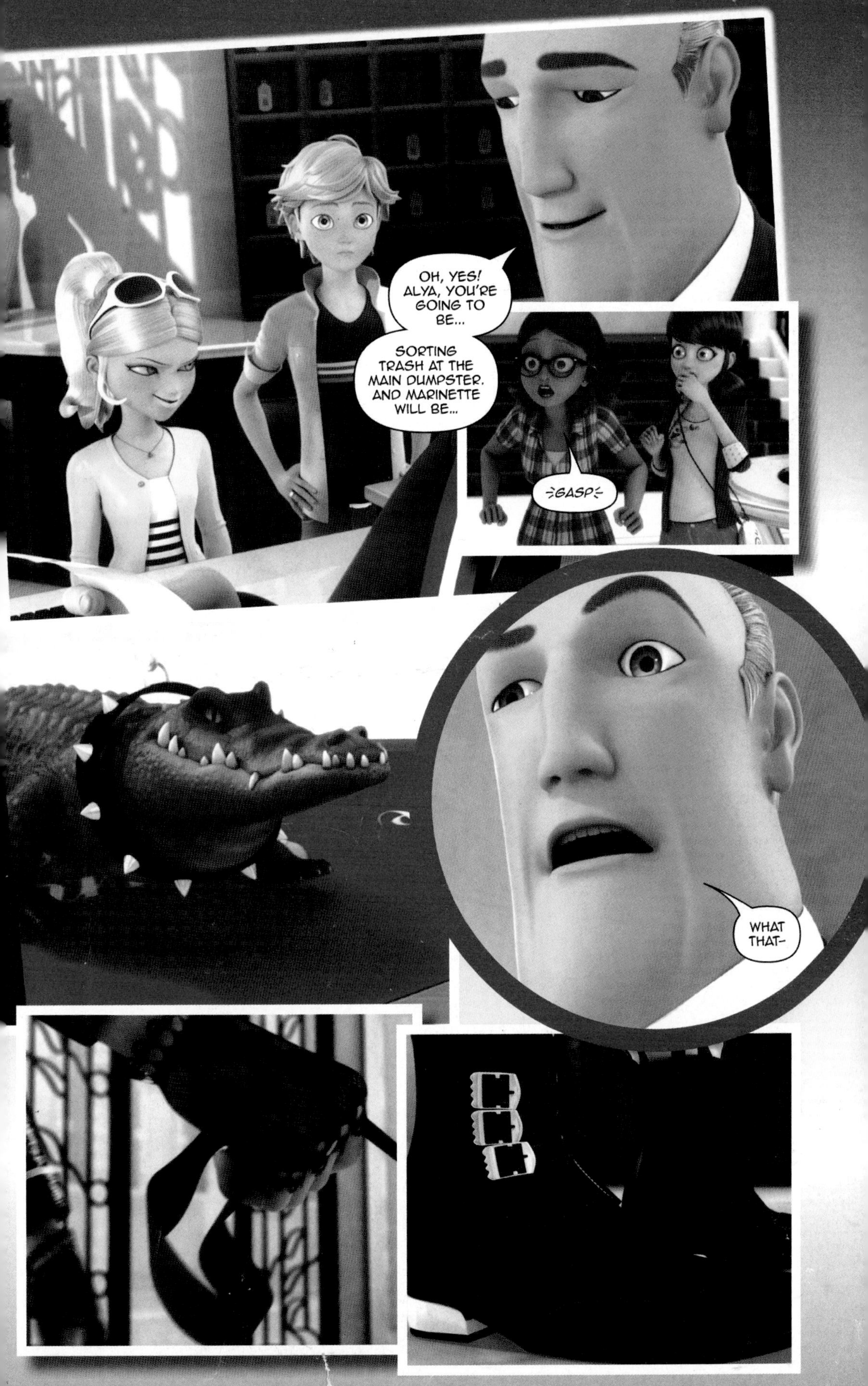

OH, YES! ALYA, YOU'RE GOING TO BE...
SORTING TRASH AT THE MAIN DUMPSTER. AND MARINETTE WILL BE...
GASP
WHAT THAT-

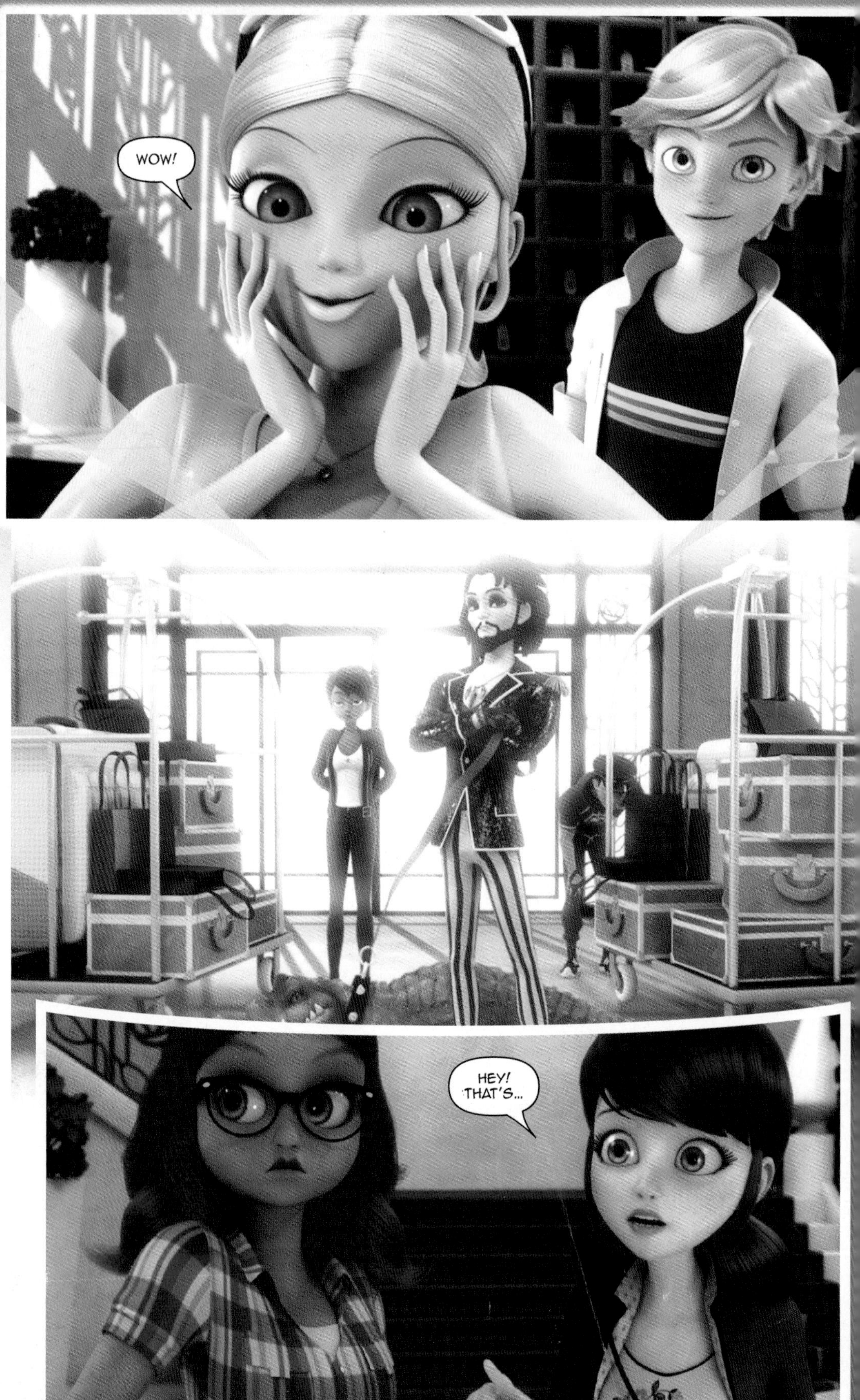
WOW!
HEY! THAT'S...

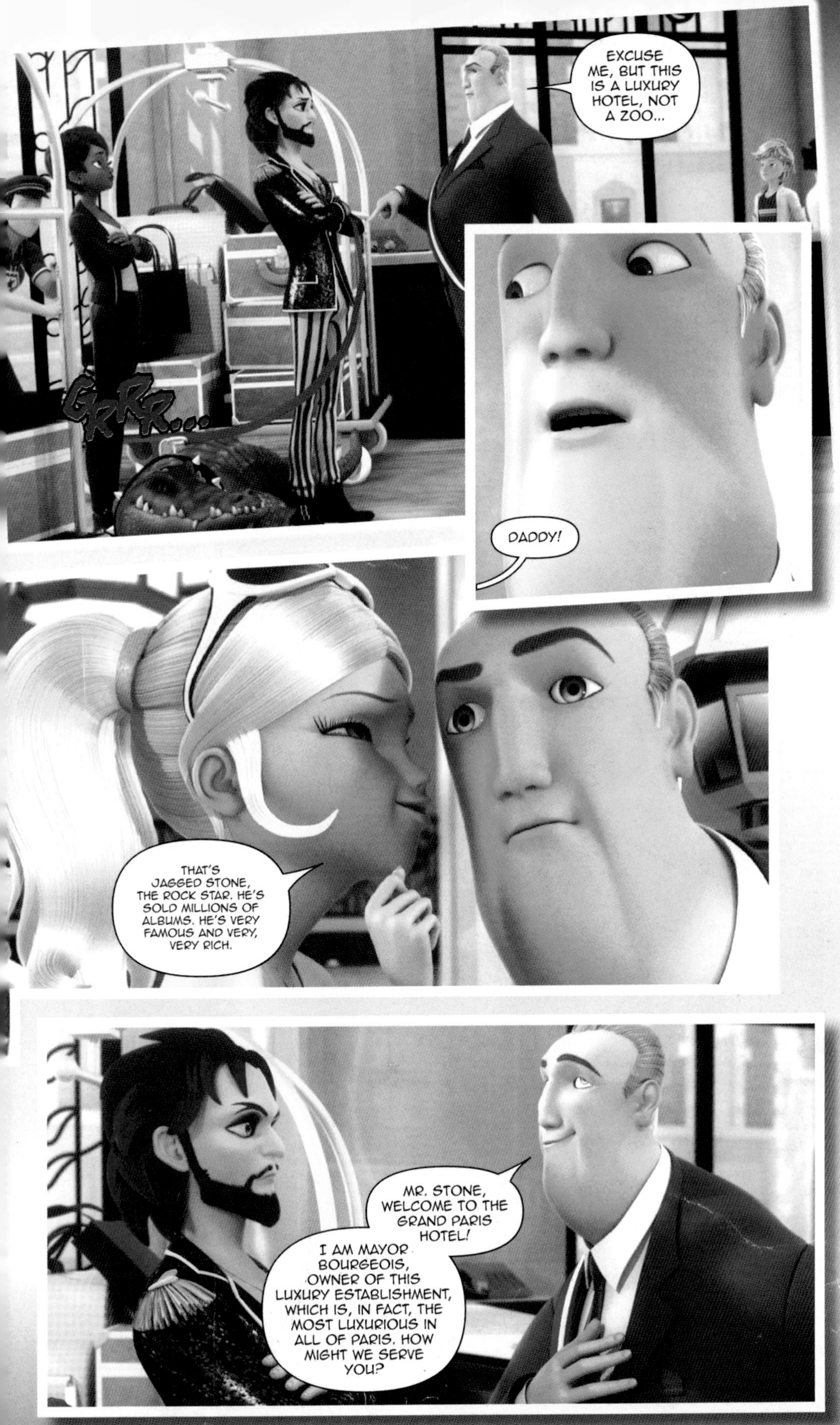
EXCUSE ME, BUT THIS IS A LUXURY HOTEL, NOT A ZOO...
GRRR...
DADDY!
THAT'S JAGGED STONE, THE ROCK STAR. HE'S SOLD MILLIONS OF ALBUMS. HE'S VERY FAMOUS AND VERY, VERY RICH.
MR. STONE, WELCOME TO THE GRAND PARIS HOTEL!
I AM MAYOR BOURGEOIS, OWNER OF THIS LUXURY ESTABLISHMENT, WHICH IS, IN FACT, THE MOST LUXURIOUS IN ALL OF PARIS. HOW MIGHT WE SERVE YOU?

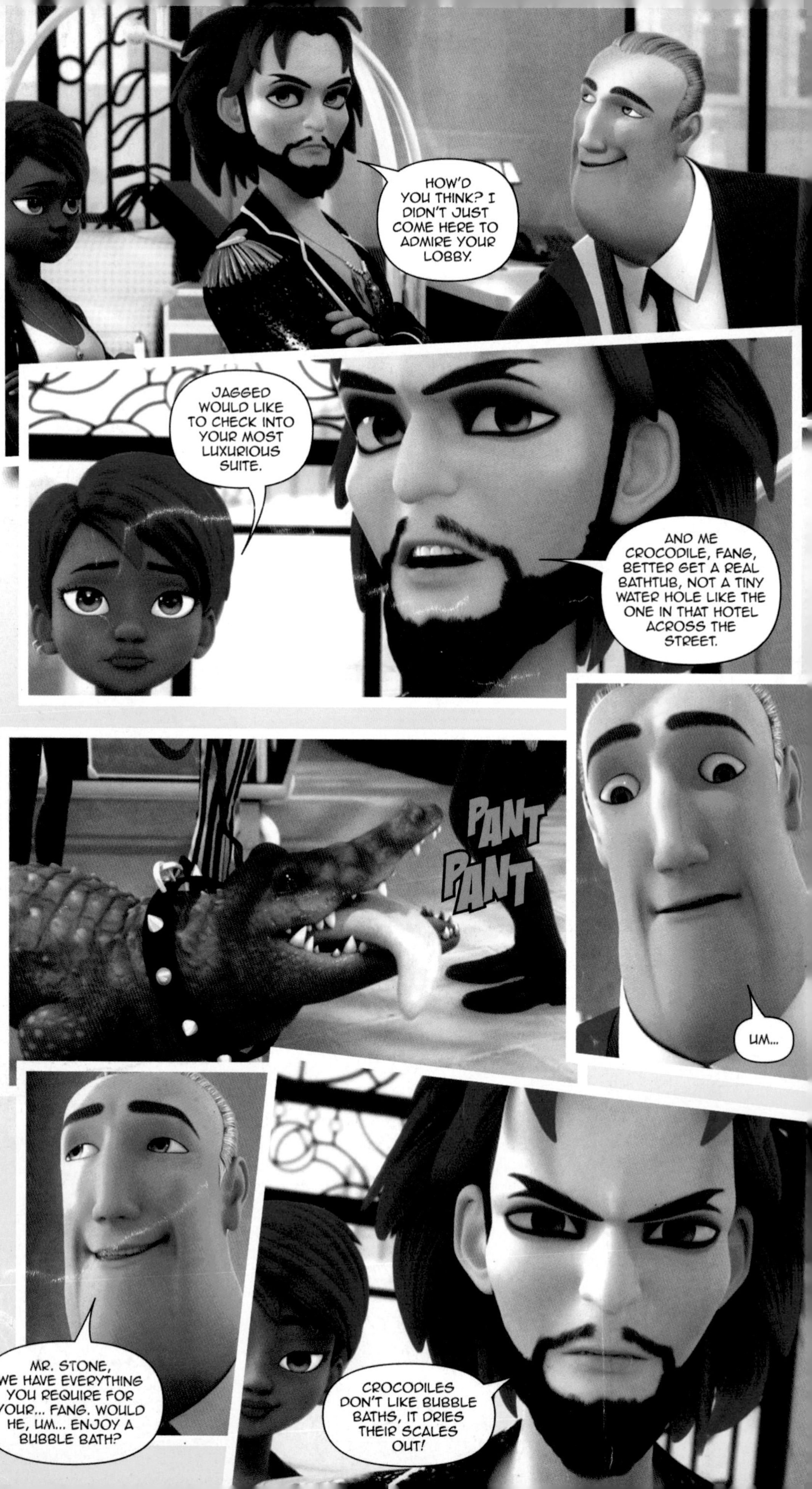
HOW'D YOU THINK? I DIDN'T JUST COME HERE TO ADMIRE YOUR LOBBY.
JAGGED WOULD LIKE TO CHECK INTO YOUR MOST LUXURIOUS SUITE.
AND ME CROCODILE, FANG, BETTER GET A REAL BATHTUB, NOT A TINY WATER HOLE LIKE THE ONE IN THAT HOTEL ACROSS THE STREET.
PANT PANT
UM...
MR. STONE, WE HAVE EVERYTHING YOU REQUIRE FOR YOUR... FANG. WOULD HE, UM... ENJOY A BUBBLE BATH?
CROCODILES DON'T LIKE BUBBLE BATHS, IT DRIES THEIR SCALES OUT!

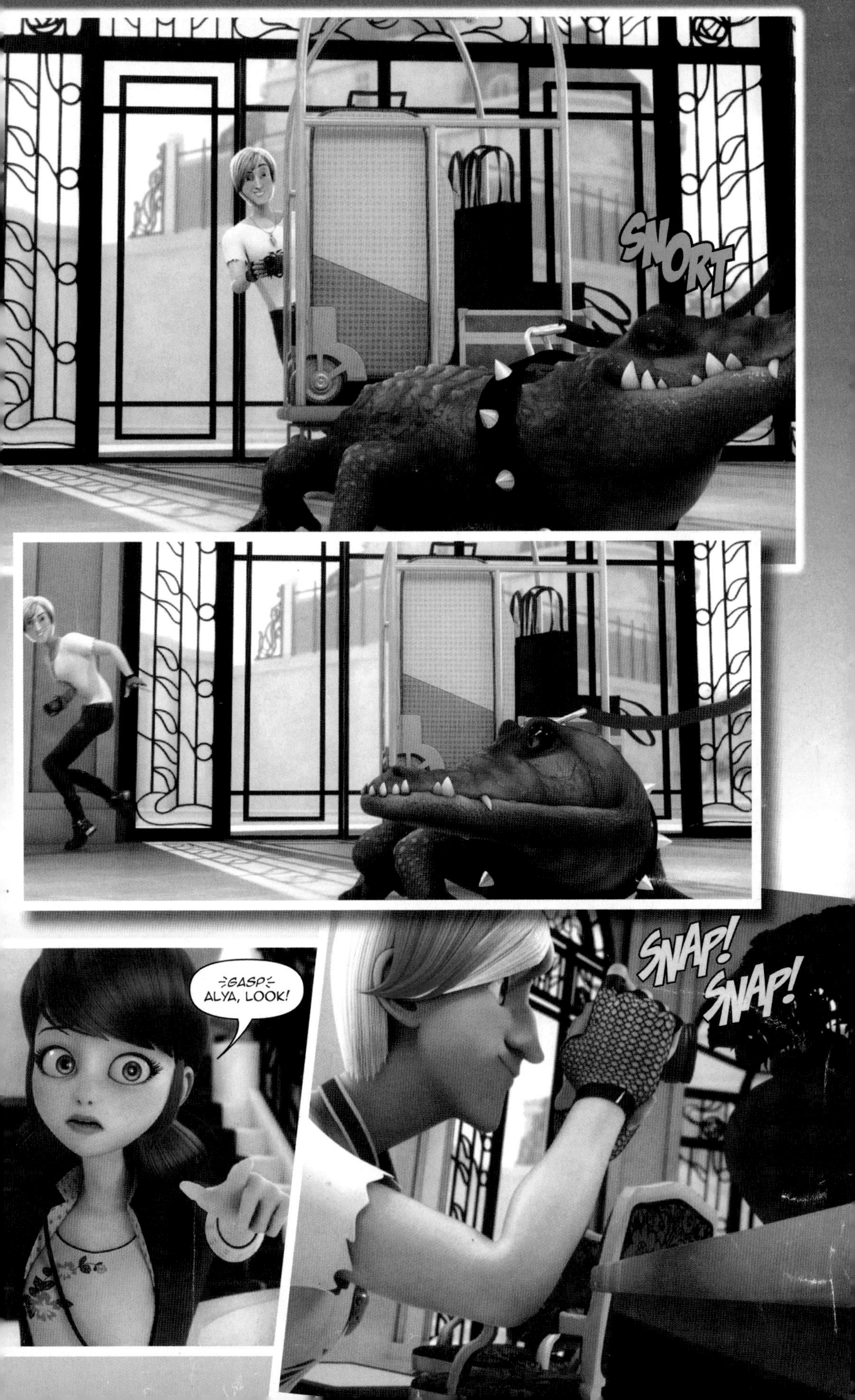
SNORT
ꟷGASPꟷ ALYA, LOOK!
SNAP! SNAP!

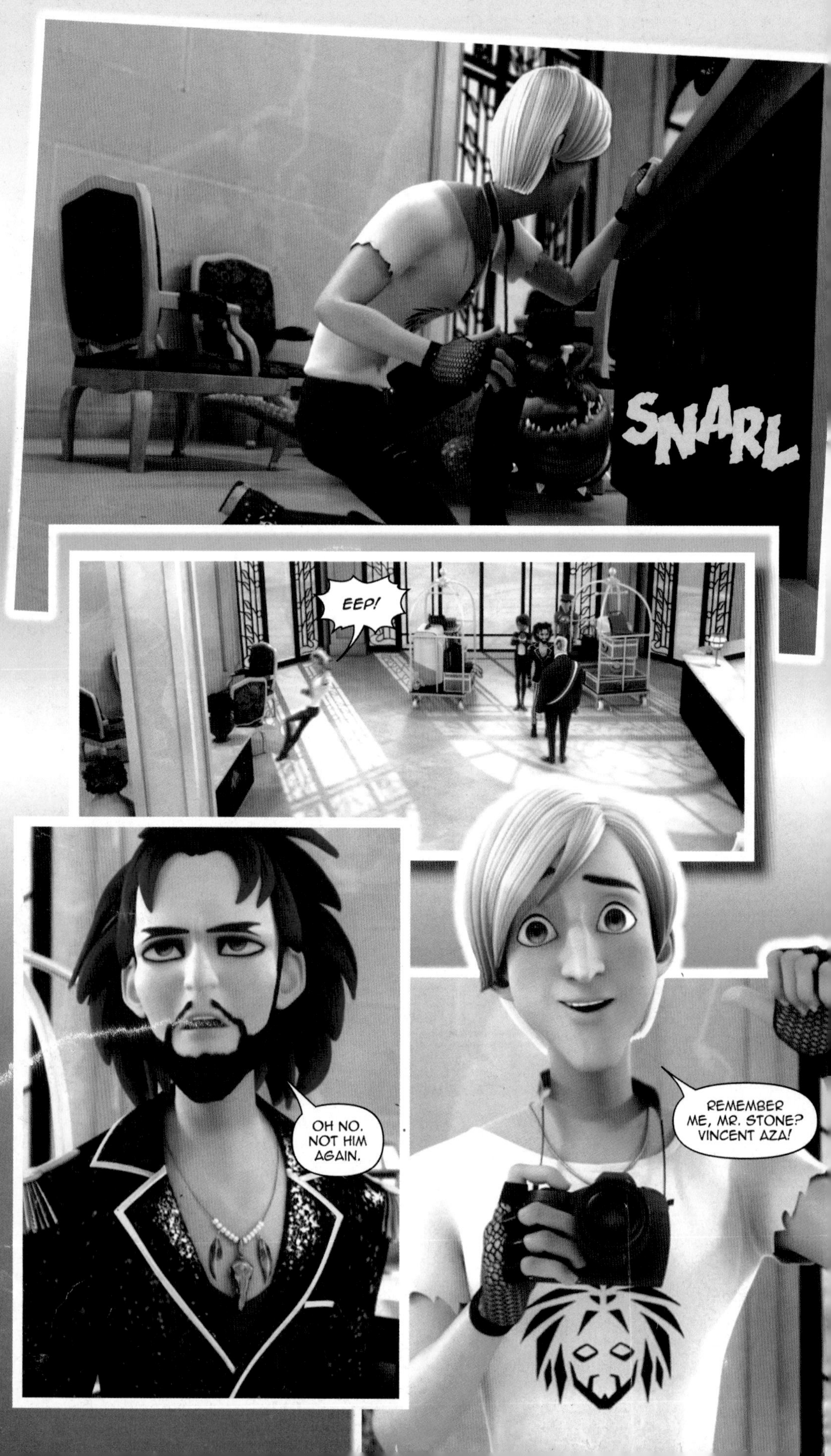
SNARL
EEP!
OH NO. NOT HIM AGAIN.
REMEMBER ME, MR. STONE? VINCENT AZA!

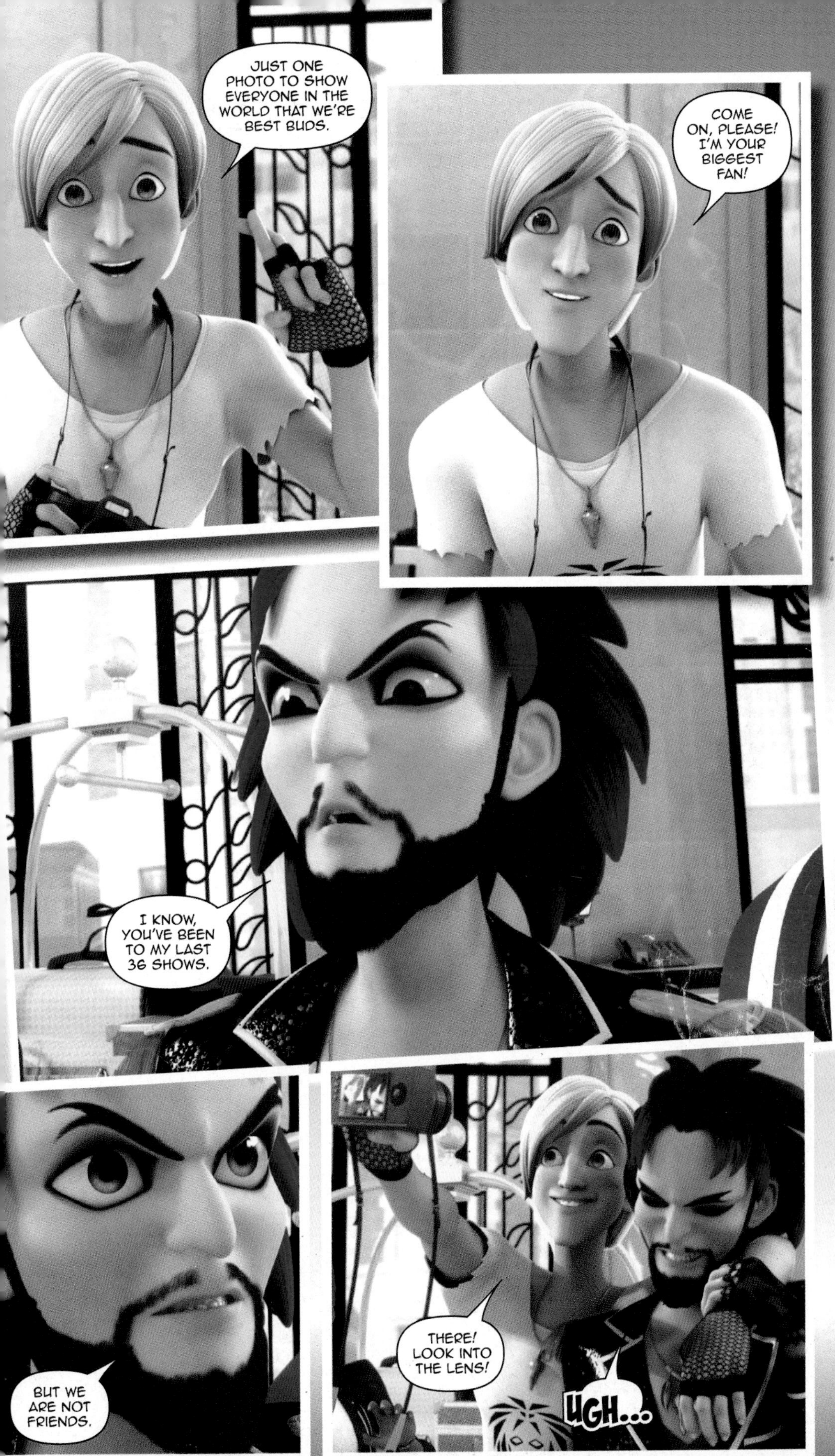
JUST ONE PHOTO TO SHOW EVERYONE IN THE WORLD THAT WE'RE BEST BUDS.
COME ON, PLEASE! I'M YOUR BIGGEST FAN!
I KNOW, YOU'VE BEEN TO MY LAST 36 SHOWS.
BUT WE ARE NOT FRIENDS.
THERE! LOOK INTO THE LENS!
UGH...

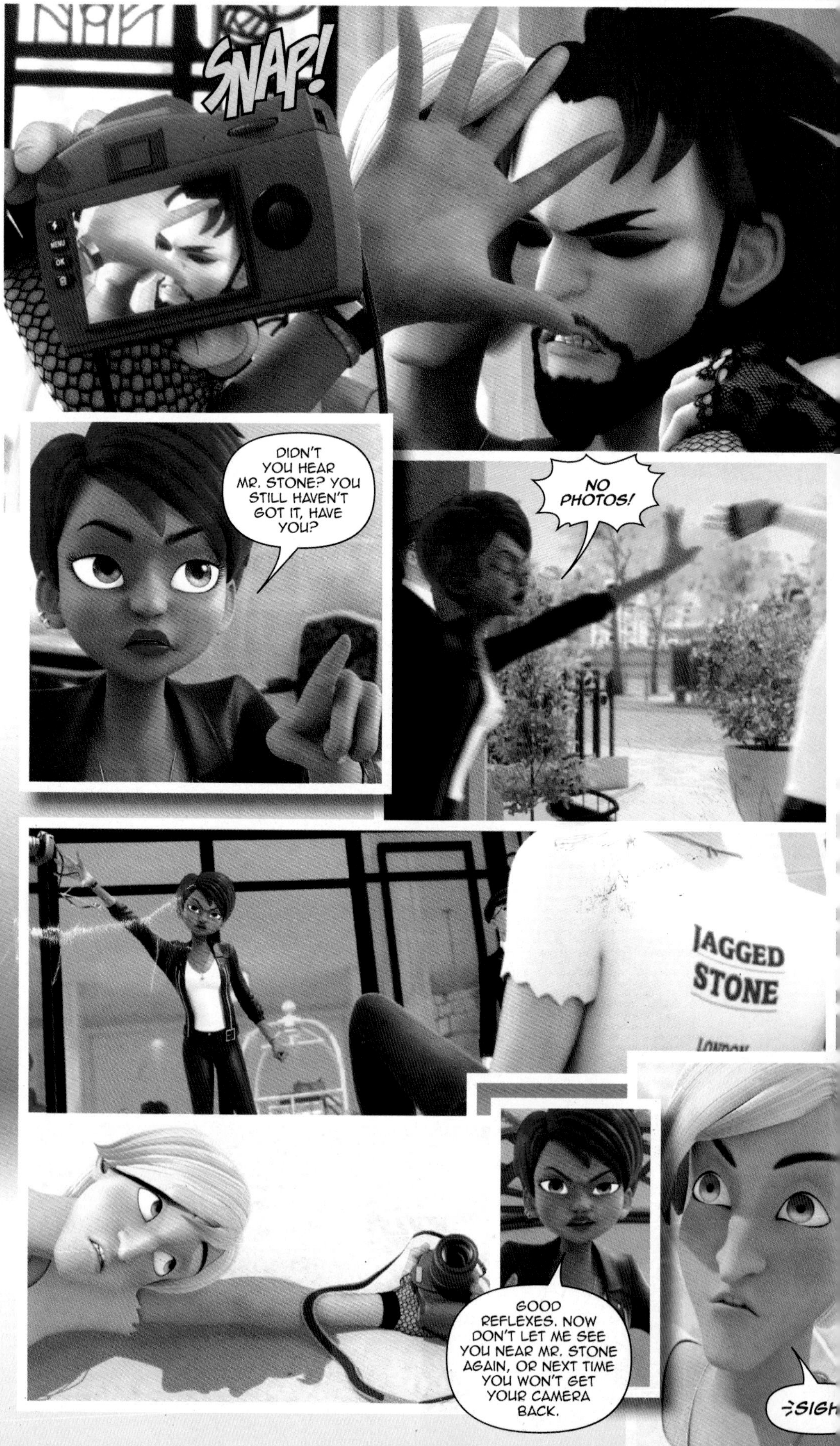
SNAP!
DIDN'T YOU HEAR MR. STONE? YOU STILL HAVEN'T GOT IT, HAVE YOU?
NO PHOTOS!
JAGGED STONE
GOOD REFLEXES. NOW DON'T LET ME SEE YOU NEAR MR. STONE AGAIN, OR NEXT TIME YOU WON'T GET YOUR CAMERA BACK.

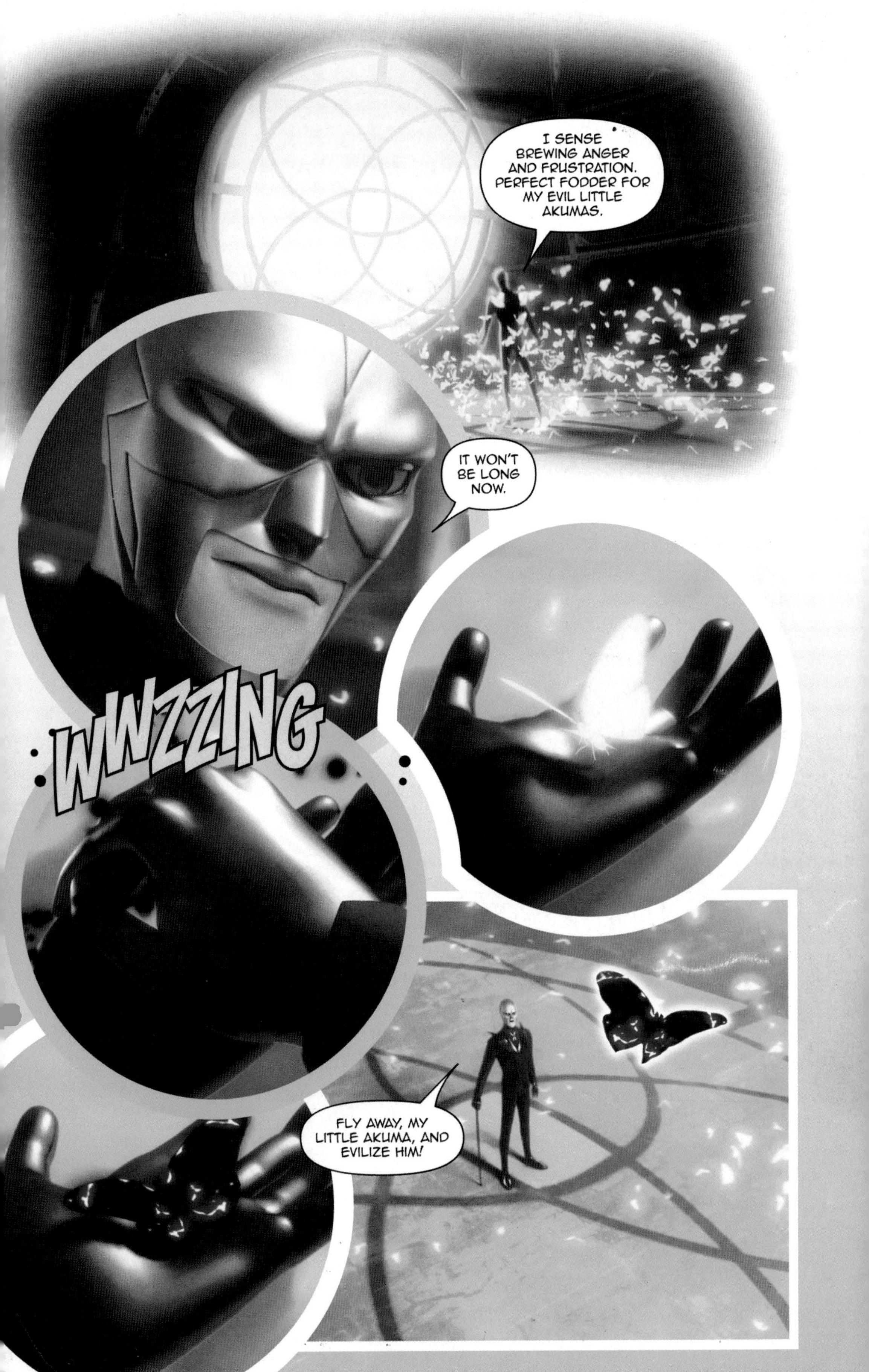
I SENSE BREWING ANGER AND FRUSTRATION. PERFECT FODDER FOR MY EVIL LITTLE AKUMAS.
IT WON'T BE LONG NOW.
WWZZING
FLY AWAY, MY LITTLE AKUMA, AND EVILIZE HIM!

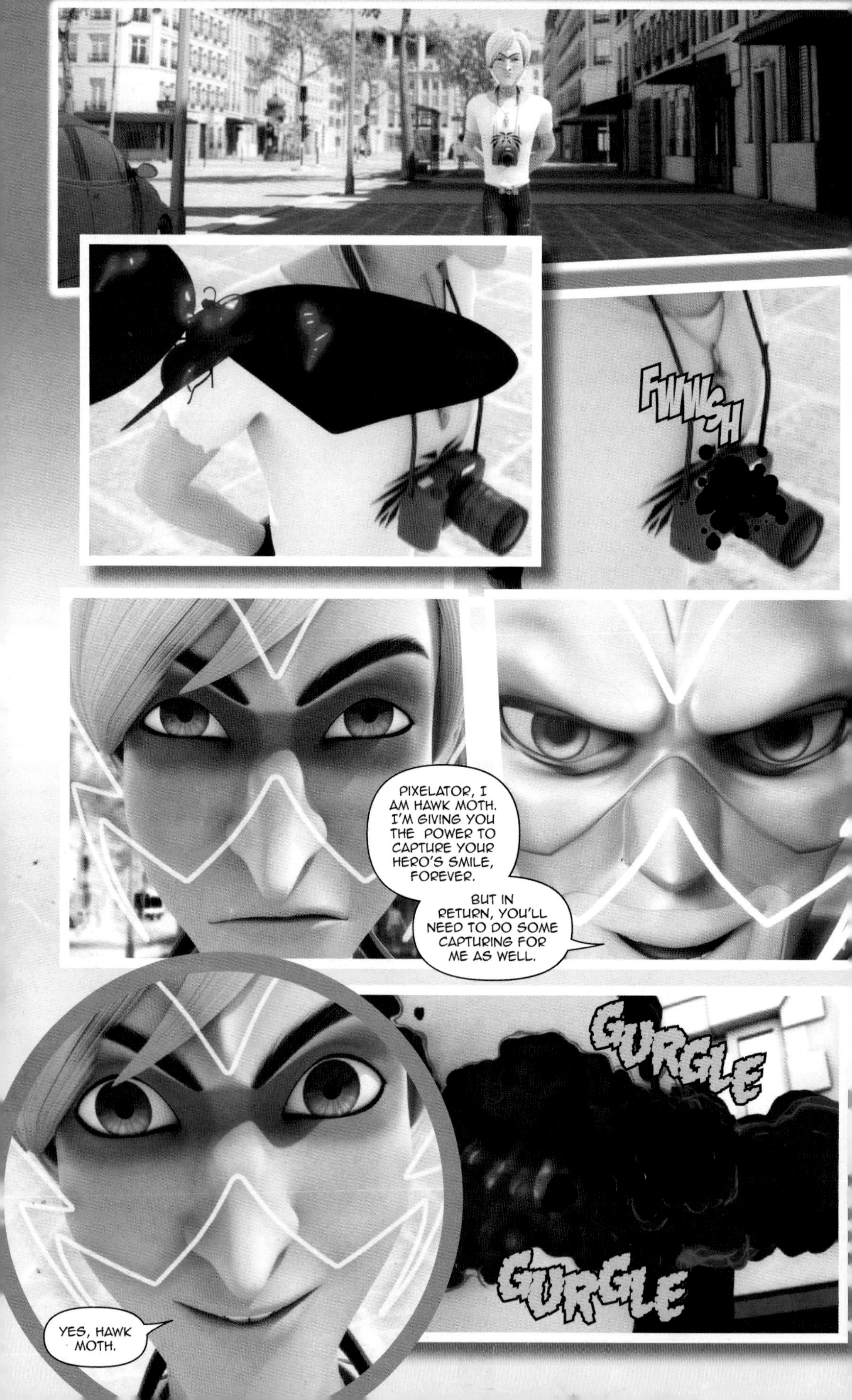
FWWSH
PIXELATOR, I AM HAWK MOTH. I'M GIVING YOU THE POWER TO CAPTURE YOUR HERO'S SMILE, FOREVER.
BUT IN RETURN, YOU'LL NEED TO DO SOME CAPTURING FOR ME AS WELL.
YES, HAWK MOTH.
GURGLE
GURGLE

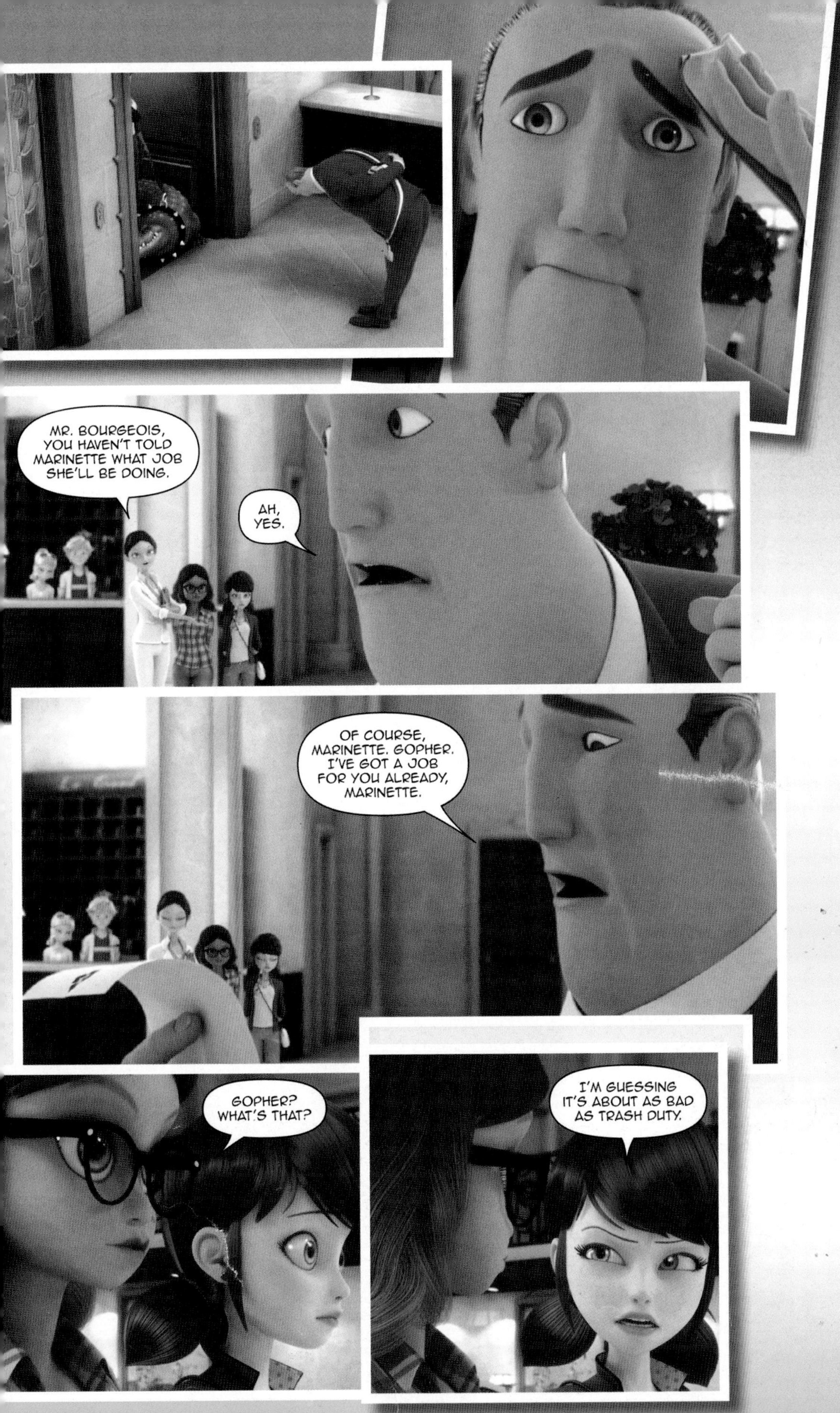
MR. BOURGEOIS, YOU HAVEN'T TOLD MARINETTE WHAT JOB SHE'LL BE DOING.
AH, YES.
OF COURSE, MARINETTE. GOPHER. I'VE GOT A JOB FOR YOU ALREADY, MARINETTE.
GOPHER? WHAT'S THAT?
I'M GUESSING IT'S ABOUT AS BAD AS TRASH DUTY.

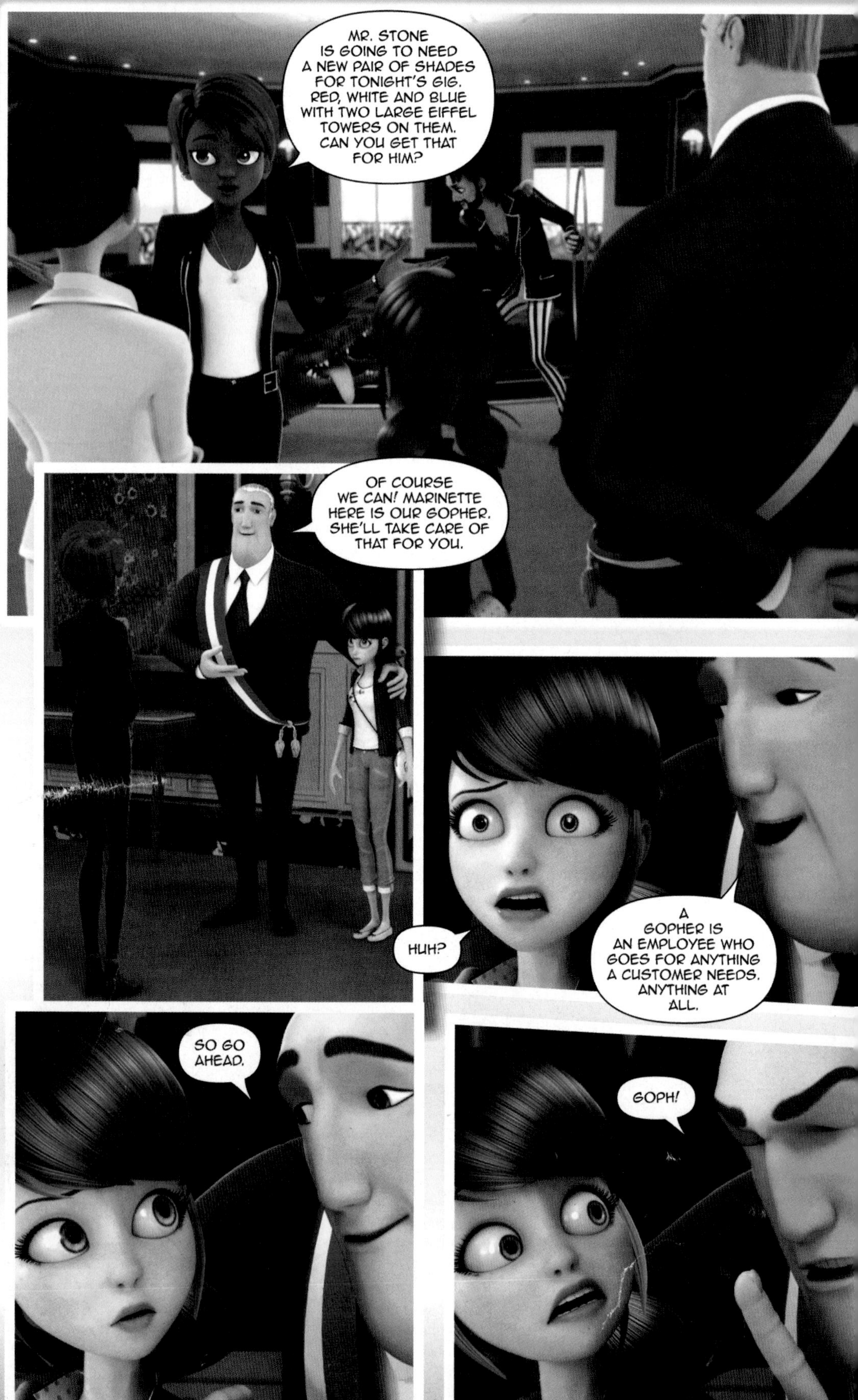
MR. STONE IS GOING TO NEED A NEW PAIR OF SHADES FOR TONIGHT'S GIG. RED, WHITE AND BLUE WITH TWO LARGE EIFFEL TOWERS ON THEM. CAN YOU GET THAT FOR HIM?
OF COURSE WE CAN! MARINETTE HERE IS OUR GOPHER. SHE'LL TAKE CARE OF THAT FOR YOU.
HUH?
A GOPHER IS AN EMPLOYEE WHO GOES FOR ANYTHING A CUSTOMER NEEDS. ANYTHING AT ALL.
SO GO AHEAD.
GOPH!

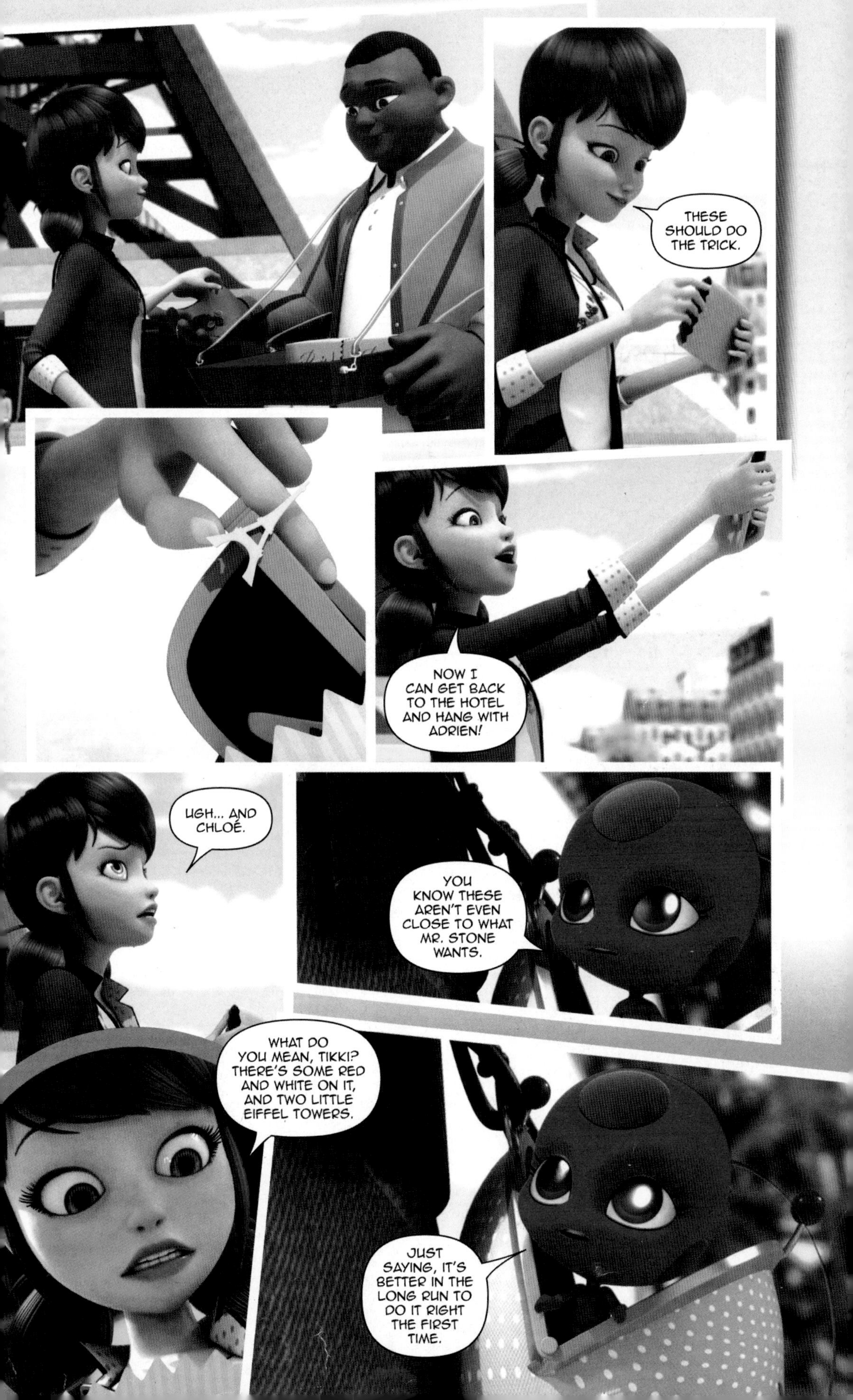
THESE SHOULD DO THE TRICK.
NOW I CAN GET BACK TO THE HOTEL AND HANG WITH ADRIEN!
UGH... AND CHLOÉ.
YOU KNOW THESE AREN'T EVEN CLOSE TO WHAT MR. STONE WANTS.
WHAT DO YOU MEAN, TIKKI? THERE'S SOME RED AND WHITE ON IT, AND TWO LITTLE EIFFEL TOWERS.
JUST SAYING, IT'S BETTER IN THE LONG RUN TO DO IT RIGHT THE FIRST TIME.

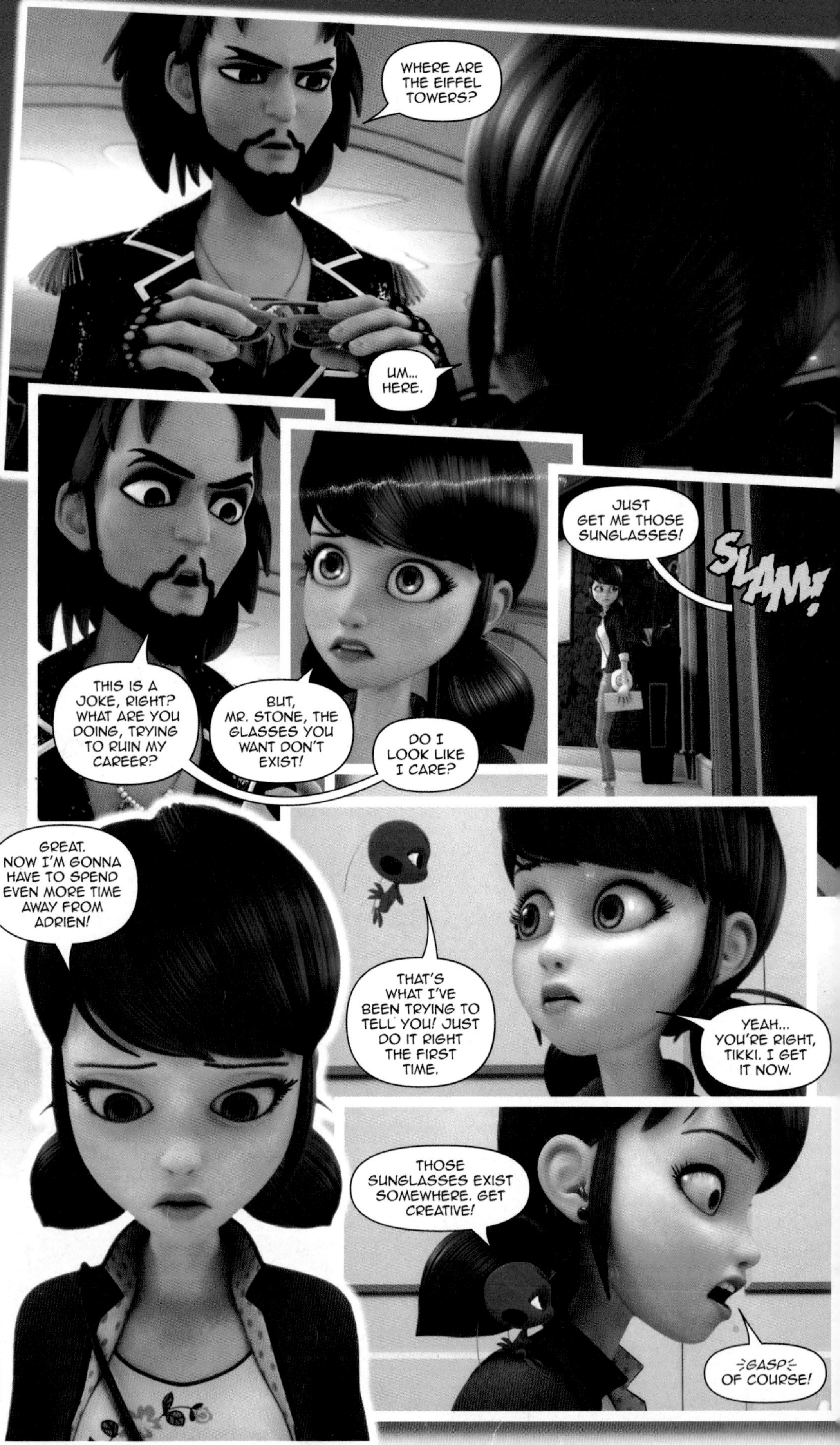
WHERE ARE THE EIFFEL TOWERS?
UM... HERE.
THIS IS A JOKE, RIGHT? WHAT ARE YOU DOING, TRYING TO RUIN MY CAREER?
BUT, MR. STONE, THE GLASSES YOU WANT DON'T EXIST!
DO I LOOK LIKE I CARE?
JUST GET ME THOSE SUNGLASSES!
SLAM!
GREAT. NOW I'M GONNA HAVE TO SPEND EVEN MORE TIME AWAY FROM ADRIEN!
THAT'S WHAT I'VE BEEN TRYING TO TELL YOU! JUST DO IT RIGHT THE FIRST TIME.
YEAH... YOU'RE RIGHT, TIKKI. I GET IT NOW.
THOSE SUNGLASSES EXIST SOMEWHERE. GET CREATIVE!
GASP OF COURSE!

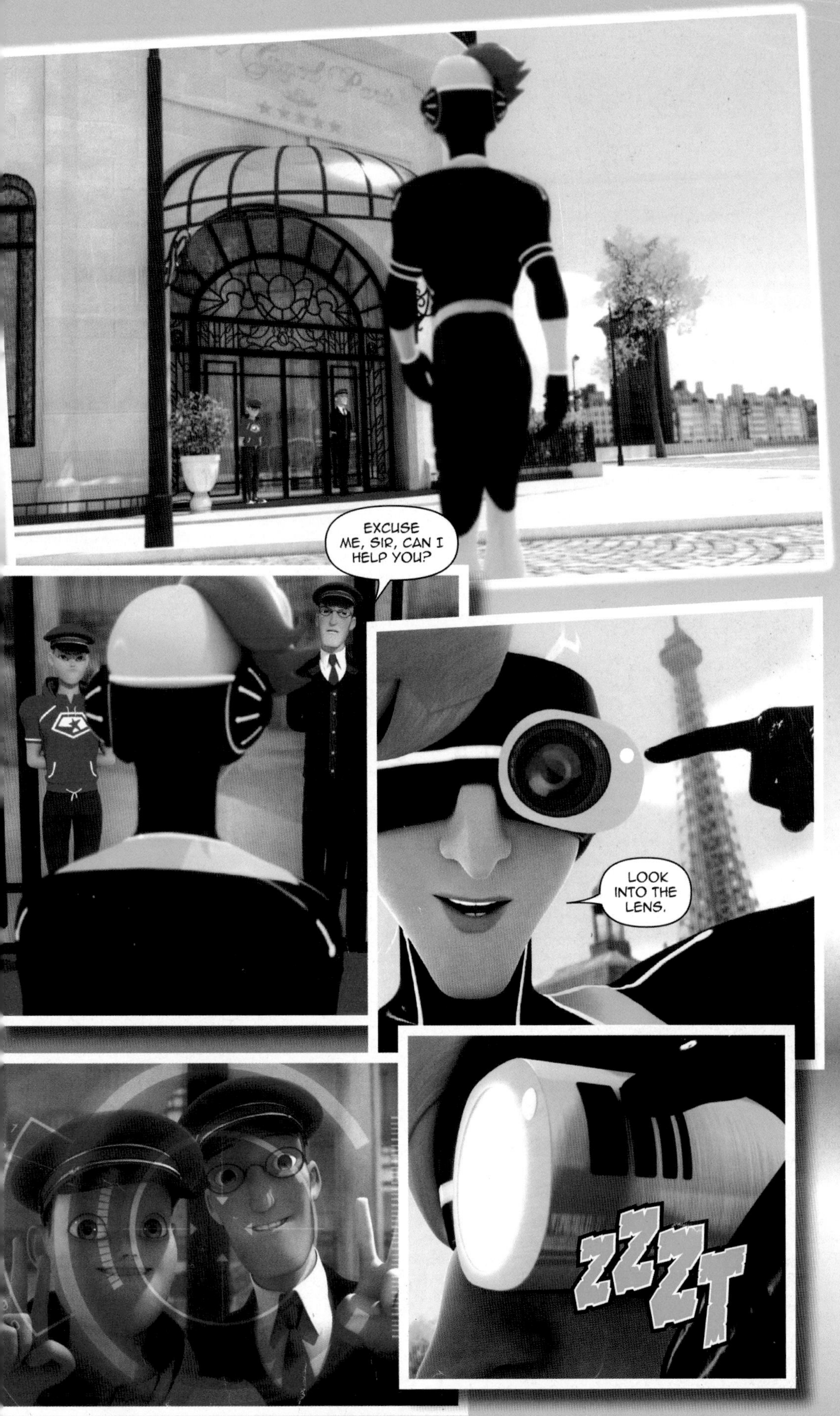
EXCUSE ME, SIR, CAN I HELP YOU?
LOOK INTO THE LENS.
ZZZT

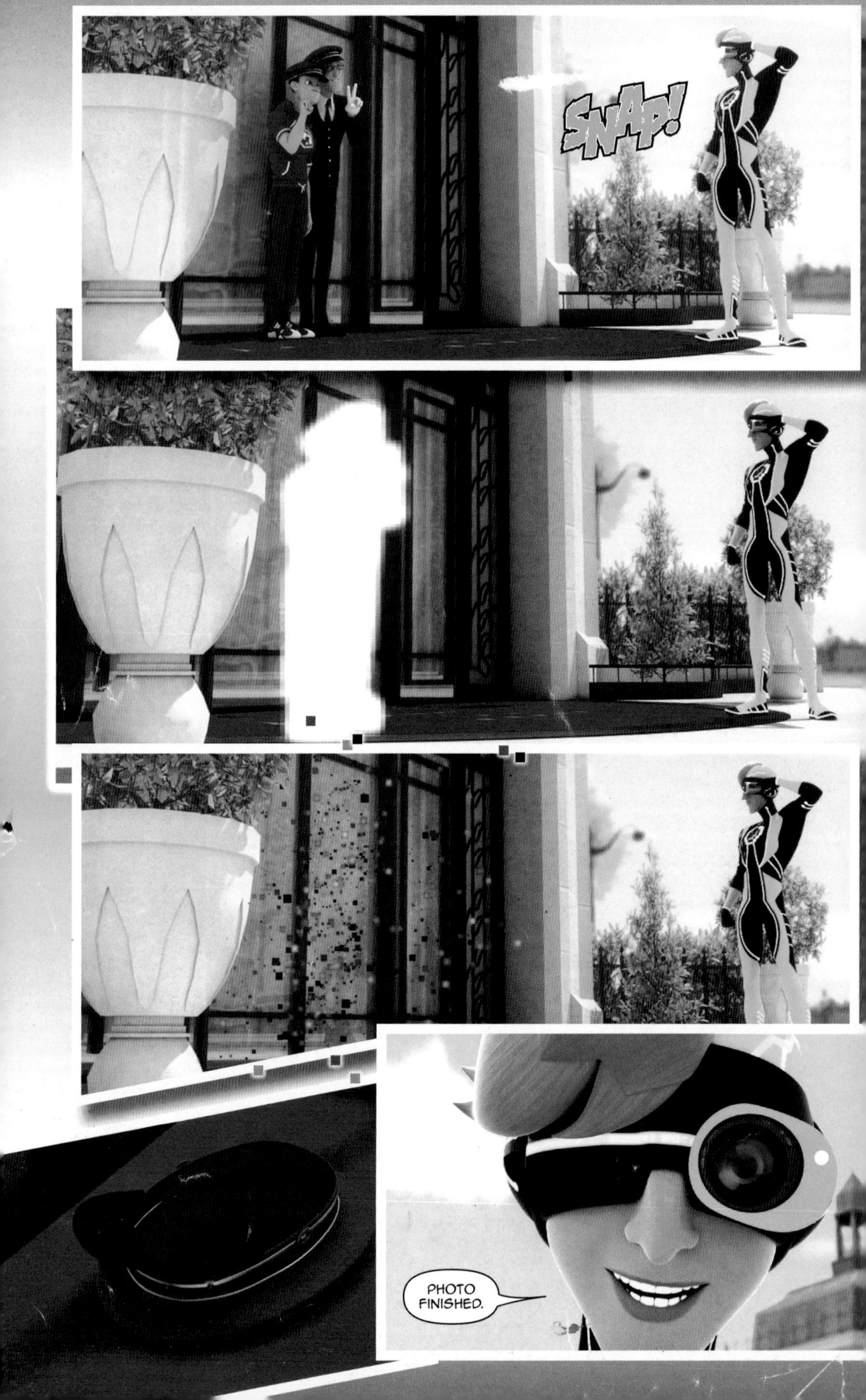
SNAP!
PHOTO FINISHED.

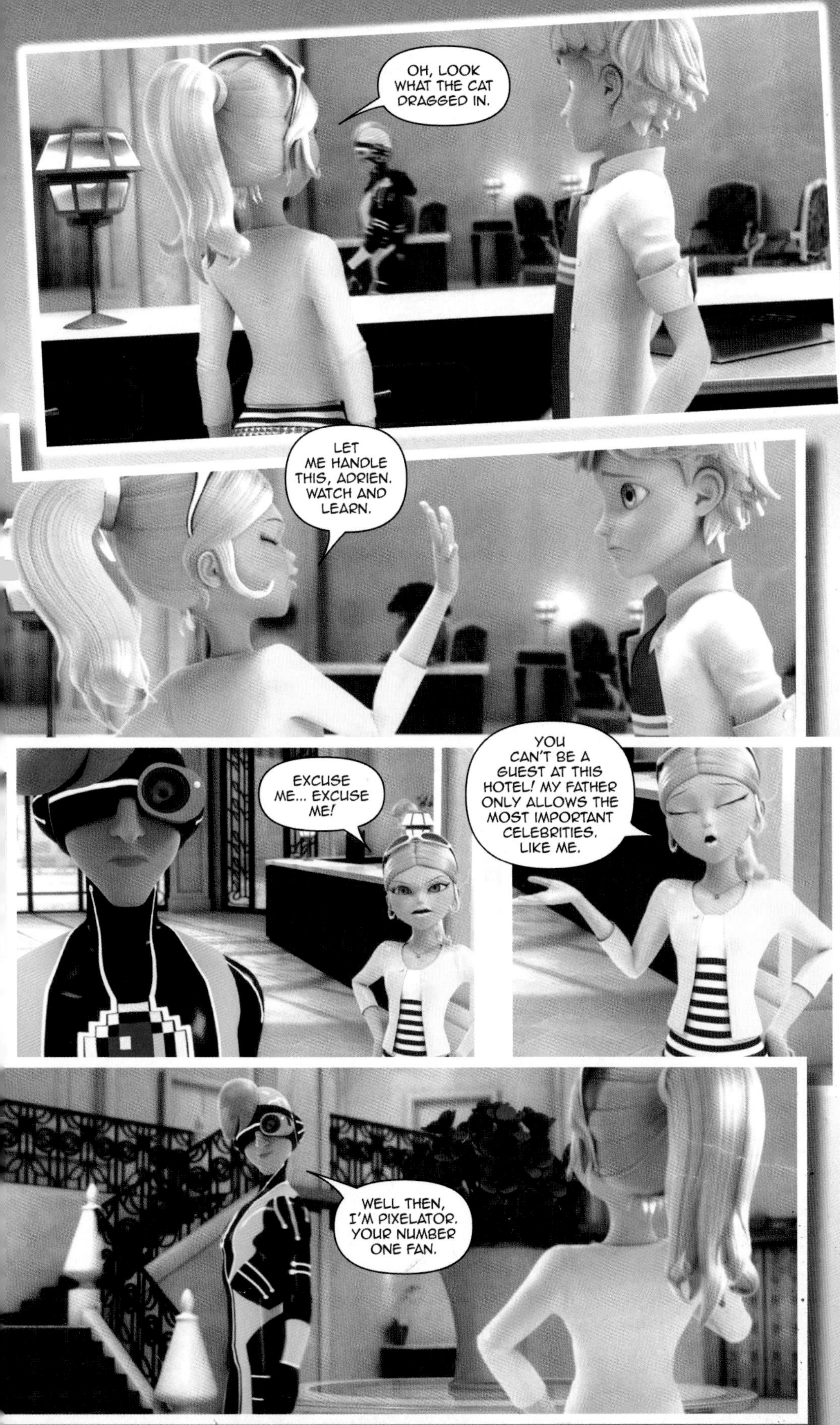
OH, LOOK WHAT THE CAT DRAGGED IN.
LET ME HANDLE THIS, ADRIEN. WATCH AND LEARN.
EXCUSE ME... EXCUSE ME!
YOU CAN'T BE A GUEST AT THIS HOTEL! MY FATHER ONLY ALLOWS THE MOST IMPORTANT CELEBRITIES. LIKE ME.
WELL THEN, I'M PIXELATOR. YOUR NUMBER ONE FAN.

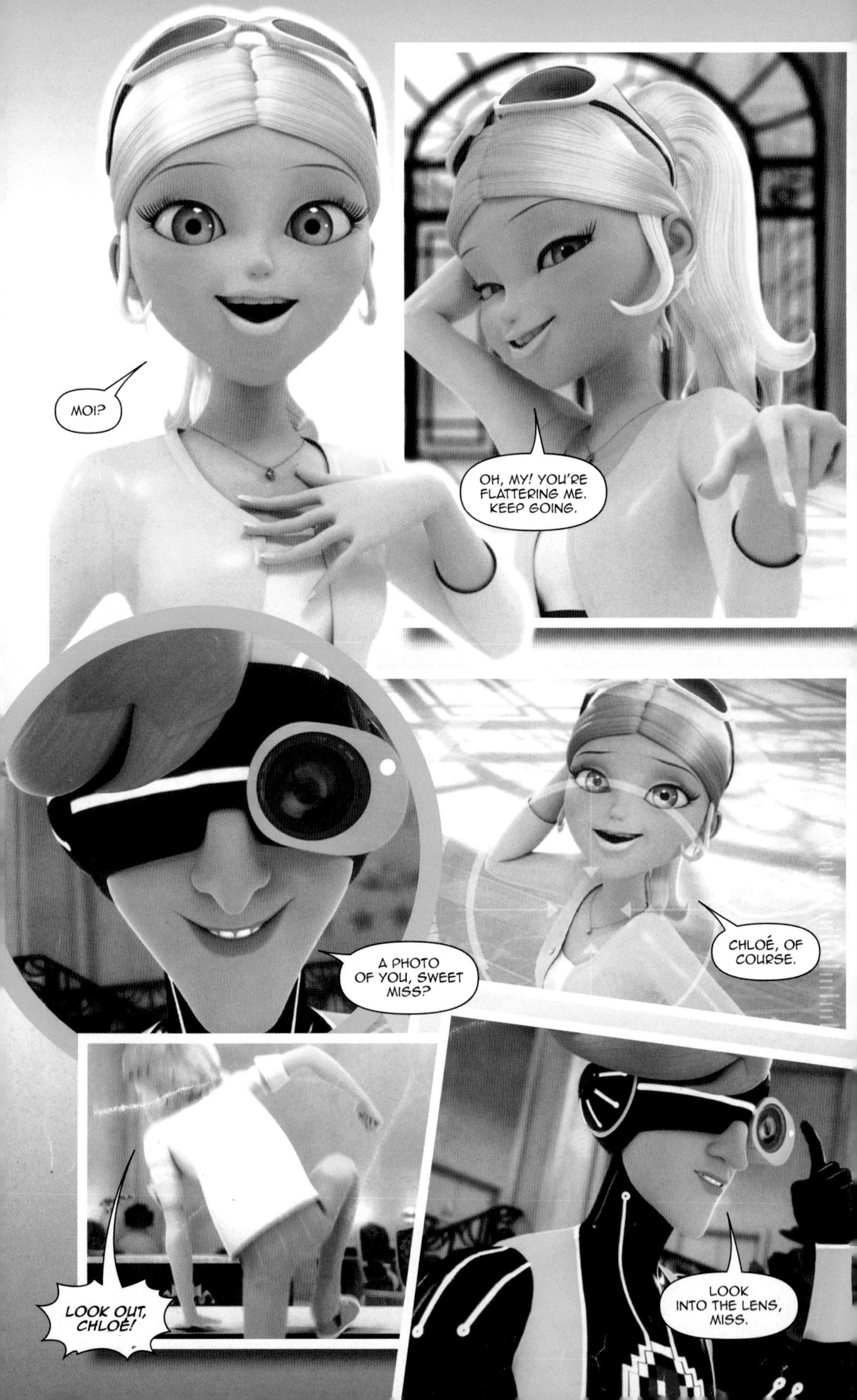
MOI?
OH, MY! YOU'RE FLATTERING ME. KEEP GOING.
A PHOTO OF YOU, SWEET MISS?
CHLOÉ, OF COURSE.
LOOK OUT, CHLOÉ!
LOOK INTO THE LENS, MISS.

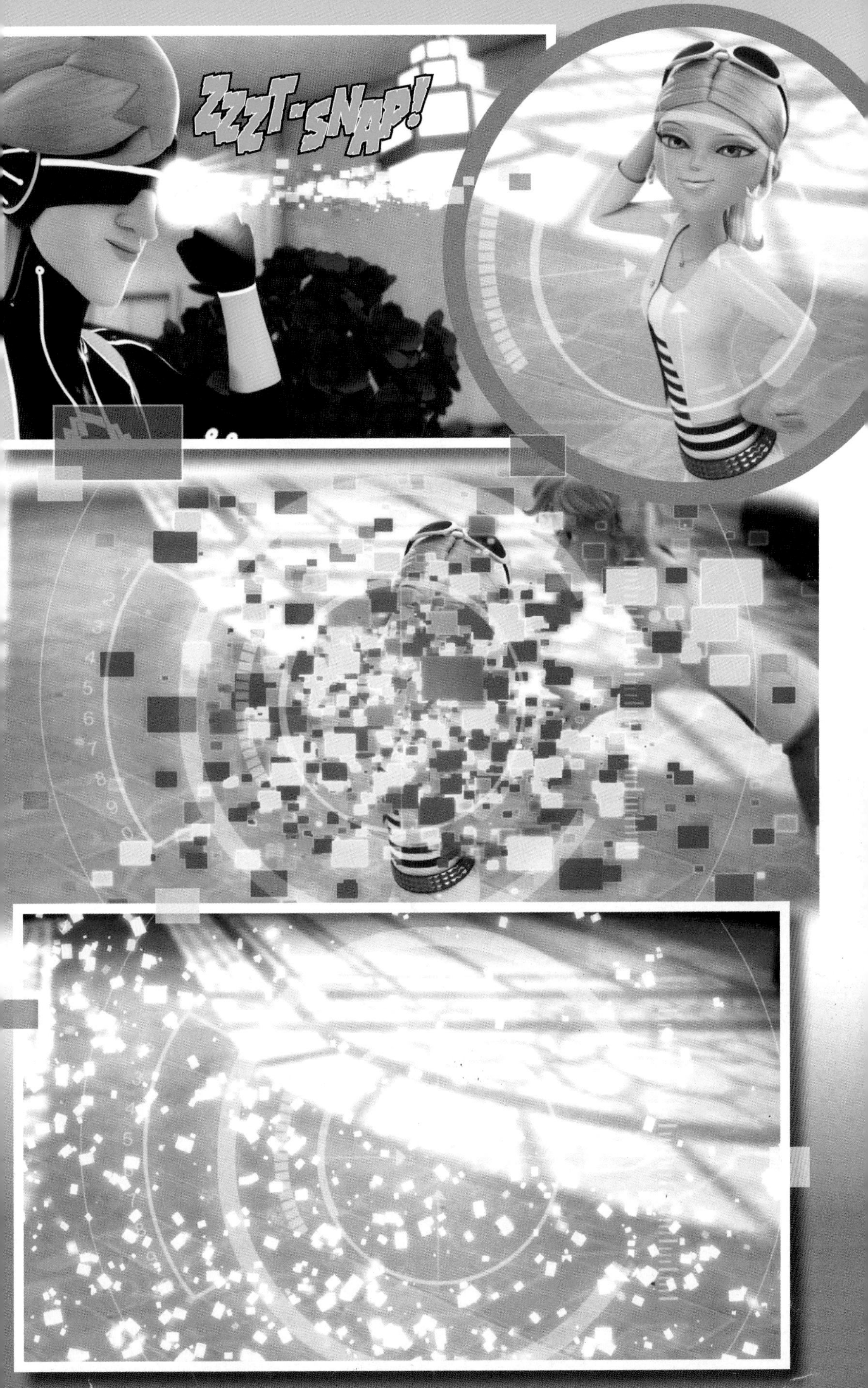
ZZZT-SNAP!

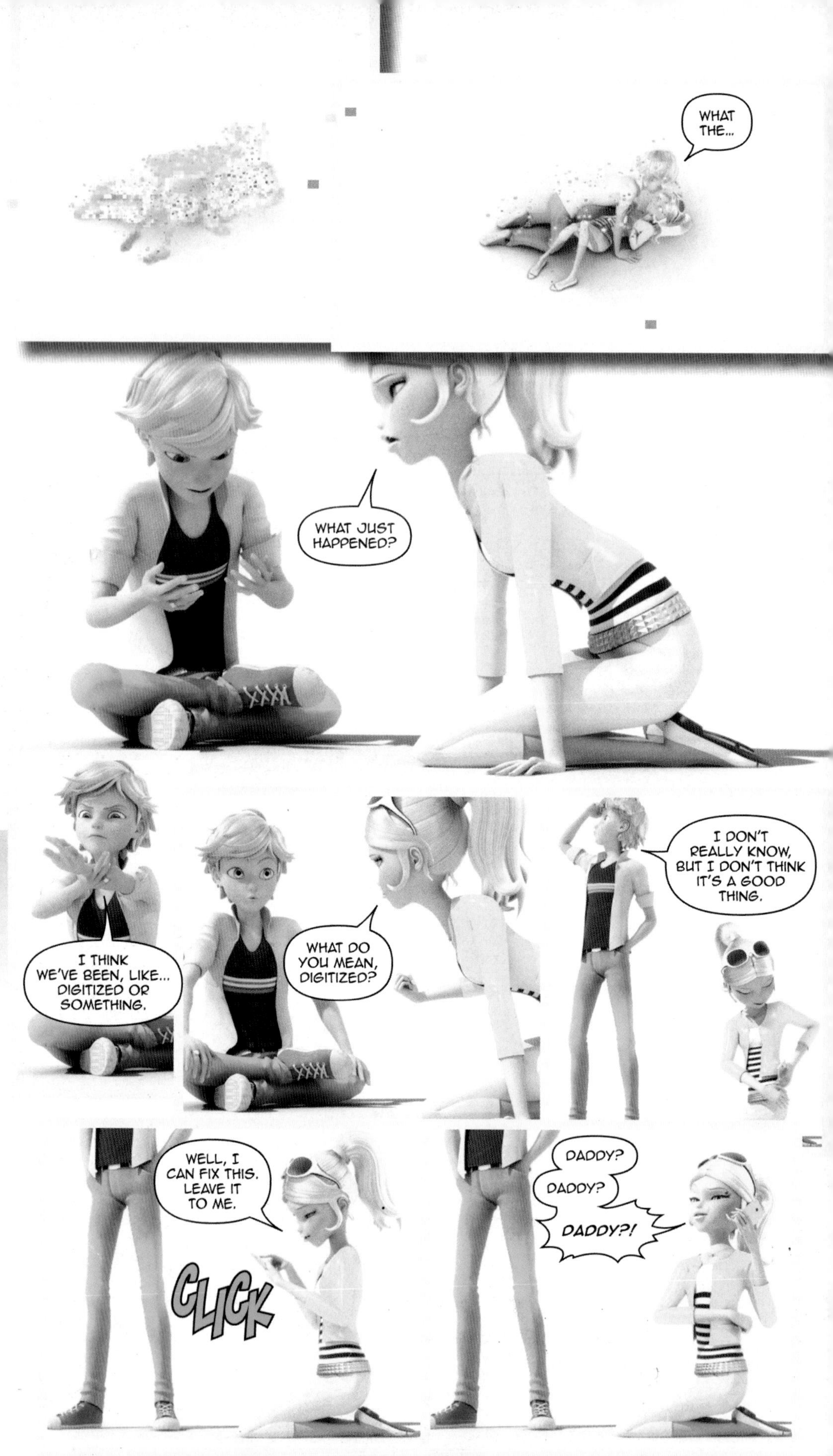
WHAT THE...
WHAT JUST HAPPENED?
I THINK WE'VE BEEN, LIKE... DIGITIZED OR SOMETHING.
WHAT DO YOU MEAN, DIGITIZED?
I DON'T REALLY KNOW, BUT I DON'T THINK IT'S A GOOD THING.
WELL, I CAN FIX THIS. LEAVE IT TO ME.
CLICK
DADDY?
DADDY?
DADDY?!

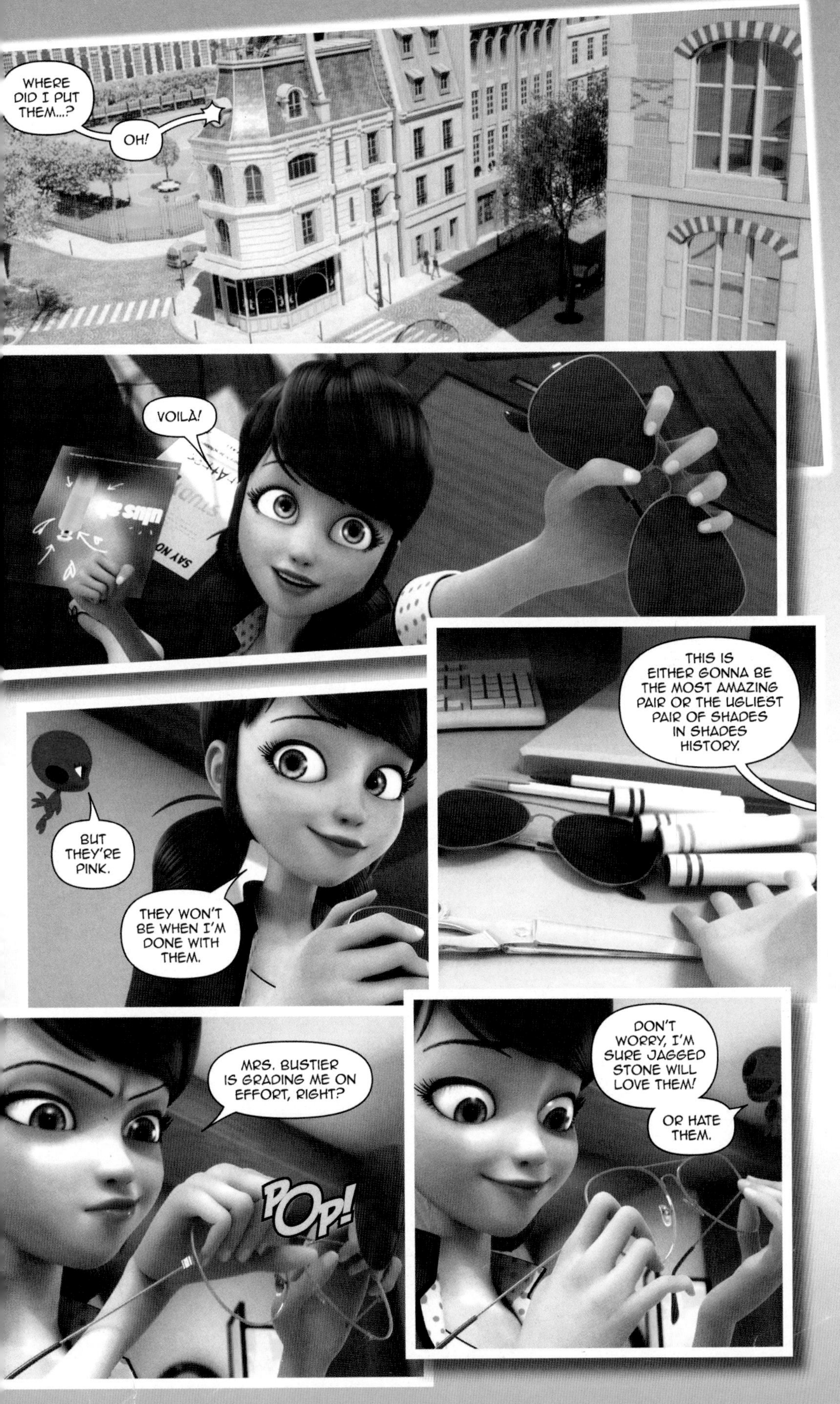
WHERE DID I PUT THEM...?
OH!
VOILÀ!
THIS IS EITHER GONNA BE THE MOST AMAZING PAIR OR THE UGLIEST PAIR OF SHADES IN SHADES HISTORY.
BUT THEY'RE PINK.
THEY WON'T BE WHEN I'M DONE WITH THEM.
MRS. BUSTIER IS GRADING ME ON EFFORT, RIGHT?
POP!
DON'T WORRY, I'M SURE JAGGED STONE WILL LOVE THEM!
OR HATE THEM.

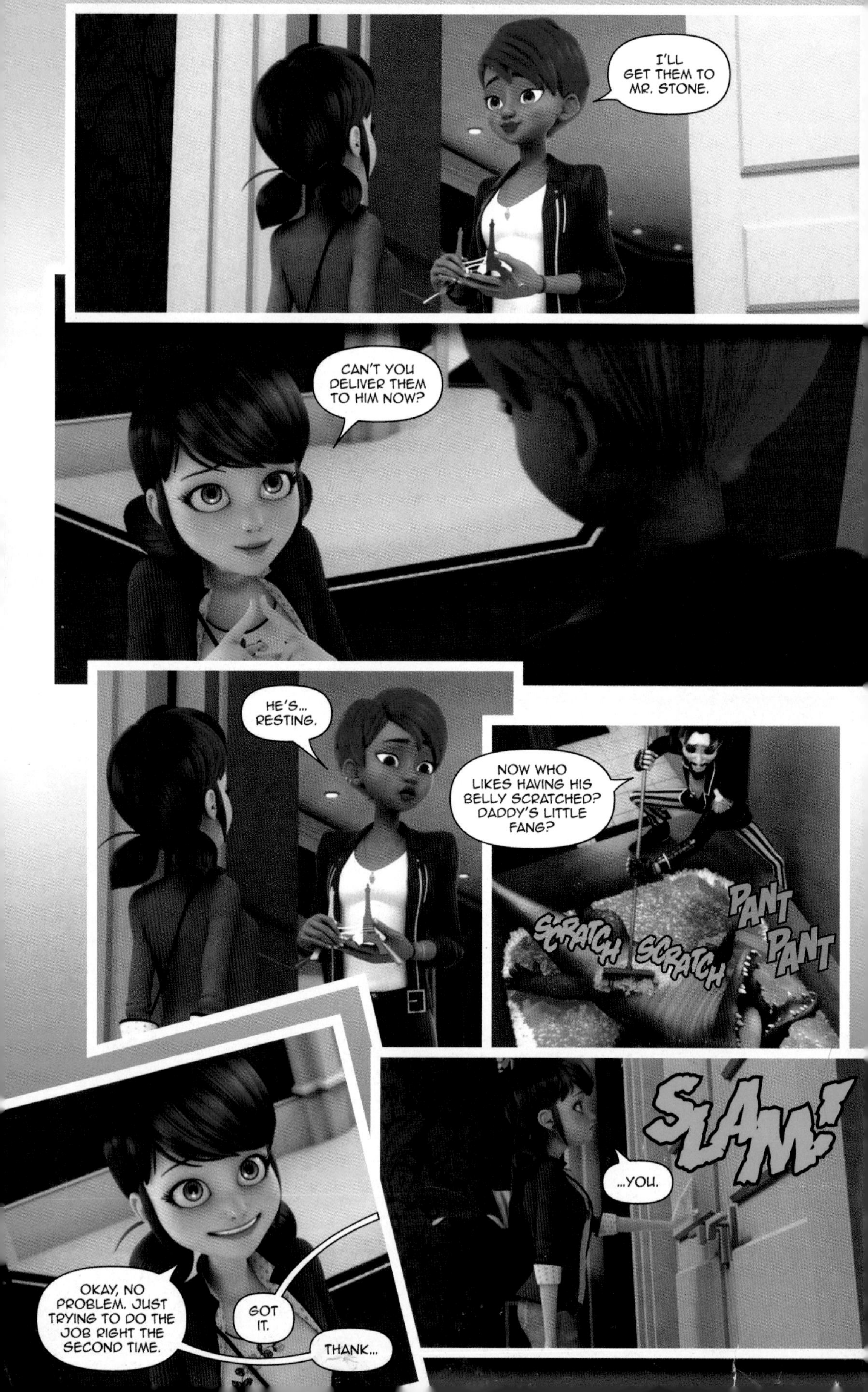
I'LL GET THEM TO MR. STONE.
CAN'T YOU DELIVER THEM TO HIM NOW?
HE'S... RESTING.
NOW WHO LIKES HAVING HIS BELLY SCRATCHED? DADDY'S LITTLE FANG?
SCRATCH SCRATCH
PANT PANT
OKAY, NO PROBLEM. JUST TRYING TO DO THE JOB RIGHT THE SECOND TIME.
GOT IT.
THANK...
...YOU.
SLAM!

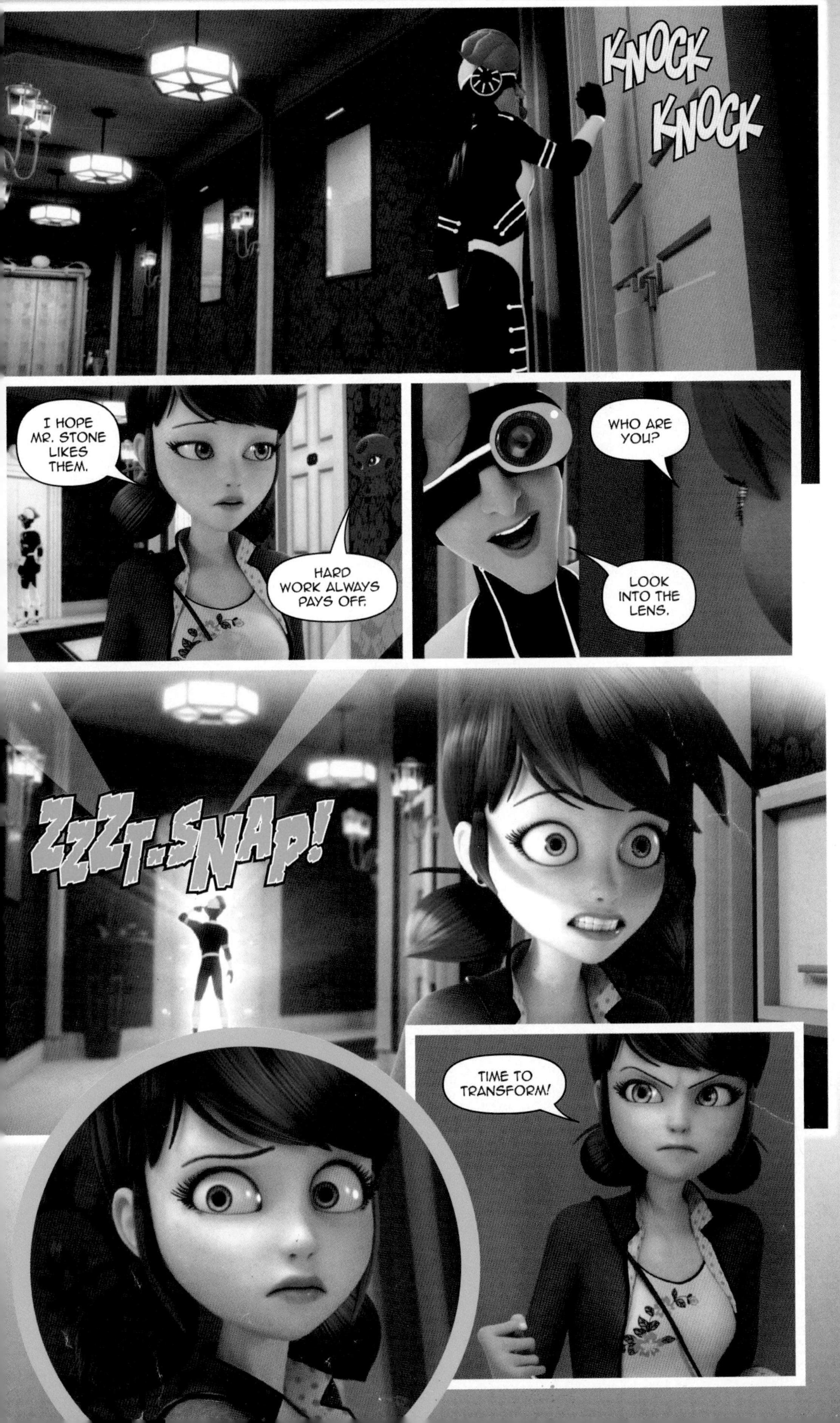
KNOCK KNOCK
I HOPE MR. STONE LIKES THEM.
HARD WORK ALWAYS PAYS OFF.
WHO ARE YOU?
LOOK INTO THE LENS.
ZZZT..SNAP!
TIME TO TRANSFORM!

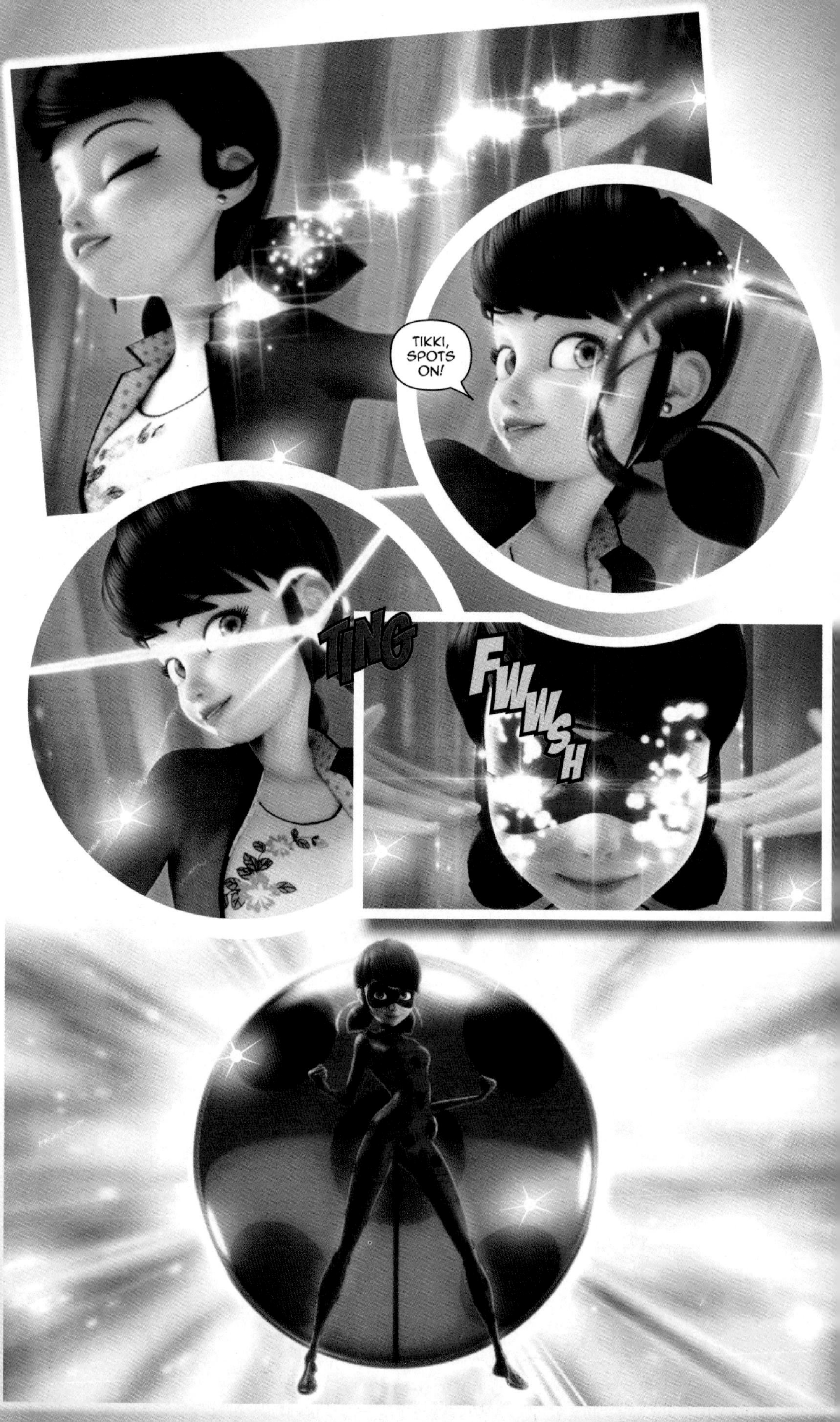
TIKKI, SPOTS ON!
TING
FWWSH

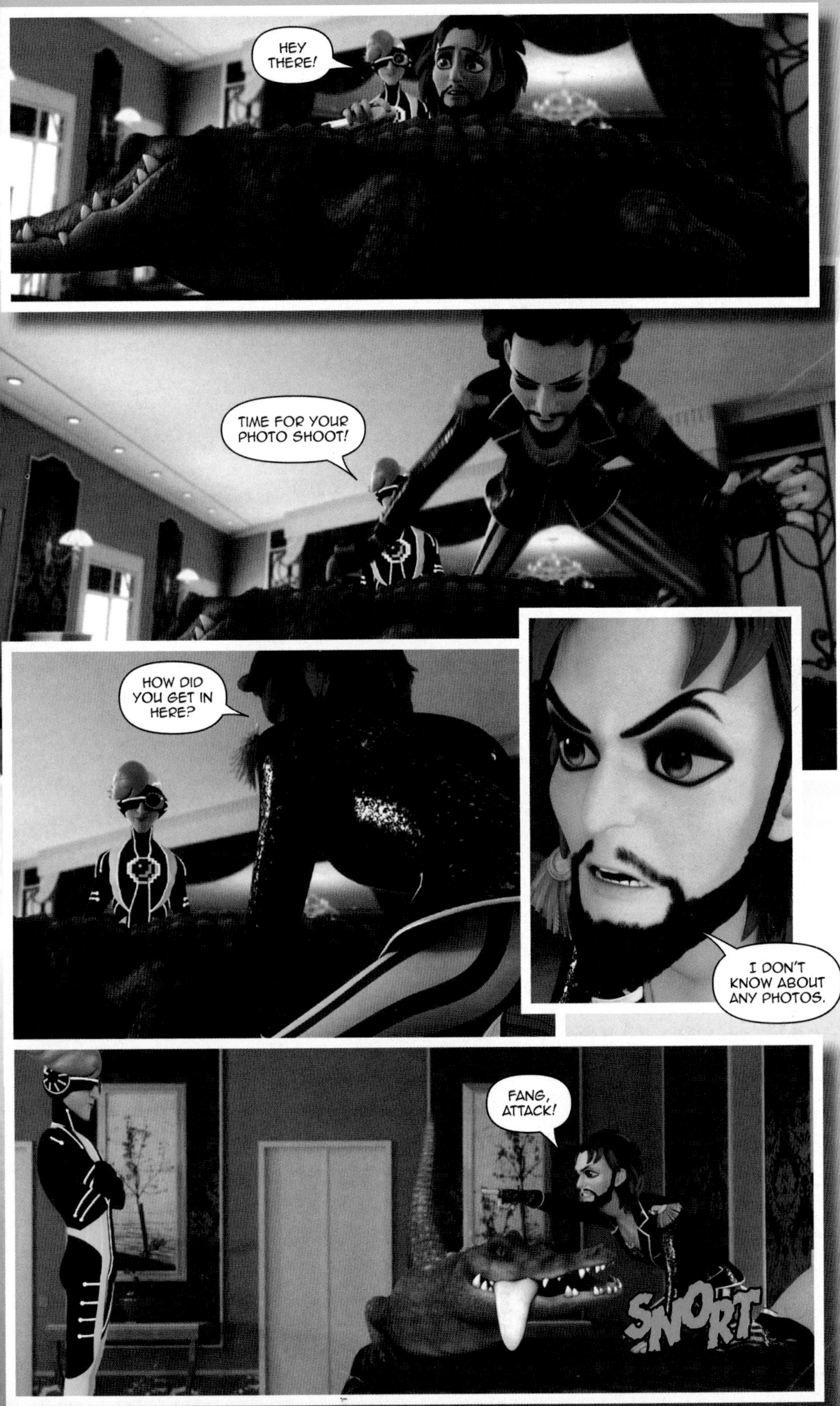
HEY THERE!
TIME FOR YOUR PHOTO SHOOT!
HOW DID YOU GET IN HERE?
I DON'T KNOW ABOUT ANY PHOTOS.
FANG, ATTACK!
SNORT

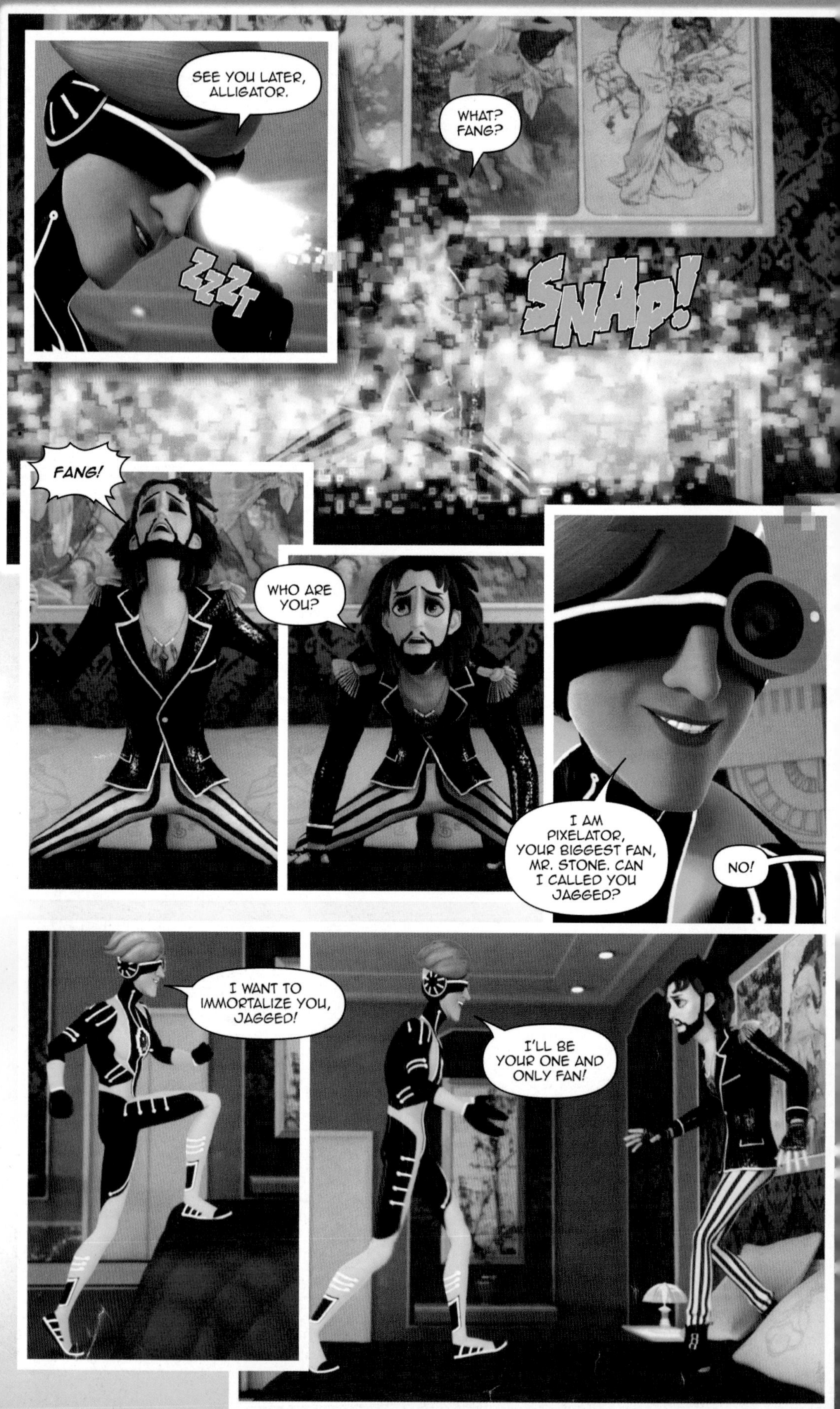
SEE YOU LATER, ALLIGATOR.
ZZZT
WHAT? FANG?
SNAP!
FANG!
WHO ARE YOU?
I AM PIXELATOR, YOUR BIGGEST FAN, MR. STONE. CAN I CALLED YOU JAGGED?
NO!
I WANT TO IMMORTALIZE YOU, JAGGED!
I'LL BE YOUR ONE AND ONLY FAN!

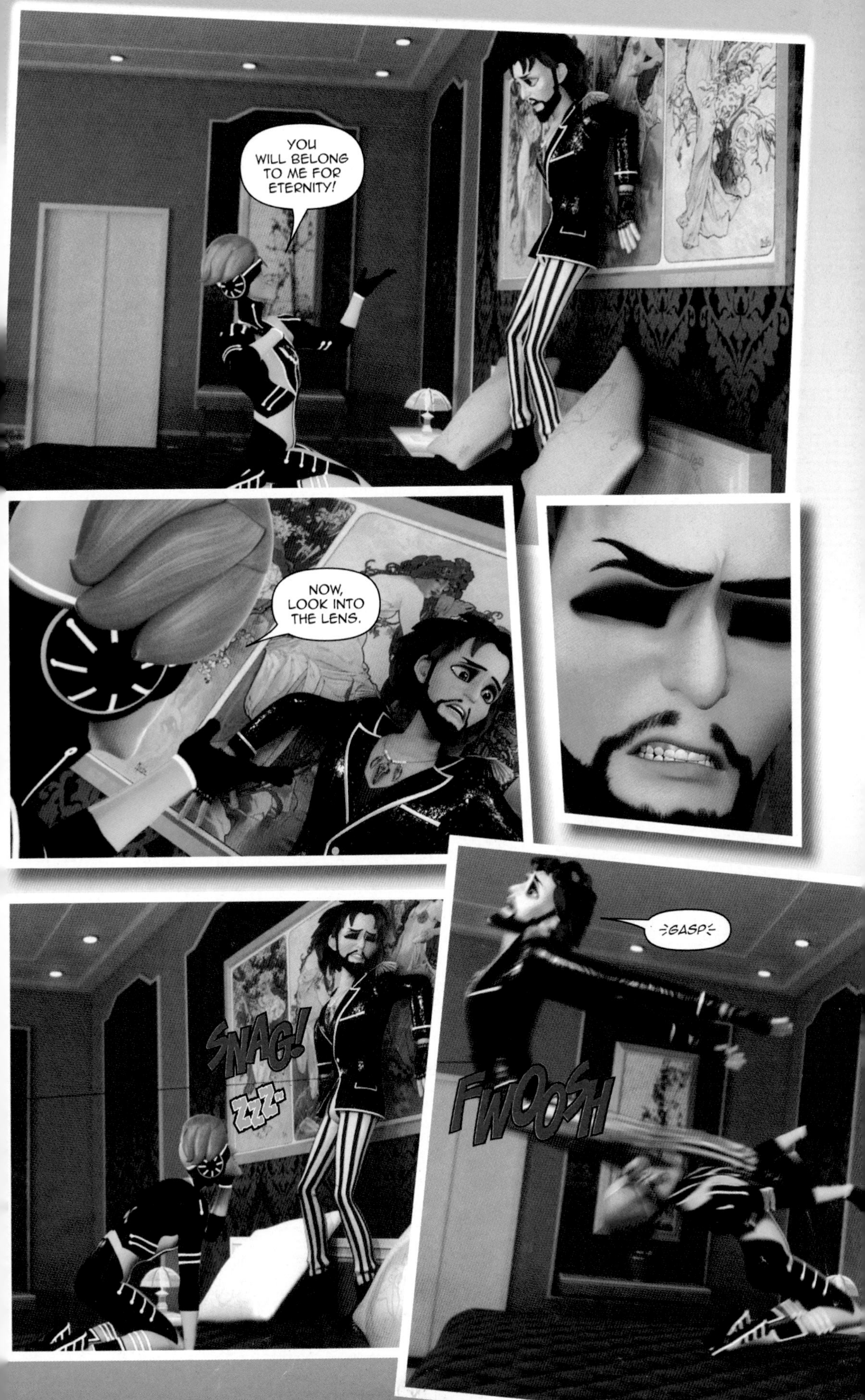
YOU WILL BELONG TO ME FOR ETERNITY!
NOW, LOOK INTO THE LENS.
SNAG!
ZZZ-
FWOOSH
GASP

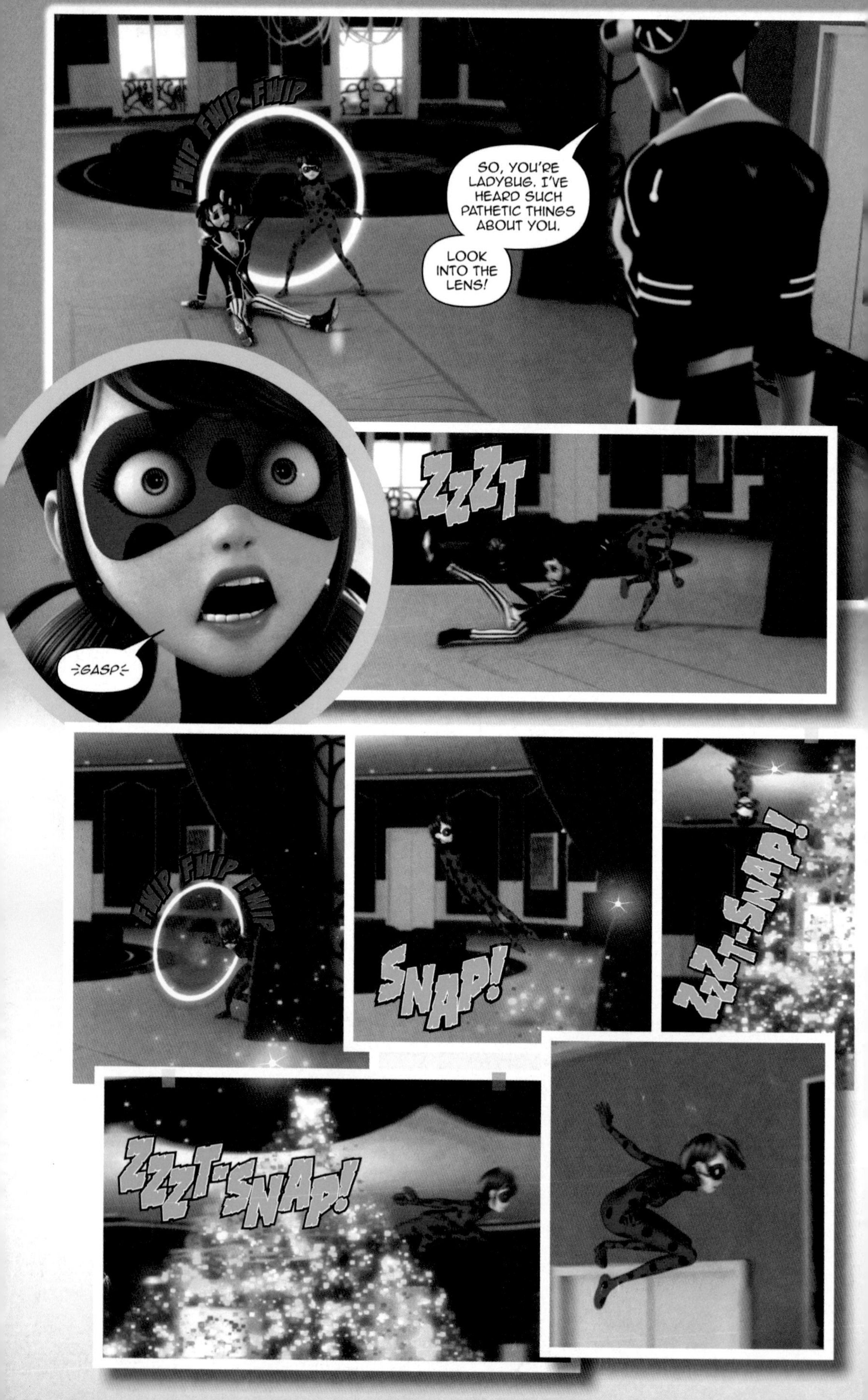

FWIP FWIP FWIP
SO, YOU'RE LADYBUG. I'VE HEARD SUCH PATHETIC THINGS ABOUT YOU.
LOOK INTO THE LENS!
GASP
ZZZT
FWIP FWIP FWIP
SNAP!
ZZZT-SNAP!
ZZZT-SNAP!

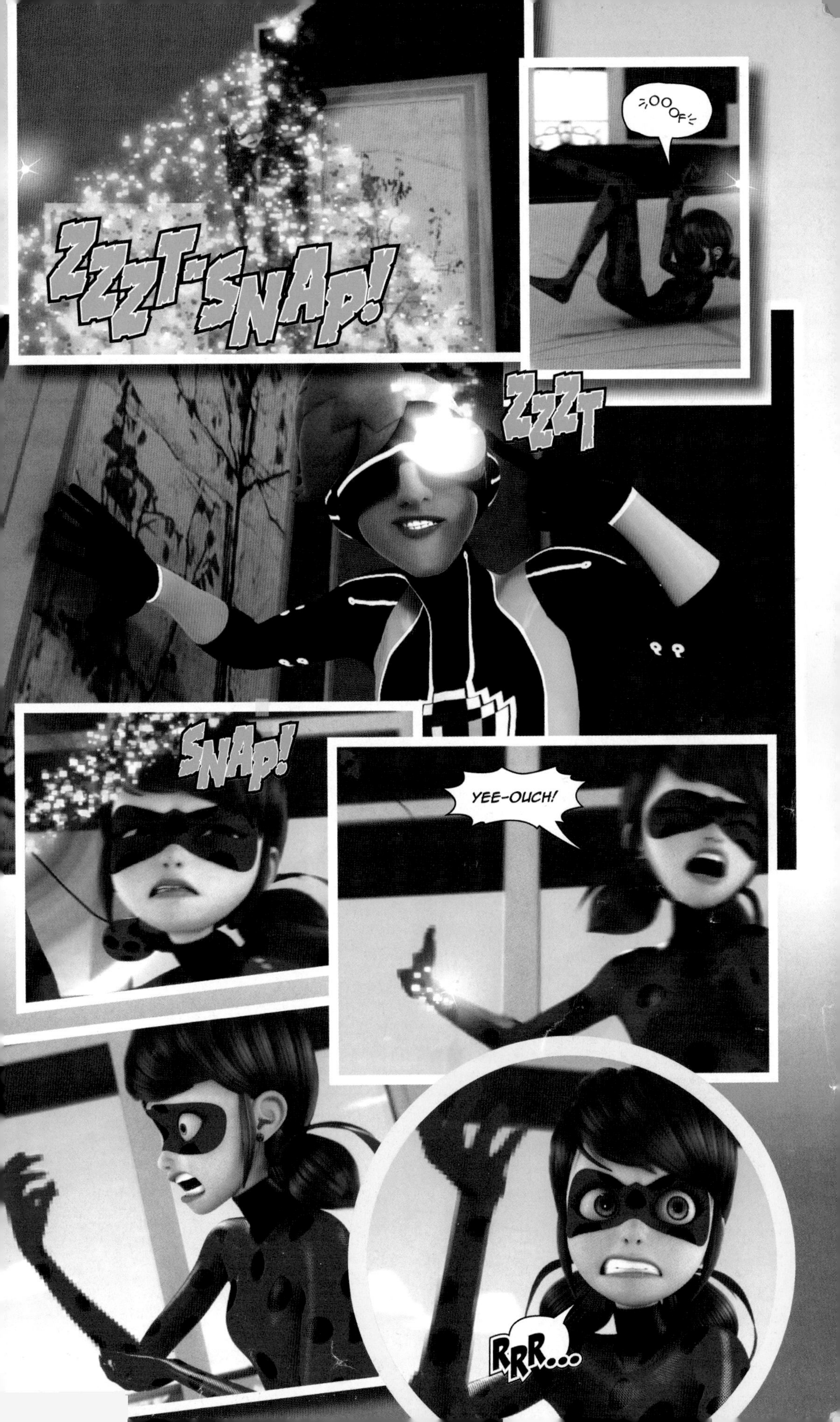
ZZZT-SNAP!
OOOF
ZZZT
SNAP!
YEE-OUCH!
RRR...

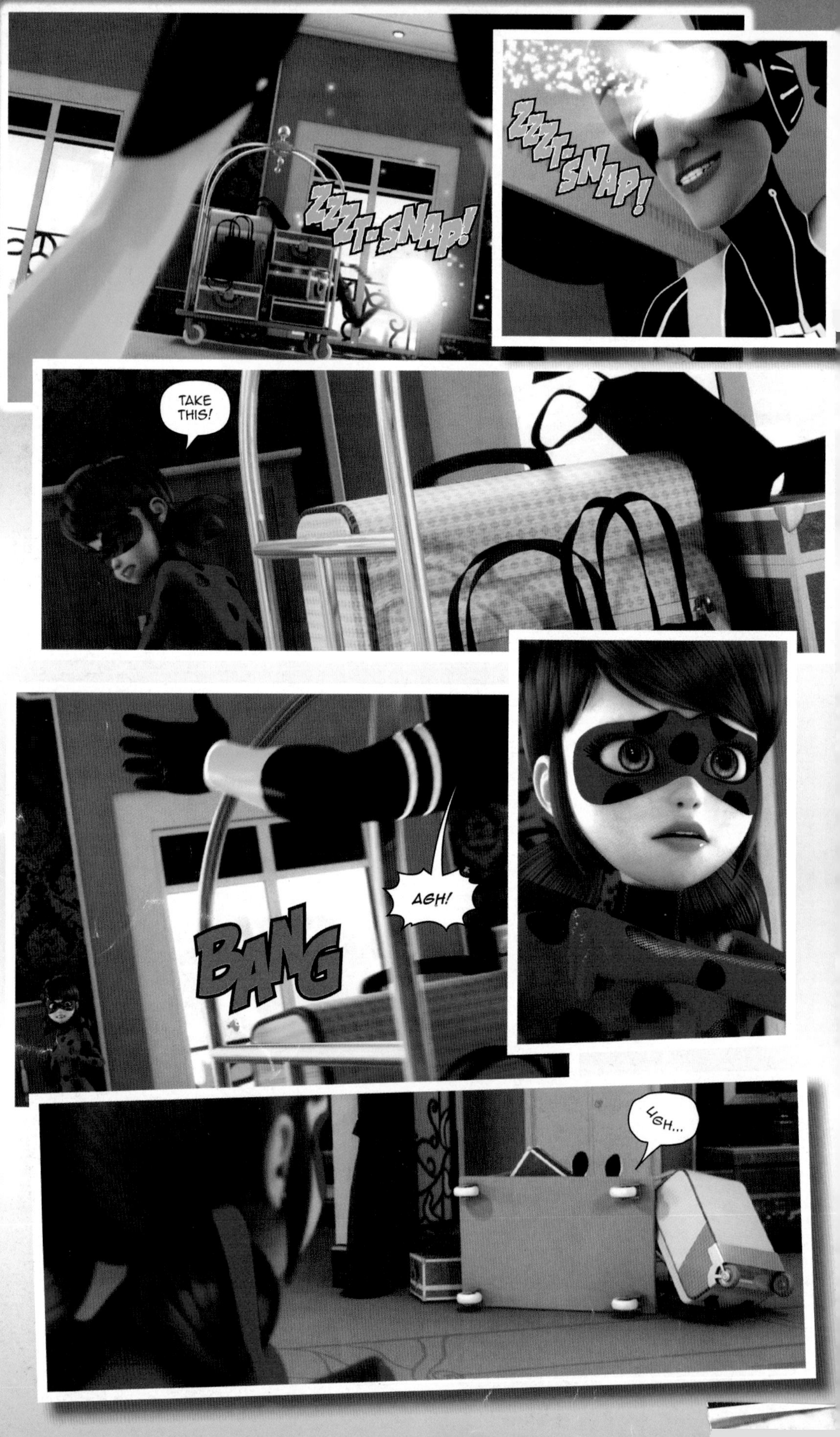
ZZZT-SNAP!
ZZZT-SNAP!
TAKE THIS!
BANG
AGH!
UGH...

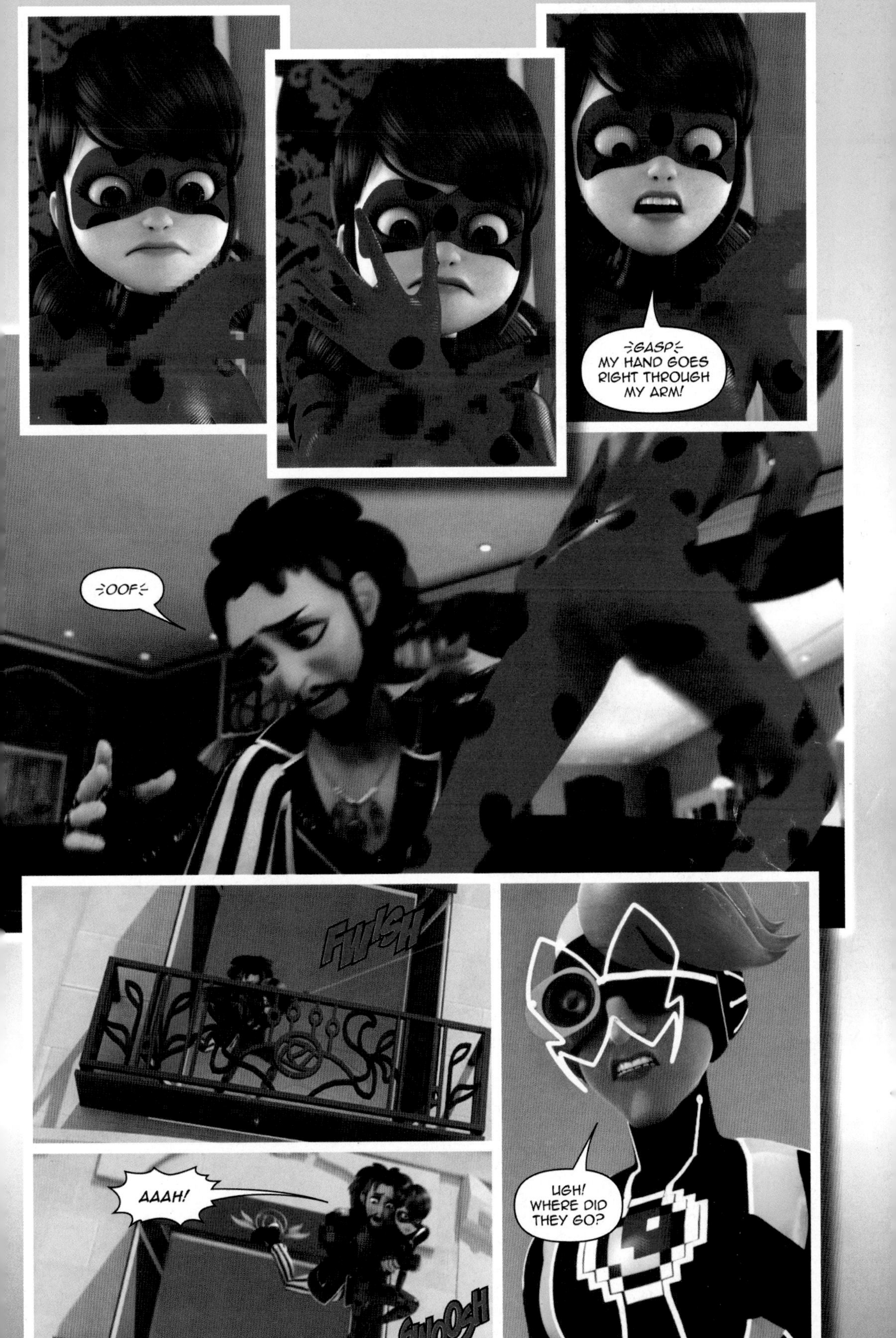

GASP
MY HAND GOES RIGHT THROUGH MY ARM!
OOF
FWISH
AAAH!
SWOOSH
UGH! WHERE DID THEY GO?

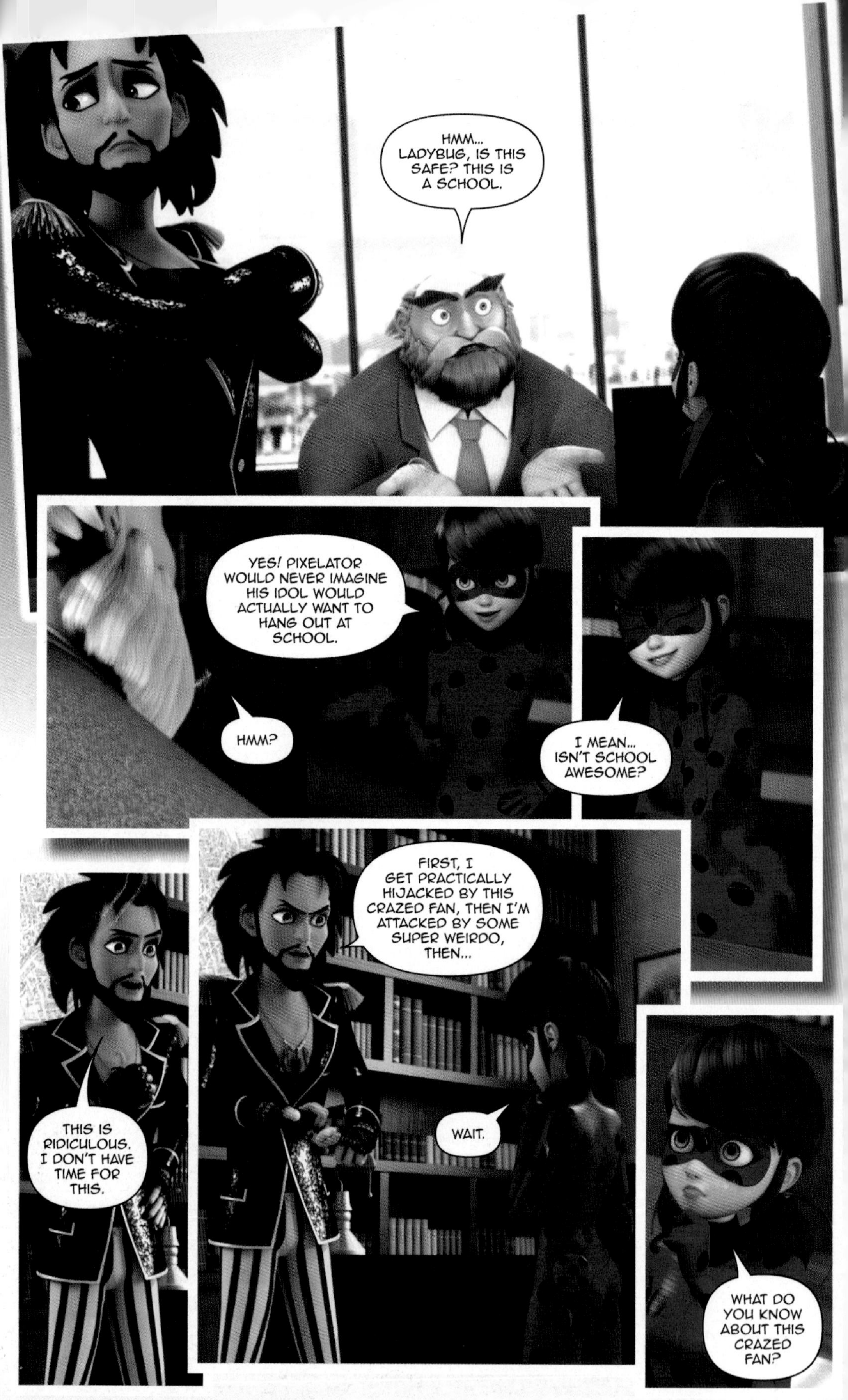
HMM... LADYBUG, IS THIS SAFE? THIS IS A SCHOOL.
YES! PIXELATOR WOULD NEVER IMAGINE HIS IDOL WOULD ACTUALLY WANT TO HANG OUT AT SCHOOL.
HMM?
I MEAN... ISN'T SCHOOL AWESOME?
FIRST, I GET PRACTICALLY HIJACKED BY THIS CRAZED FAN, THEN I'M ATTACKED BY SOME SUPER WEIRDO, THEN...
THIS IS RIDICULOUS. I DON'T HAVE TIME FOR THIS.
WAIT.
WHAT DO YOU KNOW ABOUT THIS CRAZED FAN?

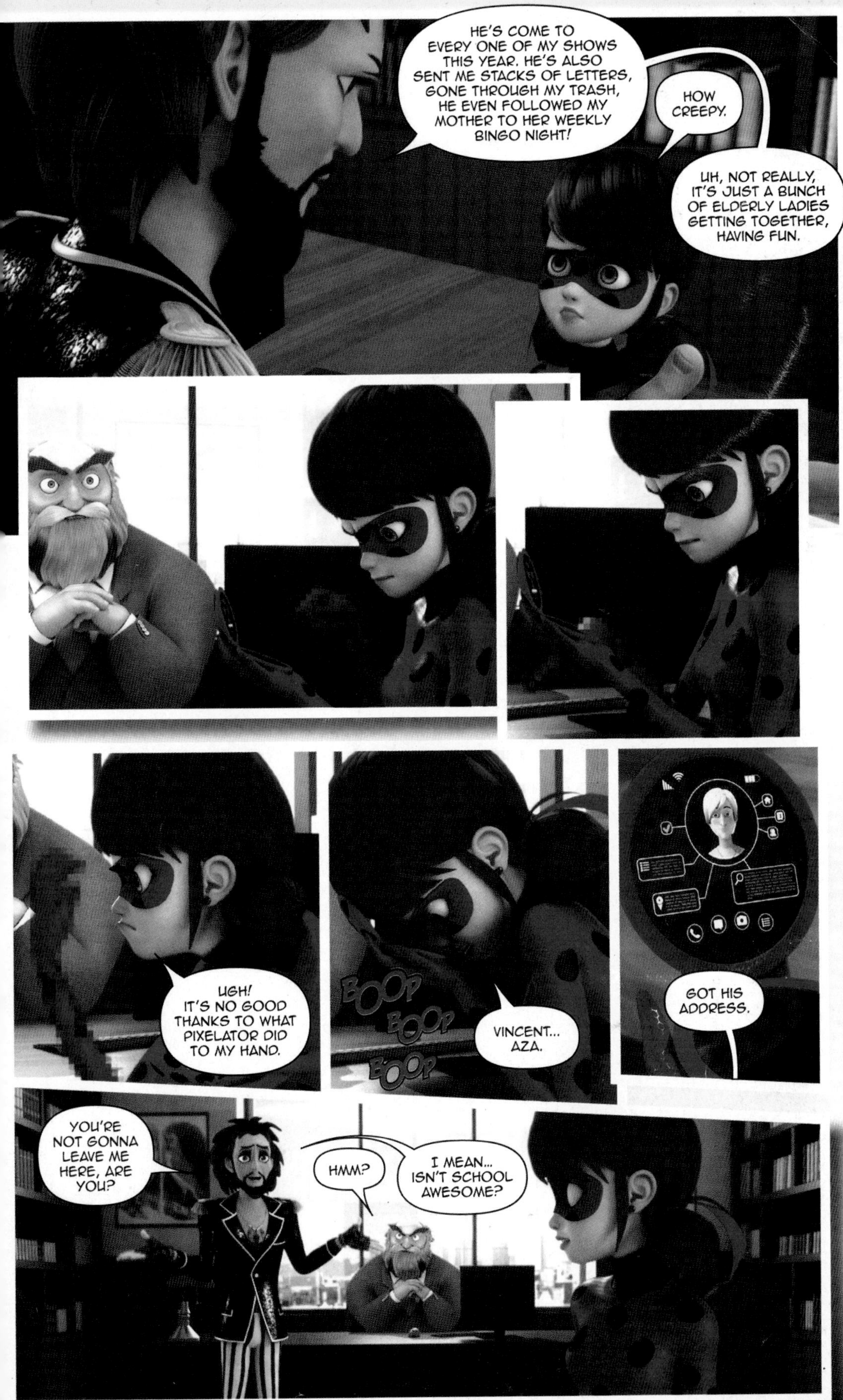
HE'S COME TO EVERY ONE OF MY SHOWS THIS YEAR. HE'S ALSO SENT ME STACKS OF LETTERS, GONE THROUGH MY TRASH, HE EVEN FOLLOWED MY MOTHER TO HER WEEKLY BINGO NIGHT!
HOW CREEPY.
UH, NOT REALLY, IT'S JUST A BUNCH OF ELDERLY LADIES GETTING TOGETHER, HAVING FUN.
UGH! IT'S NO GOOD THANKS TO WHAT PIXELATOR DID TO MY HAND.
BOOP BOOP BOOP
VINCENT... AZA.
GOT HIS ADDRESS.
YOU'RE NOT GONNA LEAVE ME HERE, ARE YOU?
HMM?
I MEAN... ISN'T SCHOOL AWESOME?

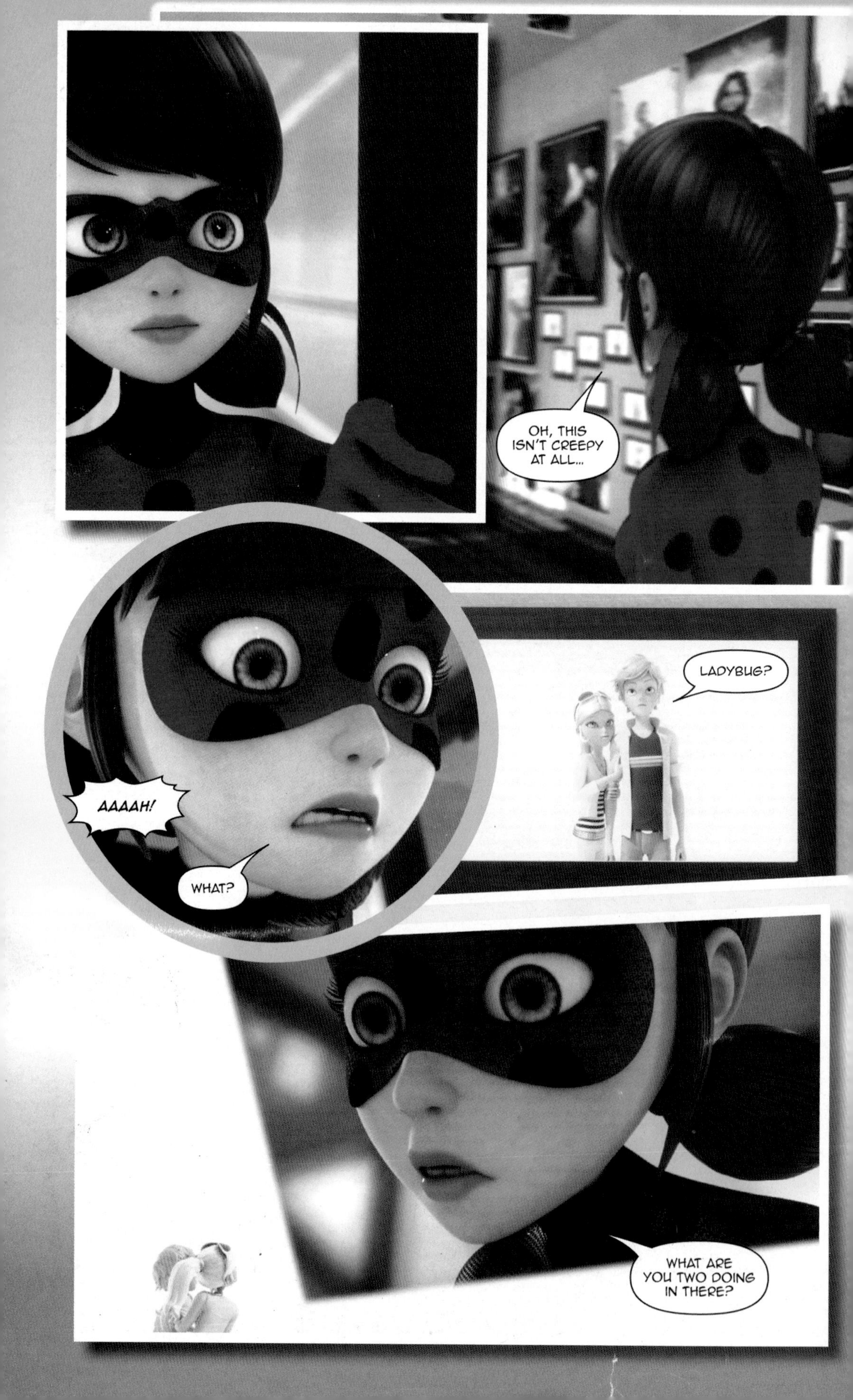
OH, THIS ISN'T CREEPY AT ALL...
LADYBUG?
AAAAH!
WHAT?
WHAT ARE YOU TWO DOING IN THERE?

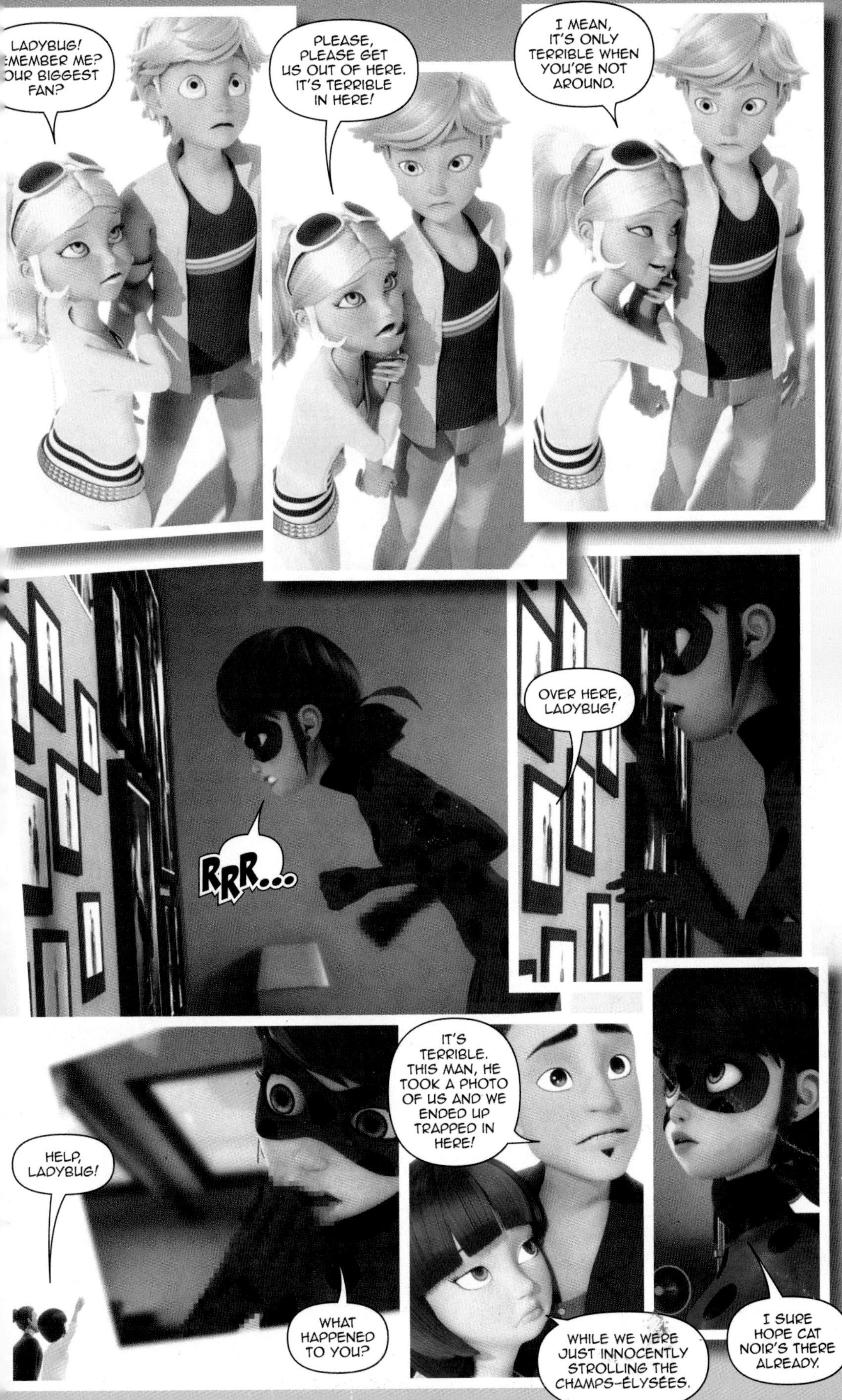
LADYBUG! EMEMBER ME? OUR BIGGEST FAN?
PLEASE, PLEASE GET US OUT OF HERE. IT'S TERRIBLE IN HERE!
I MEAN, IT'S ONLY TERRIBLE WHEN YOU'RE NOT AROUND.
RRR...
OVER HERE, LADYBUG!
HELP, LADYBUG!
WHAT HAPPENED TO YOU?
IT'S TERRIBLE. THIS MAN, HE TOOK A PHOTO OF US AND WE ENDED UP TRAPPED IN HERE!
WHILE WE WERE JUST INNOCENTLY STROLLING THE CHAMPS-ÉLYSÉES.
I SURE HOPE CAT NOIR'S THERE ALREADY.

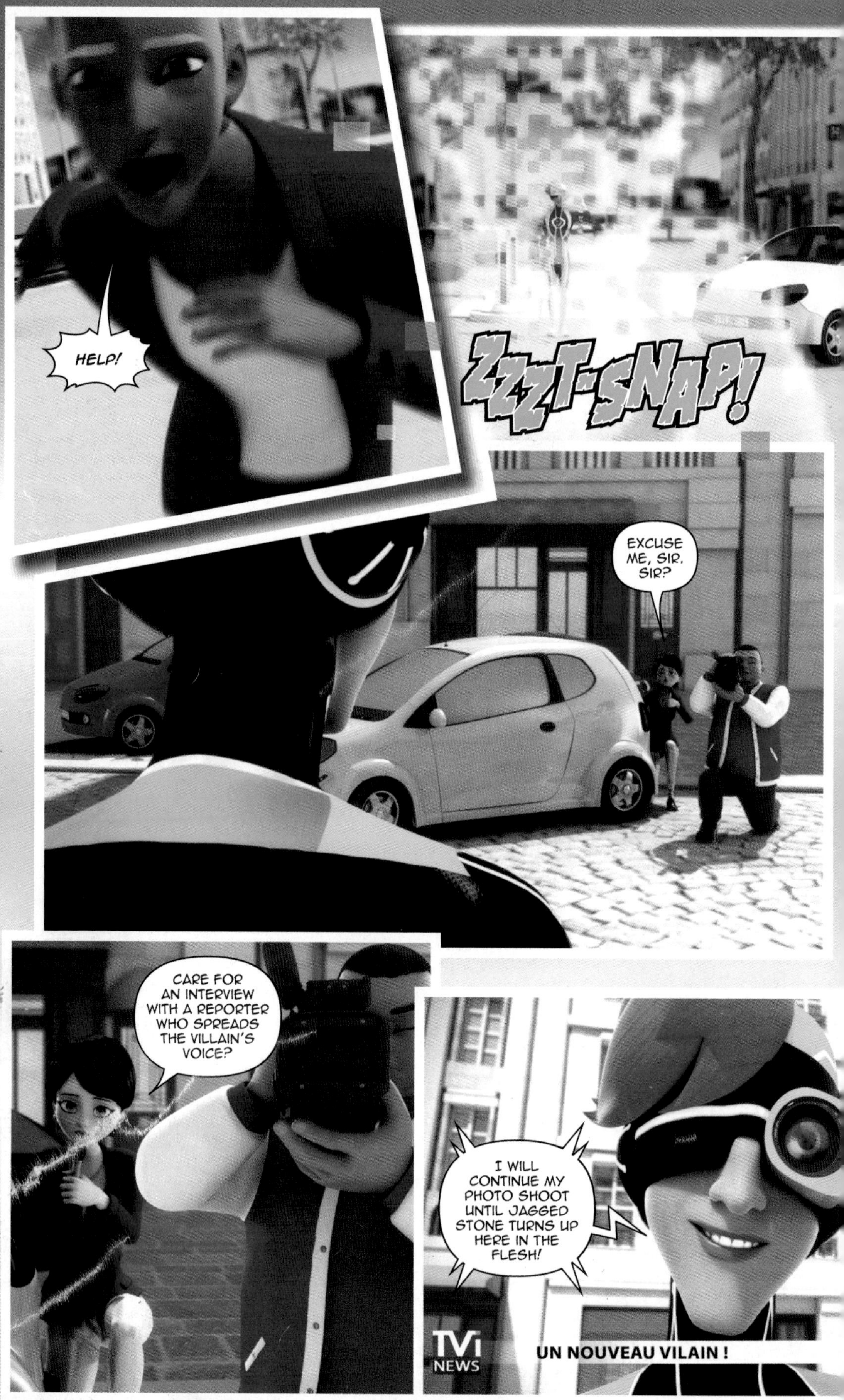
HELP!
ZZZT-SNAP!
EXCUSE ME, SIR. SIR?
CARE FOR AN INTERVIEW WITH A REPORTER WHO SPREADS THE VILLAIN'S VOICE?
I WILL CONTINUE MY PHOTO SHOOT UNTIL JAGGED STONE TURNS UP HERE IN THE FLESH!
TVi NEWS
UN NOUVEAU VILAIN !

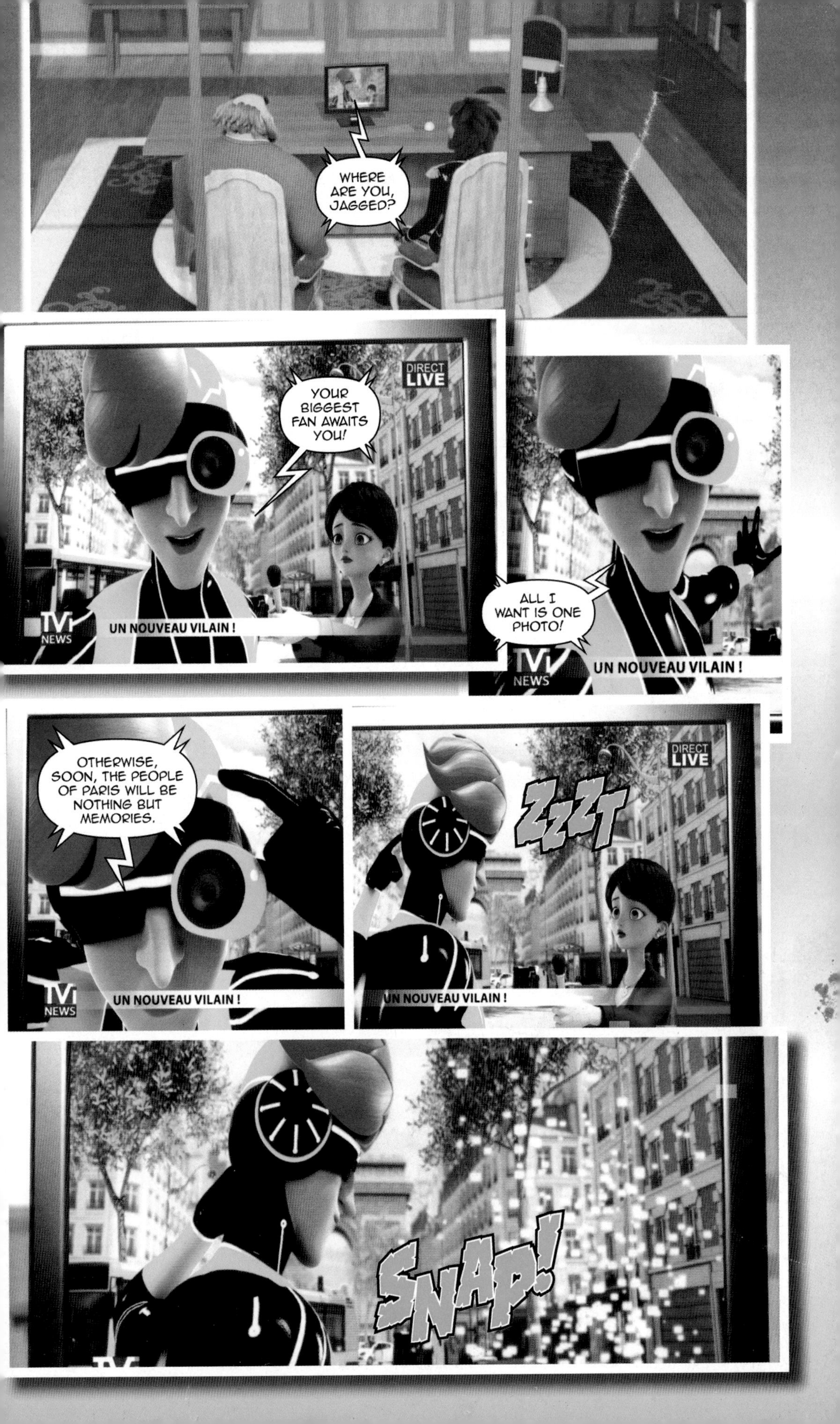
WHERE ARE YOU, JAGGED?
DIRECT LIVE
YOUR BIGGEST FAN AWAITS YOU!
TVi NEWS
UN NOUVEAU VILAIN !
ALL I WANT IS ONE PHOTO!
TVi NEWS
UN NOUVEAU VILAIN !
OTHERWISE, SOON, THE PEOPLE OF PARIS WILL BE NOTHING BUT MEMORIES.
TVi NEWS
UN NOUVEAU VILAIN !
DIRECT LIVE
ZZZT
UN NOUVEAU VILAIN !
SNAP!

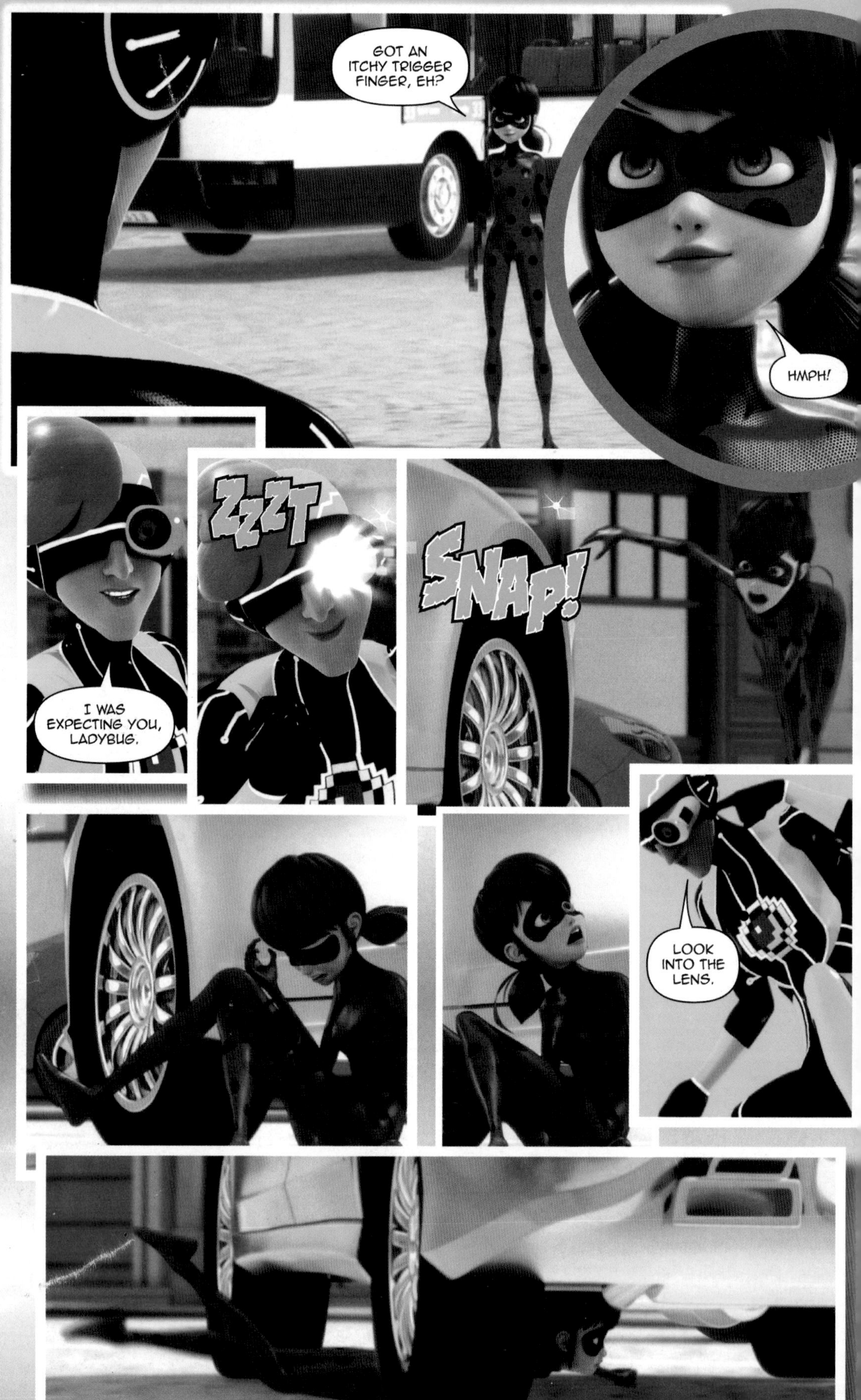

GOT AN ITCHY TRIGGER FINGER, EH?
HMPH!
I WAS EXPECTING YOU, LADYBUG.
ZZZT
SNAP!
LOOK INTO THE LENS.

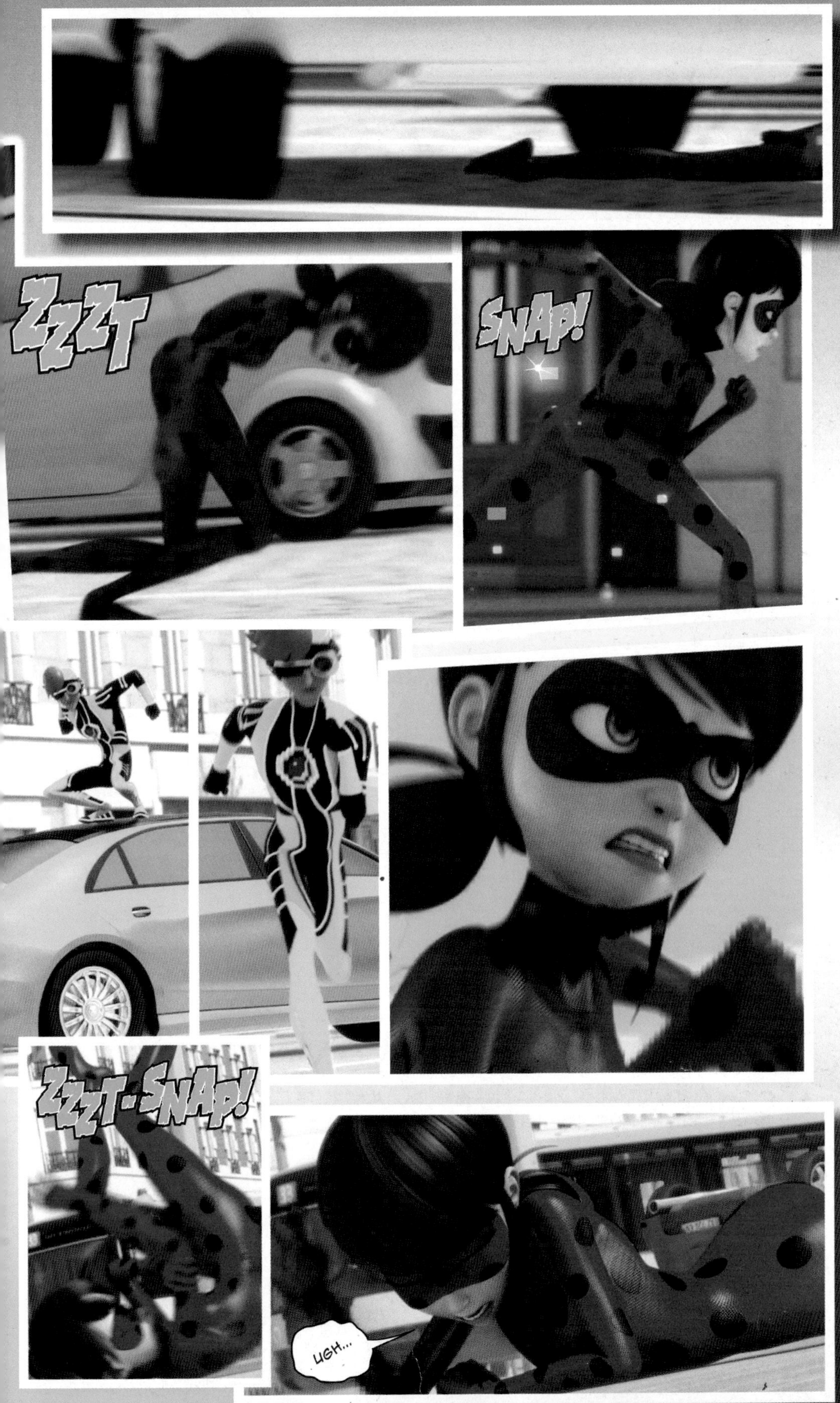
ZZZT
SNAP!
ZZZT-SNAP!
UGH...

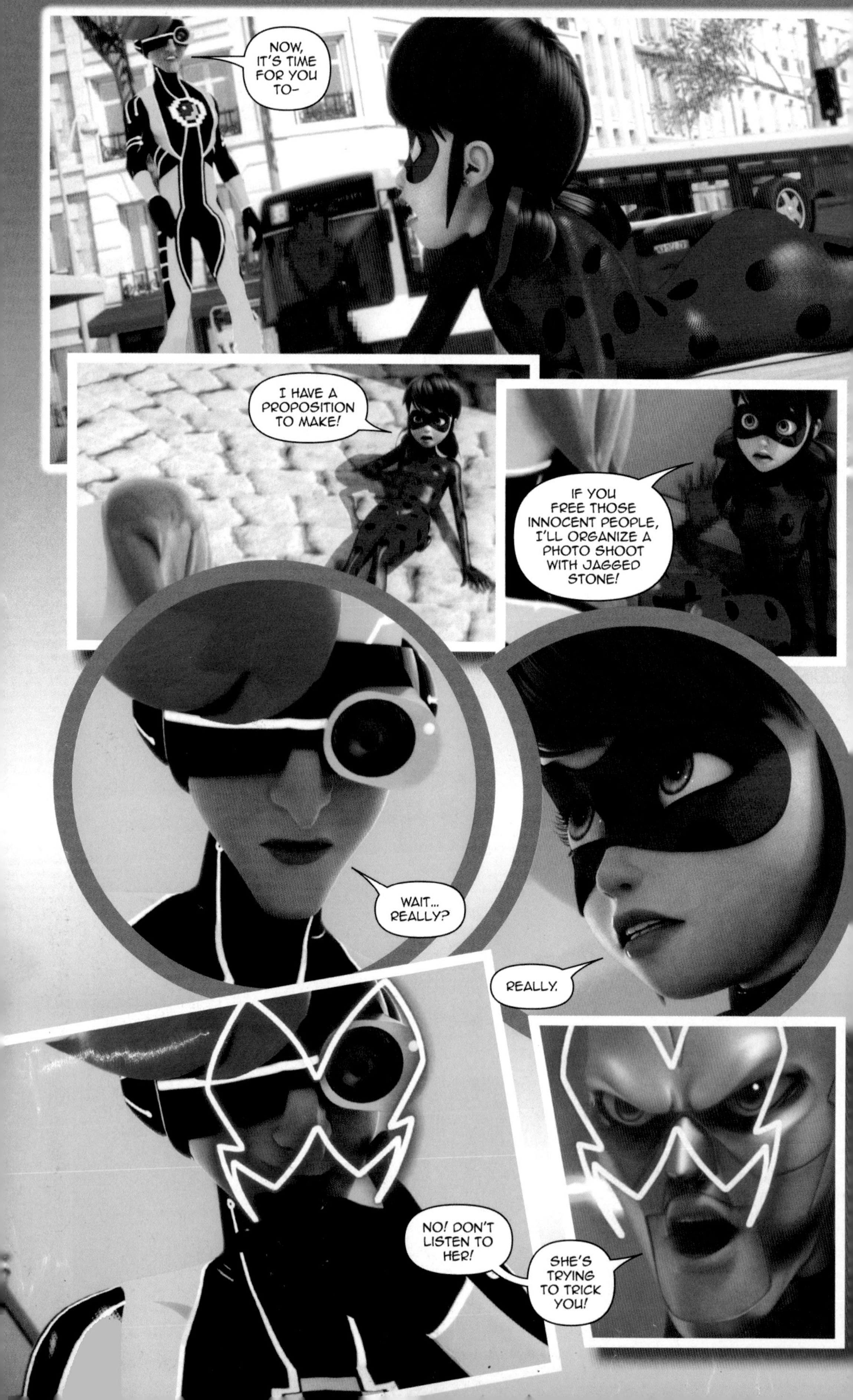
NOW, IT'S TIME FOR YOU TO-
I HAVE A PROPOSITION TO MAKE!
IF YOU FREE THOSE INNOCENT PEOPLE, I'LL ORGANIZE A PHOTO SHOOT WITH JAGGED STONE!
WAIT... REALLY?
REALLY.
NO! DON'T LISTEN TO HER!
SHE'S TRYING TO TRICK YOU!

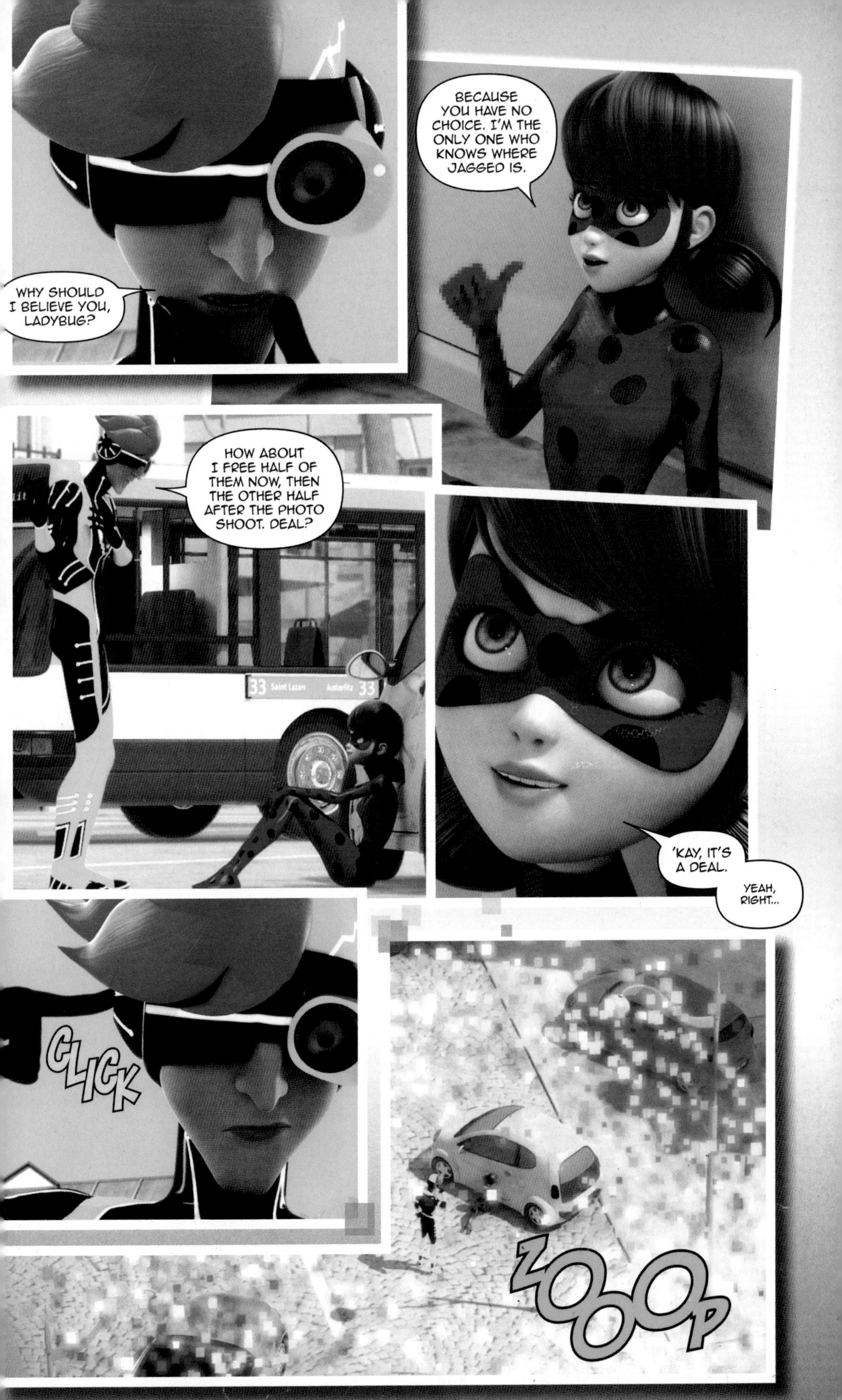

WHY SHOULD I BELIEVE YOU, LADYBUG?
BECAUSE YOU HAVE NO CHOICE. I'M THE ONLY ONE WHO KNOWS WHERE JAGGED IS.
HOW ABOUT I FREE HALF OF THEM NOW, THEN THE OTHER HALF AFTER THE PHOTO SHOOT. DEAL?
33 Saint Lazare Austerlitz 33
'KAY, IT'S A DEAL.
YEAH, RIGHT...
CLICK
ZOOOP

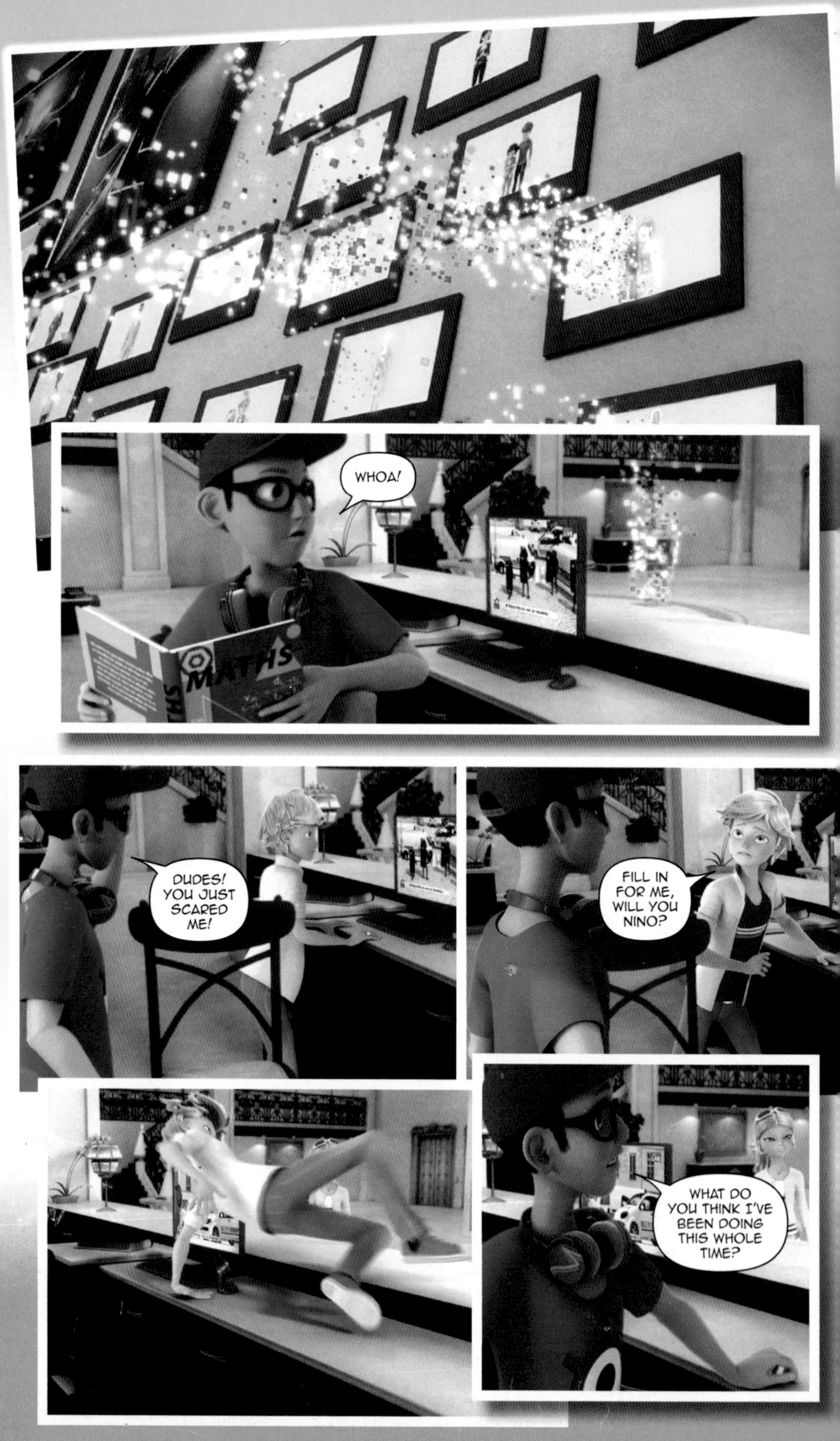
WHOA!
DUDES! YOU JUST SCARED ME!
FILL IN FOR ME, WILL YOU NINO?
WHAT DO YOU THINK I'VE BEEN DOING THIS WHOLE TIME?

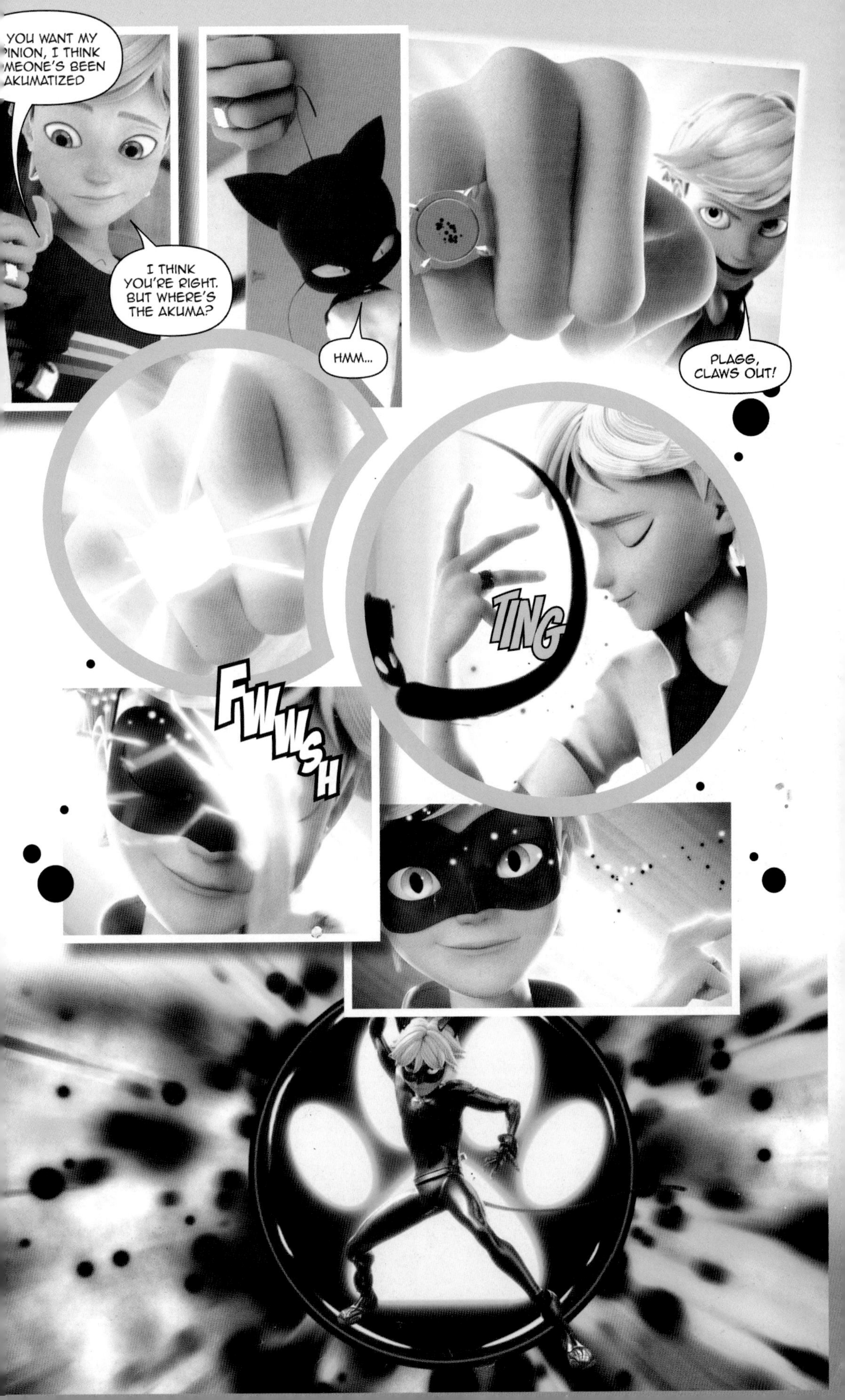
YOU WANT MY PINION, I THINK MEONE'S BEEN AKUMATIZED
I THINK YOU'RE RIGHT. BUT WHERE'S THE AKUMA?
HMM...
PLAGG, CLAWS OUT!
TING
FWWSH

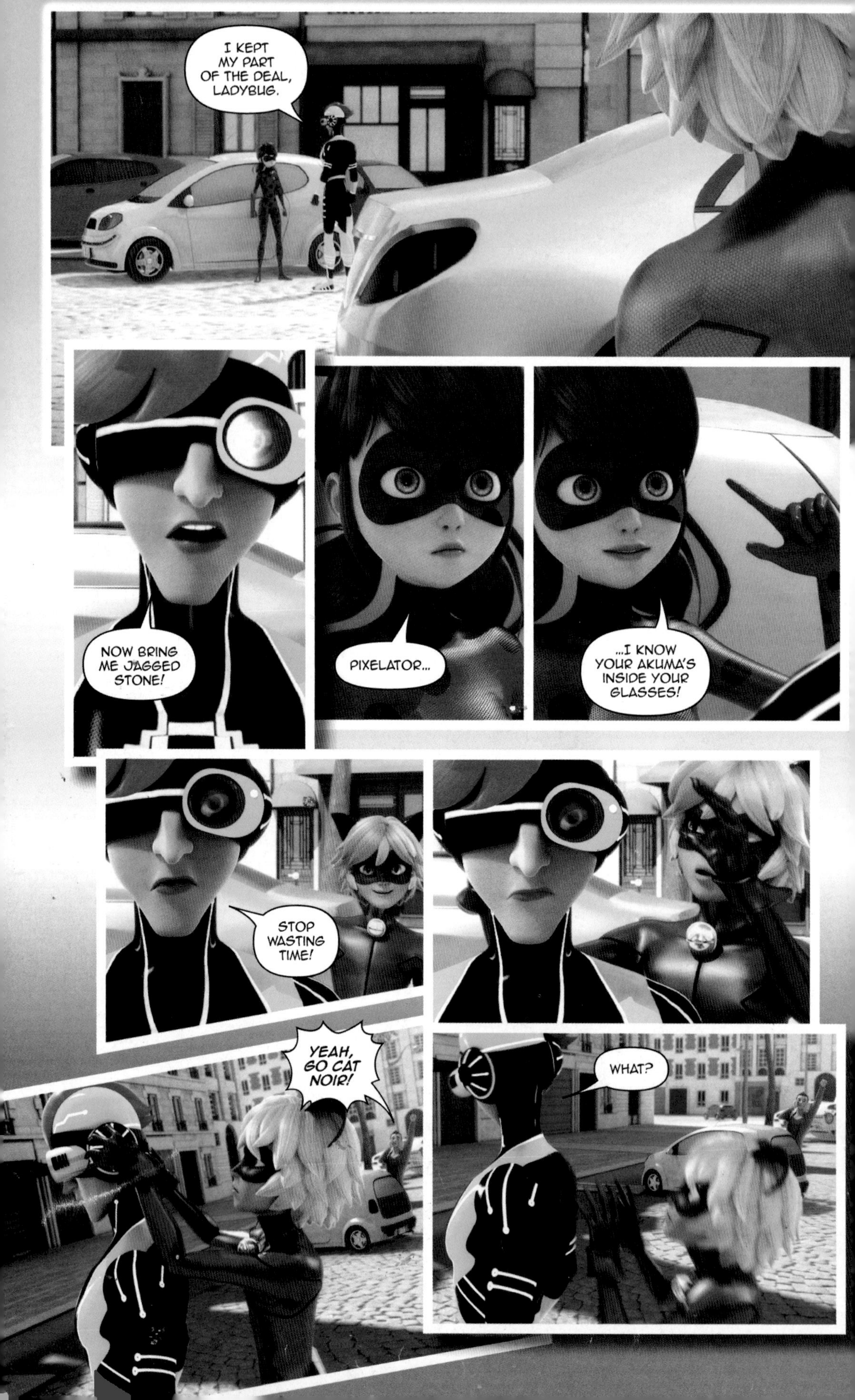
I KEPT MY PART OF THE DEAL, LADYBUG.
NOW BRING ME JAGGED STONE!
PIXELATOR...
...I KNOW YOUR AKUMA'S INSIDE YOUR GLASSES!
STOP WASTING TIME!
YEAH, GO CAT NOIR!
WHAT?

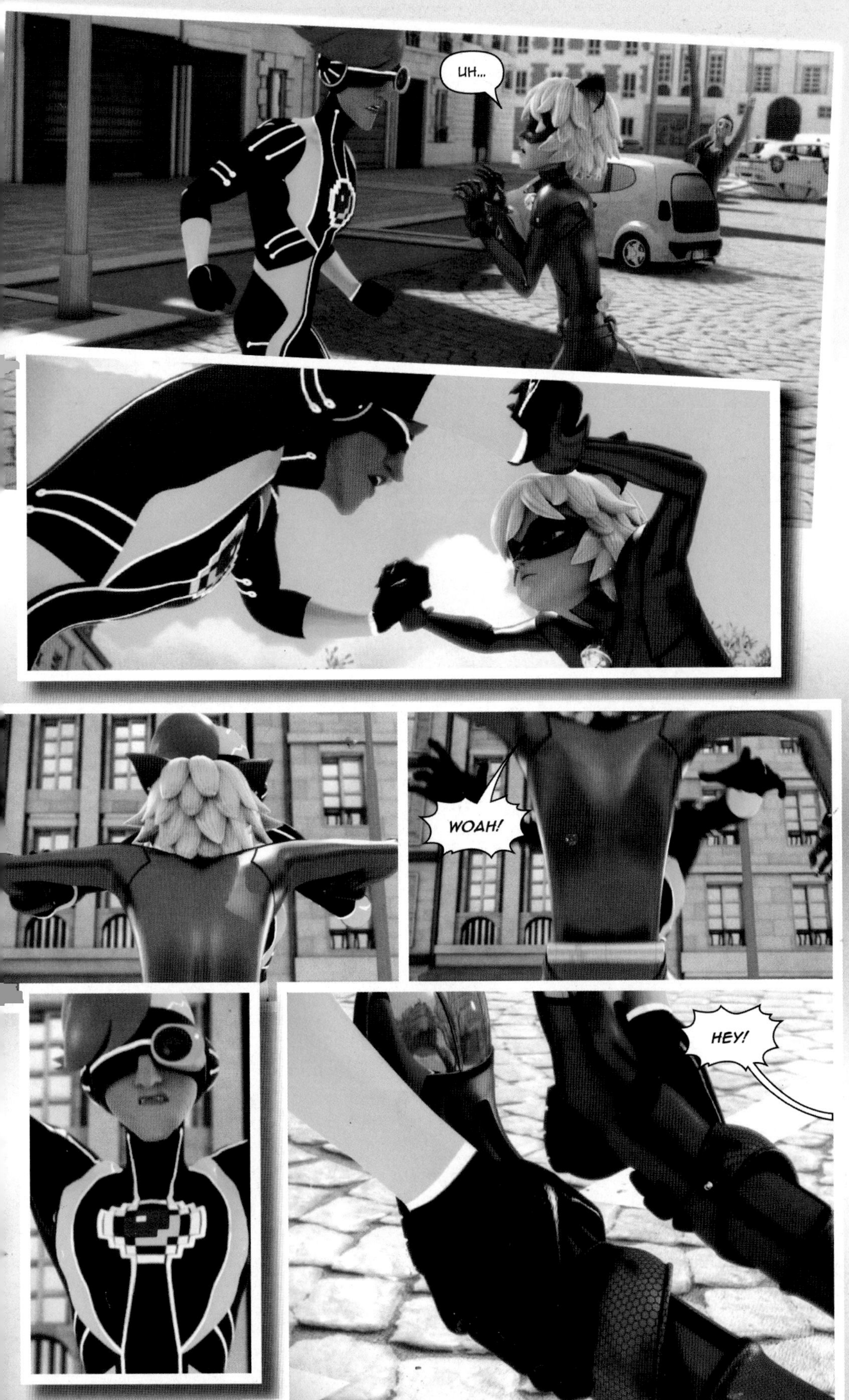
UH...
WOAH!
HEY!

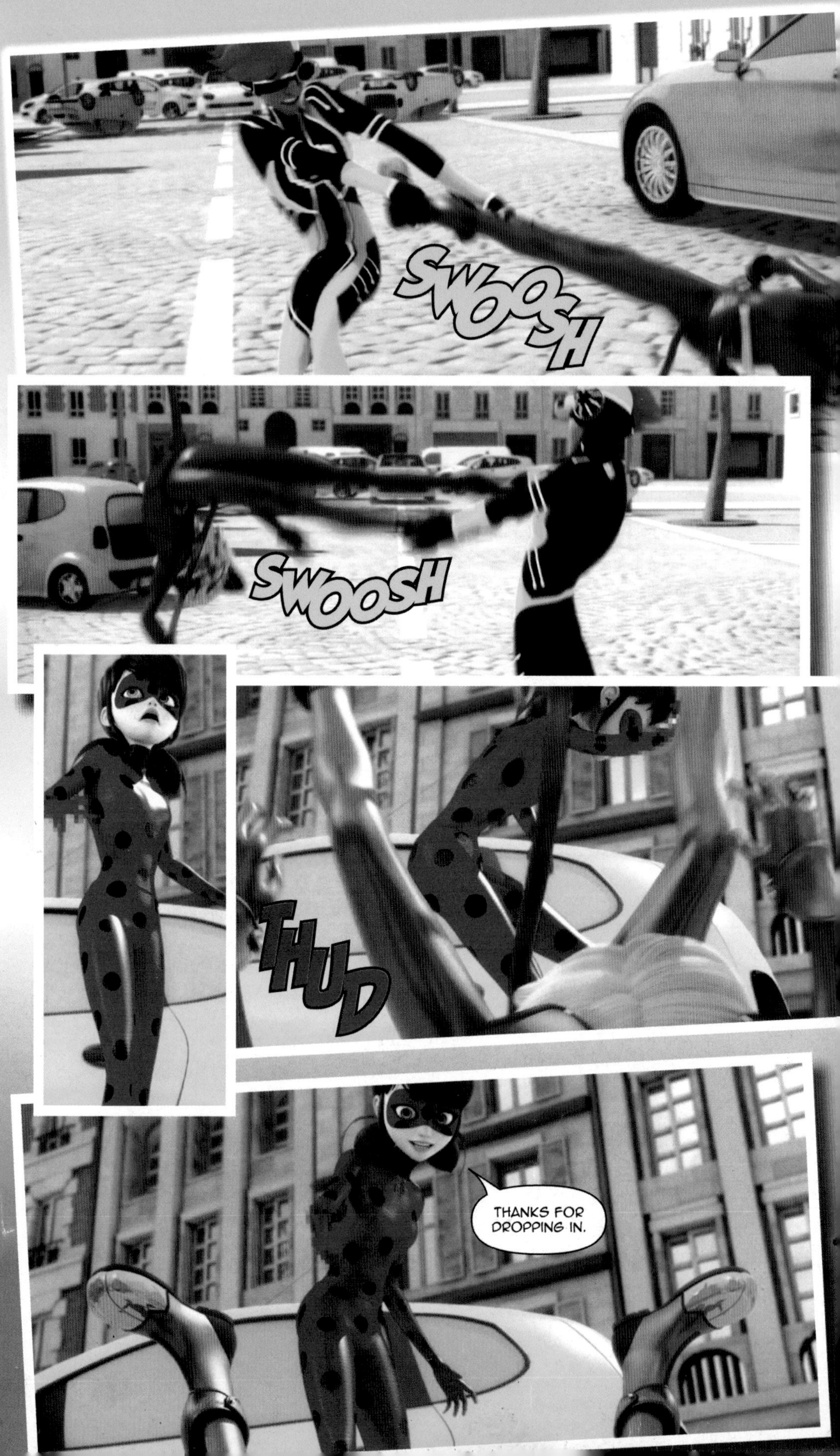
SWOOSH
SWOOSH
THUD
THANKS FOR DROPPING IN.

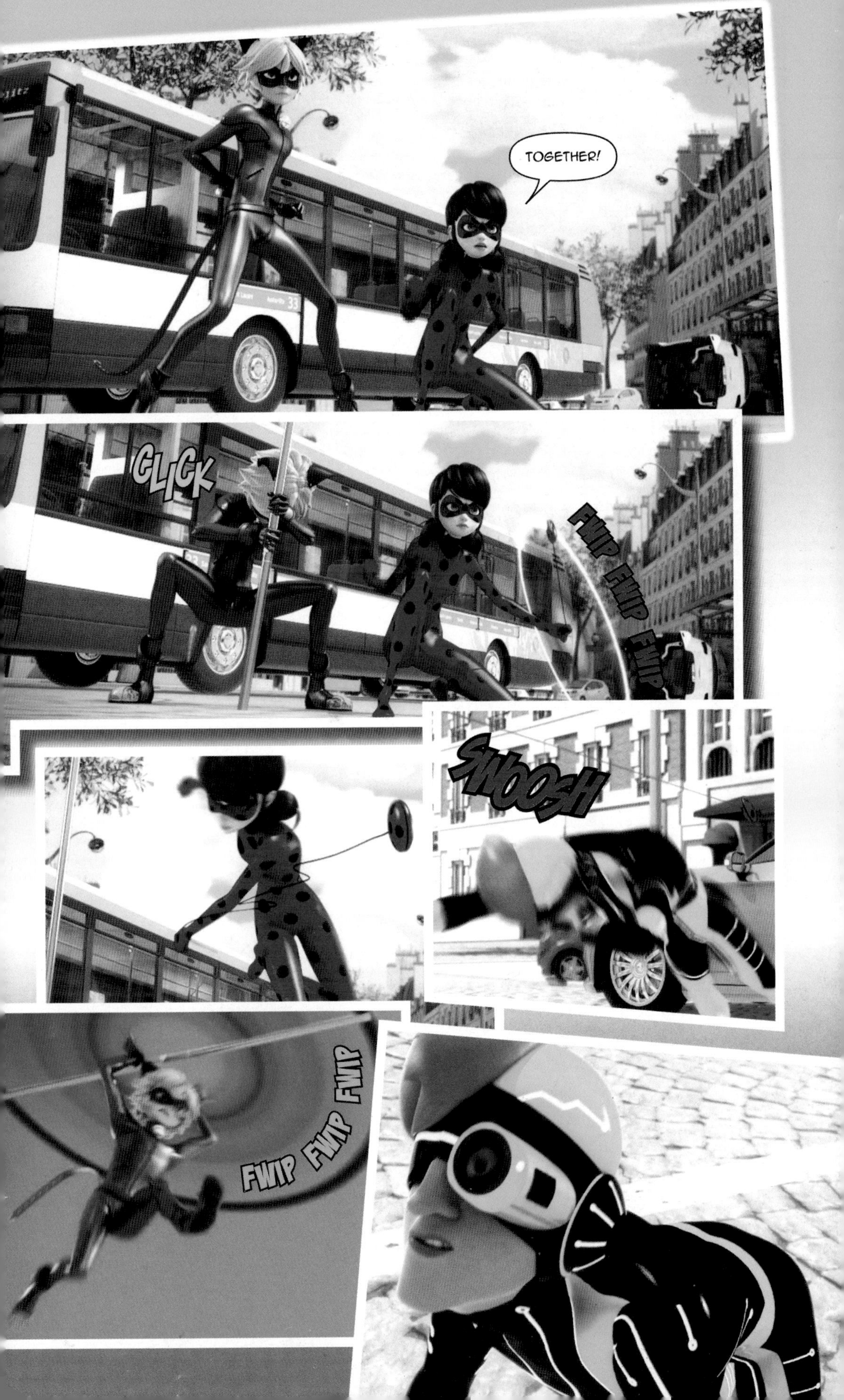
TOGETHER!
CLICK
FWIP FWIP FWIP
SWOOSH
FWIP FWIP FWIP

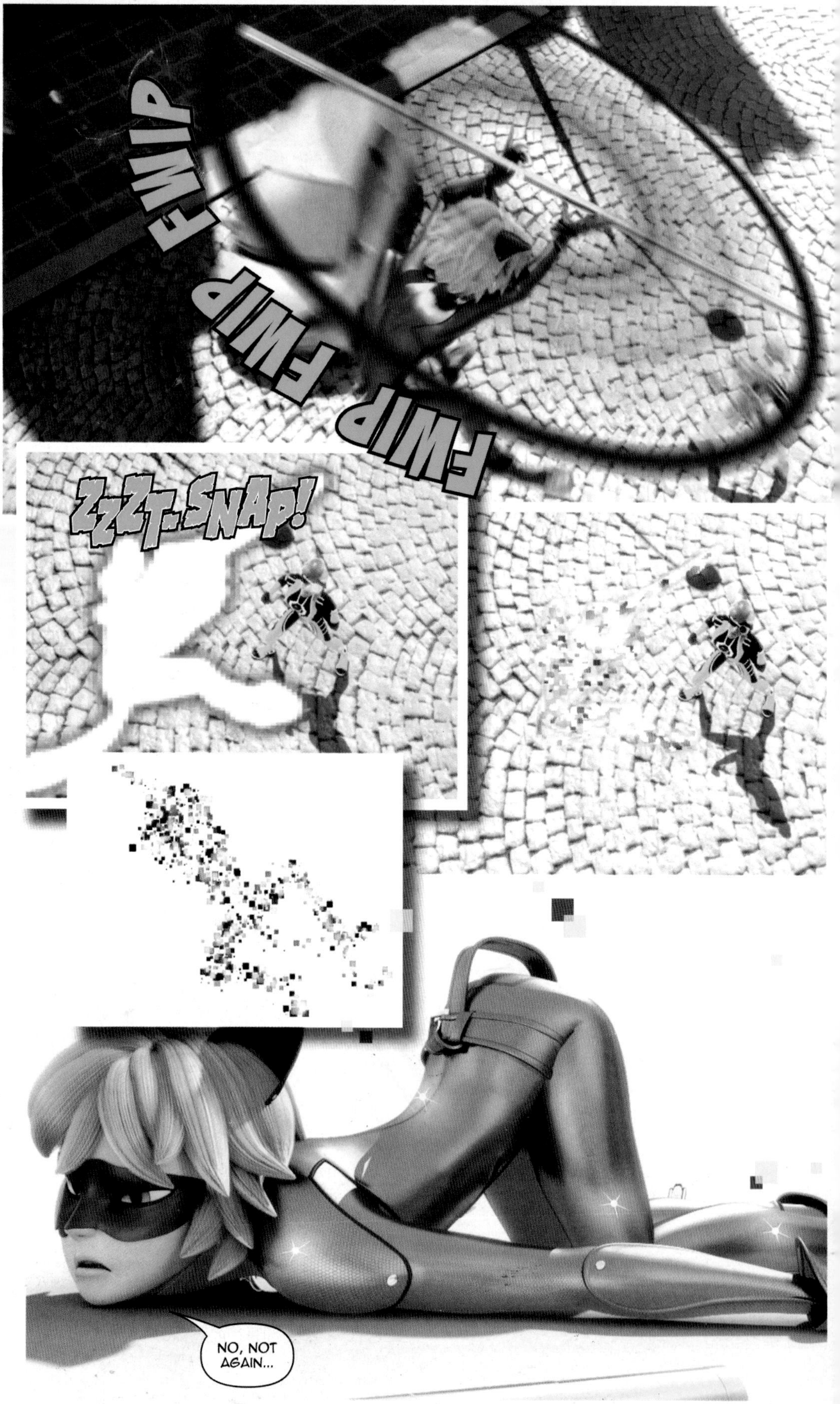
FWIP FWIP FWIP
ZZZT-SNAP!
NO, NOT AGAIN...

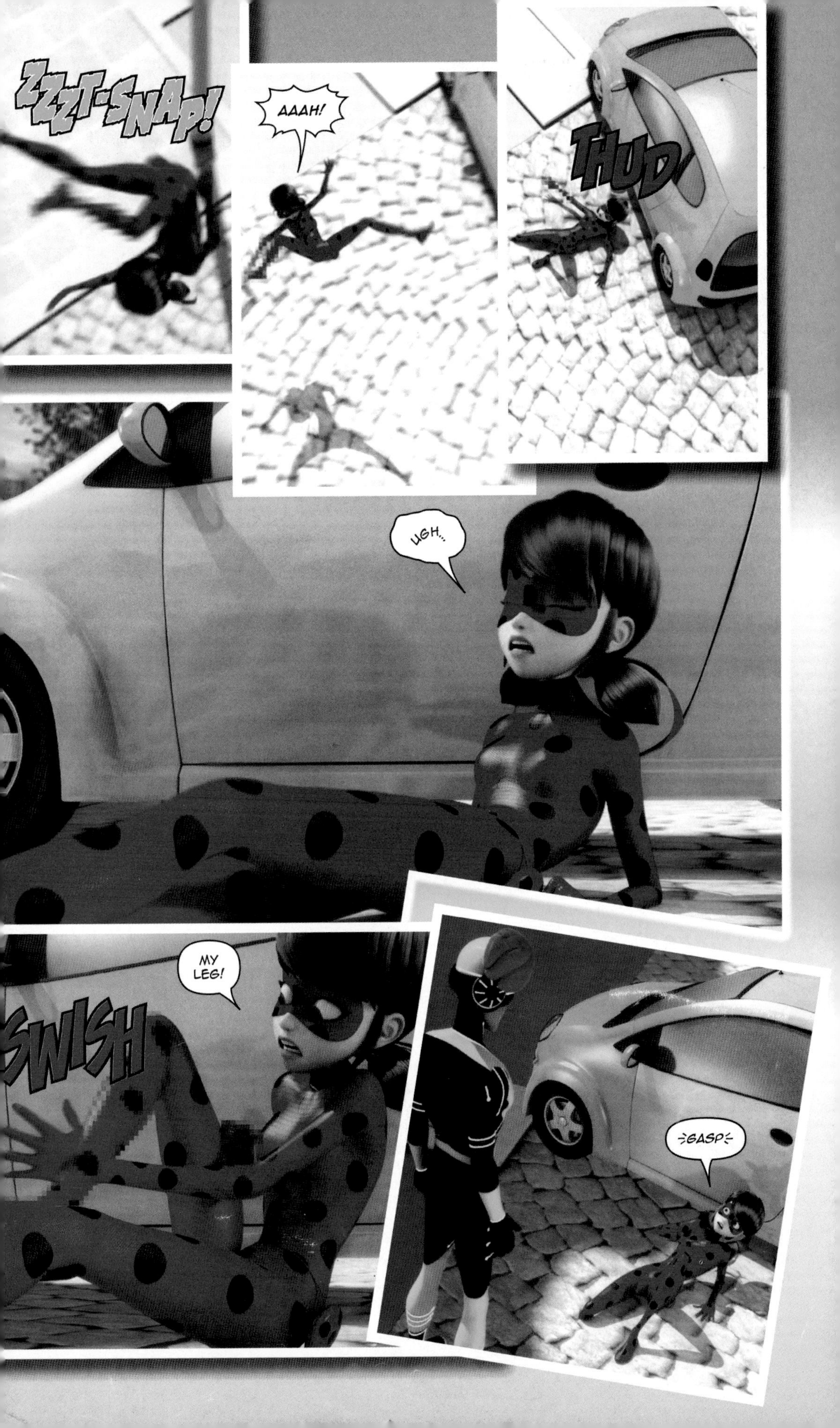
ZZZT-SNAP!
AAAH!
THUD
UGH...
MY LEG!
SWISH
GASP

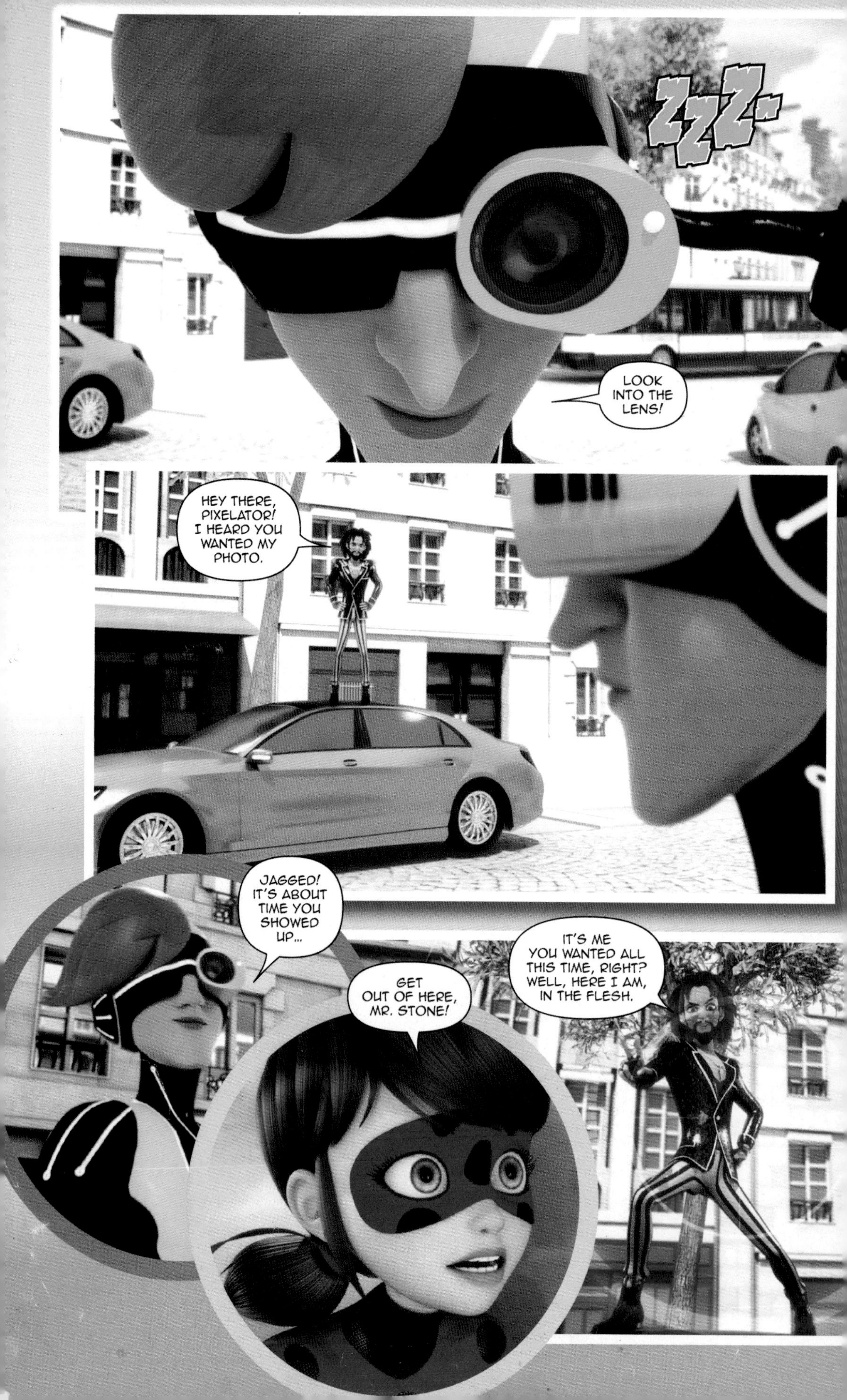
ZZZ-
LOOK INTO THE LENS!
HEY THERE, PIXELATOR! I HEARD YOU WANTED MY PHOTO.
JAGGED! IT'S ABOUT TIME YOU SHOWED UP...
GET OUT OF HERE, MR. STONE!
IT'S ME YOU WANTED ALL THIS TIME, RIGHT? WELL, HERE I AM, IN THE FLESH.

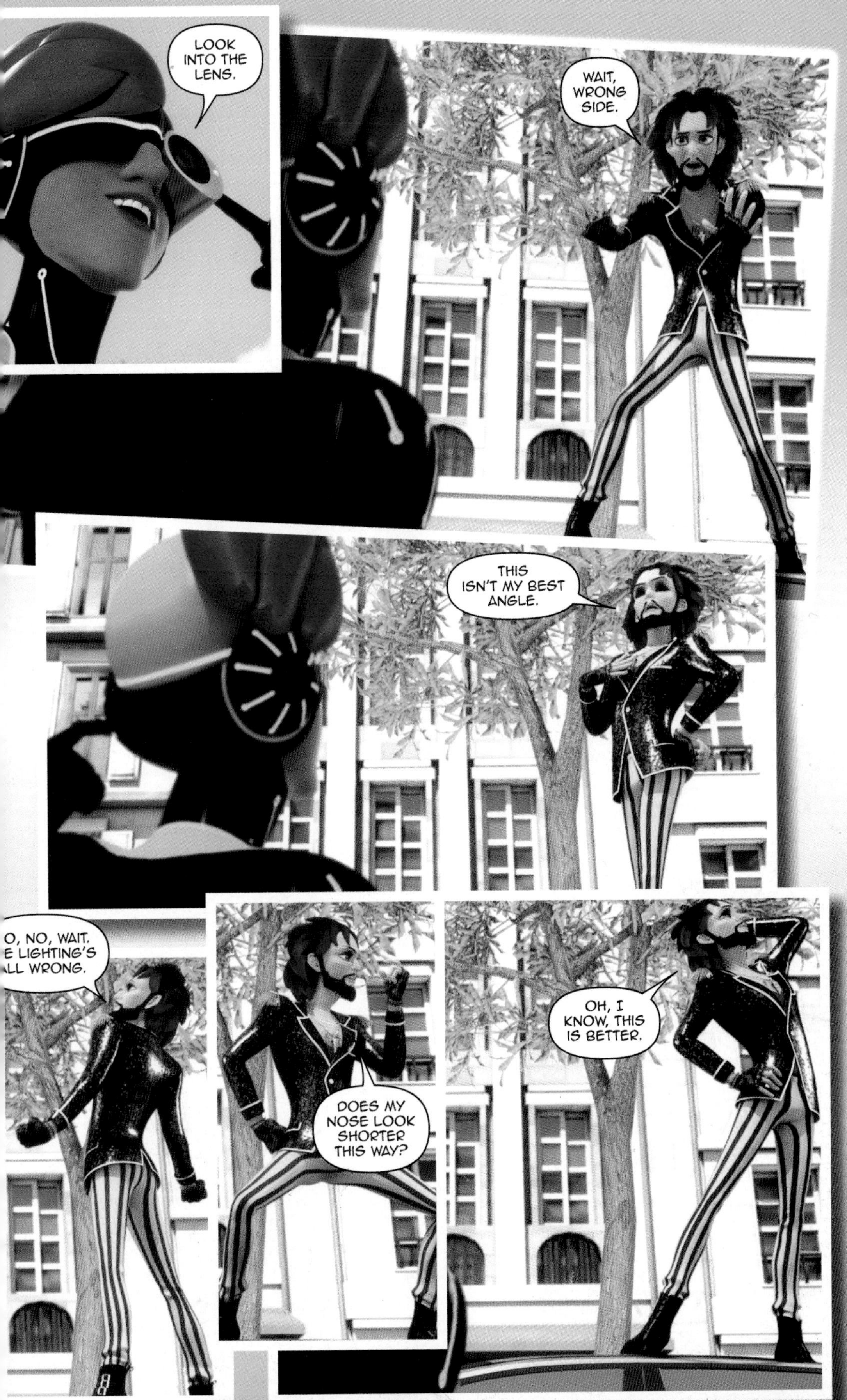
LOOK INTO THE LENS.
WAIT, WRONG SIDE.
THIS ISN'T MY BEST ANGLE.
O, NO, WAIT. E LIGHTING'S LL WRONG.
DOES MY NOSE LOOK SHORTER THIS WAY?
OH, I KNOW, THIS IS BETTER.

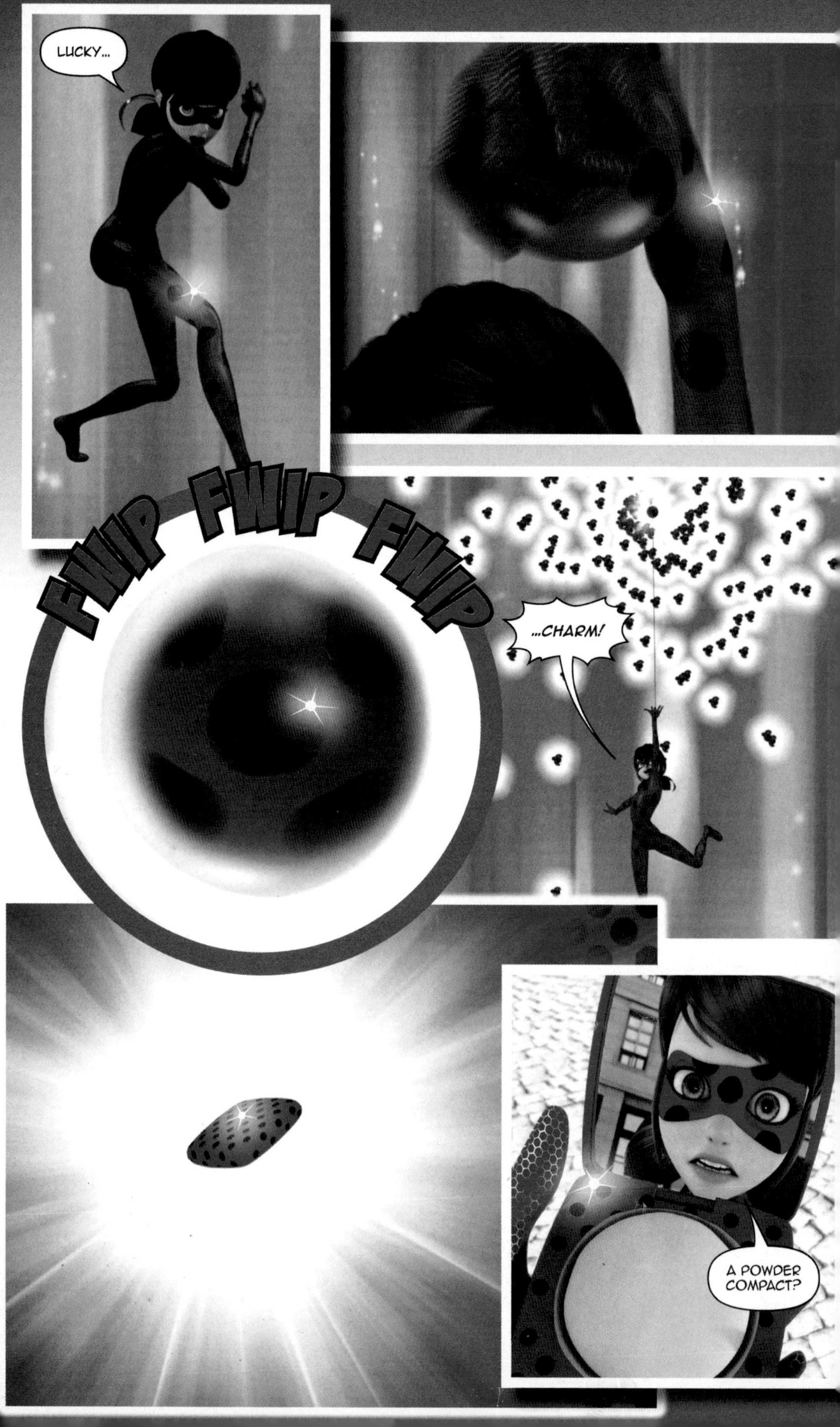
LUCKY...
FWIP FWIP FWIP
...CHARM!
A POWDER COMPACT?

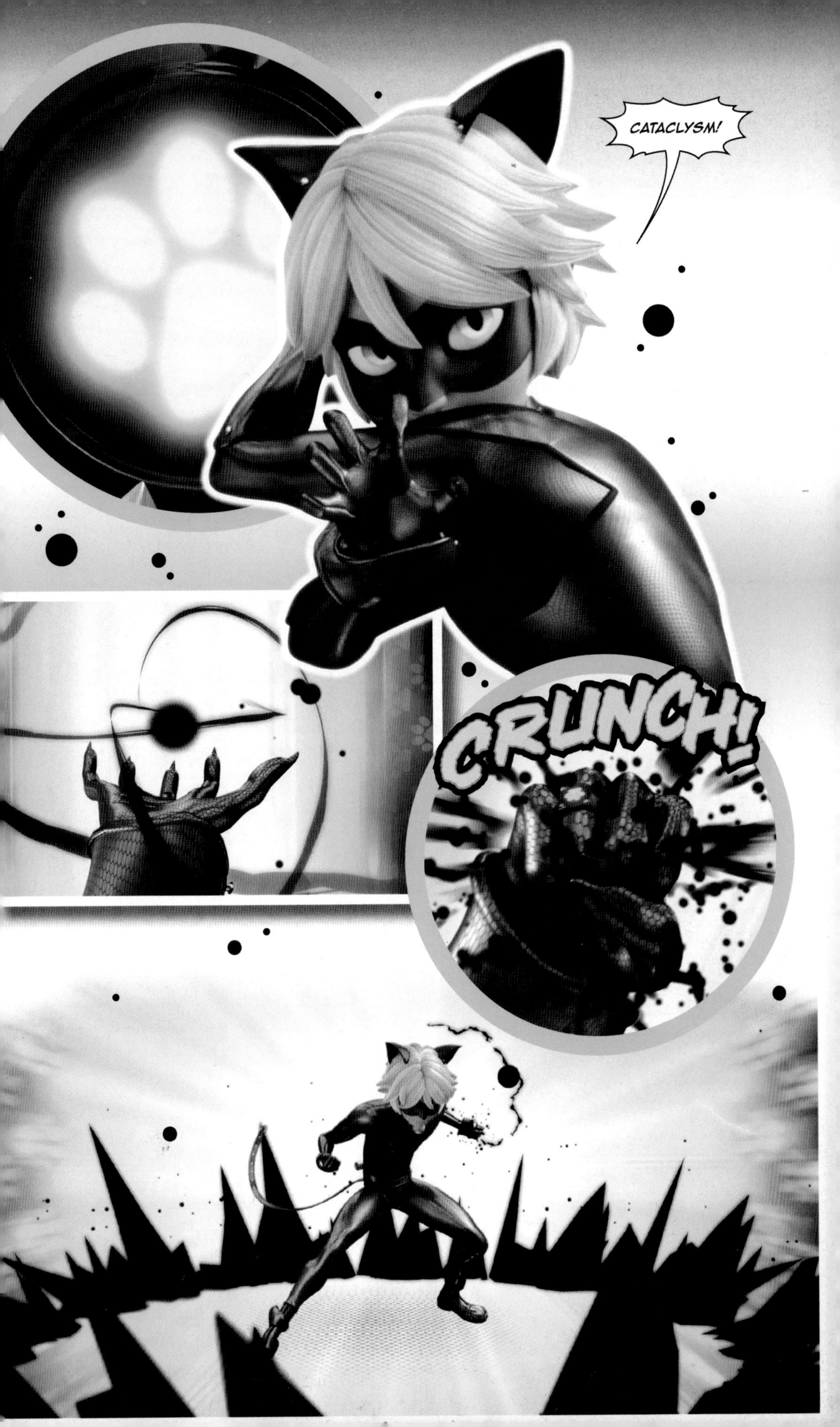
CATACLYSM!
CRUNCH!

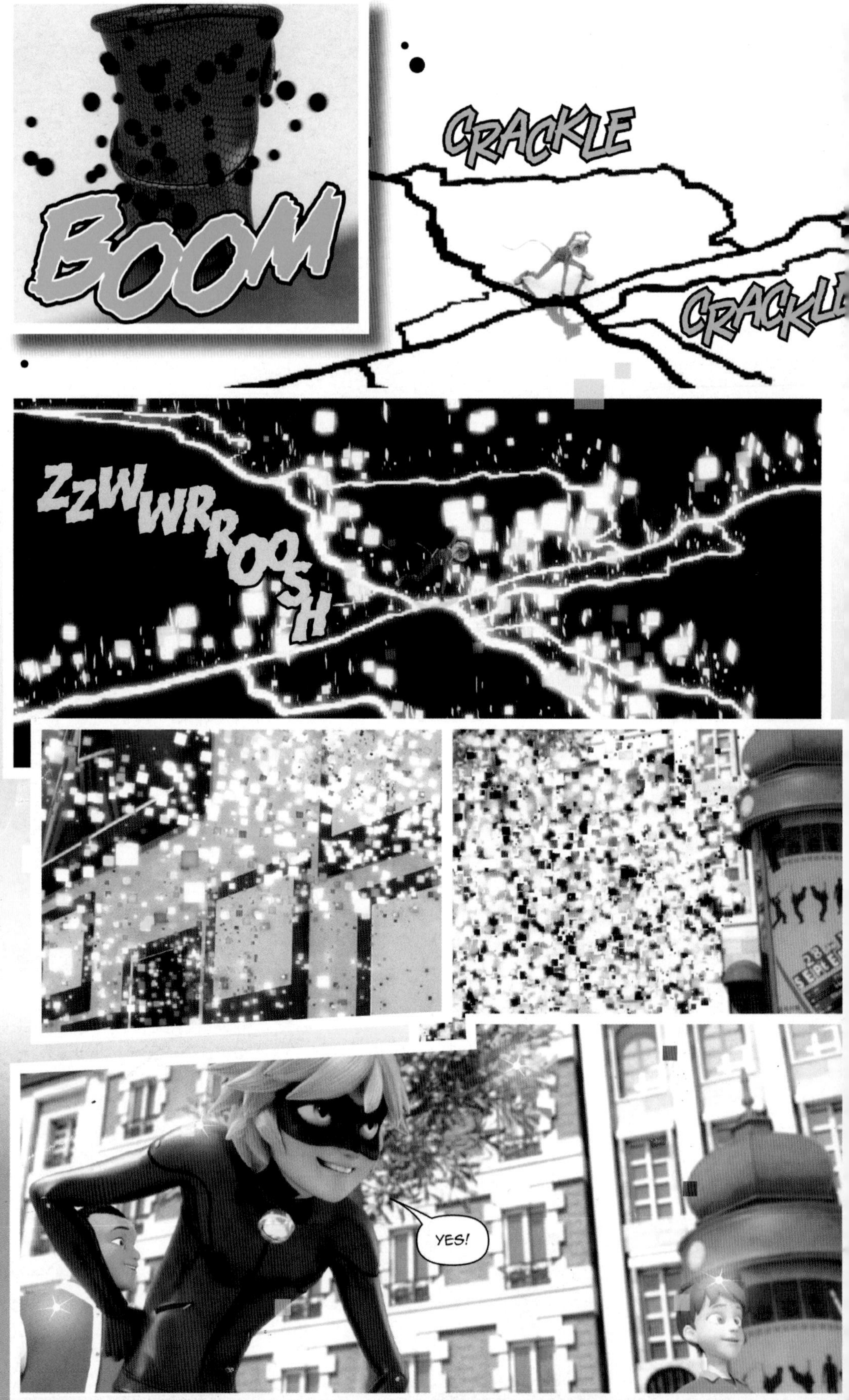

BOOM
CRACKLE
CRACKLE
ZZWWRROOSH
YES!

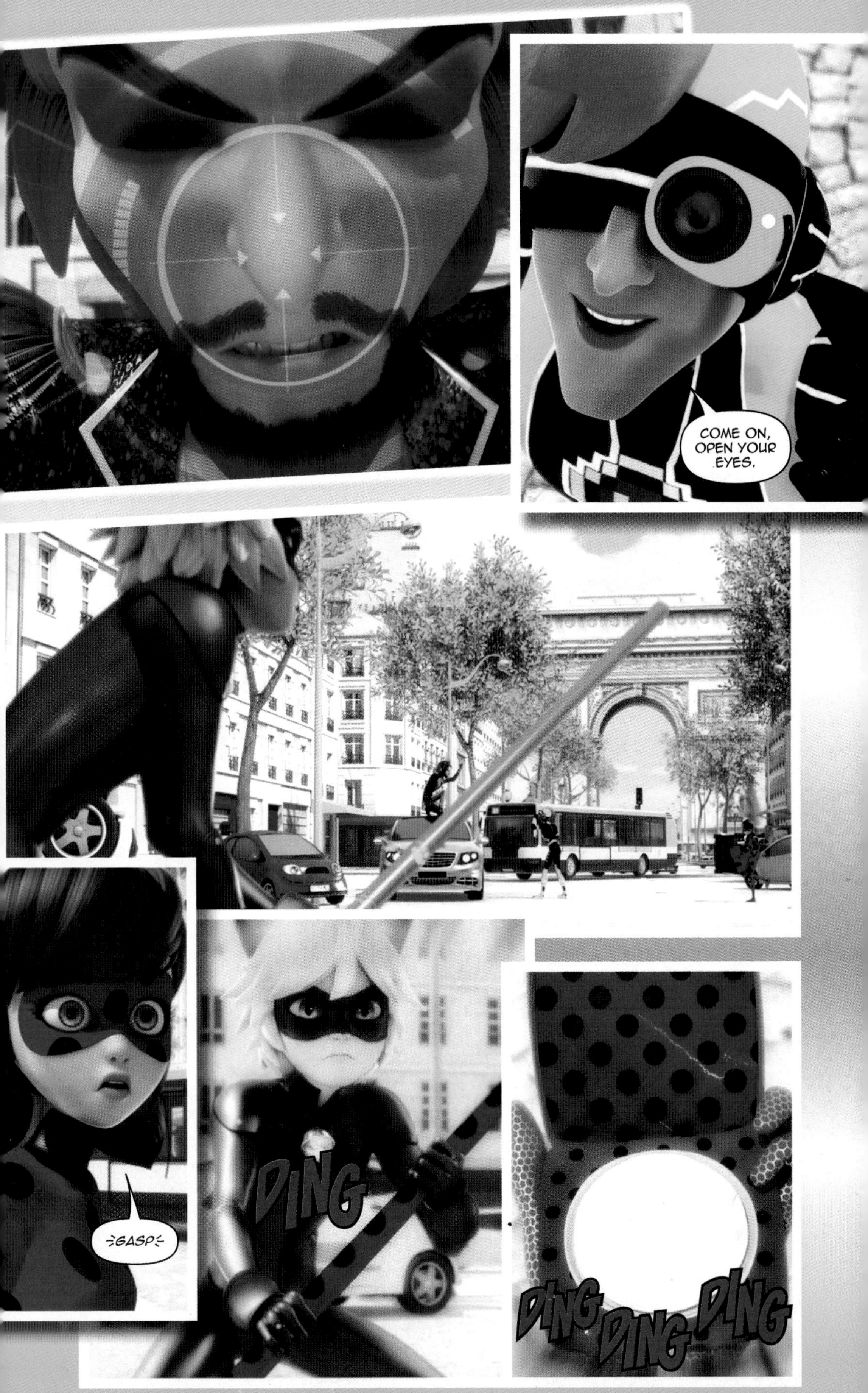
COME ON, OPEN YOUR EYES.
GASP
DING
DING DING DING

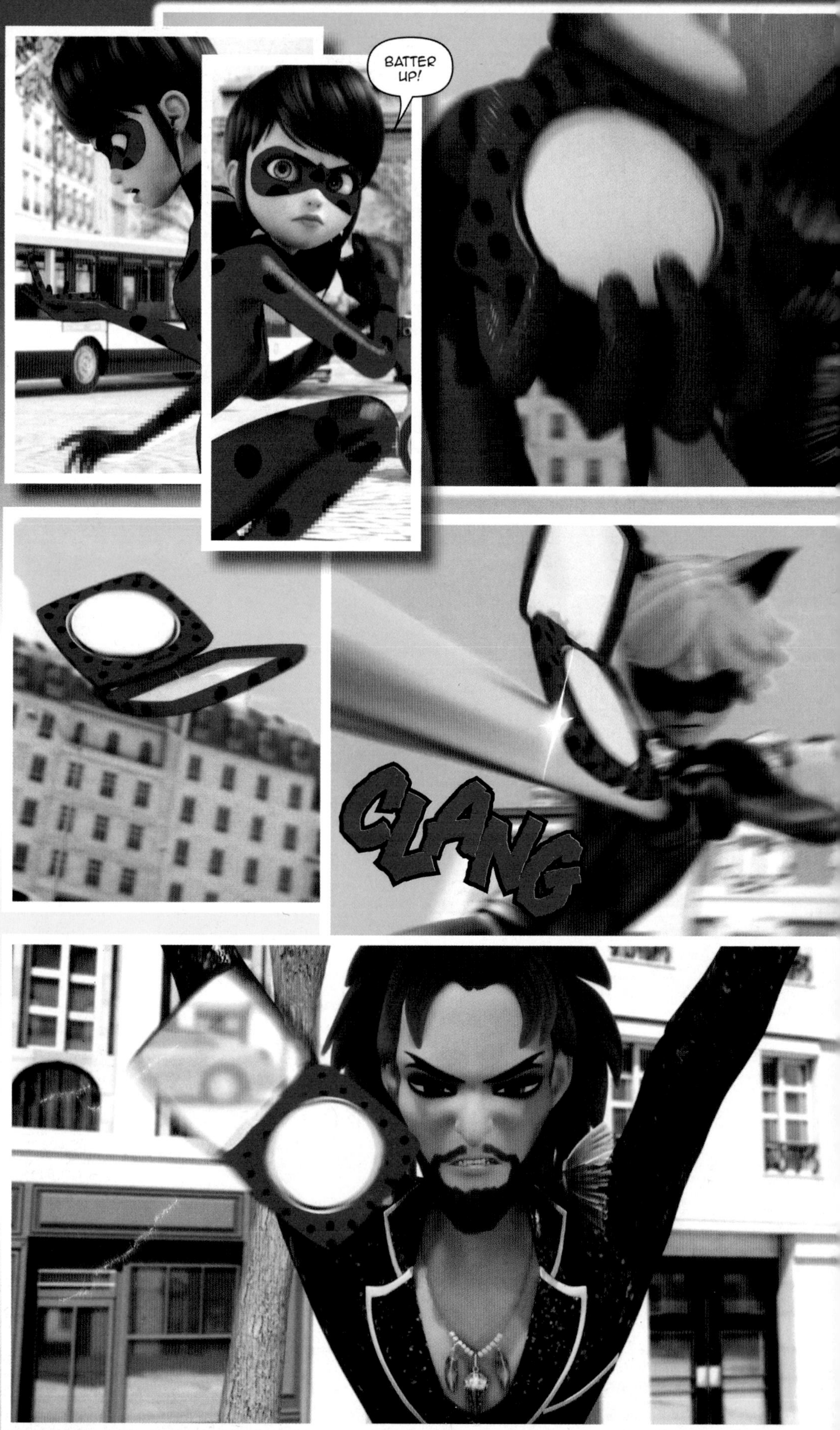
BATTER UP!
CLANG

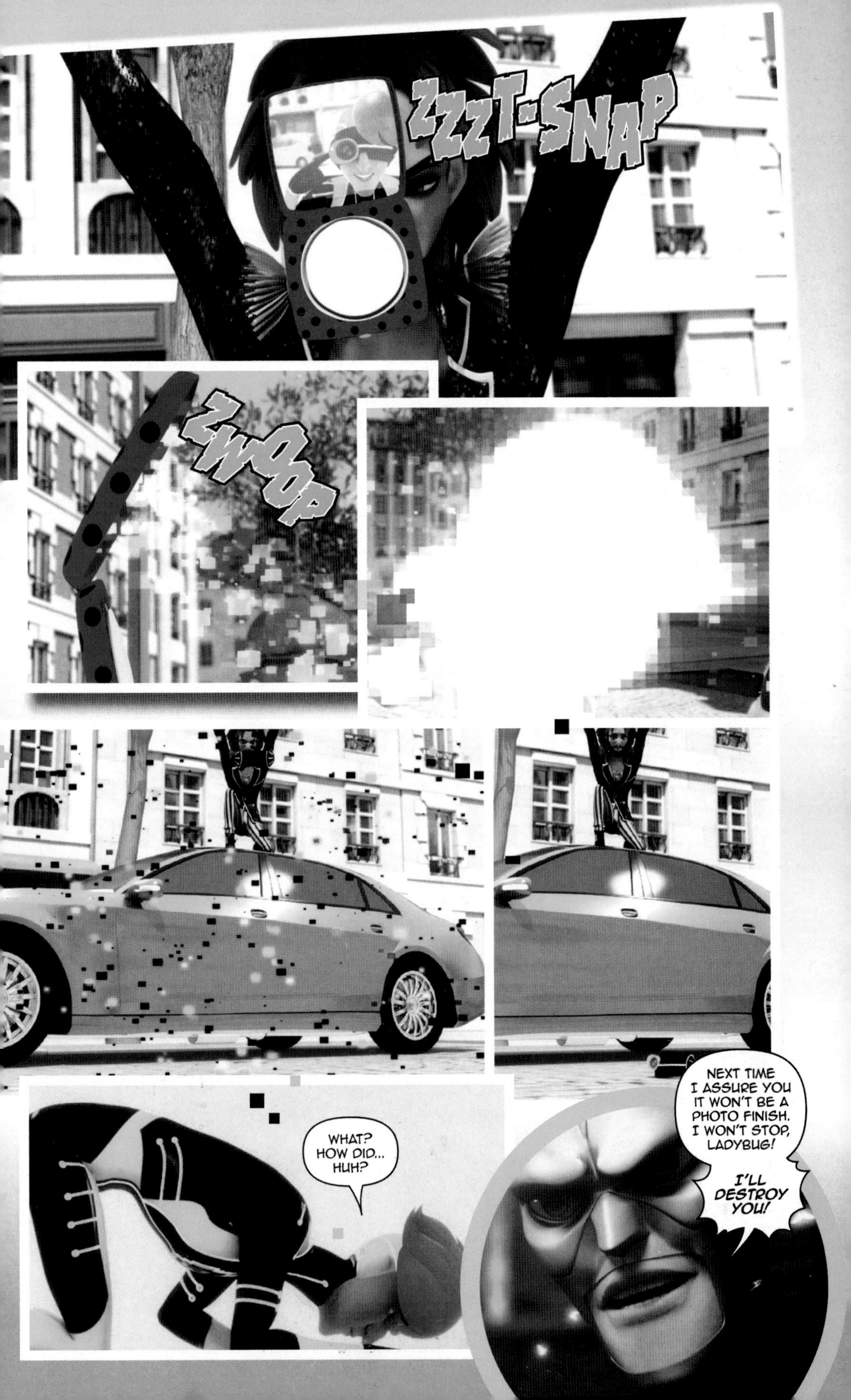
ZZZT-SNAP
ZWOOP
WHAT? HOW DID... HUH?
NEXT TIME I ASSURE YOU IT WON'T BE A PHOTO FINISH. I WON'T STOP, LADYBUG!
I'LL DESTROY YOU!

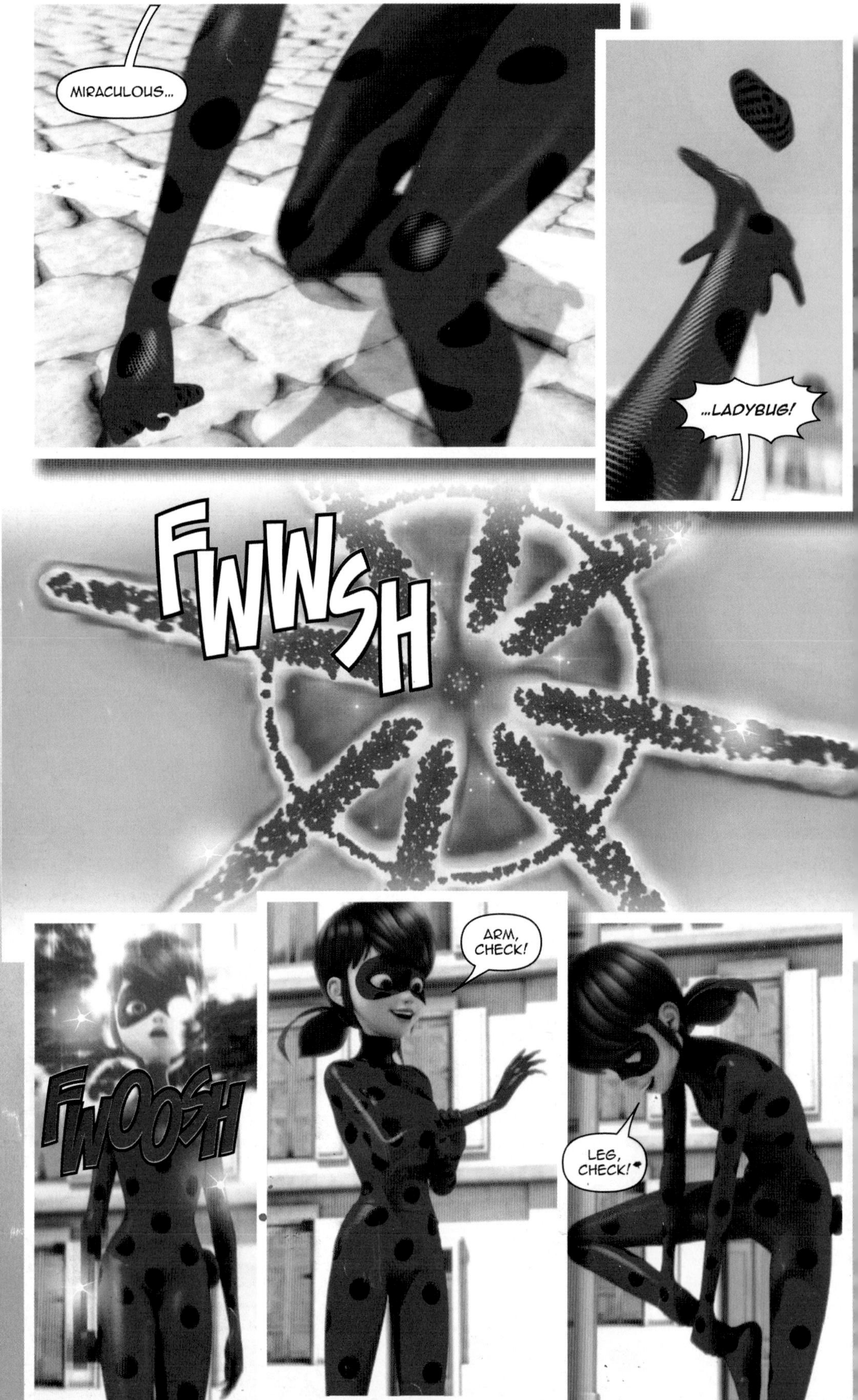
MIRACULOUS...
...LADYBUG!
FWWSH
FWOOSH
ARM, CHECK!
LEG, CHECK!

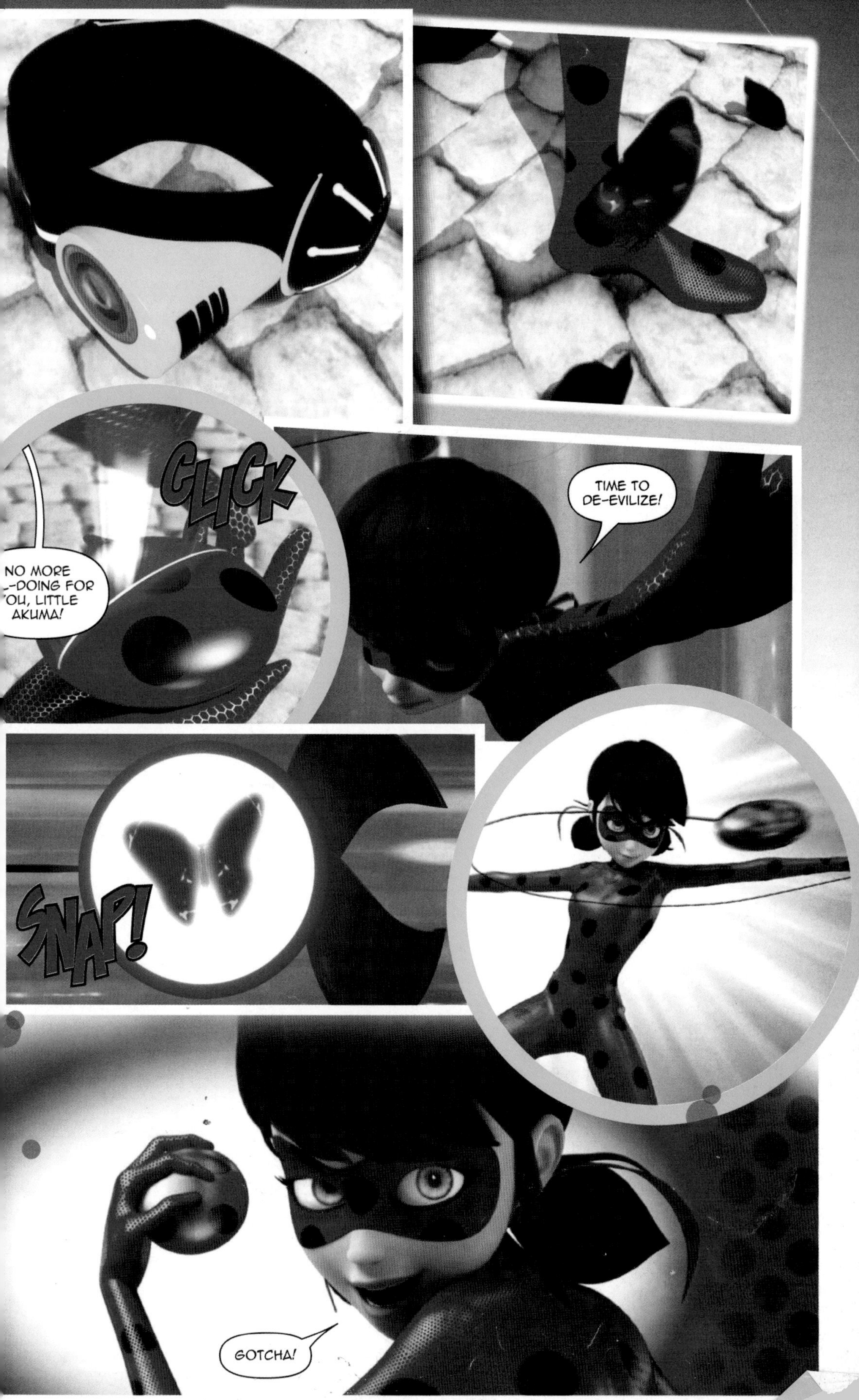
CLICK
NO MORE -DOING FOR OU, LITTLE AKUMA!
TIME TO DE-EVILIZE!
SNAP!
GOTCHA!

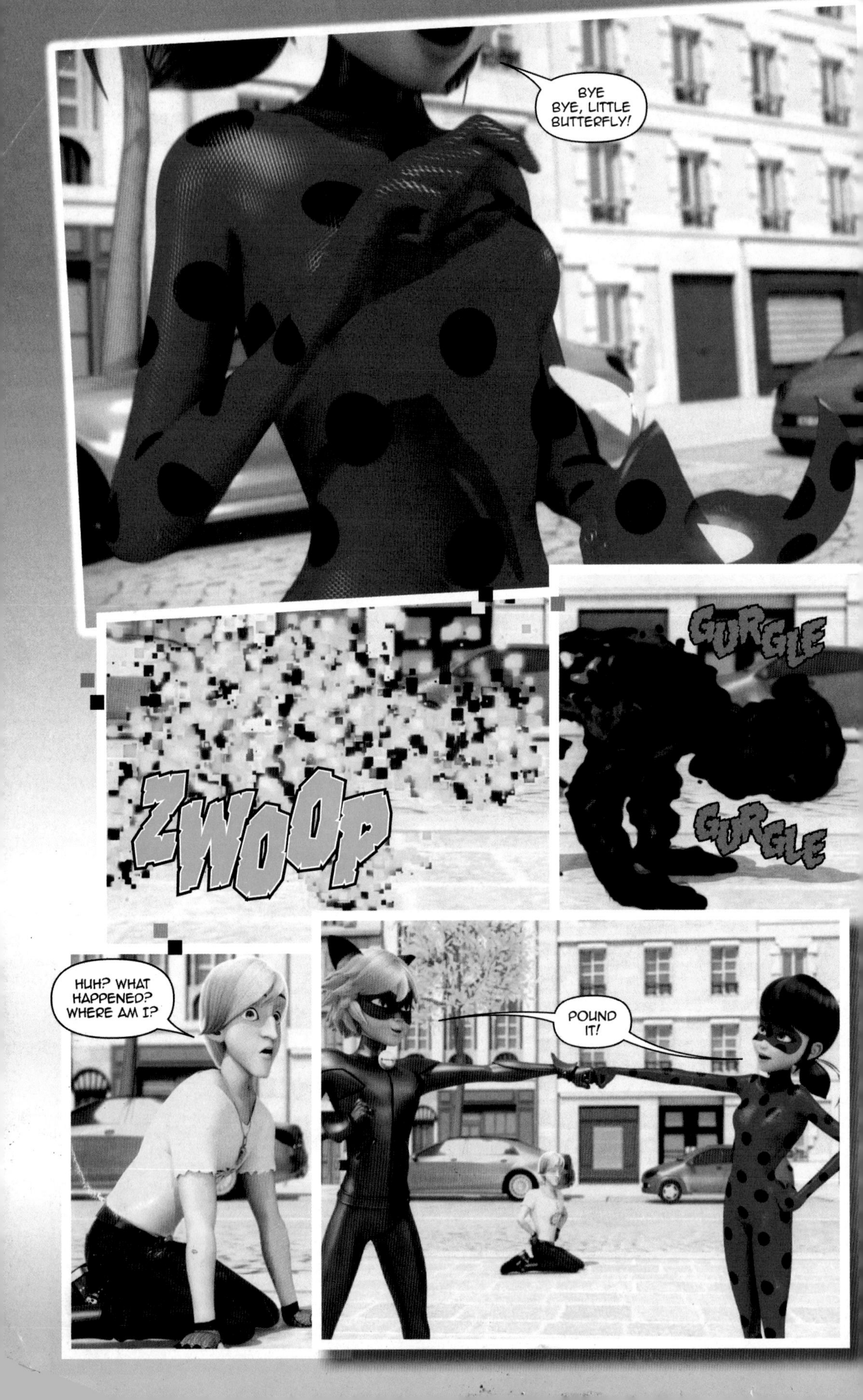
BYE BYE, LITTLE BUTTERFLY!
ZWOOP
GURGLE
GURGLE
HUH? WHAT HAPPENED? WHERE AM I?
POUND IT!

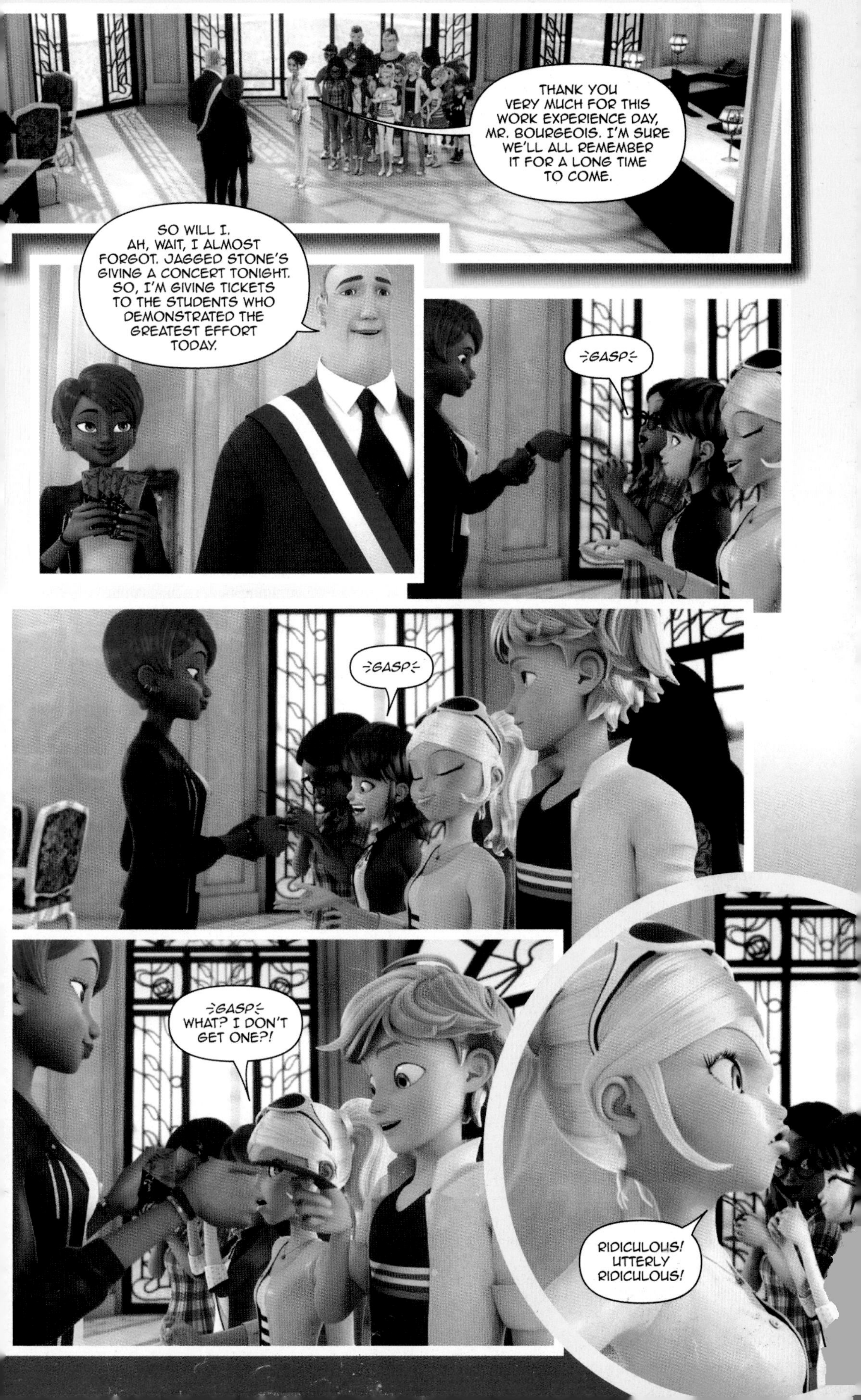
THANK YOU VERY MUCH FOR THIS WORK EXPERIENCE DAY, MR. BOURGEOIS. I'M SURE WE'LL ALL REMEMBER IT FOR A LONG TIME TO COME.
SO WILL I. AH, WAIT, I ALMOST FORGOT. JAGGED STONE'S GIVING A CONCERT TONIGHT. SO, I'M GIVING TICKETS TO THE STUDENTS WHO DEMONSTRATED THE GREATEST EFFORT TODAY.
GASP
GASP
GASP WHAT? I DON'T GET ONE?!
RIDICULOUS! UTTERLY RIDICULOUS!

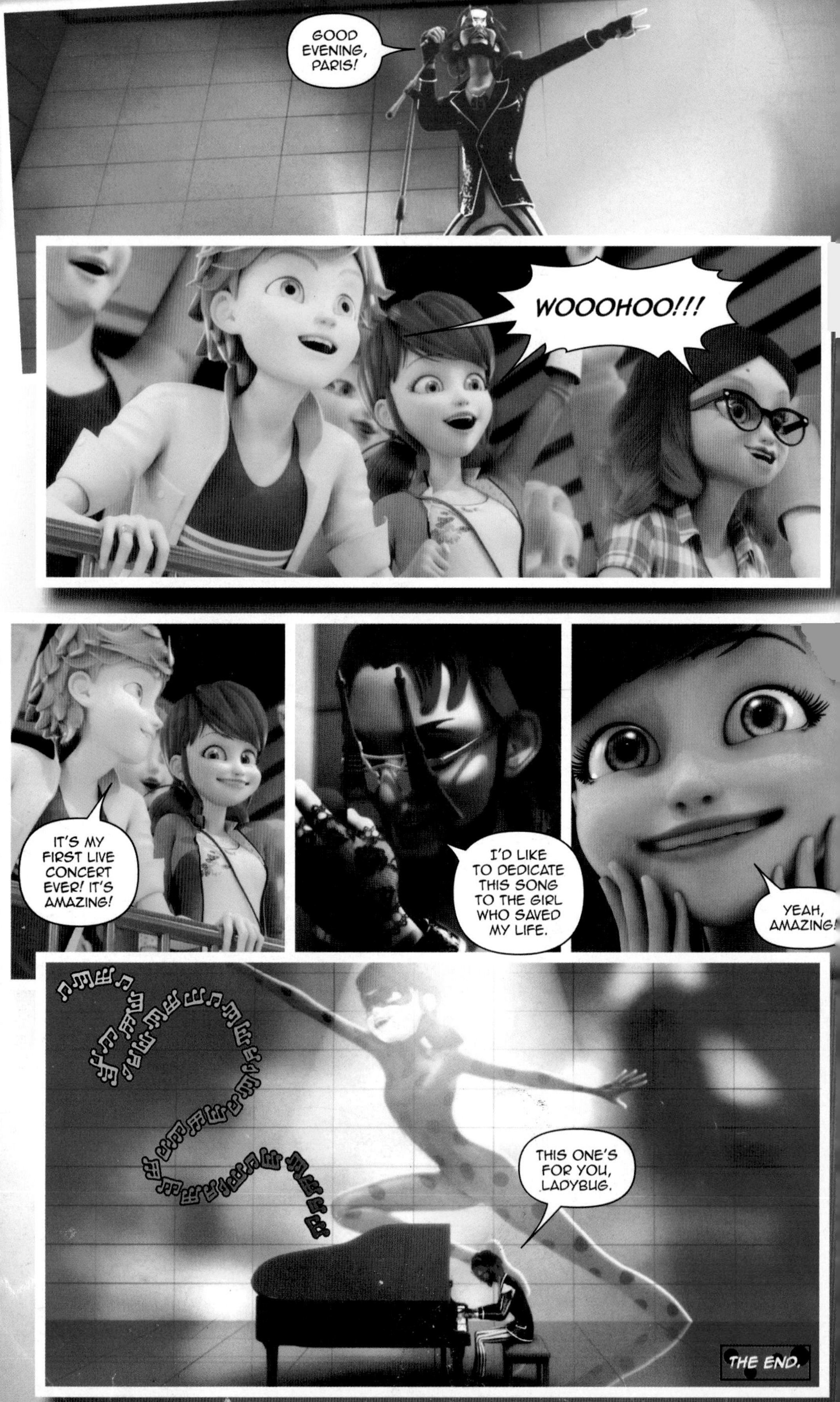
GOOD EVENING, PARIS!
WOOOHOO!!!
IT'S MY FIRST LIVE CONCERT EVER! IT'S AMAZING!
I'D LIKE TO DEDICATE THIS SONG TO THE GIRL WHO SAVED MY LIFE.
YEAH, AMAZING!
THIS ONE'S FOR YOU, LADYBUG.
THE END.

Guitar Villain

reated by: Thomas Astruc
mics adaptation by: Nicole D'Andria
ritten by: Sébastien Thibaudeau
rt arranged by: Cheryl Black
ttered by: Justin Birch

Bryan Seaton: Publisher/ CEO
Shawn Gabborin: Editor In Chief
Jason Martin: Publisher-Danger Zone
Nicole D'Andria: Marketing Director/Editor
Jim Dietz: Social Media Manager
Danielle Davison: Executive Administrator
Chad Cicconi: Akumatized
Shawn Pryor: President of Creator Relations

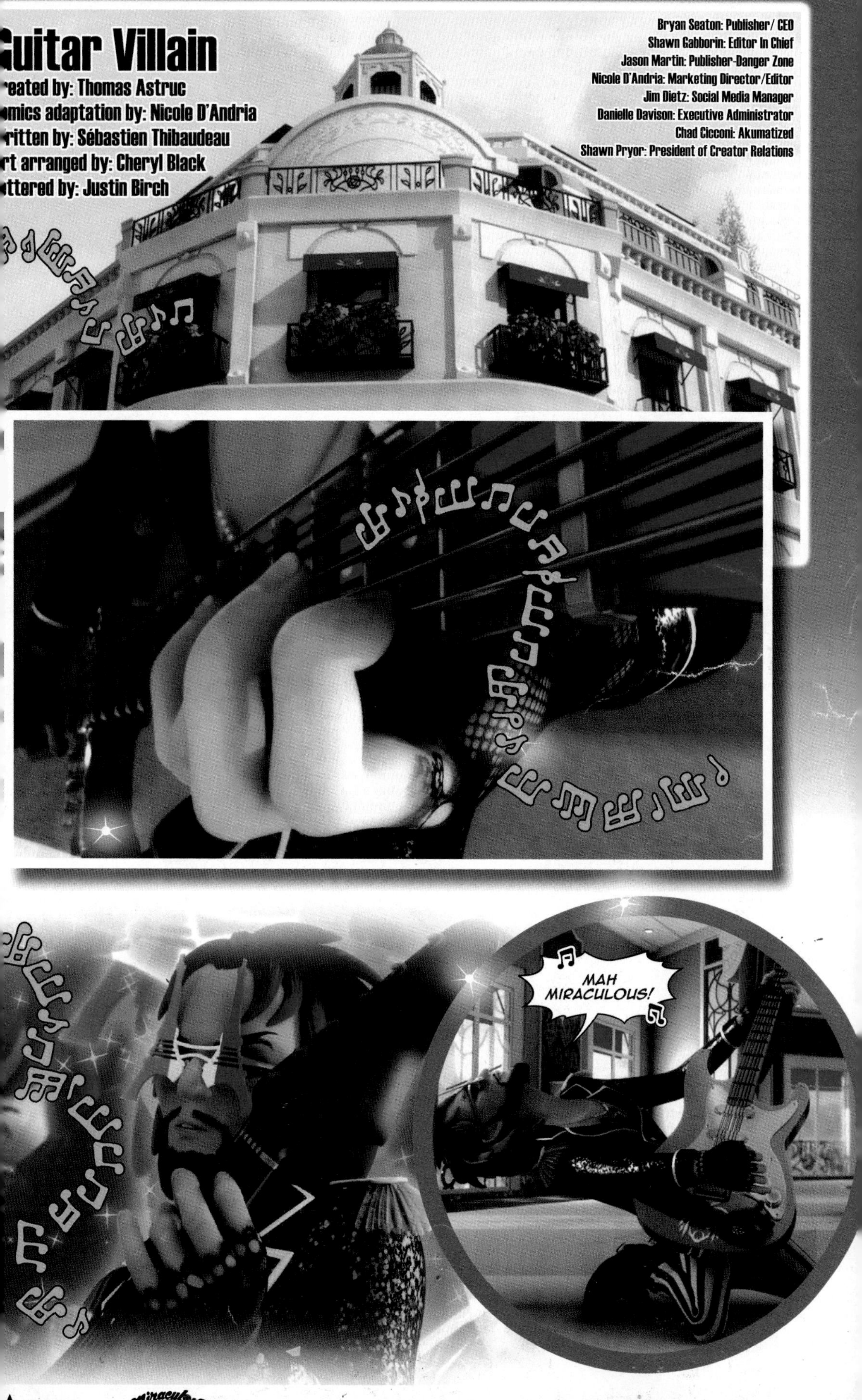

MAH MIRACULOUS!

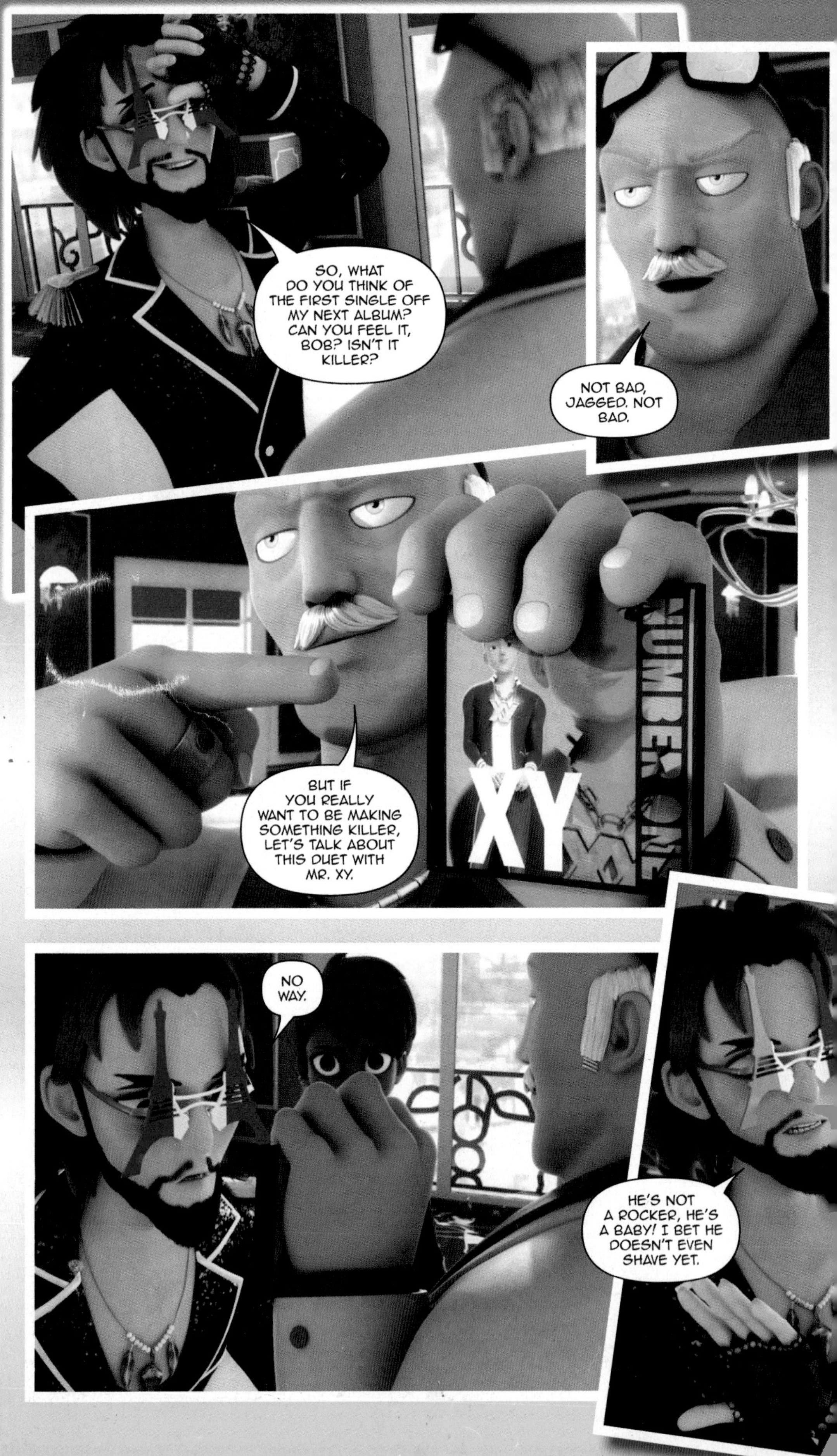
SO, WHAT DO YOU THINK OF THE FIRST SINGLE OFF MY NEXT ALBUM? CAN YOU FEEL IT, BOB? ISN'T IT KILLER?
NOT BAD, JAGGED. NOT BAD.
BUT IF YOU REALLY WANT TO BE MAKING SOMETHING KILLER, LET'S TALK ABOUT THIS DUET WITH MR. XY.
XY
NUMBER ONE
NO WAY.
HE'S NOT A ROCKER, HE'S A BABY! I BET HE DOESN'T EVEN SHAVE YET.

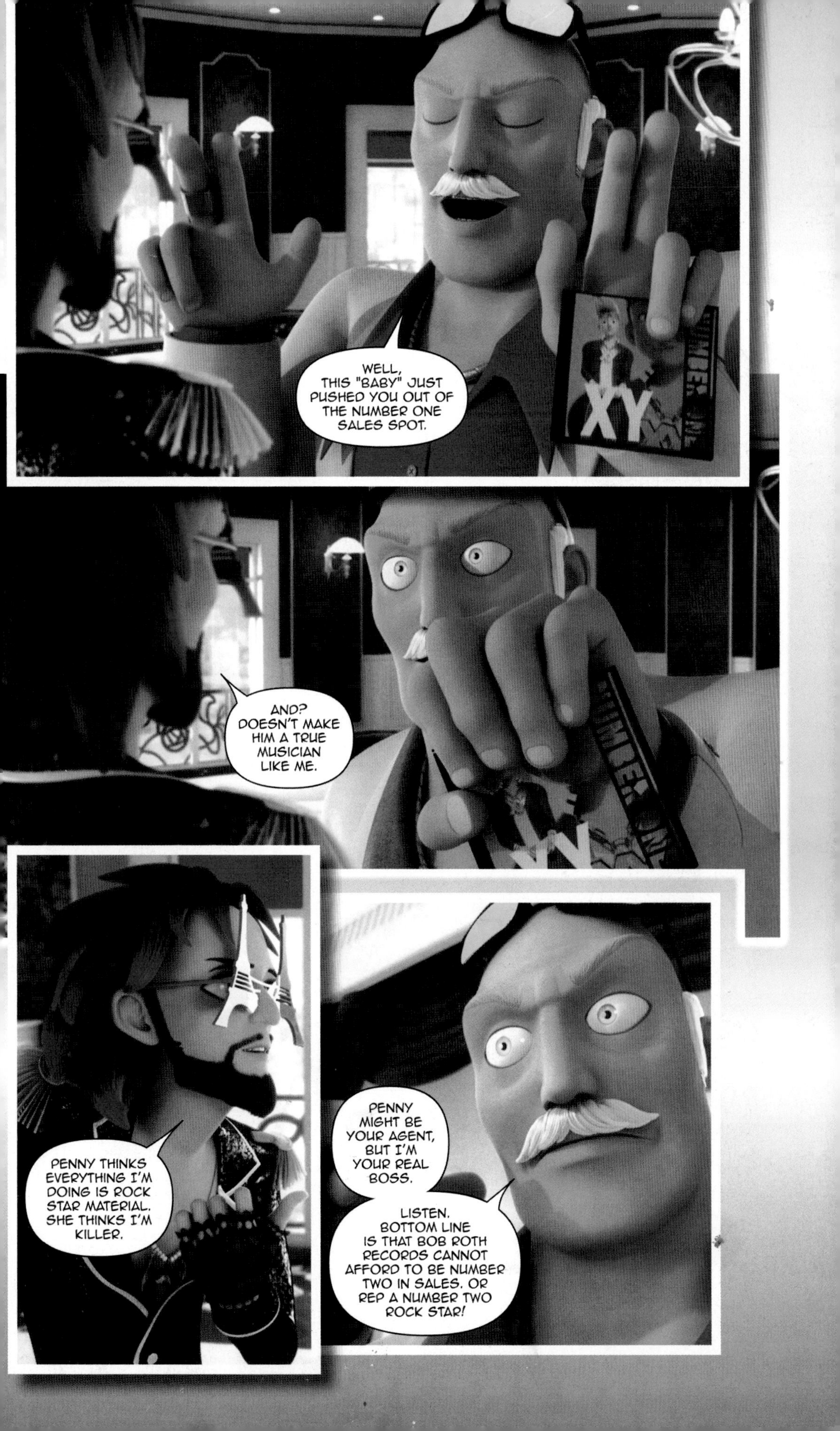
WELL, THIS "BABY" JUST PUSHED YOU OUT OF THE NUMBER ONE SALES SPOT.
AND? DOESN'T MAKE HIM A TRUE MUSICIAN LIKE ME.
PENNY THINKS EVERYTHING I'M DOING IS ROCK STAR MATERIAL. SHE THINKS I'M KILLER.
PENNY MIGHT BE YOUR AGENT, BUT I'M YOUR REAL BOSS.
LISTEN. BOTTOM LINE IS THAT BOB ROTH RECORDS CANNOT AFFORD TO BE NUMBER TWO IN SALES. OR REP A NUMBER TWO ROCK STAR!

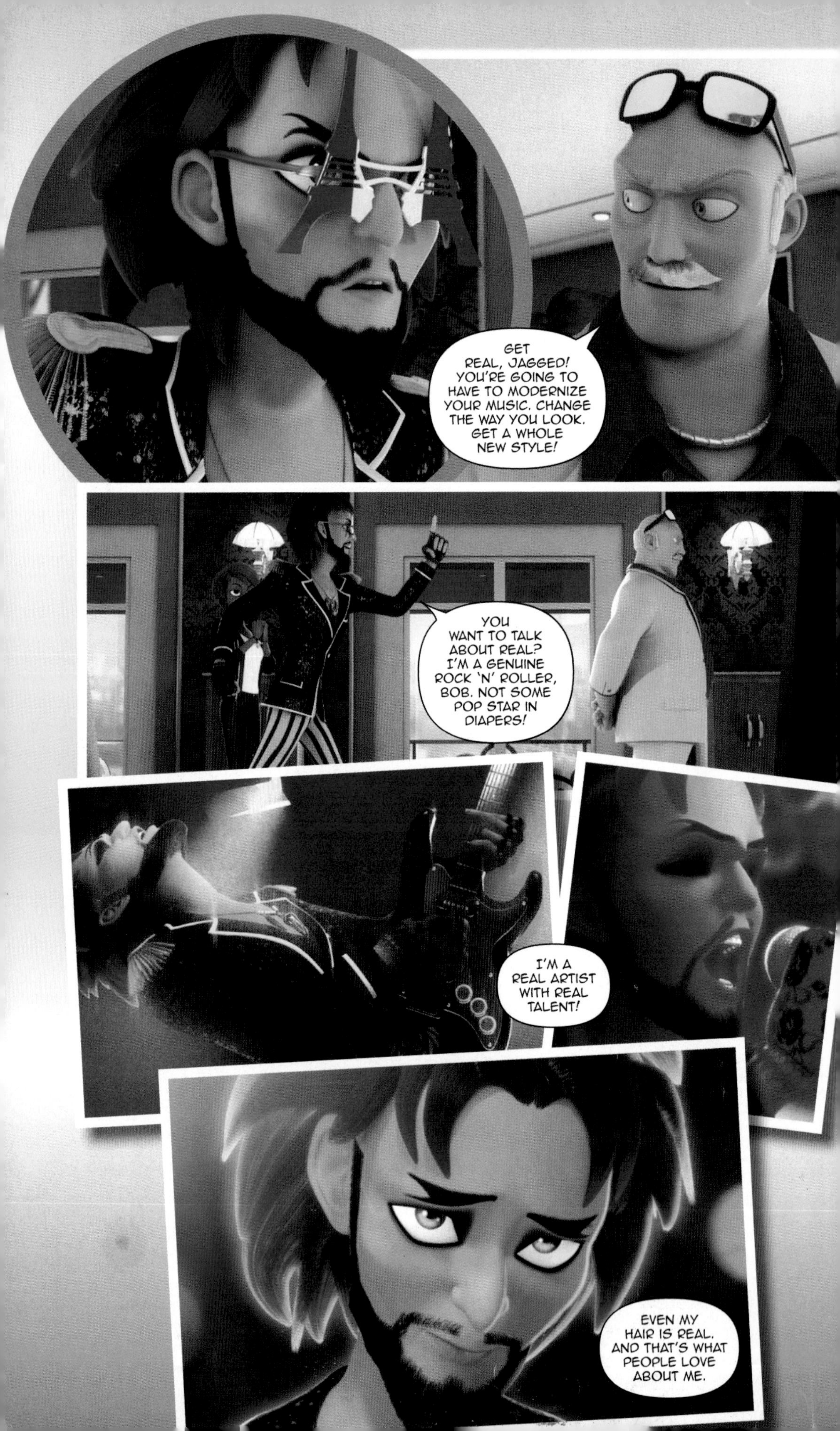
GET REAL, JAGGED! YOU'RE GOING TO HAVE TO MODERNIZE YOUR MUSIC. CHANGE THE WAY YOU LOOK. GET A WHOLE NEW STYLE!
YOU WANT TO TALK ABOUT REAL? I'M A GENUINE ROCK 'N' ROLLER, BOB. NOT SOME POP STAR IN DIAPERS!
I'M A REAL ARTIST WITH REAL TALENT!
EVEN MY HAIR IS REAL. AND THAT'S WHAT PEOPLE LOVE ABOUT ME.

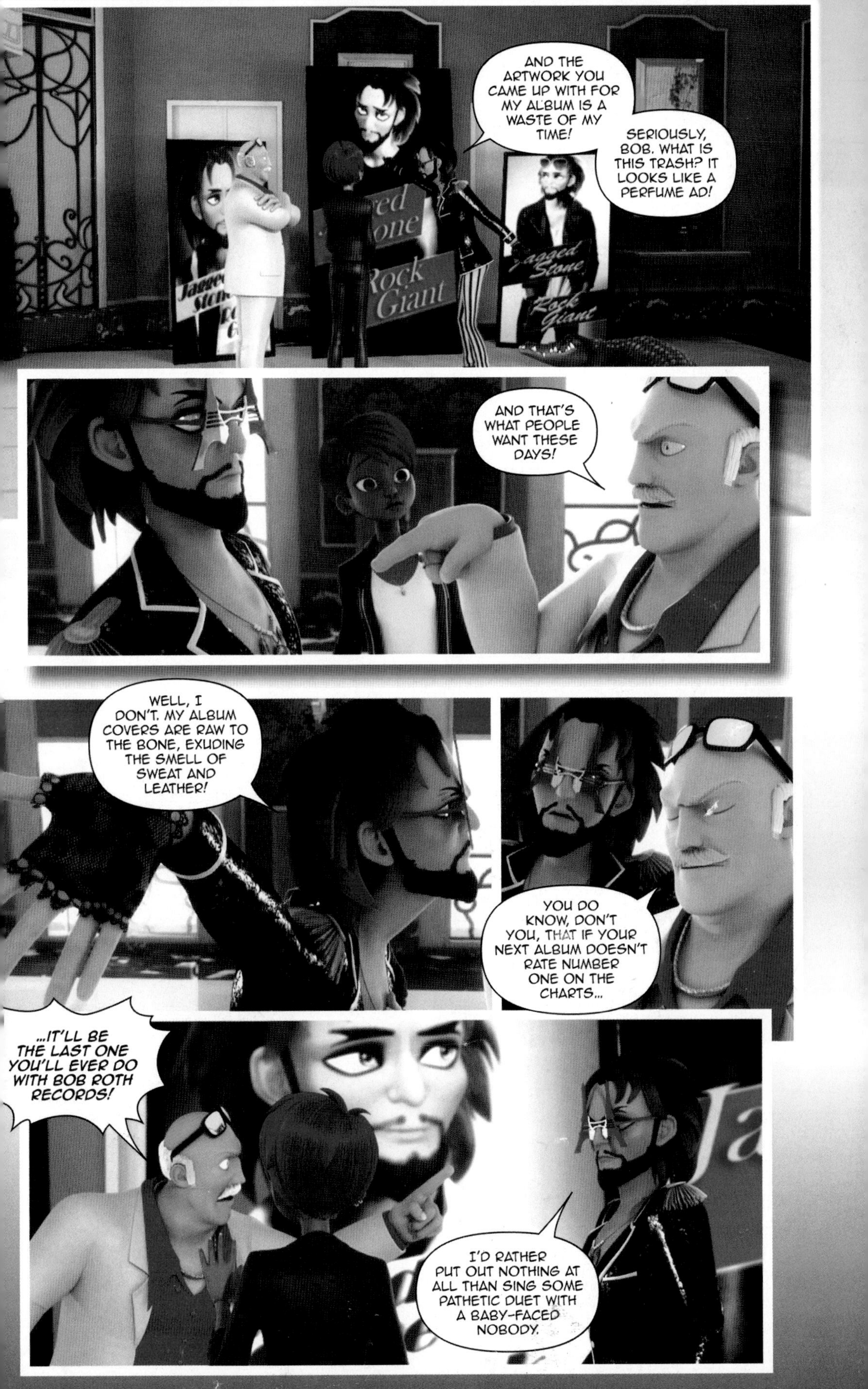
AND THE ARTWORK YOU CAME UP WITH FOR MY ALBUM IS A WASTE OF MY TIME!
SERIOUSLY, BOB. WHAT IS THIS TRASH? IT LOOKS LIKE A PERFUME AD!
Jagged Stone
Rock Giant
Jagged Stone
Rock Giant
AND THAT'S WHAT PEOPLE WANT THESE DAYS!
WELL, I DON'T. MY ALBUM COVERS ARE RAW TO THE BONE, EXUDING THE SMELL OF SWEAT AND LEATHER!
YOU DO KNOW, DON'T YOU, THAT IF YOUR NEXT ALBUM DOESN'T RATE NUMBER ONE ON THE CHARTS...
...IT'LL BE THE LAST ONE YOU'LL EVER DO WITH BOB ROTH RECORDS!
I'D RATHER PUT OUT NOTHING AT ALL THAN SING SOME PATHETIC DUET WITH A BABY-FACED NOBODY.

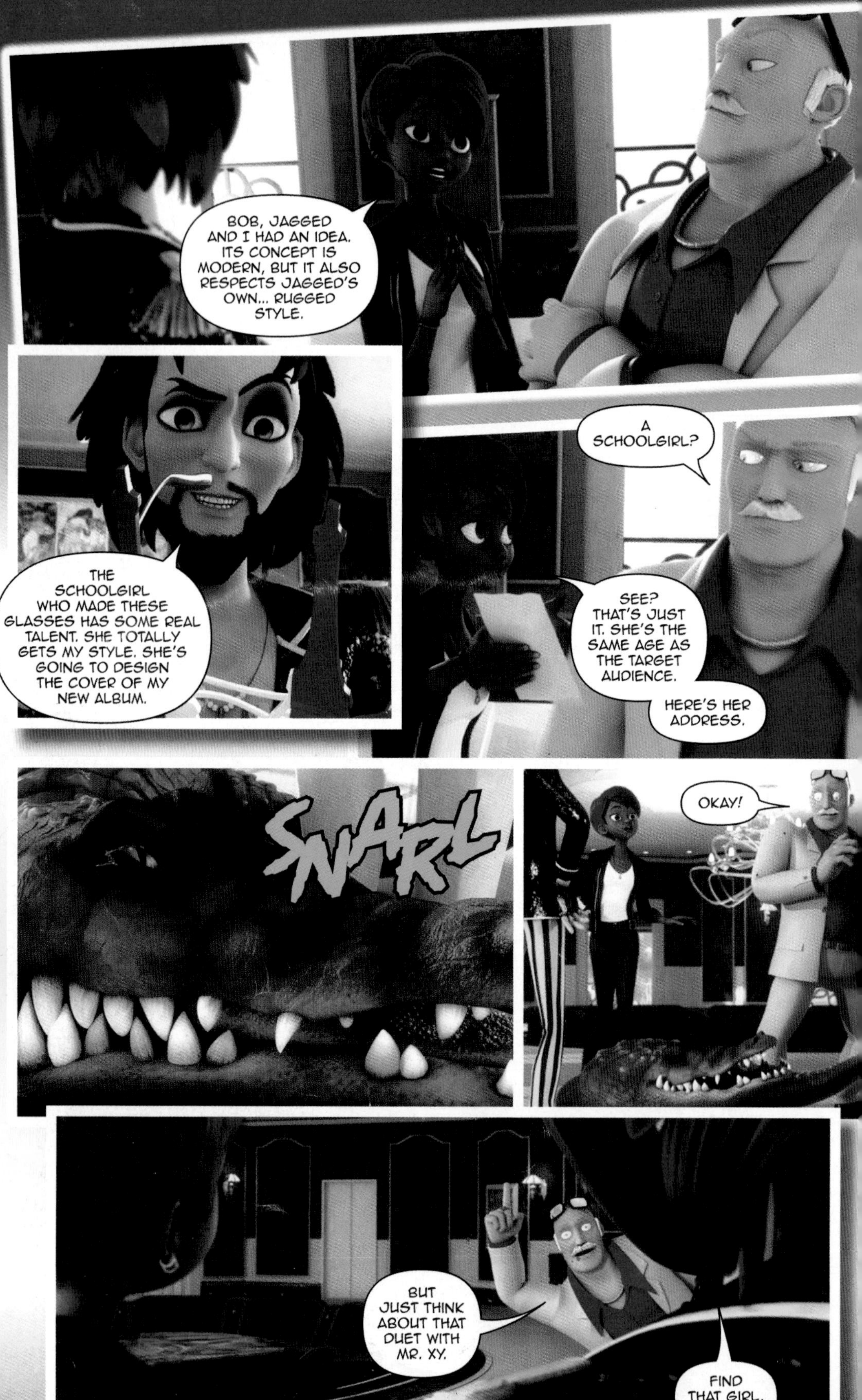

BOB, JAGGED AND I HAD AN IDEA. ITS CONCEPT IS MODERN, BUT IT ALSO RESPECTS JAGGED'S OWN... RUGGED STYLE.
THE SCHOOLGIRL WHO MADE THESE GLASSES HAS SOME REAL TALENT. SHE TOTALLY GETS MY STYLE. SHE'S GOING TO DESIGN THE COVER OF MY NEW ALBUM.
A SCHOOLGIRL?
SEE? THAT'S JUST IT. SHE'S THE SAME AGE AS THE TARGET AUDIENCE.
HERE'S HER ADDRESS.
SNARL
OKAY!
BUT JUST THINK ABOUT THAT DUET WITH MR. XY.
FIND THAT GIRL, BOB!

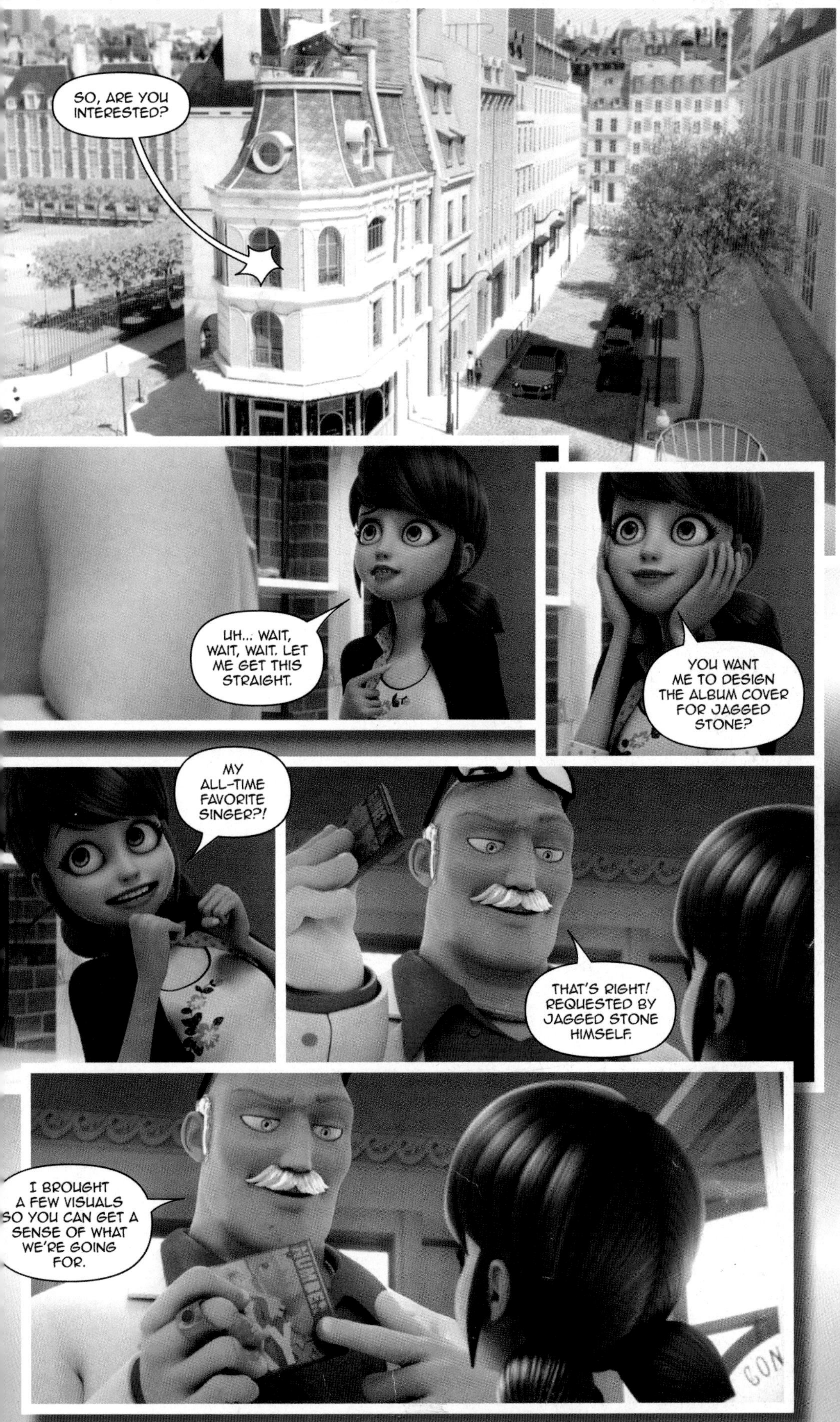
SO, ARE YOU INTERESTED?
UH... WAIT, WAIT, WAIT. LET ME GET THIS STRAIGHT.
YOU WANT ME TO DESIGN THE ALBUM COVER FOR JAGGED STONE?
MY ALL-TIME FAVORITE SINGER?!
THAT'S RIGHT! REQUESTED BY JAGGED STONE HIMSELF.
I BROUGHT A FEW VISUALS SO YOU CAN GET A SENSE OF WHAT WE'RE GOING FOR.

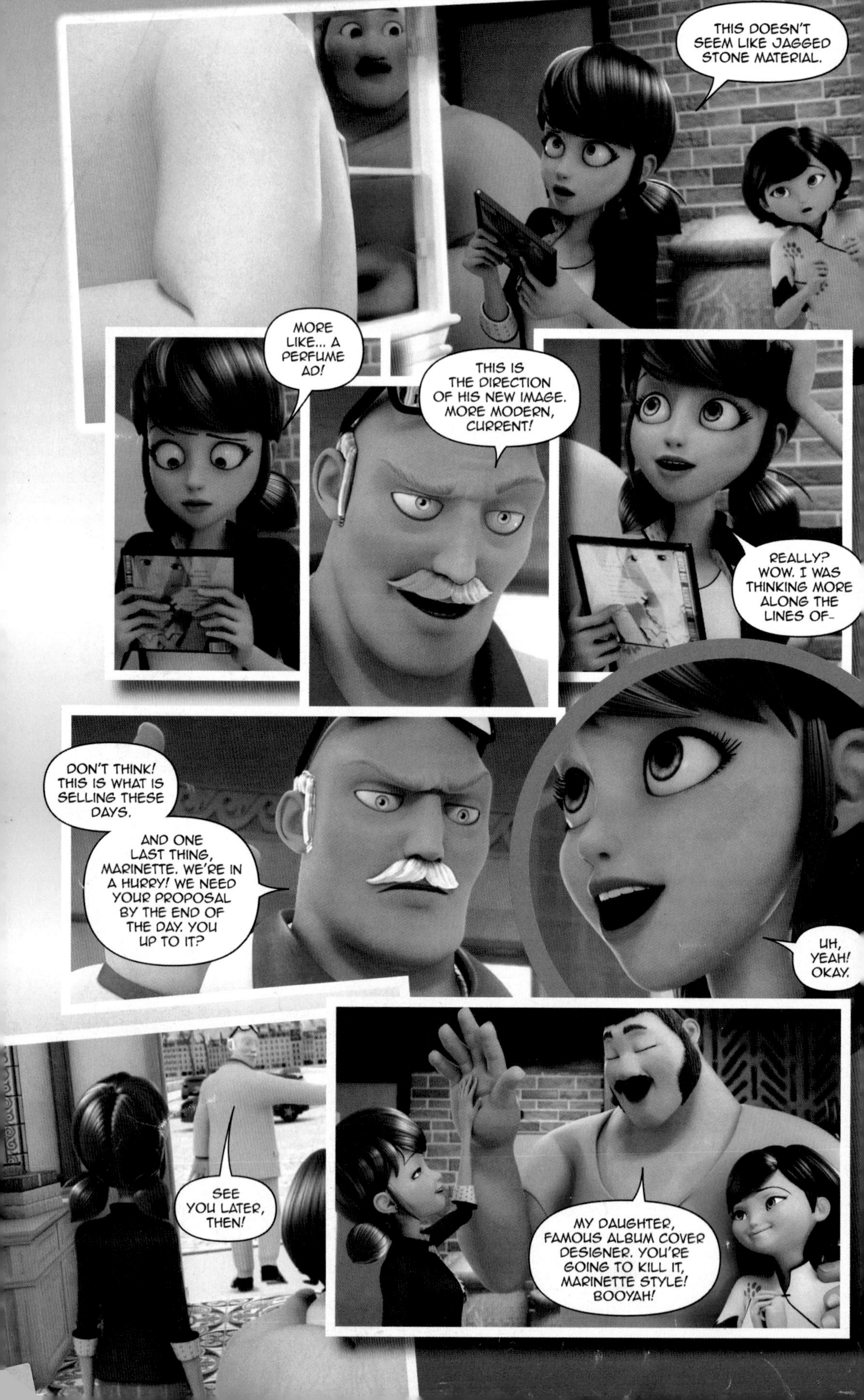
THIS DOESN'T SEEM LIKE JAGGED STONE MATERIAL.
MORE LIKE... A PERFUME AD!
THIS IS THE DIRECTION OF HIS NEW IMAGE. MORE MODERN, CURRENT!
REALLY? WOW. I WAS THINKING MORE ALONG THE LINES OF-
DON'T THINK! THIS IS WHAT IS SELLING THESE DAYS.
AND ONE LAST THING, MARINETTE. WE'RE IN A HURRY! WE NEED YOUR PROPOSAL BY THE END OF THE DAY. YOU UP TO IT?
UH, YEAH! OKAY.
SEE YOU LATER, THEN!
MY DAUGHTER, FAMOUS ALBUM COVER DESIGNER. YOU'RE GOING TO KILL IT, MARINETTE STYLE! BOOYAH!

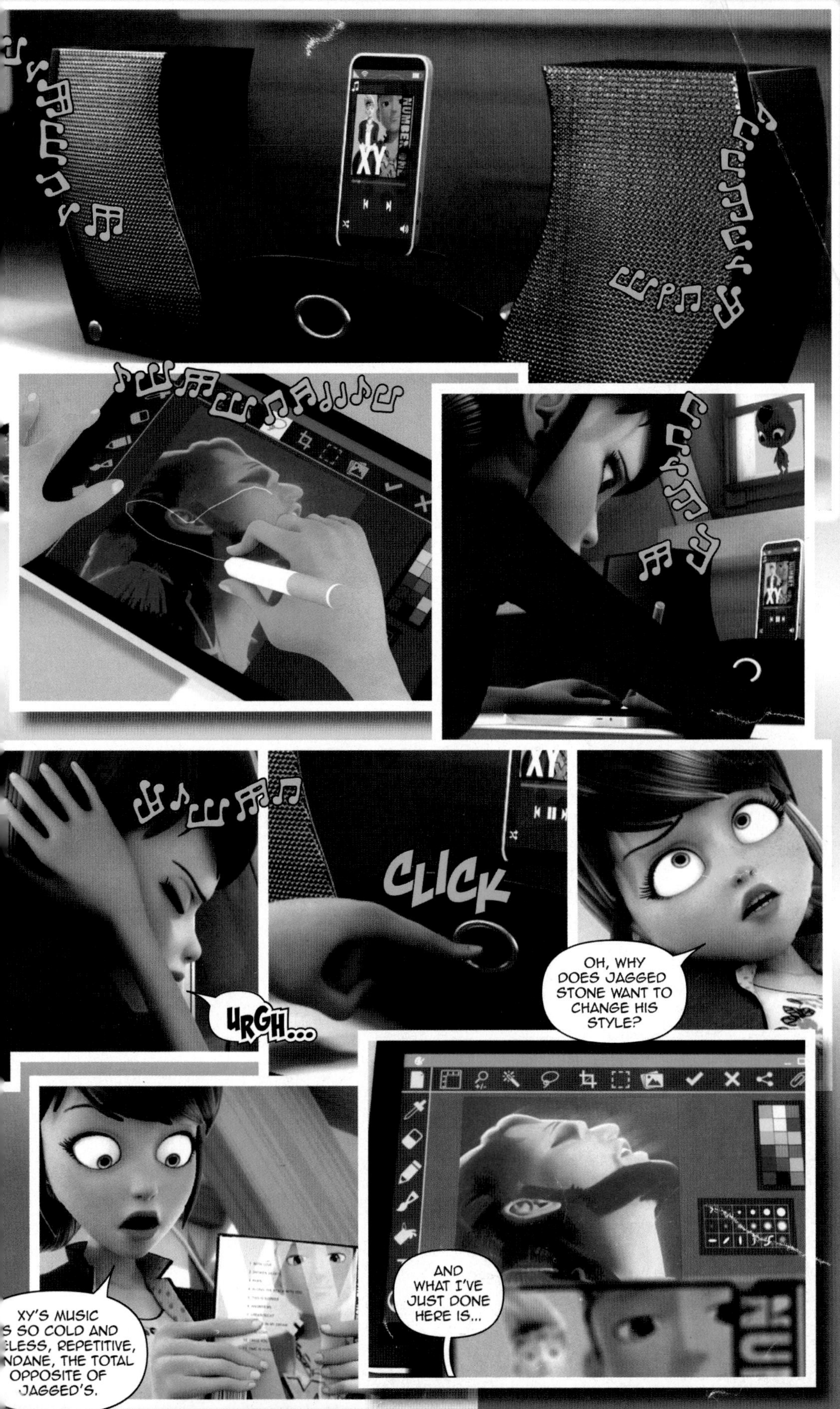
CLICK
URGH...
OH, WHY DOES JAGGED STONE WANT TO CHANGE HIS STYLE?
XY'S MUSIC
S SO COLD AND
ELESS, REPETITIVE,
NDANE, THE TOTAL
OPPOSITE OF
JAGGED'S.
AND WHAT I'VE JUST DONE HERE IS...

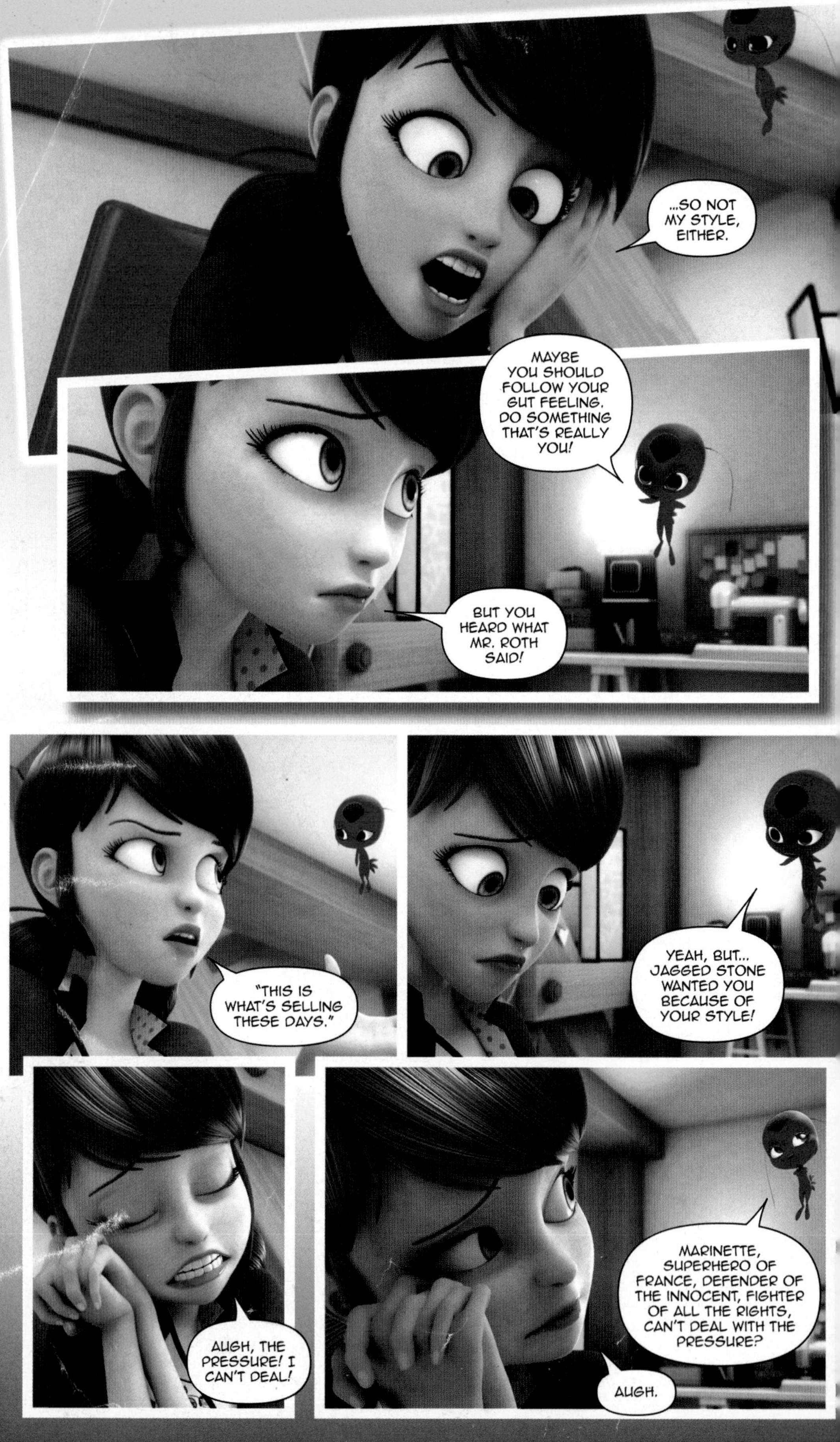
...SO NOT MY STYLE, EITHER.
MAYBE YOU SHOULD FOLLOW YOUR GUT FEELING. DO SOMETHING THAT'S REALLY YOU!
BUT YOU HEARD WHAT MR. ROTH SAID!
"THIS IS WHAT'S SELLING THESE DAYS."
YEAH, BUT... JAGGED STONE WANTED YOU BECAUSE OF YOUR STYLE!
AUGH, THE PRESSURE! I CAN'T DEAL!
MARINETTE, SUPERHERO OF FRANCE, DEFENDER OF THE INNOCENT, FIGHTER OF ALL THE RIGHTS, CAN'T DEAL WITH THE PRESSURE?
AUGH.

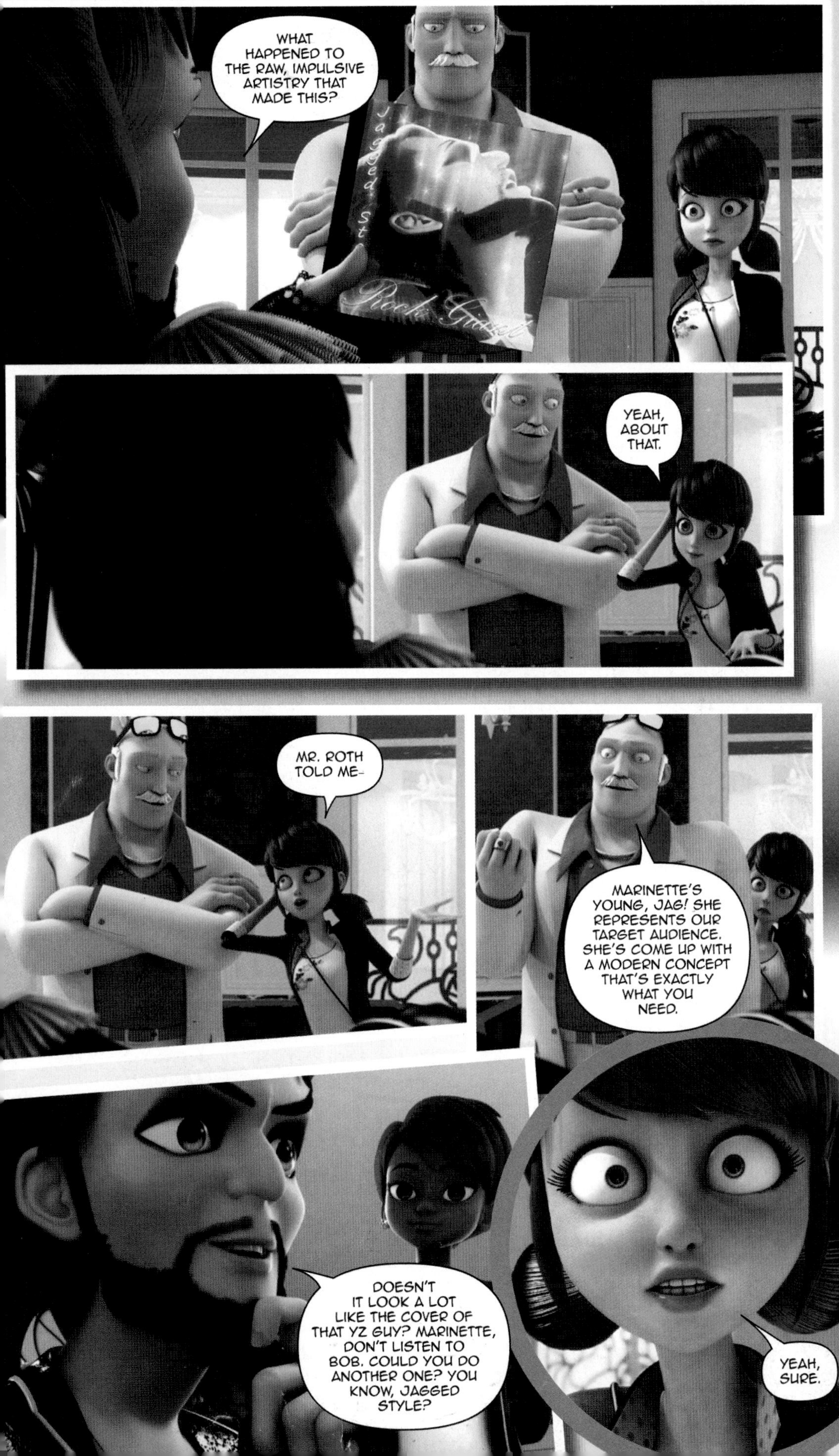
WHAT HAPPENED TO THE RAW, IMPULSIVE ARTISTRY THAT MADE THIS?
YEAH, ABOUT THAT.
MR. ROTH TOLD ME-
MARINETTE'S YOUNG, JAG! SHE REPRESENTS OUR TARGET AUDIENCE. SHE'S COME UP WITH A MODERN CONCEPT THAT'S EXACTLY WHAT YOU NEED.
DOESN'T IT LOOK A LOT LIKE THE COVER OF THAT YZ GUY? MARINETTE, DON'T LISTEN TO BOB. COULD YOU DO ANOTHER ONE? YOU KNOW, JAGGED STYLE?
YEAH, SURE.

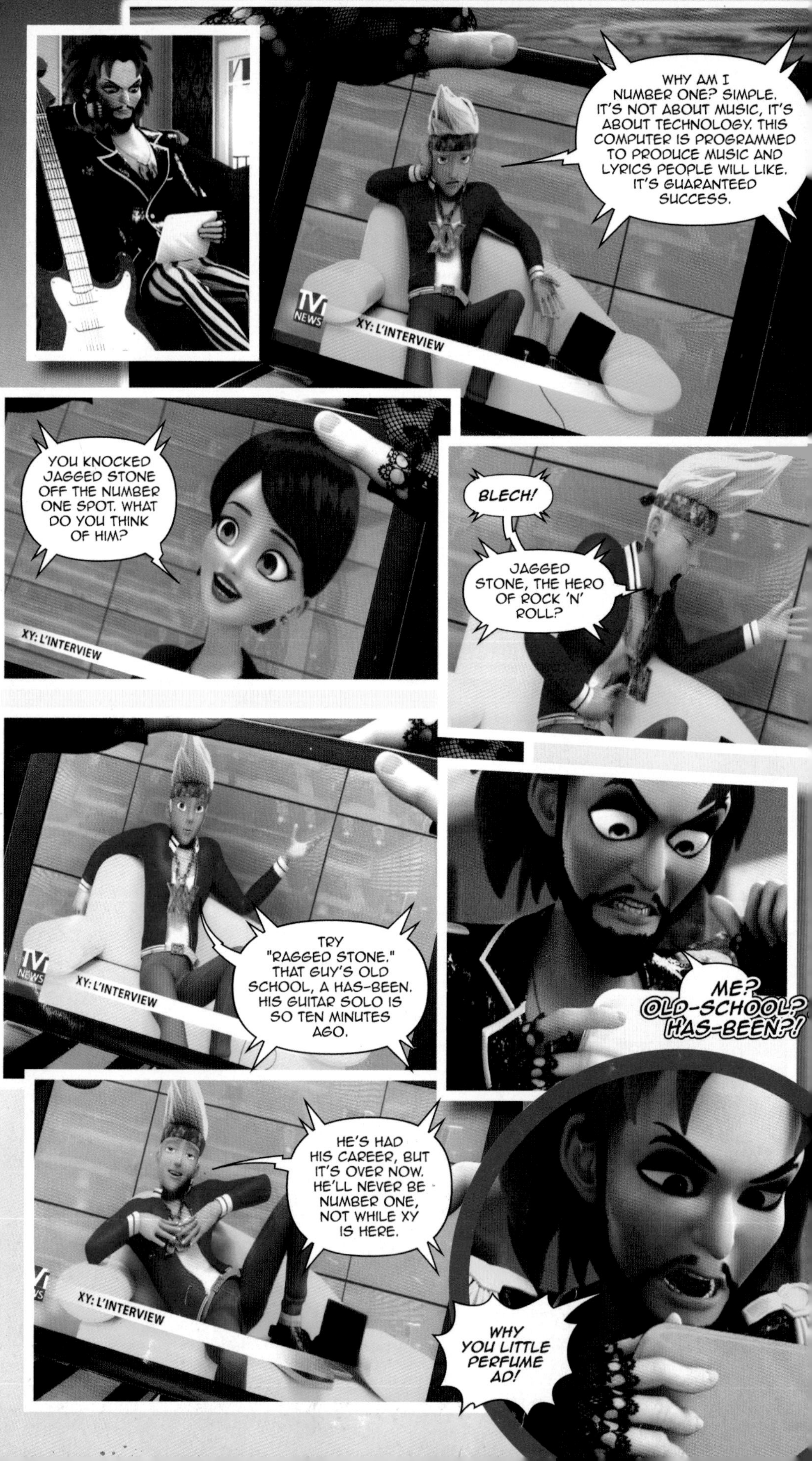
WHY AM I NUMBER ONE? SIMPLE. IT'S NOT ABOUT MUSIC, IT'S ABOUT TECHNOLOGY. THIS COMPUTER IS PROGRAMMED TO PRODUCE MUSIC AND LYRICS PEOPLE WILL LIKE. IT'S GUARANTEED SUCCESS.
TV NEWS
XY: L'INTERVIEW
YOU KNOCKED JAGGED STONE OFF THE NUMBER ONE SPOT. WHAT DO YOU THINK OF HIM?
XY: L'INTERVIEW
BLECH!
JAGGED STONE, THE HERO OF ROCK 'N' ROLL?
TRY "RAGGED STONE." THAT GUY'S OLD SCHOOL, A HAS-BEEN. HIS GUITAR SOLO IS SO TEN MINUTES AGO.
TV NEWS
XY: L'INTERVIEW
ME? OLD-SCHOOL? HAS-BEEN?!
HE'S HAD HIS CAREER, BUT IT'S OVER NOW. HE'LL NEVER BE NUMBER ONE, NOT WHILE XY IS HERE.
XY: L'INTERVIEW
WHY YOU LITTLE PERFUME AD!

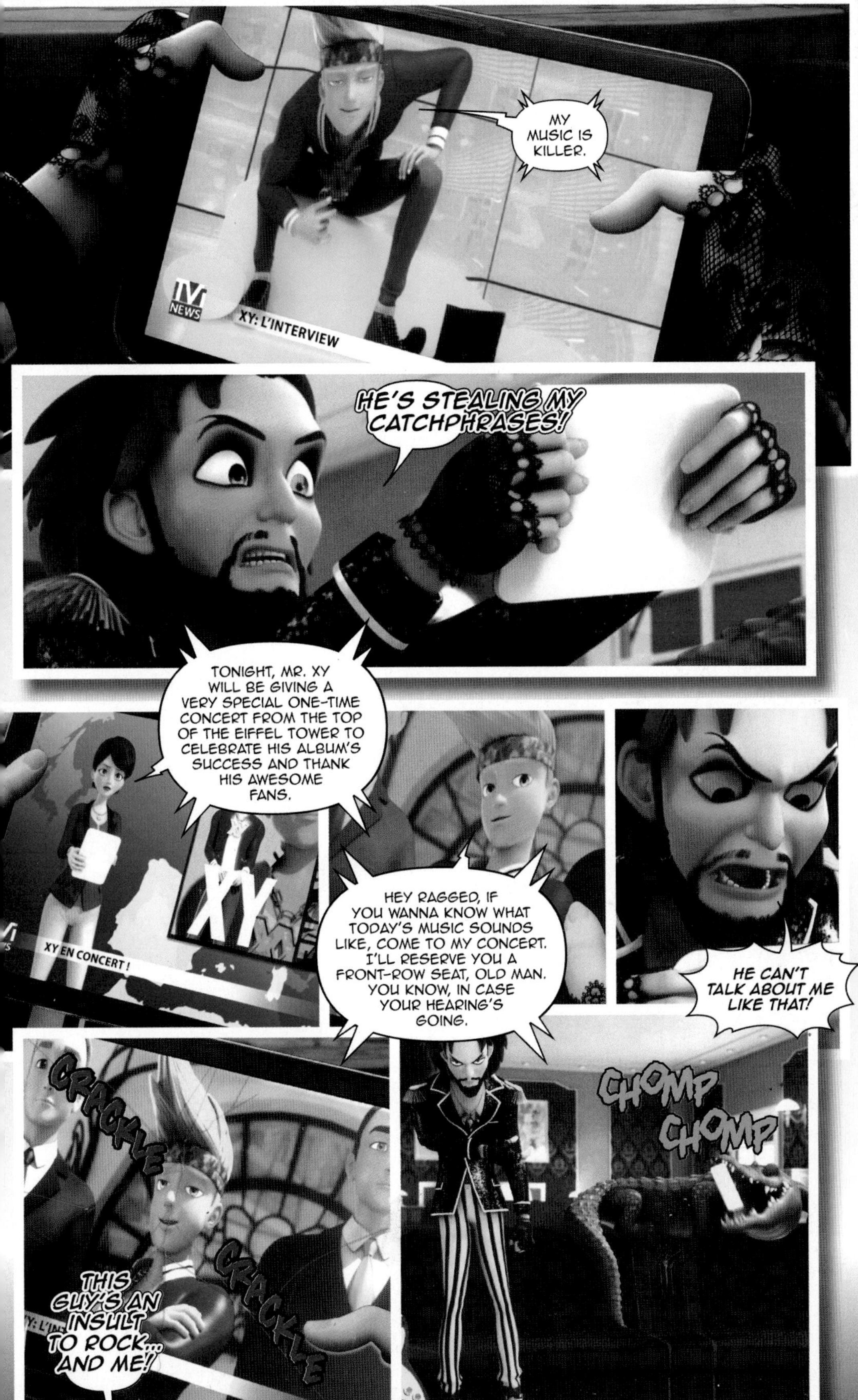
MY MUSIC IS KILLER.
TVI NEWS
XY: L'INTERVIEW
HE'S STEALING MY CATCHPHRASES!
TONIGHT, MR. XY WILL BE GIVING A VERY SPECIAL ONE-TIME CONCERT FROM THE TOP OF THE EIFFEL TOWER TO CELEBRATE HIS ALBUM'S SUCCESS AND THANK HIS AWESOME FANS.
XY EN CONCERT !
XY
HEY RAGGED, IF YOU WANNA KNOW WHAT TODAY'S MUSIC SOUNDS LIKE, COME TO MY CONCERT. I'LL RESERVE YOU A FRONT-ROW SEAT, OLD MAN. YOU KNOW, IN CASE YOUR HEARING'S GOING.
HE CAN'T TALK ABOUT ME LIKE THAT!
CRACKLE
CRACKLE
THIS GUY'S AN INSULT TO ROCK... AND ME!
CHOMP
CHOMP

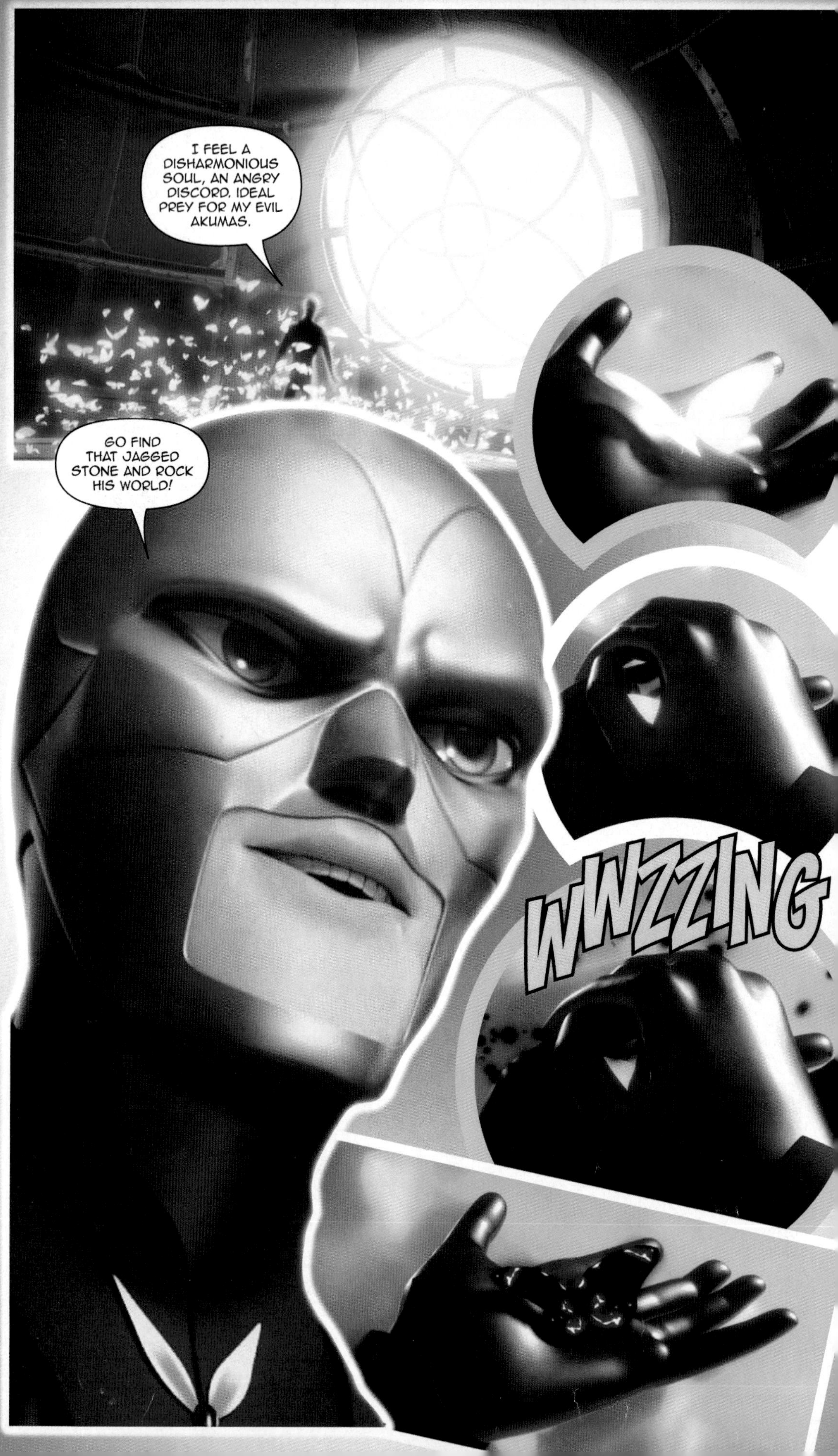
I FEEL A DISHARMONIOUS SOUL, AN ANGRY DISCORD. IDEAL PREY FOR MY EVIL AKUMAS.
GO FIND THAT JAGGED STONE AND ROCK HIS WORLD!
WWZZING

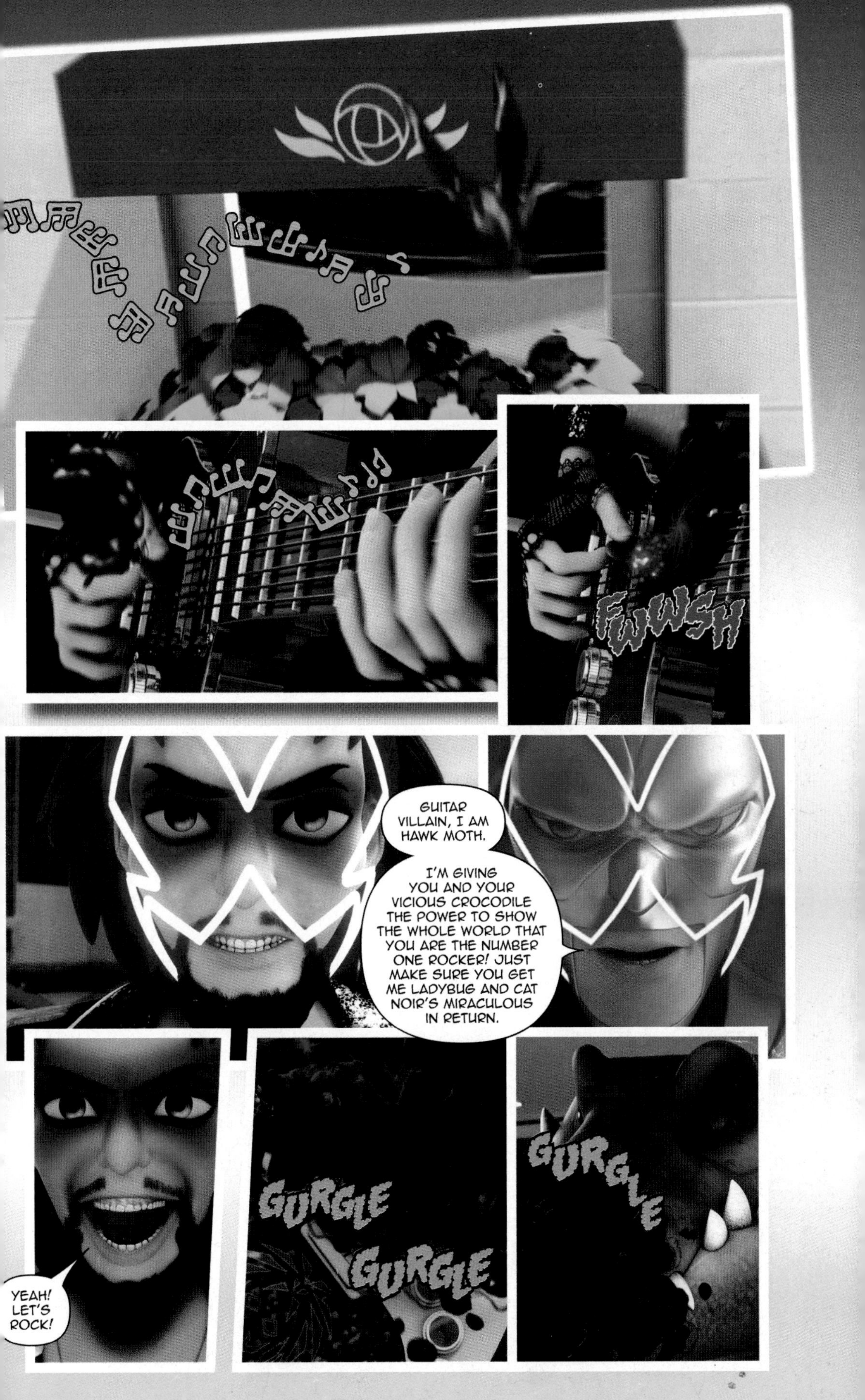
FWWSH
GUITAR VILLAIN, I AM HAWK MOTH.
I'M GIVING YOU AND YOUR VICIOUS CROCODILE THE POWER TO SHOW THE WHOLE WORLD THAT YOU ARE THE NUMBER ONE ROCKER! JUST MAKE SURE YOU GET ME LADYBUG AND CAT NOIR'S MIRACULOUS IN RETURN.
YEAH! LET'S ROCK!
GURGLE
GURGLE
GURGLE

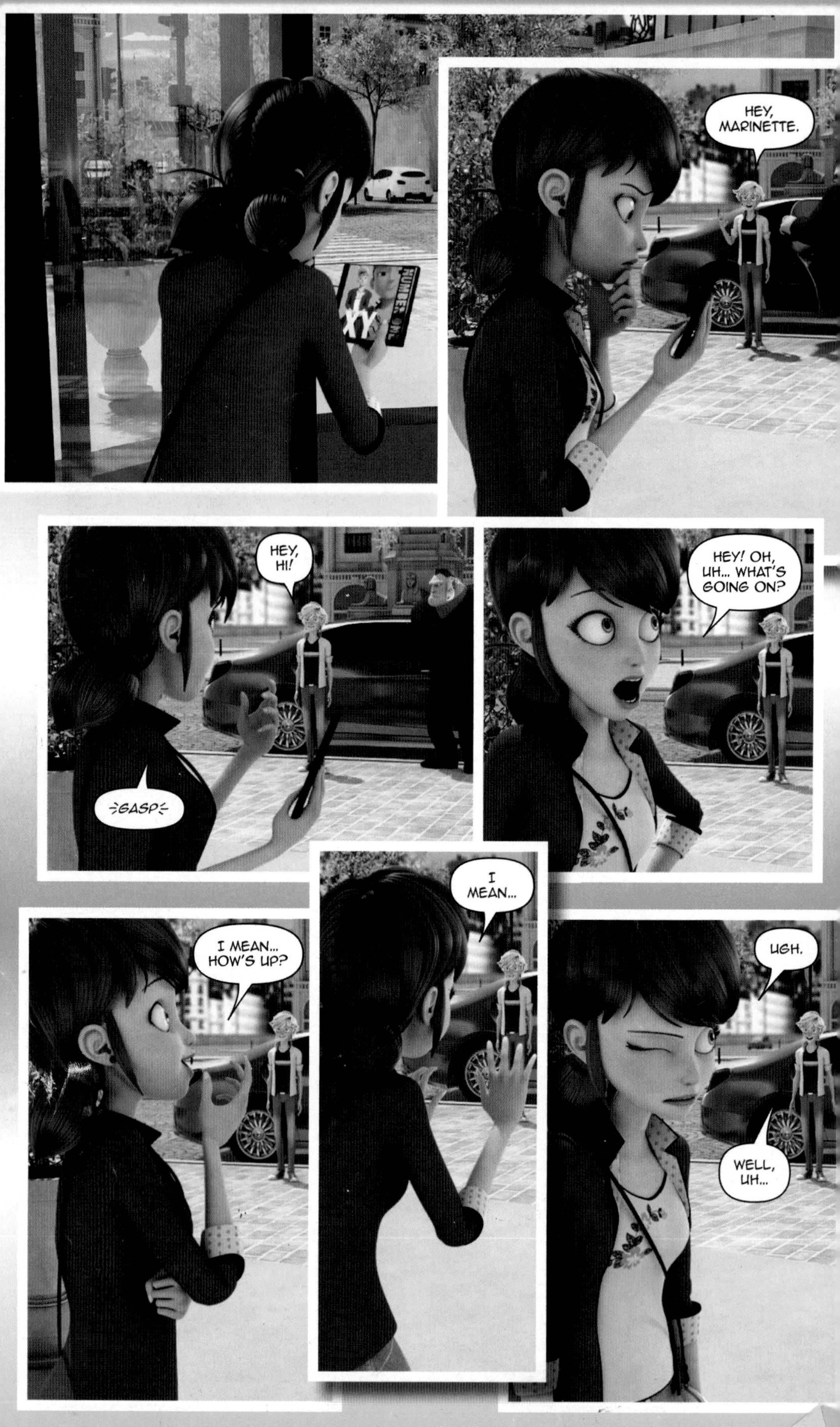
HUMMER
XY
HEY, MARINETTE.
HEY, HI!
=GASP=
HEY! OH, UH... WHAT'S GOING ON?
I MEAN... HOW'S UP?
I MEAN...
UGH.
WELL, UH...

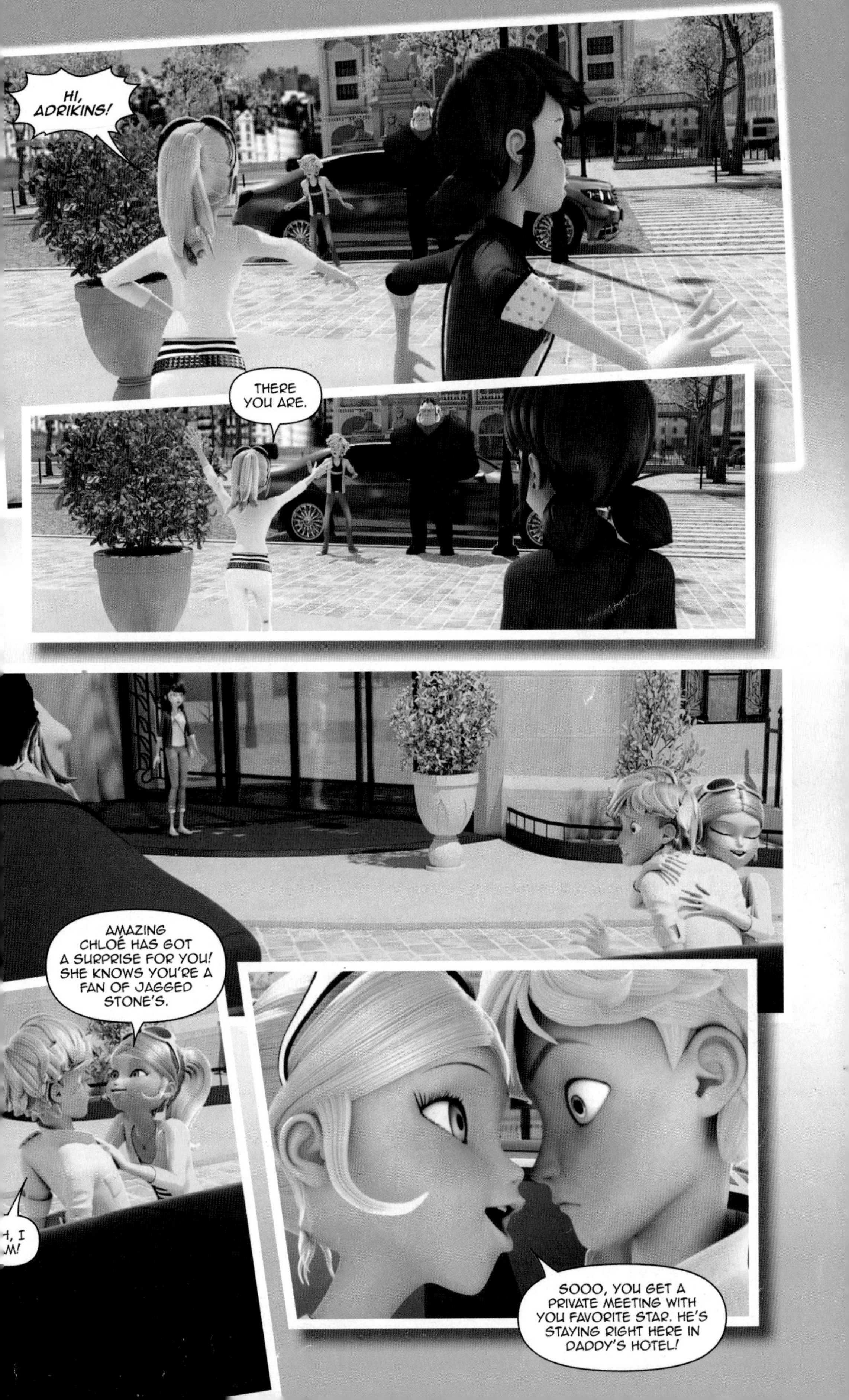
HI, ADRIKINS!
THERE YOU ARE.
AMAZING CHLOÉ HAS GOT A SURPRISE FOR YOU! SHE KNOWS YOU'RE A FAN OF JAGGED STONE'S.
SOOO, YOU GET A PRIVATE MEETING WITH YOU FAVORITE STAR. HE'S STAYING RIGHT HERE IN DADDY'S HOTEL!

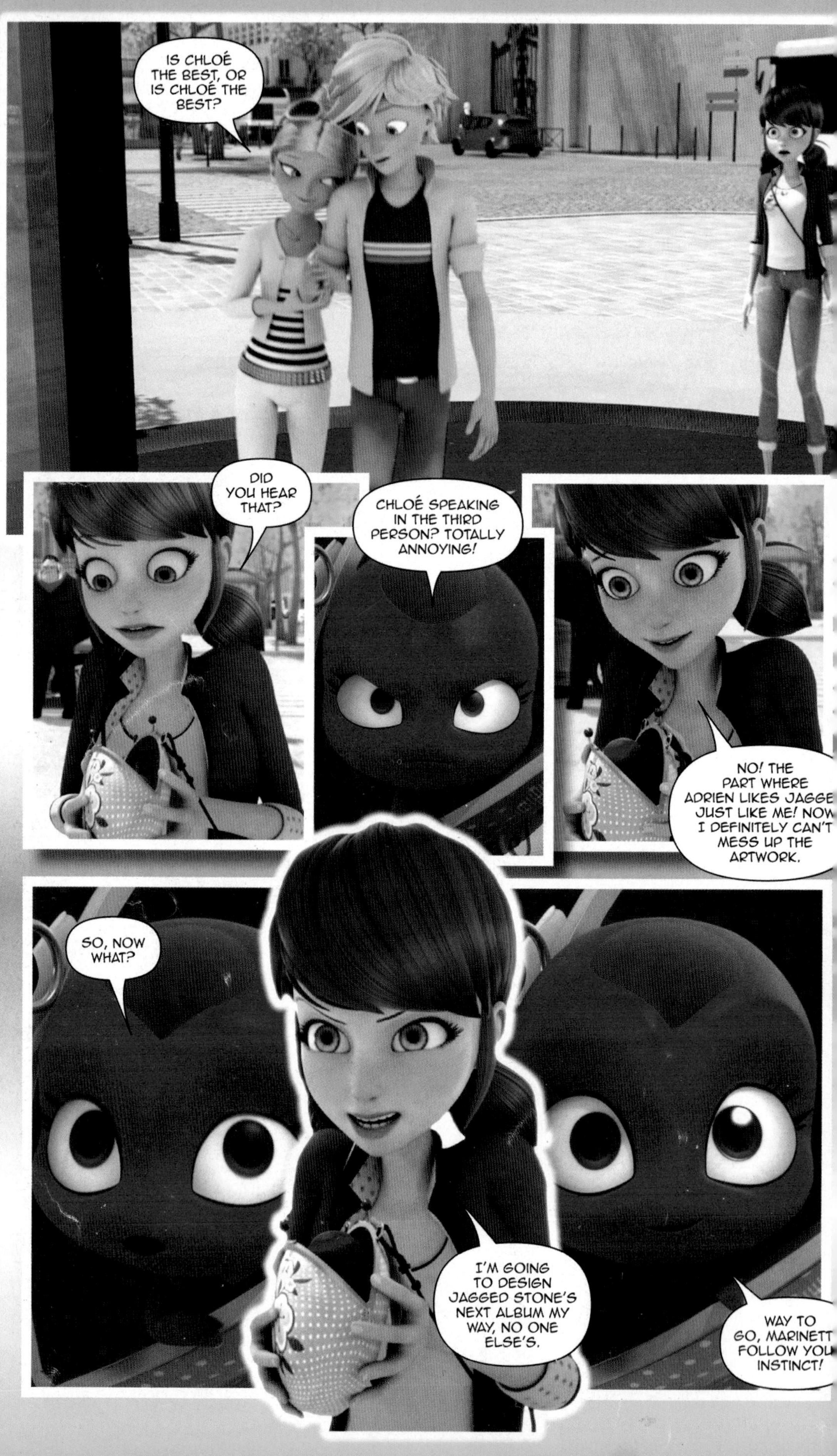
IS CHLOÉ THE BEST, OR IS CHLOÉ THE BEST?
DID YOU HEAR THAT?
CHLOÉ SPEAKING IN THE THIRD PERSON? TOTALLY ANNOYING!
NO! THE PART WHERE ADRIEN LIKES JAGGE JUST LIKE ME! NOW I DEFINITELY CAN'T MESS UP THE ARTWORK.
SO, NOW WHAT?
I'M GOING TO DESIGN JAGGED STONE'S NEXT ALBUM MY WAY, NO ONE ELSE'S.
WAY TO GO, MARINETT FOLLOW YOU INSTINCT!

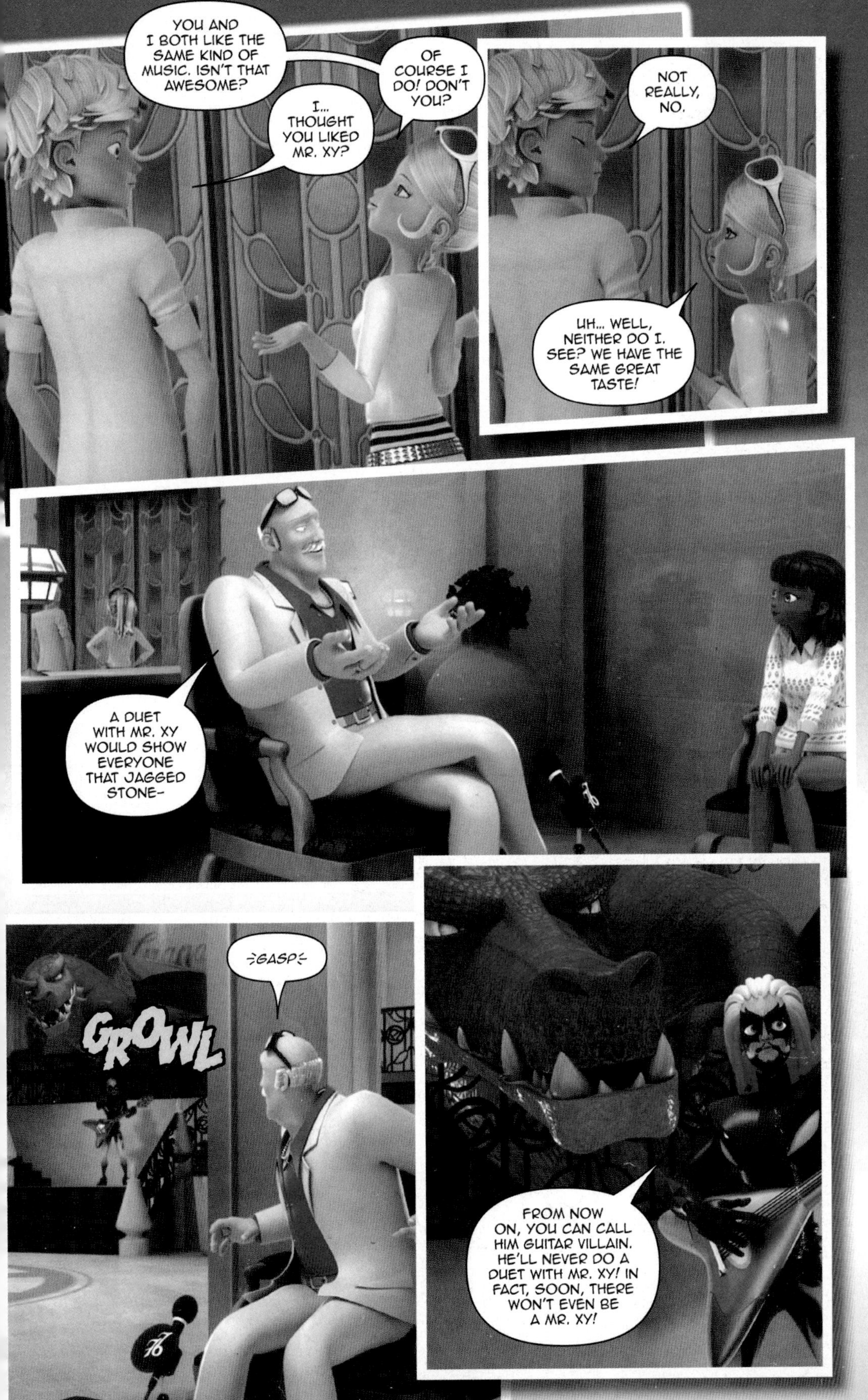
YOU AND I BOTH LIKE THE SAME KIND OF MUSIC. ISN'T THAT AWESOME?
I... THOUGHT YOU LIKED MR. XY?
OF COURSE I DO! DON'T YOU?
NOT REALLY, NO.
UH... WELL, NEITHER DO I. SEE? WE HAVE THE SAME GREAT TASTE!
A DUET WITH MR. XY WOULD SHOW EVERYONE THAT JAGGED STONE-
GROWL
GASP
FROM NOW ON, YOU CAN CALL HIM GUITAR VILLAIN. HE'LL NEVER DO A DUET WITH MR. XY! IN FACT, SOON, THERE WON'T EVEN BE A MR. XY!

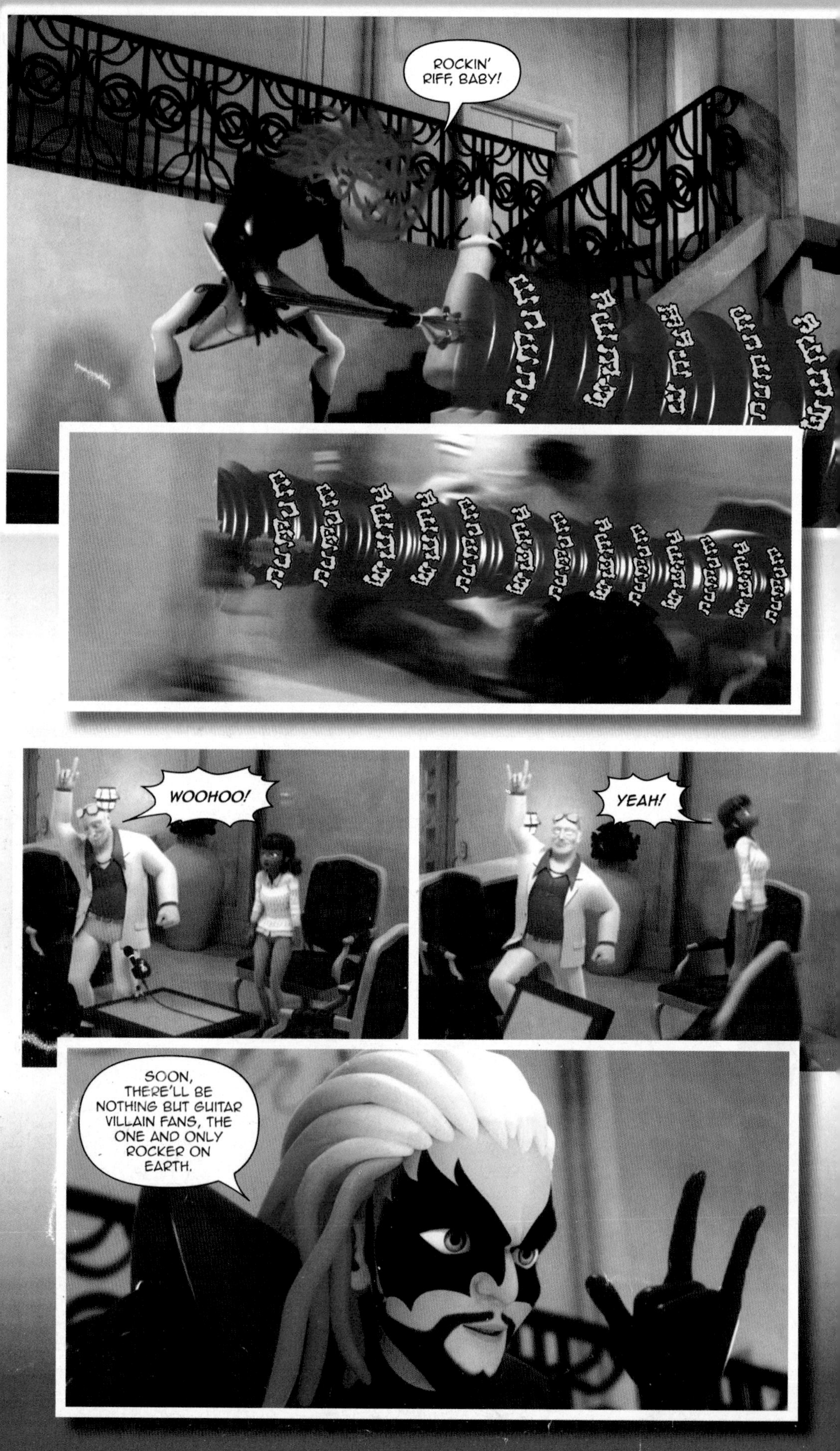
ROCKIN' RIFF, BABY!
WOOHOO!
YEAH!
SOON, THERE'LL BE NOTHING BUT GUITAR VILLAIN FANS, THE ONE AND ONLY ROCKER ON EARTH.

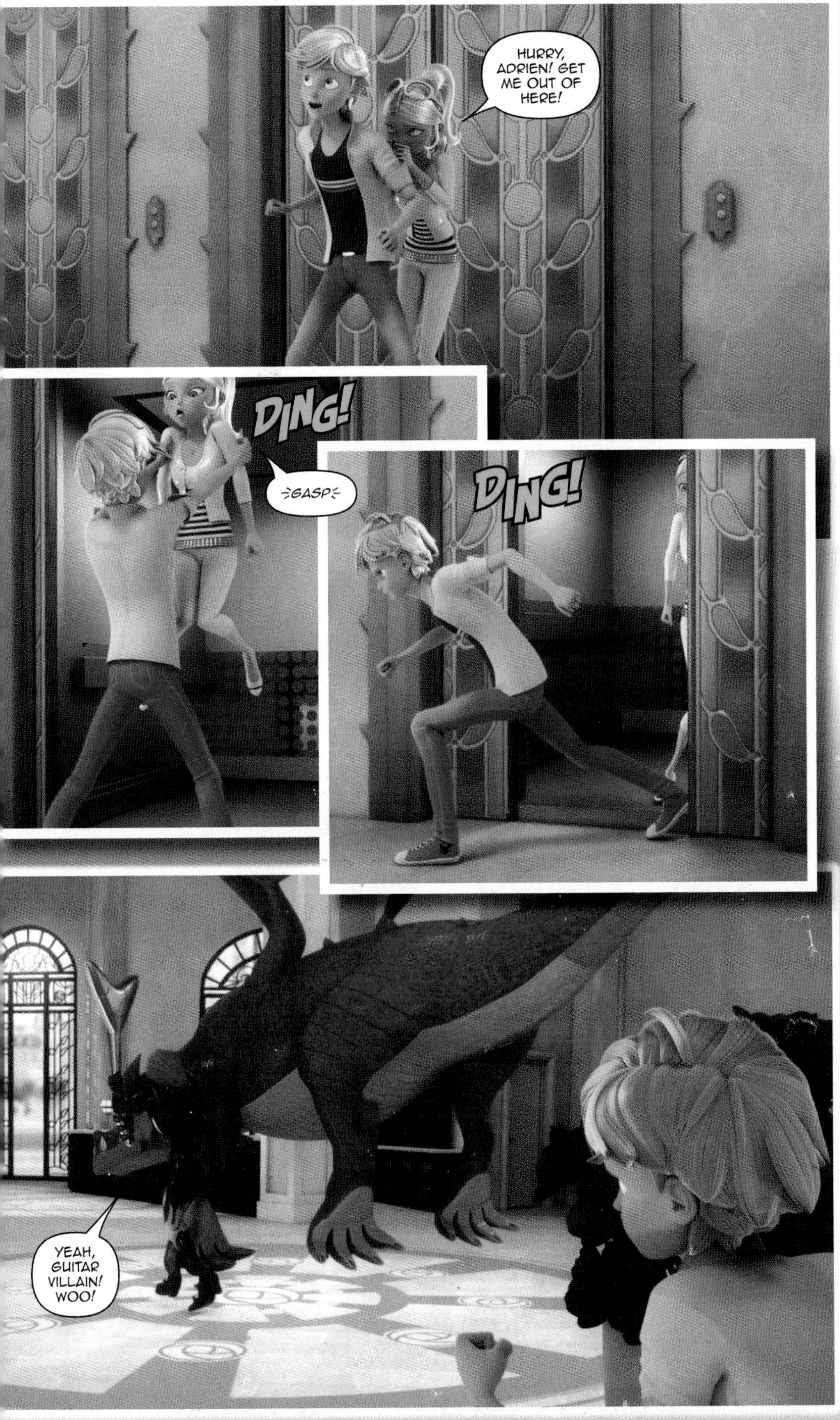
HURRY, ADRIEN! GET ME OUT OF HERE!
DING!
GASP
DING!
YEAH, GUITAR VILLAIN! WOO!

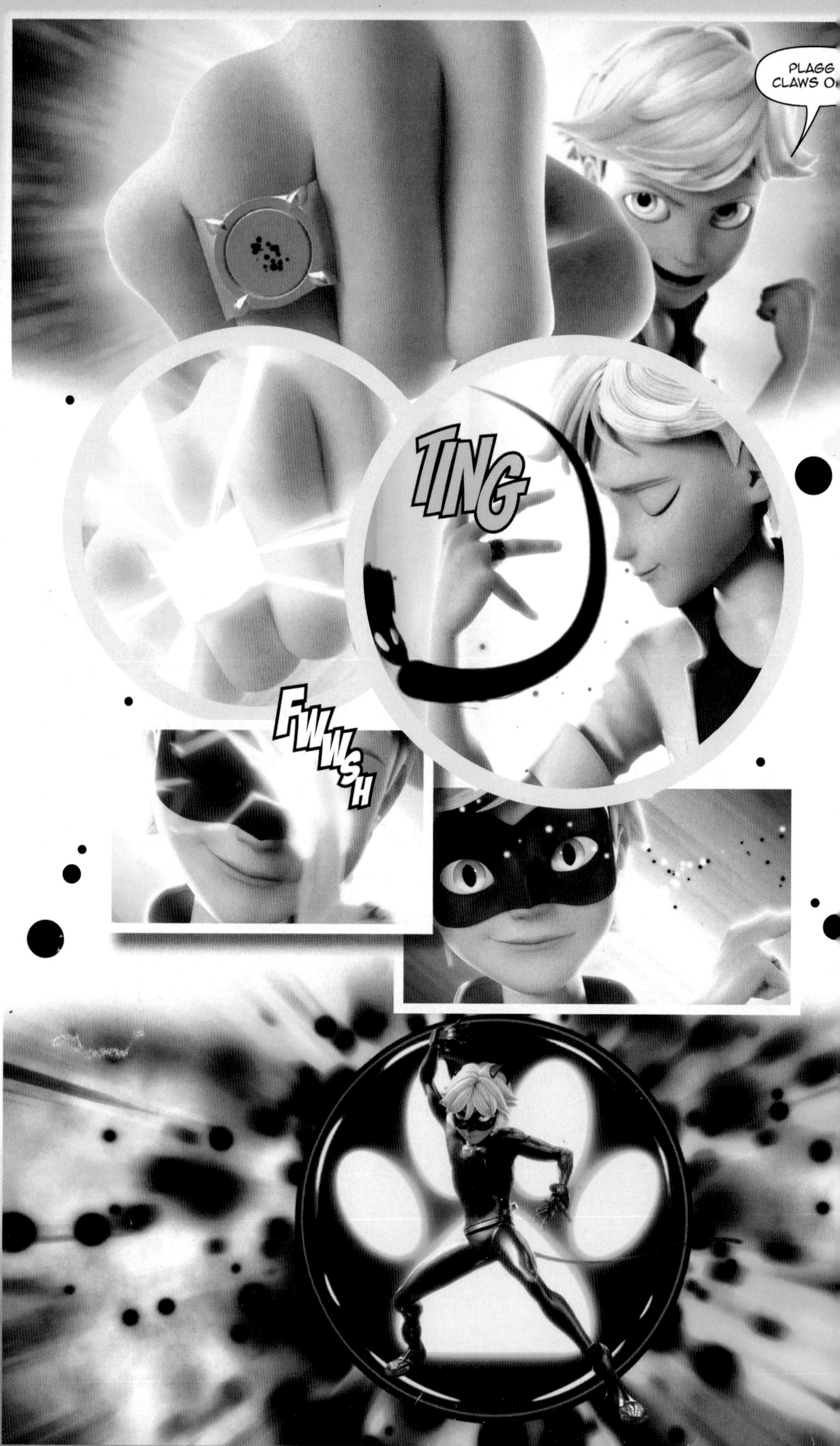
PLAGG
CLAWS O
TING
FWWSH

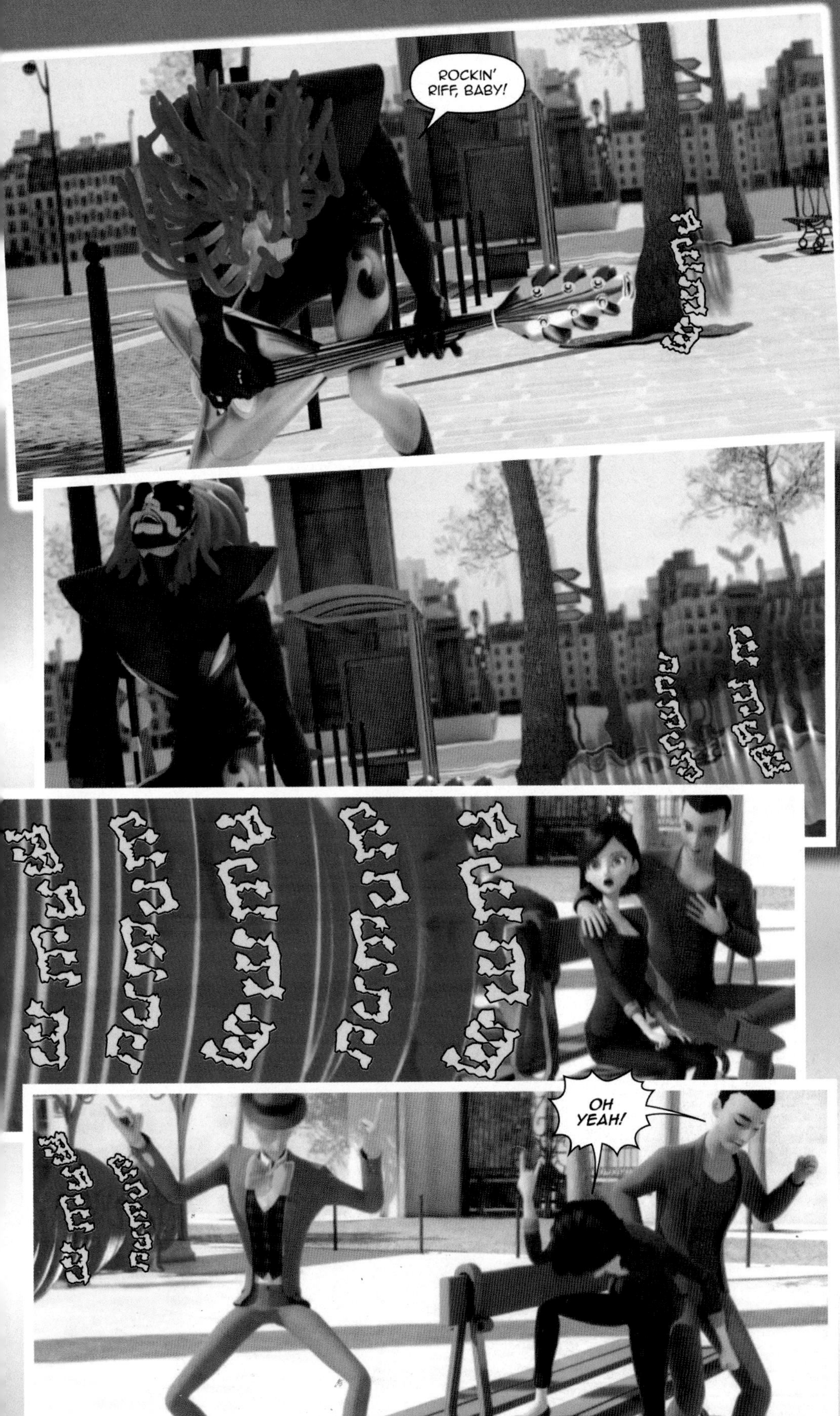
ROCKIN' RIFF, BABY!
OH YEAH!

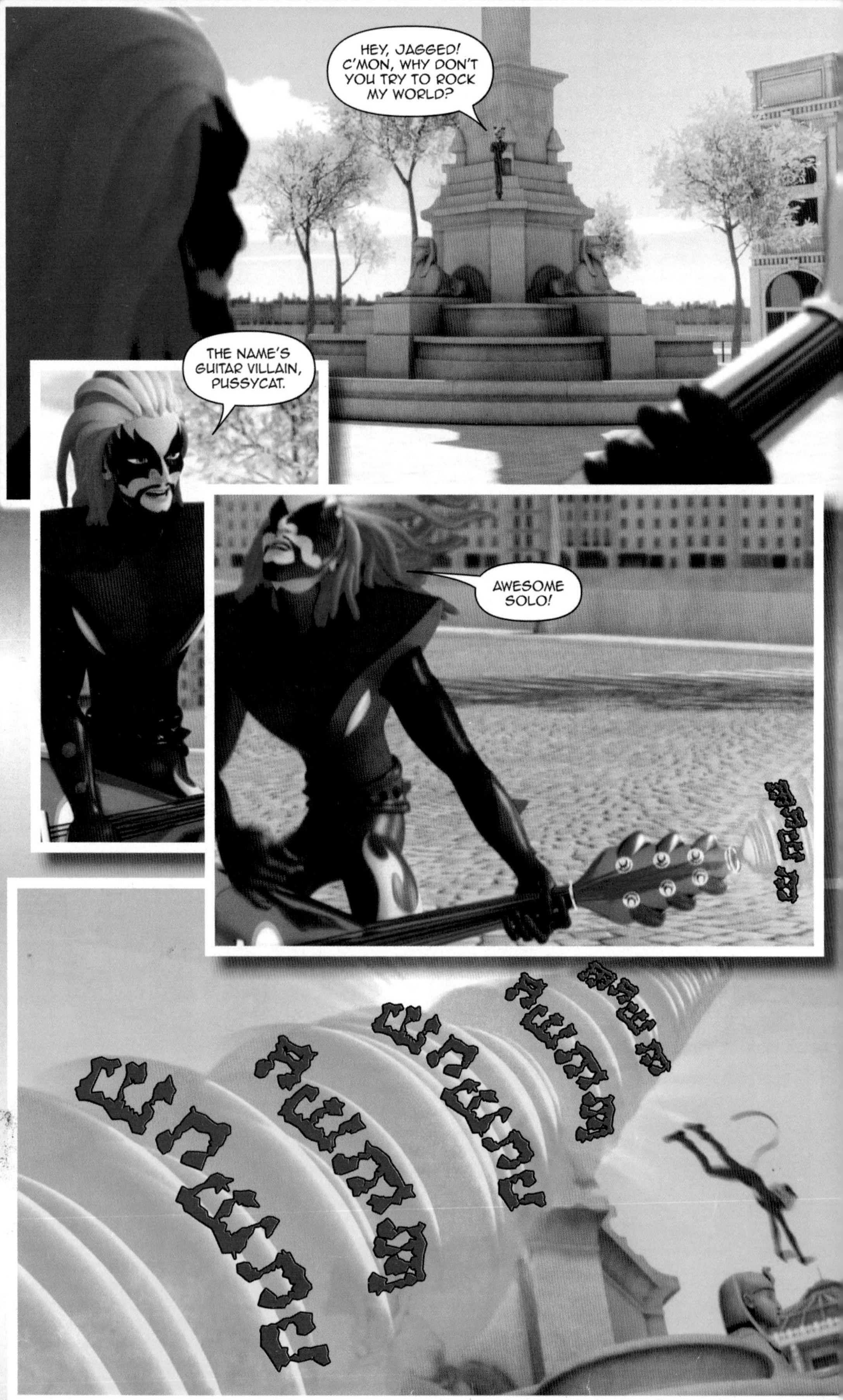
HEY, JAGGED! C'MON, WHY DON'T YOU TRY TO ROCK MY WORLD?
THE NAME'S GUITAR VILLAIN, PUSSYCAT.
AWESOME SOLO!

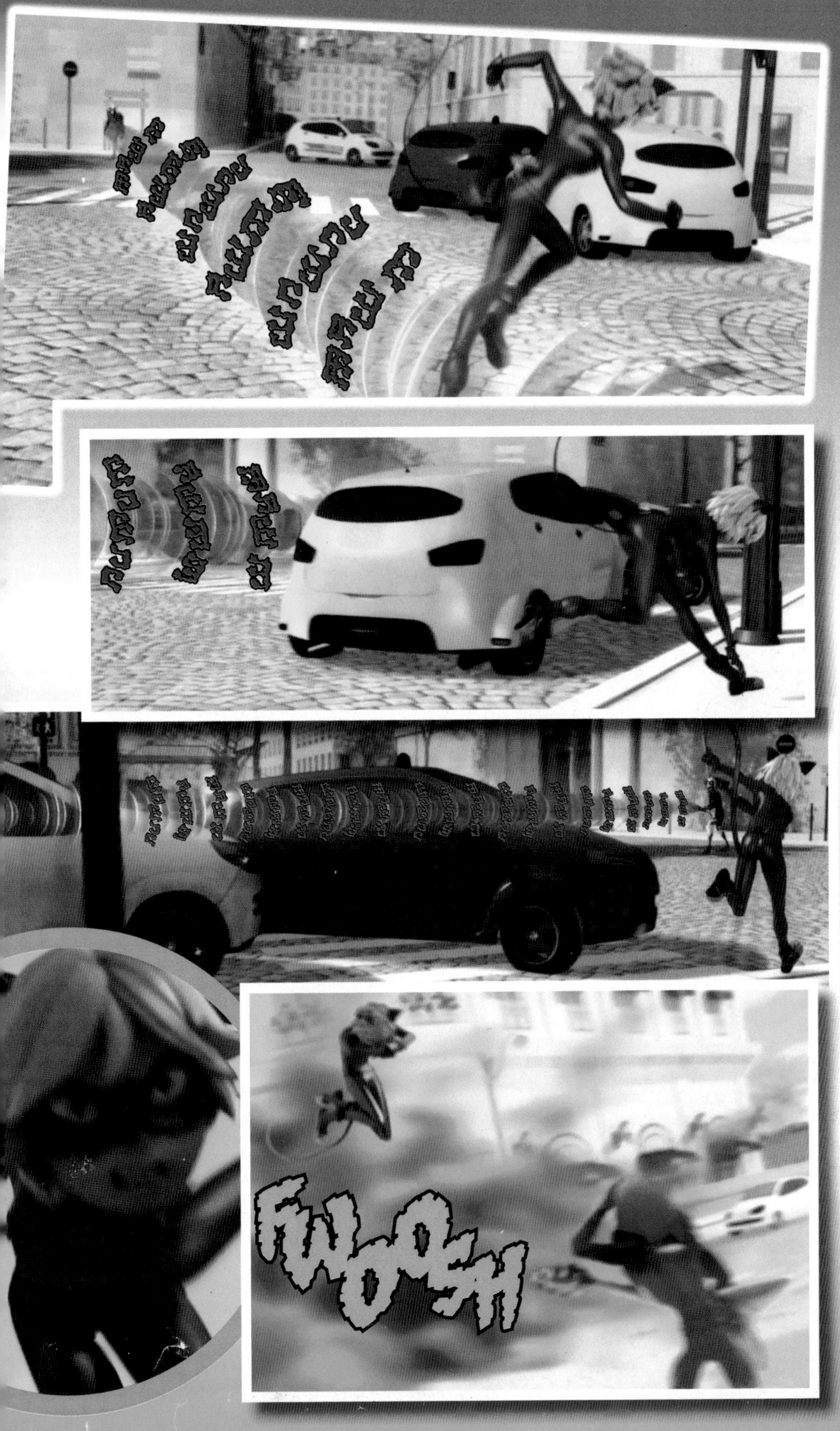
FWOOSH

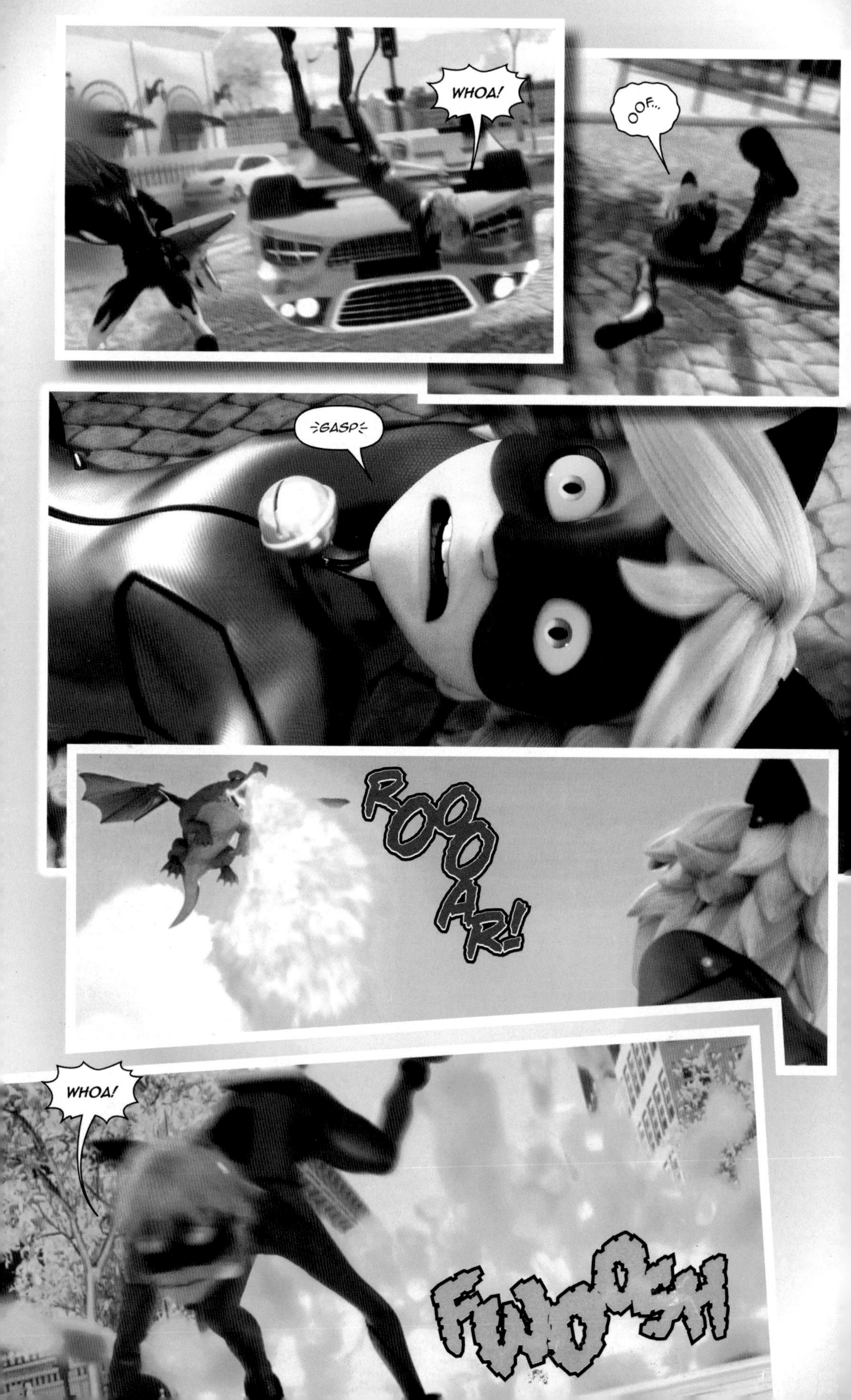
WHOA!
OOF...
GASP
ROOOAR!
WHOA!
FWOOSH

AWESOME SOLO!
BLAM
WELCOME TO MY FAN CLUB, BABY!
BOOM
UGH...

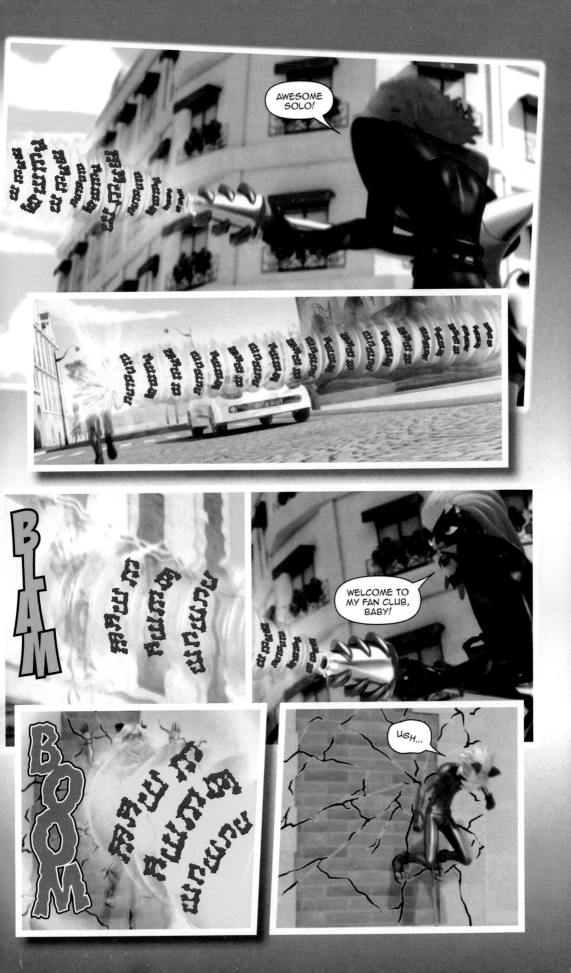

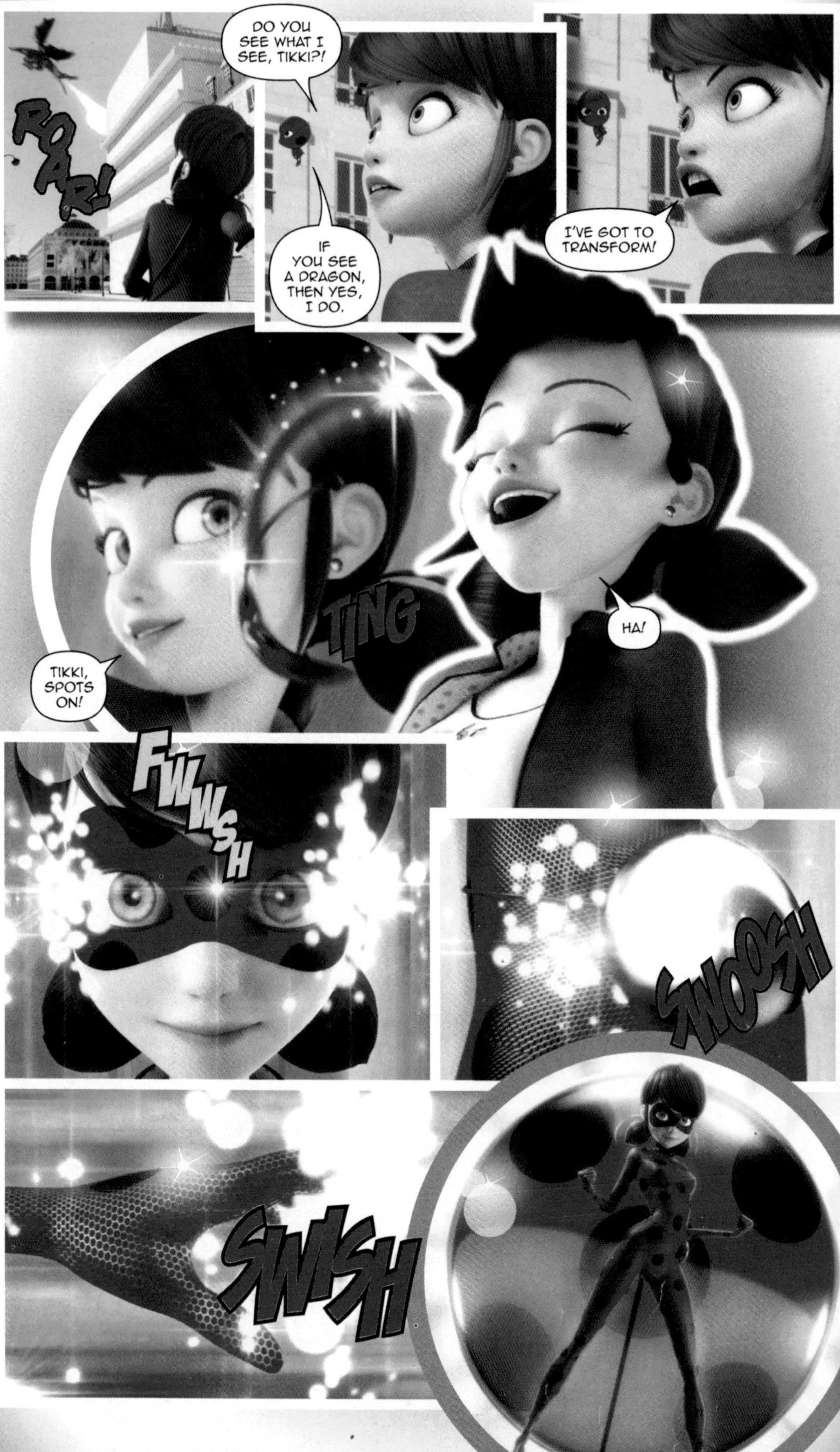
ROAR!
DO YOU SEE WHAT I SEE, TIKKI?!
IF YOU SEE A DRAGON, THEN YES, I DO.
I'VE GOT TO TRANSFORM!
TIKKI, SPOTS ON!
TING
HA!
FWWSH
SWOOSH
SWISH

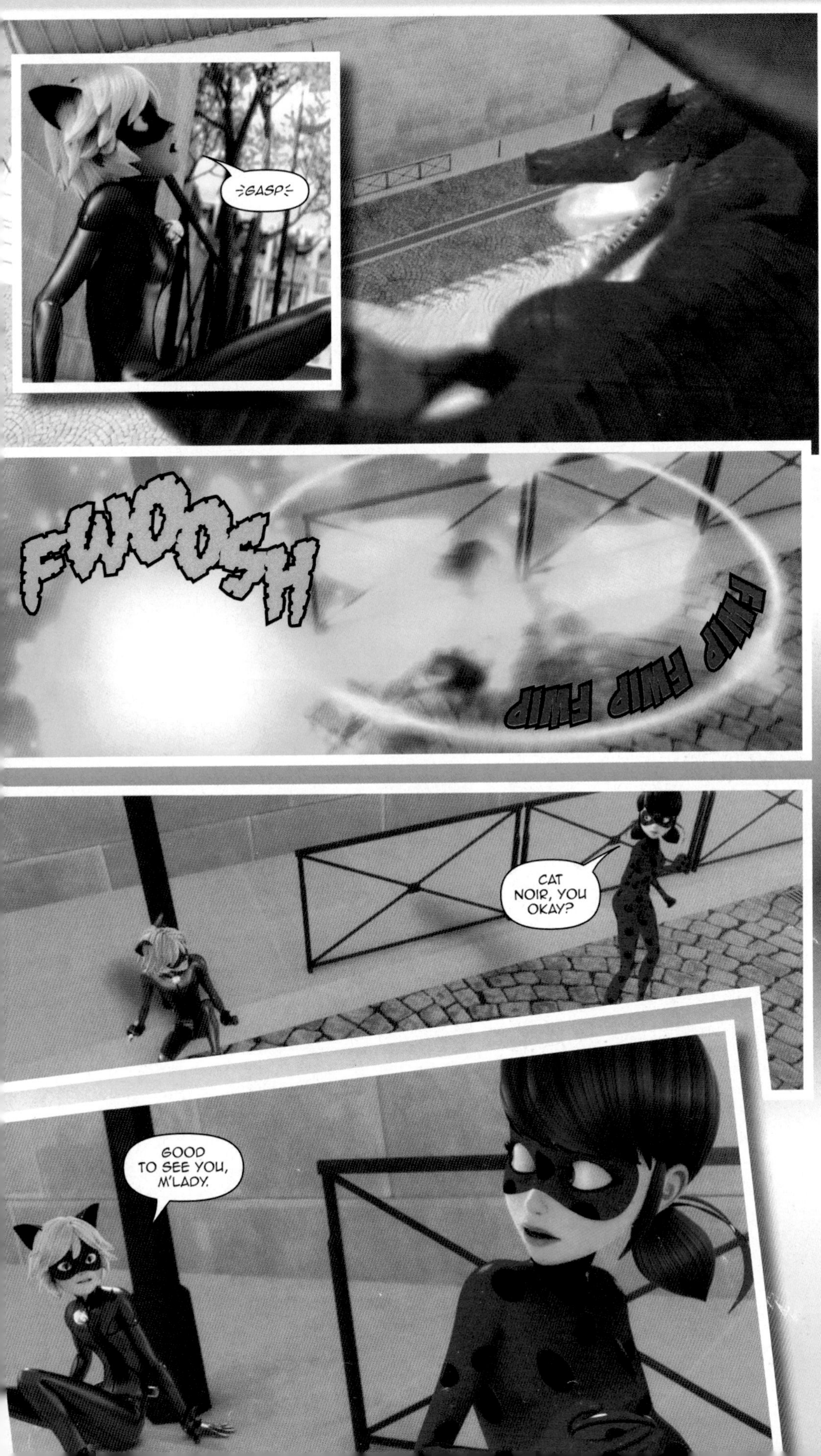

GASP
FWOOSH
FWIP FWIP FWIP
CAT NOIR, YOU OKAY?
GOOD TO SEE YOU, M'LADY.

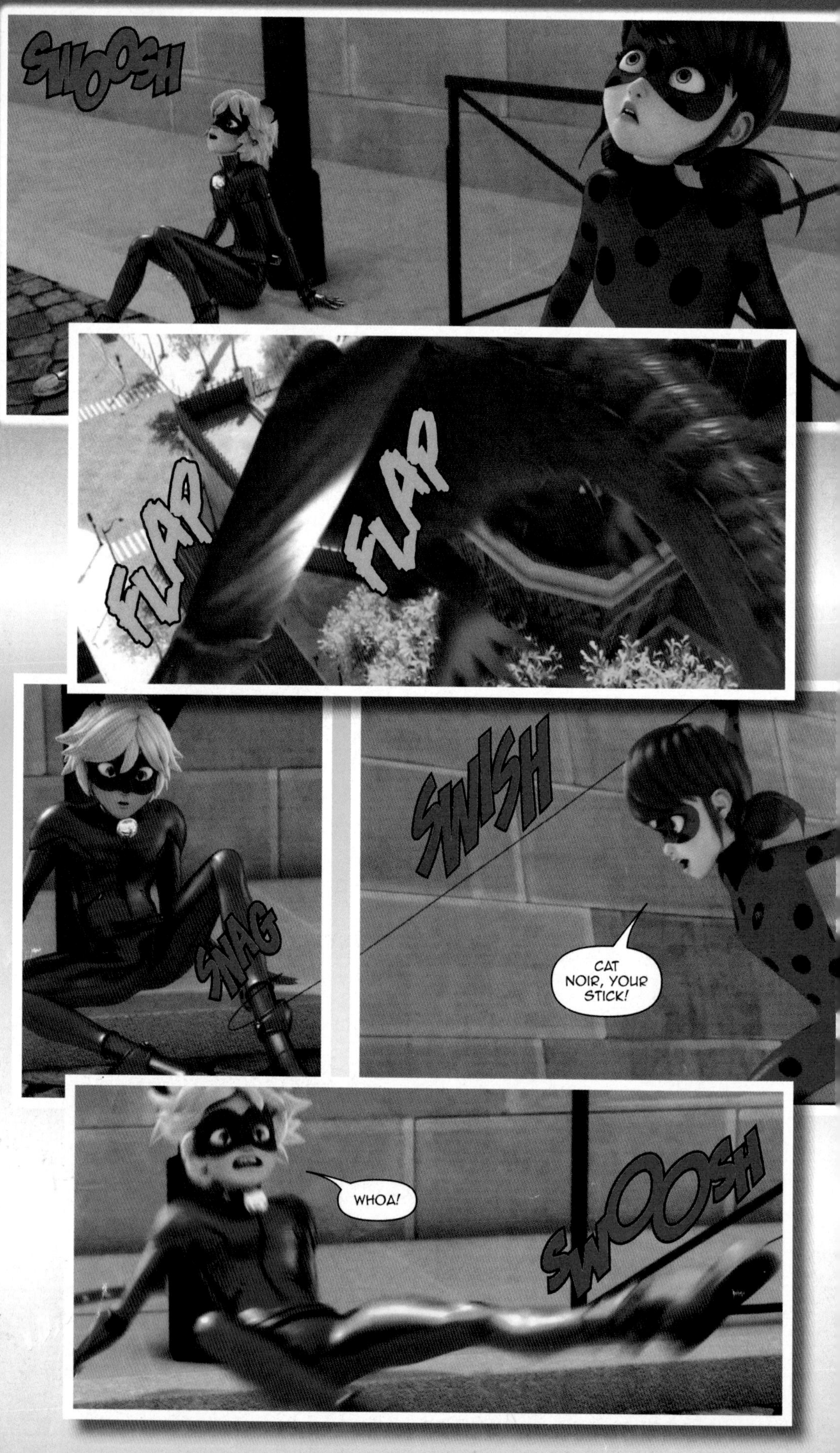
SWOOSH
FLAP
FLAP
SNAG
SWISH
CAT NOIR, YOUR STICK!
WHOA!
SWOOSH

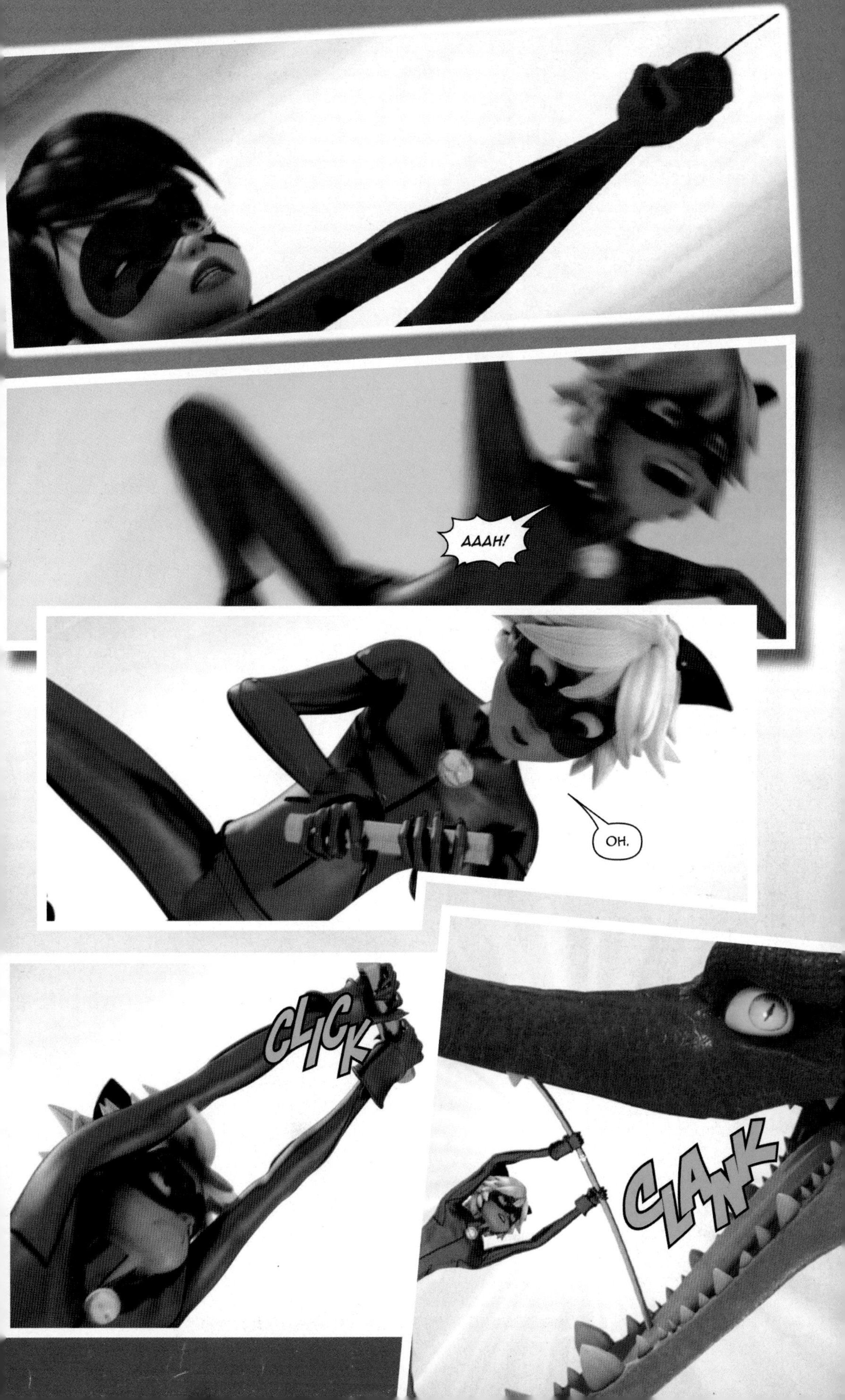
AAAH!
OH.
CLICK
CLANK

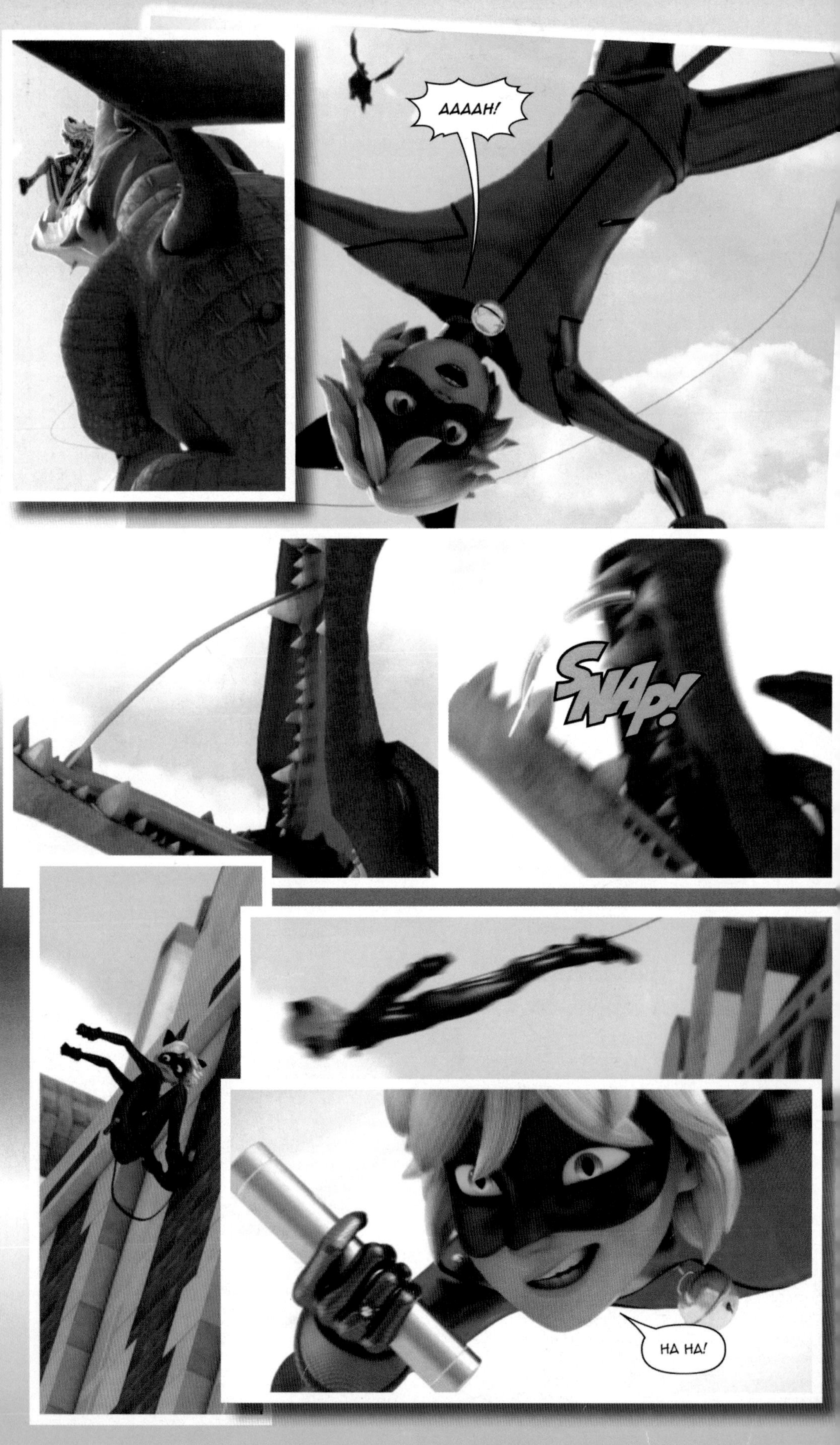
AAAAH!
SNAP!
HA HA!

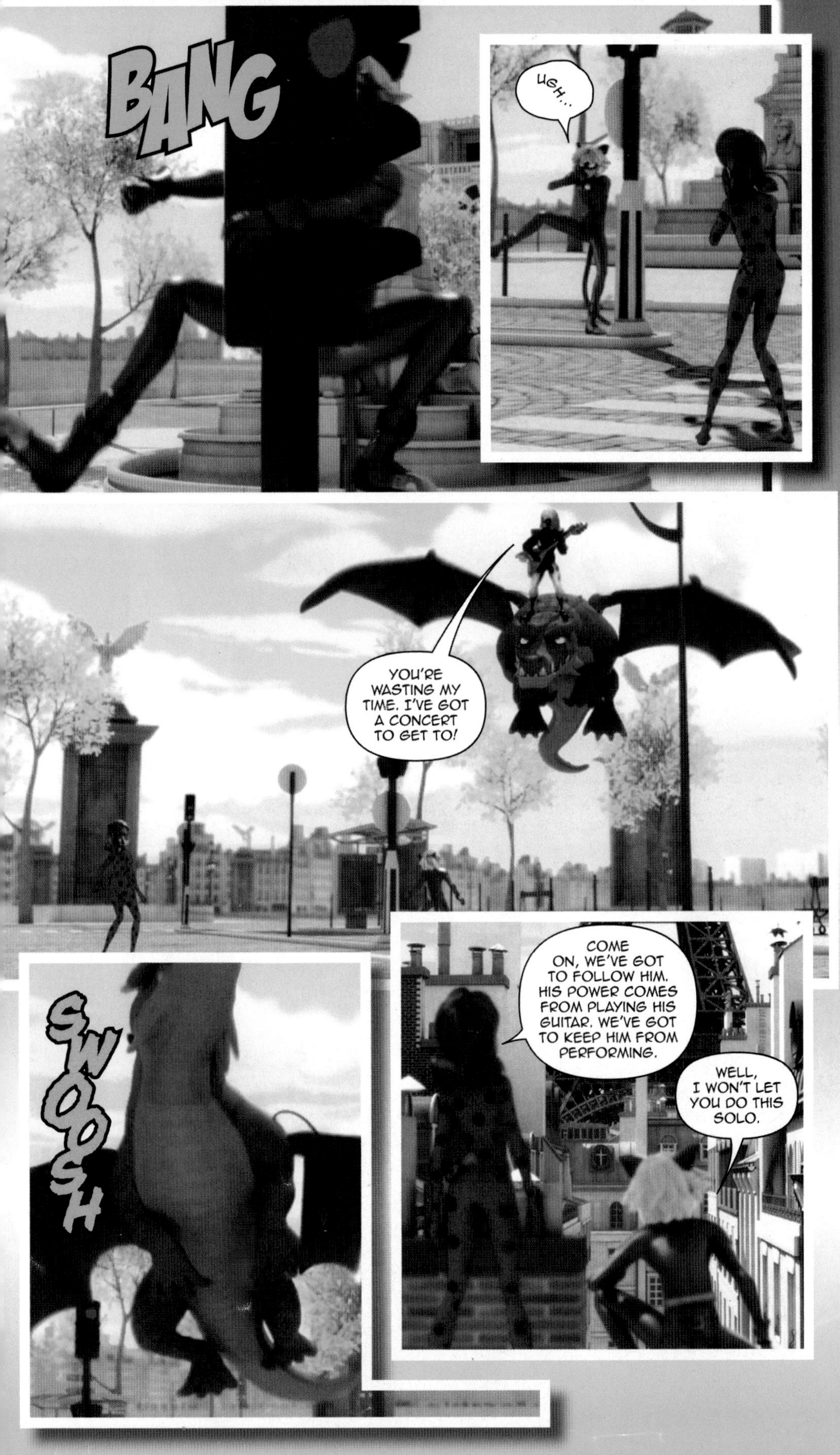
BANG
UGH...
YOU'RE WASTING MY TIME. I'VE GOT A CONCERT TO GET TO!
SWOOSH
COME ON, WE'VE GOT TO FOLLOW HIM. HIS POWER COMES FROM PLAYING HIS GUITAR. WE'VE GOT TO KEEP HIM FROM PERFORMING.
WELL, I WON'T LET YOU DO THIS SOLO.

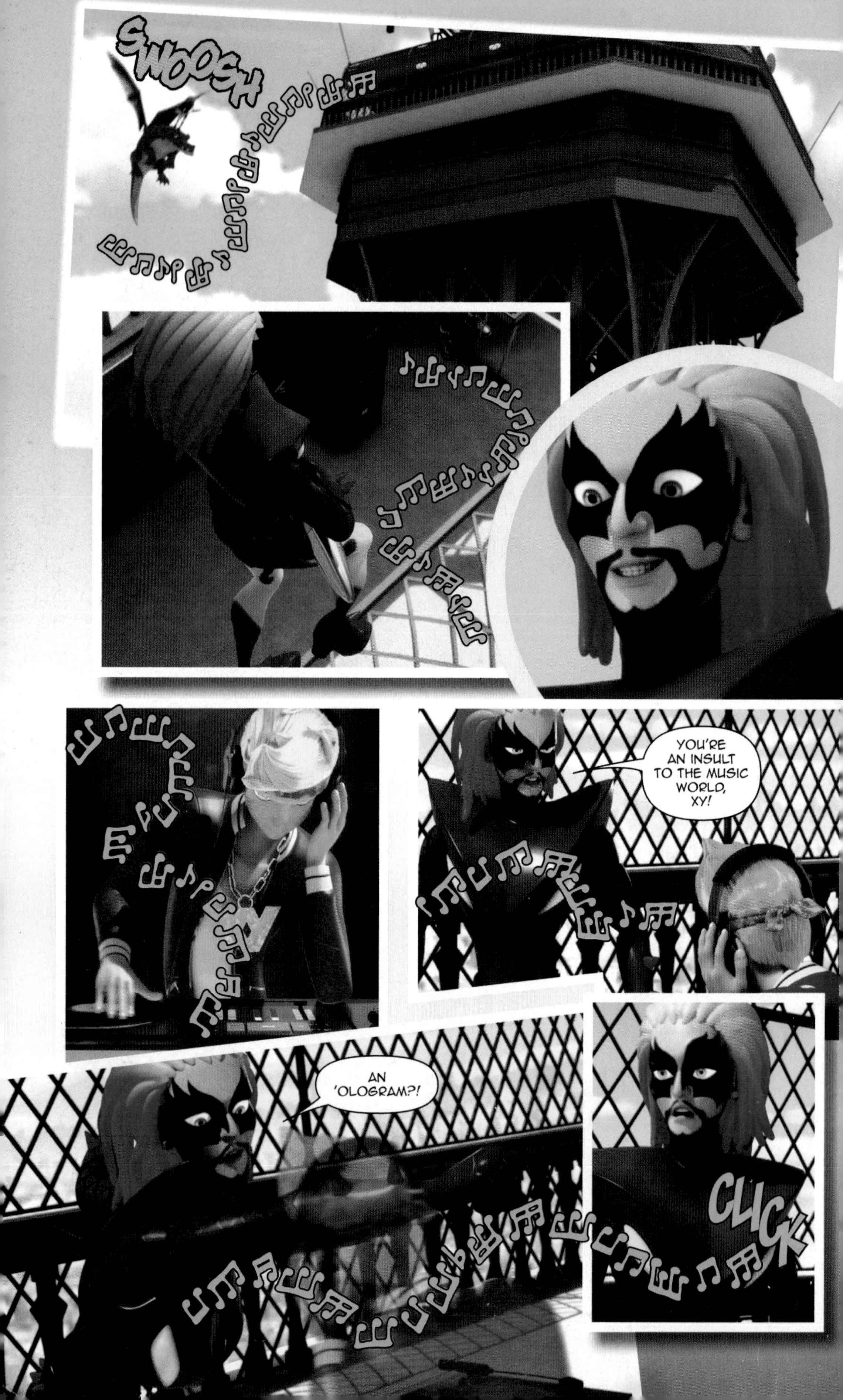
SWOOSH
YOU'RE AN INSULT TO THE MUSIC WORLD, XY!
AN 'OLOGRAM?!
CLICK

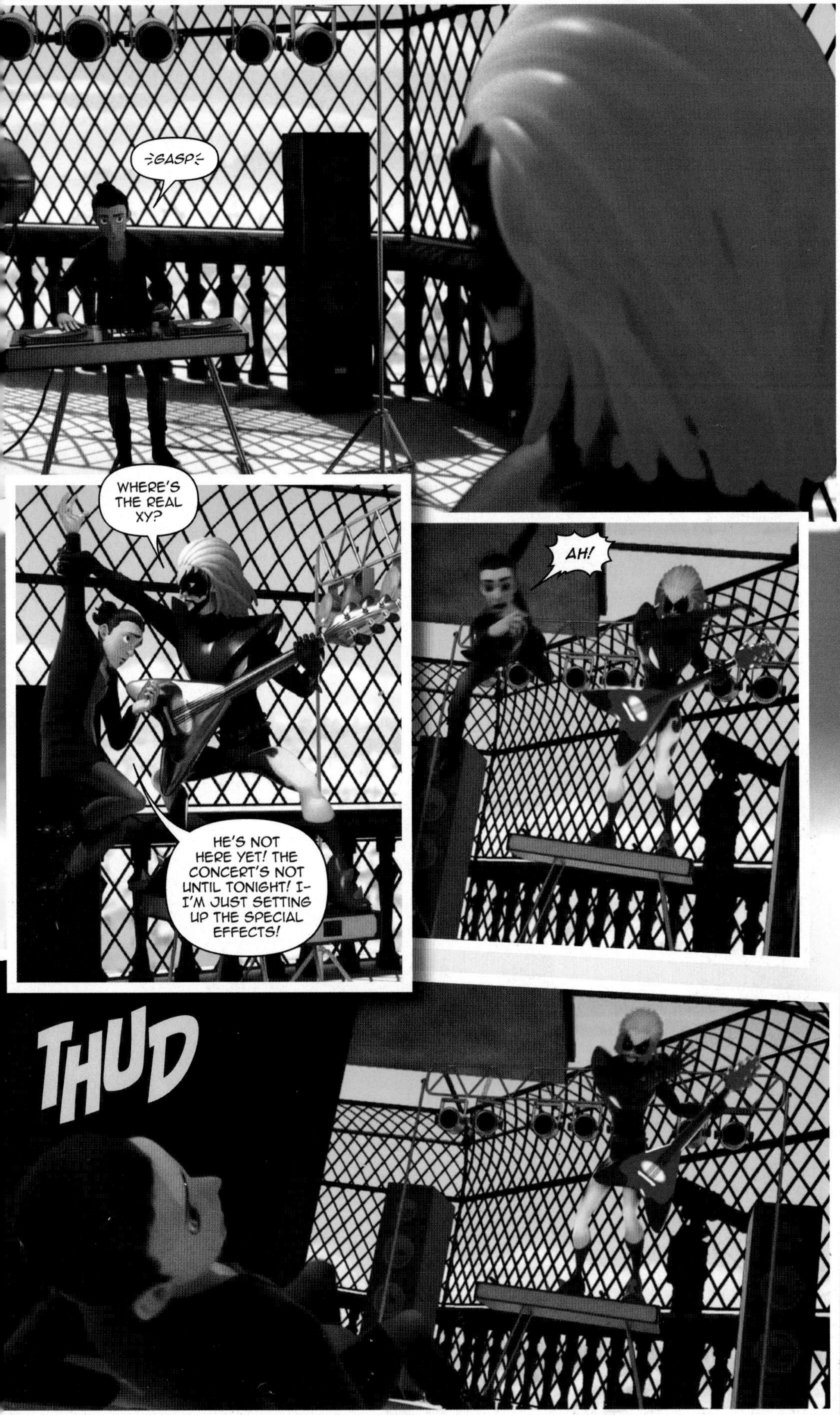

-GASP-
WHERE'S THE REAL XY?
HE'S NOT HERE YET! THE CONCERT'S NOT UNTIL TONIGHT! I-I'M JUST SETTING UP THE SPECIAL EFFECTS!
AH!
THUD

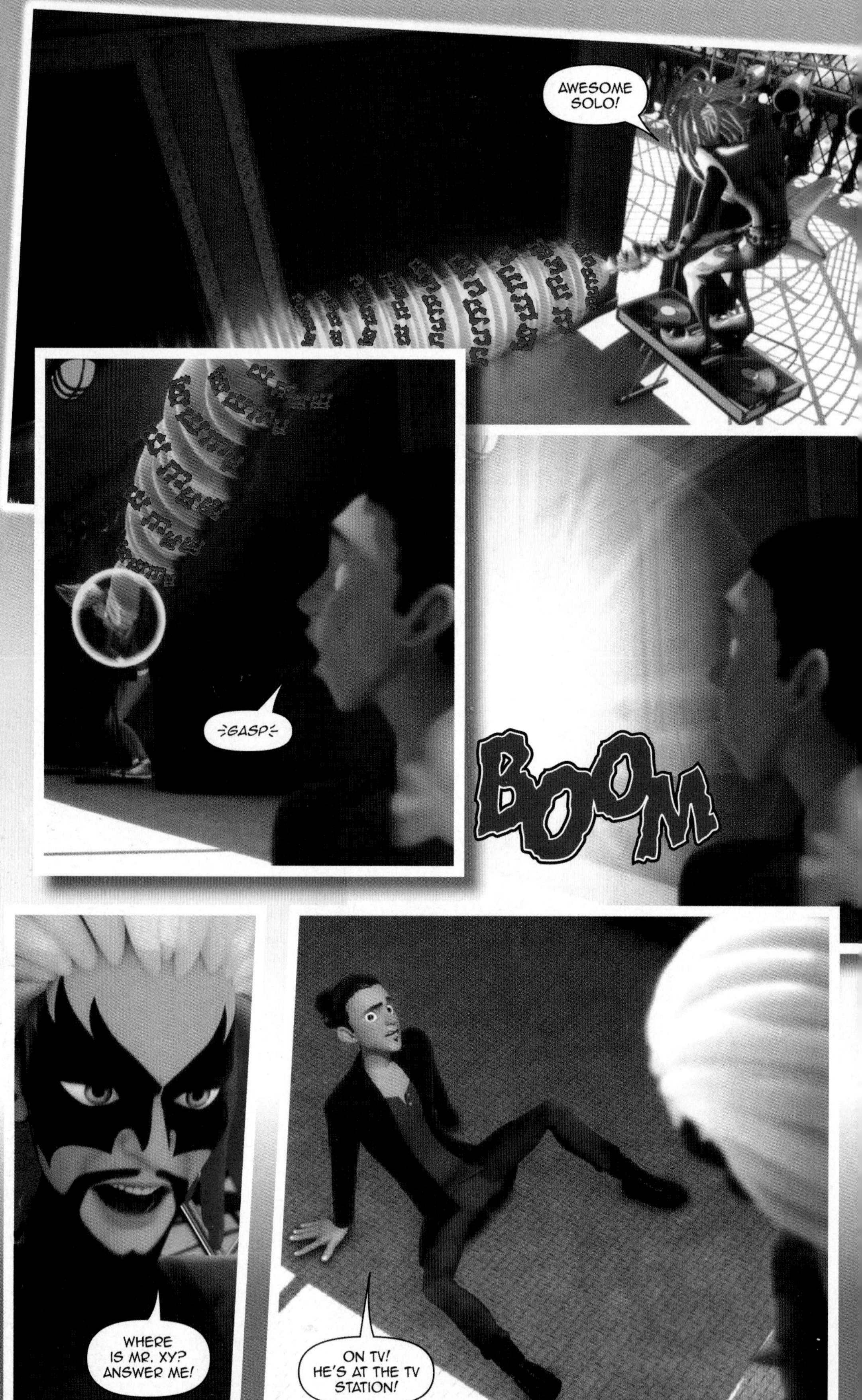
AWESOME SOLO!
GASP
BOOM
WHERE IS MR. XY? ANSWER ME!
ON TV! HE'S AT THE TV STATION!

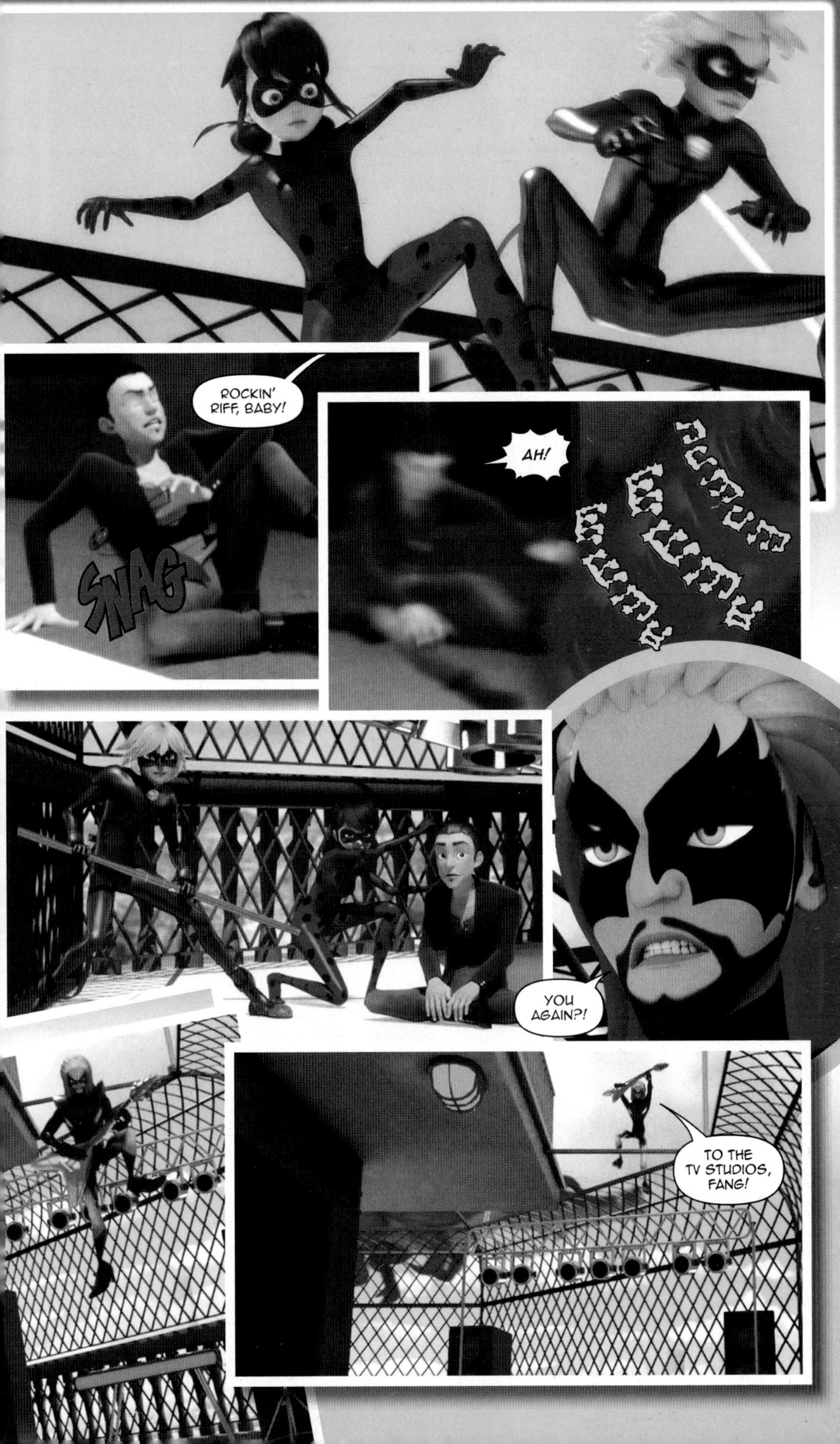
ROCKIN' RIFF, BABY!
SNAG
AH!
YOU AGAIN?!
TO THE TV STUDIOS, FANG!

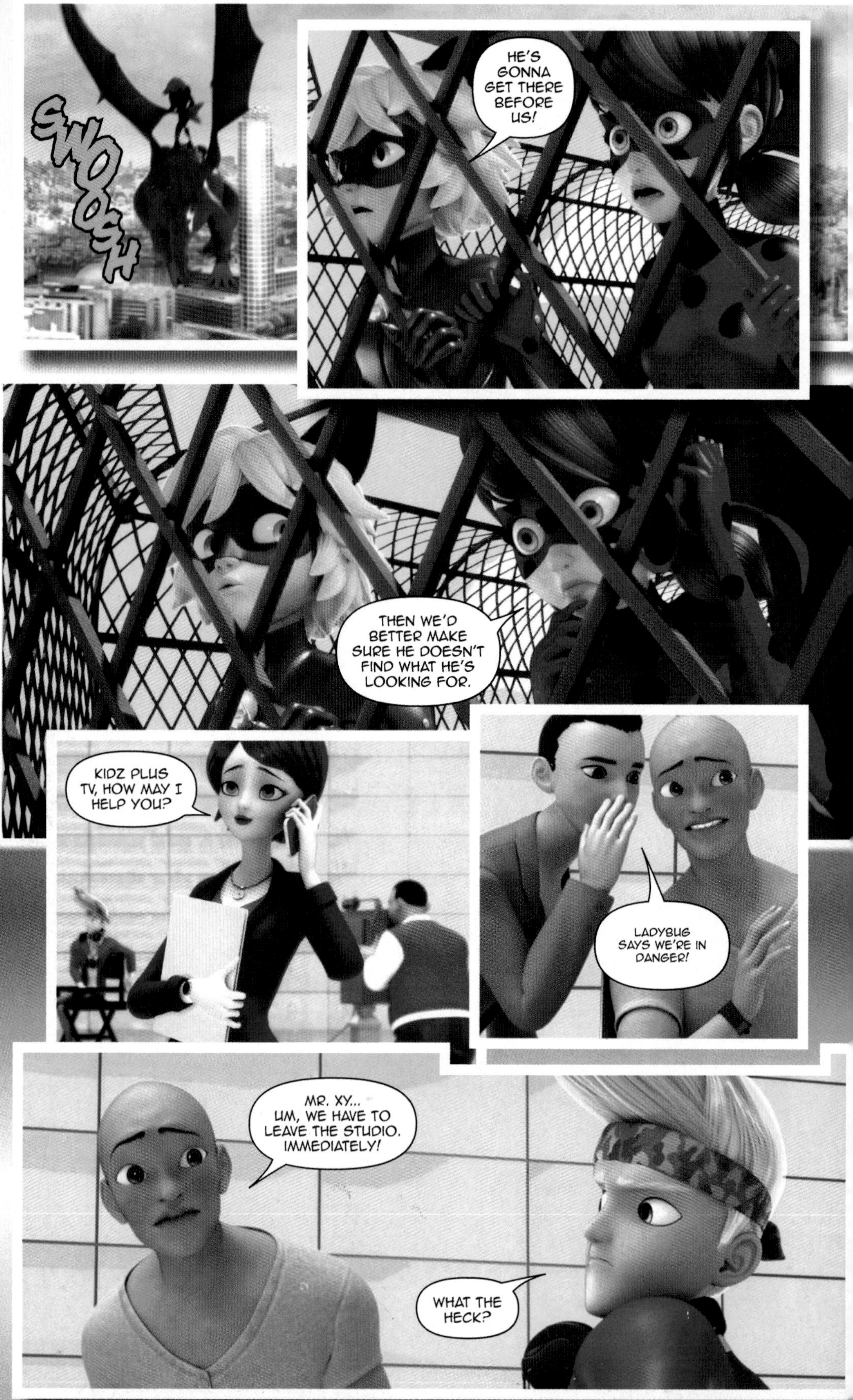
SWOOSH
HE'S GONNA GET THERE BEFORE US!
THEN WE'D BETTER MAKE SURE HE DOESN'T FIND WHAT HE'S LOOKING FOR.
KIDZ PLUS TV, HOW MAY I HELP YOU?
LADYBUG SAYS WE'RE IN DANGER!
MR. XY... UM, WE HAVE TO LEAVE THE STUDIO. IMMEDIATELY!
WHAT THE HECK?

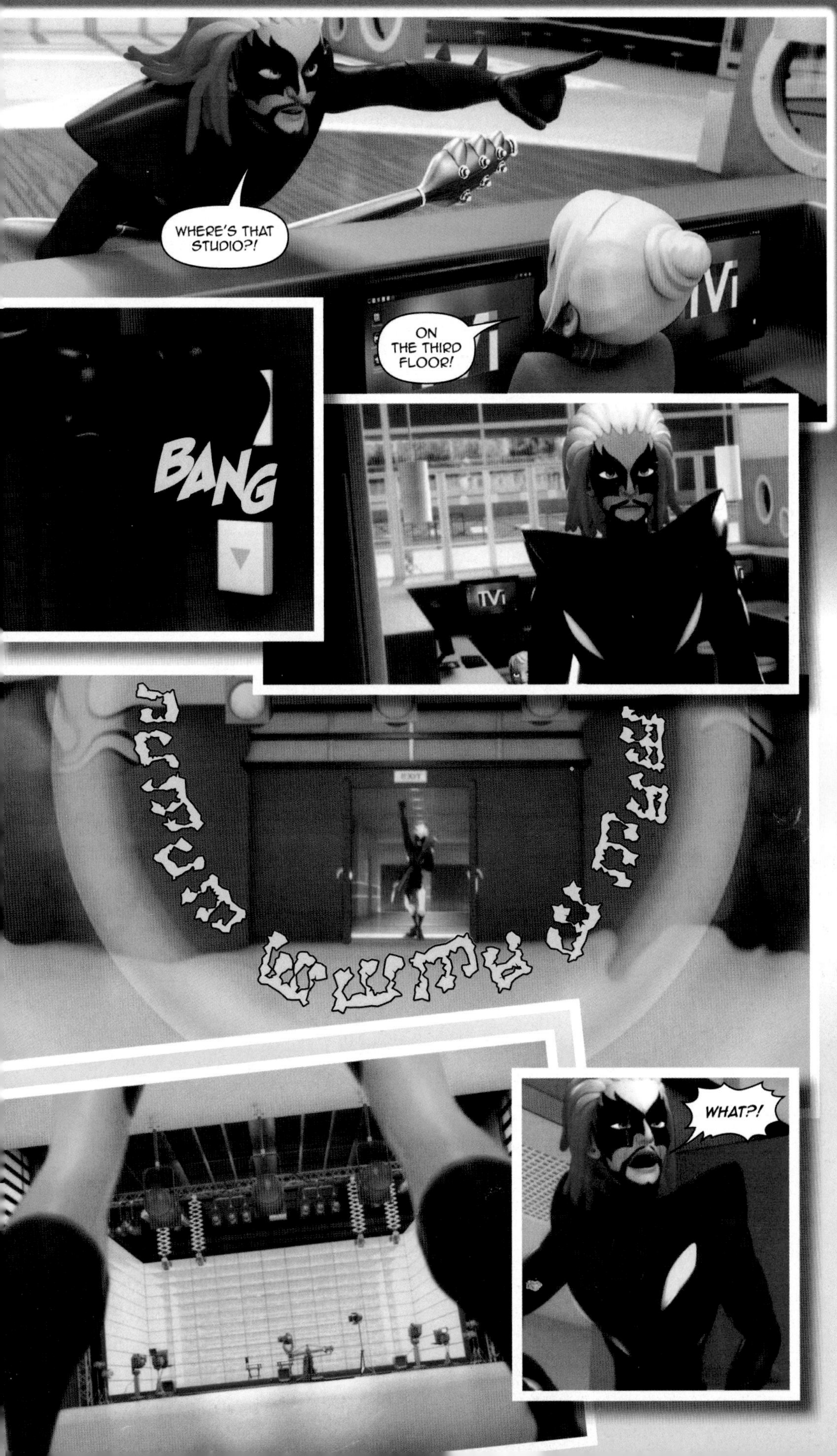
WHERE'S THAT STUDIO?!
ON THE THIRD FLOOR!
BANG
WHAT?!

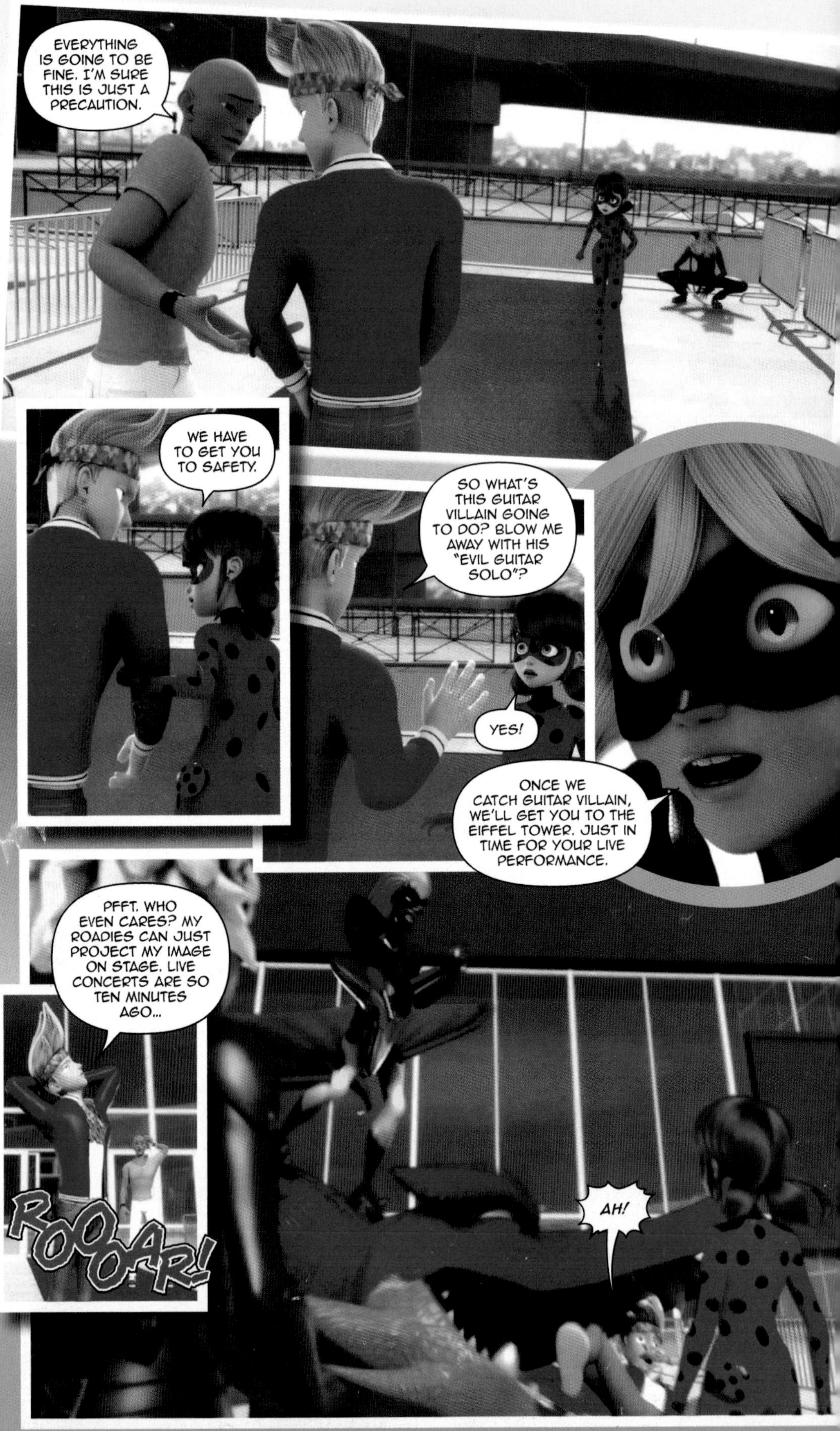
EVERYTHING IS GOING TO BE FINE. I'M SURE THIS IS JUST A PRECAUTION.
WE HAVE TO GET YOU TO SAFETY.
SO WHAT'S THIS GUITAR VILLAIN GOING TO DO? BLOW ME AWAY WITH HIS "EVIL GUITAR SOLO"?
YES!
ONCE WE CATCH GUITAR VILLAIN, WE'LL GET YOU TO THE EIFFEL TOWER. JUST IN TIME FOR YOUR LIVE PERFORMANCE.
PFFT. WHO EVEN CARES? MY ROADIES CAN JUST PROJECT MY IMAGE ON STAGE. LIVE CONCERTS ARE SO TEN MINUTES AGO...
ROOOAR!
AH!

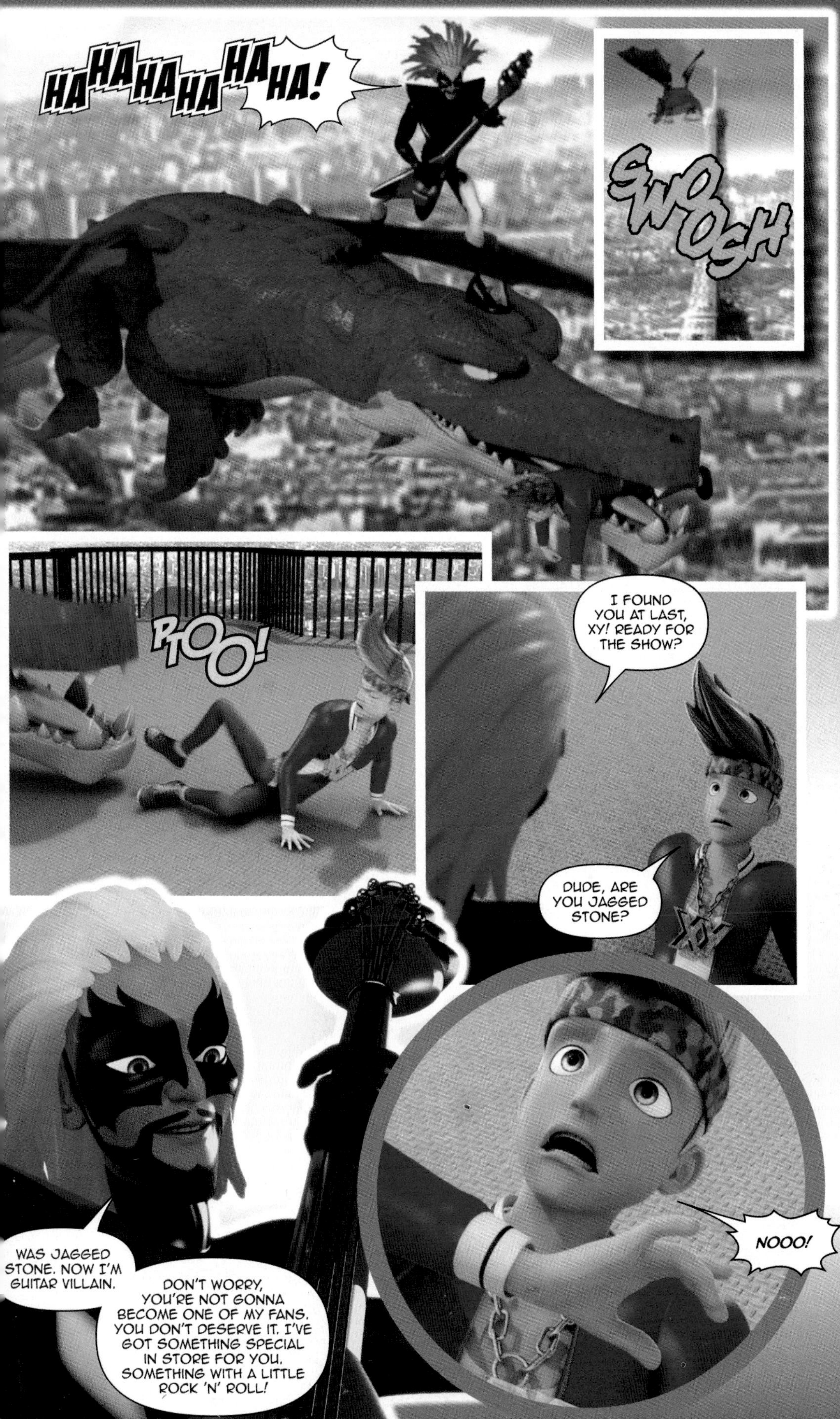
HAHAHAHAHAHAHA!
SWOOSH
PTOO!
I FOUND YOU AT LAST, XY! READY FOR THE SHOW?
DUDE, ARE YOU JAGGED STONE?
WAS JAGGED STONE. NOW I'M GUITAR VILLAIN.
DON'T WORRY, YOU'RE NOT GONNA BECOME ONE OF MY FANS. YOU DON'T DESERVE IT. I'VE GOT SOMETHING SPECIAL IN STORE FOR YOU. SOMETHING WITH A LITTLE ROCK 'N' ROLL!
NOOO!

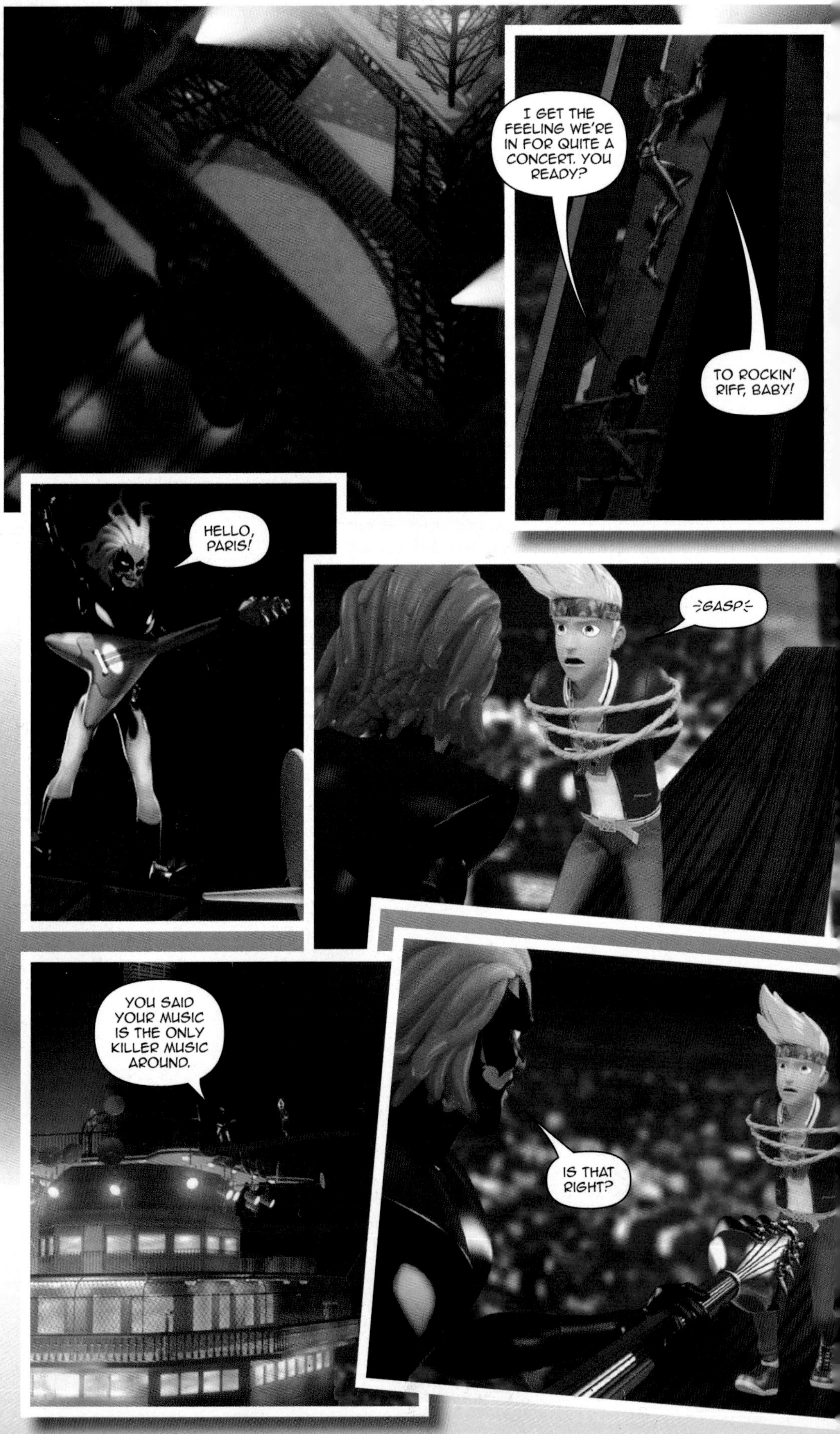
I GET THE FEELING WE'RE IN FOR QUITE A CONCERT. YOU READY?
TO ROCKIN' RIFF, BABY!
HELLO, PARIS!
GASP
YOU SAID YOUR MUSIC IS THE ONLY KILLER MUSIC AROUND.
IS THAT RIGHT?

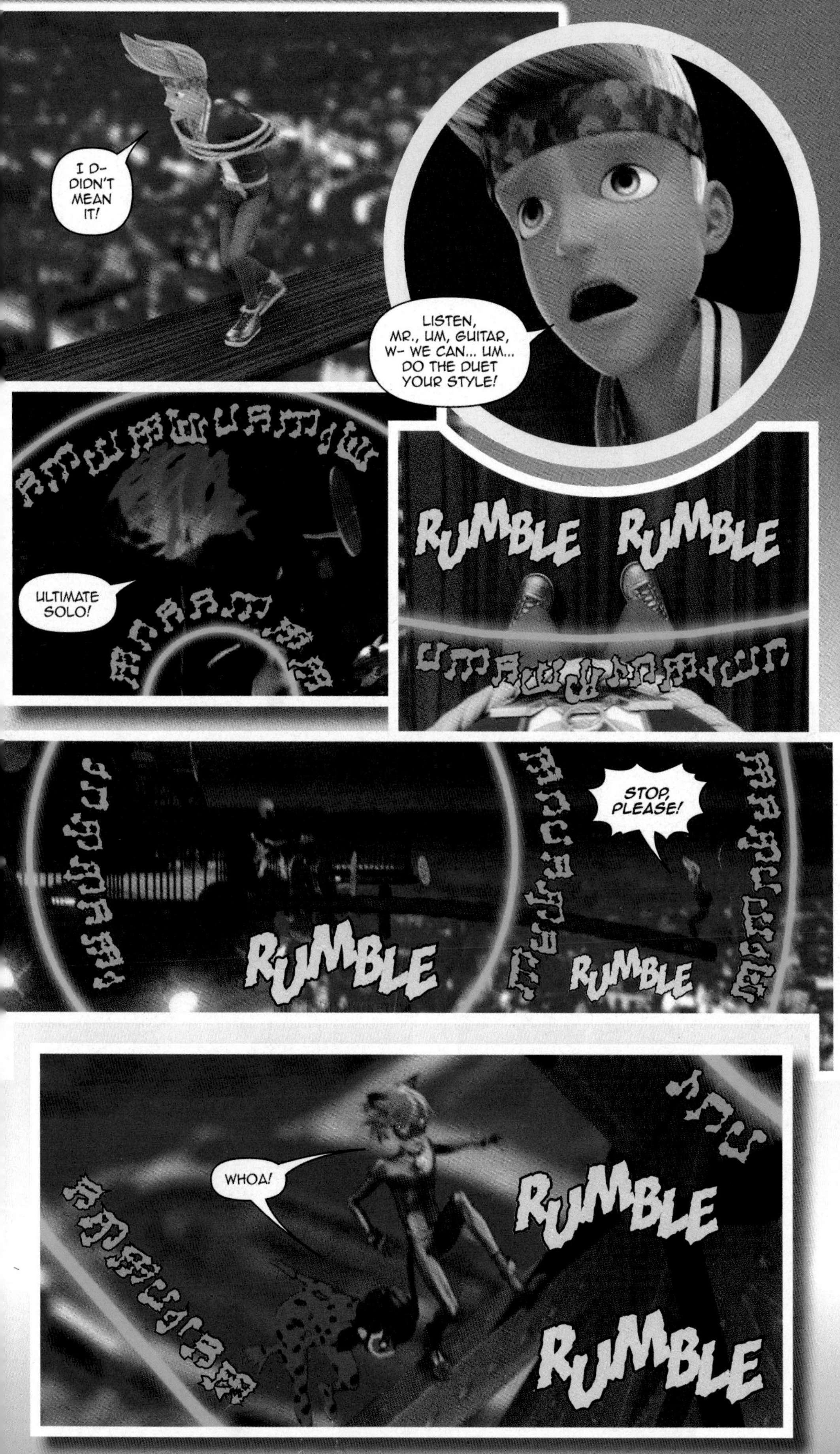
I D- DIDN'T MEAN IT!
LISTEN, MR., UM, GUITAR, W- WE CAN... UM... DO THE DUET YOUR STYLE!
ULTIMATE SOLO!
RUMBLE RUMBLE
RUMBLE
STOP, PLEASE!
RUMBLE
WHOA!
RUMBLE
RUMBLE

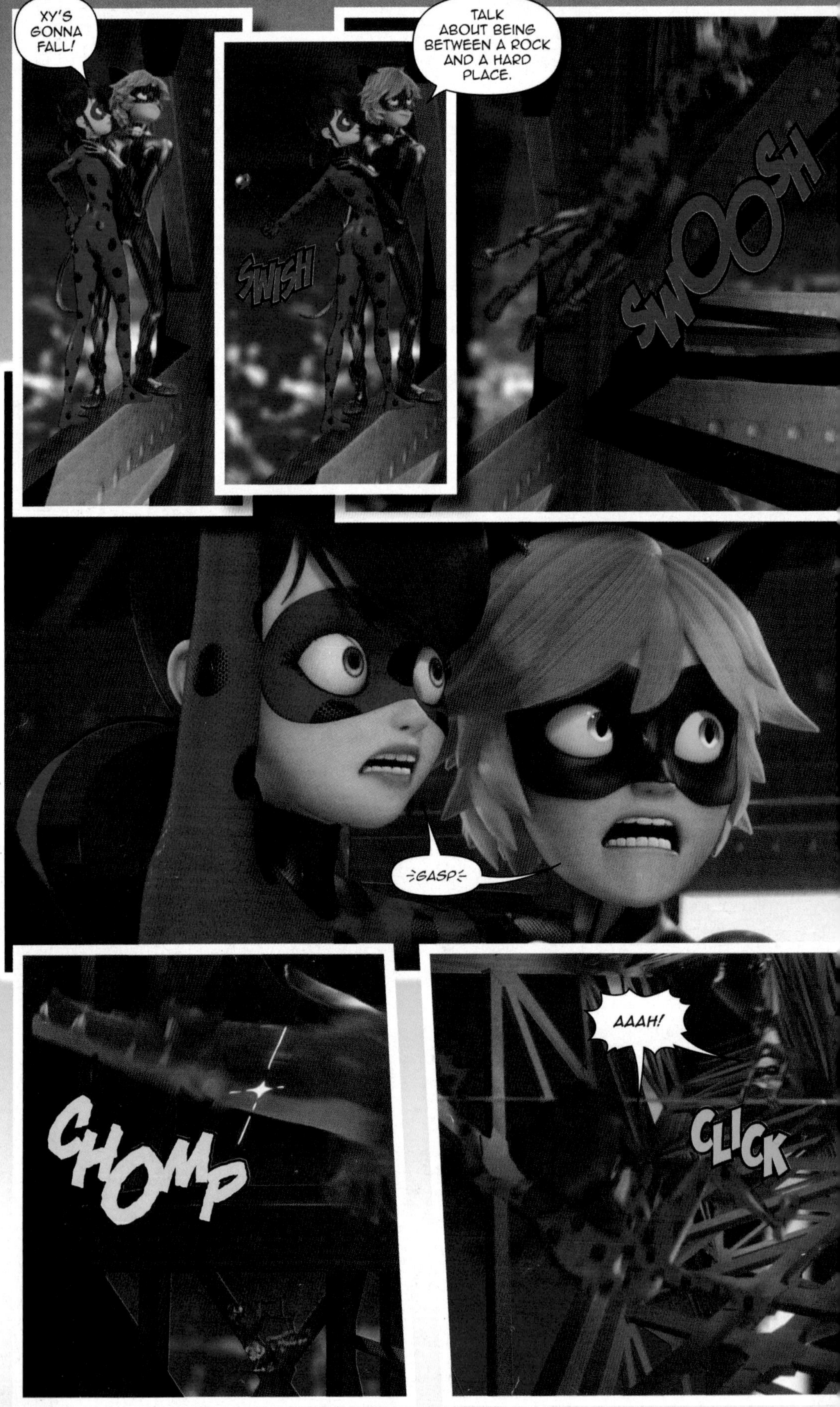
XY'S GONNA FALL!
TALK ABOUT BEING BETWEEN A ROCK AND A HARD PLACE.
SWISH
SWOOSH
GASP
CHOMP
AAAH!
CLICK

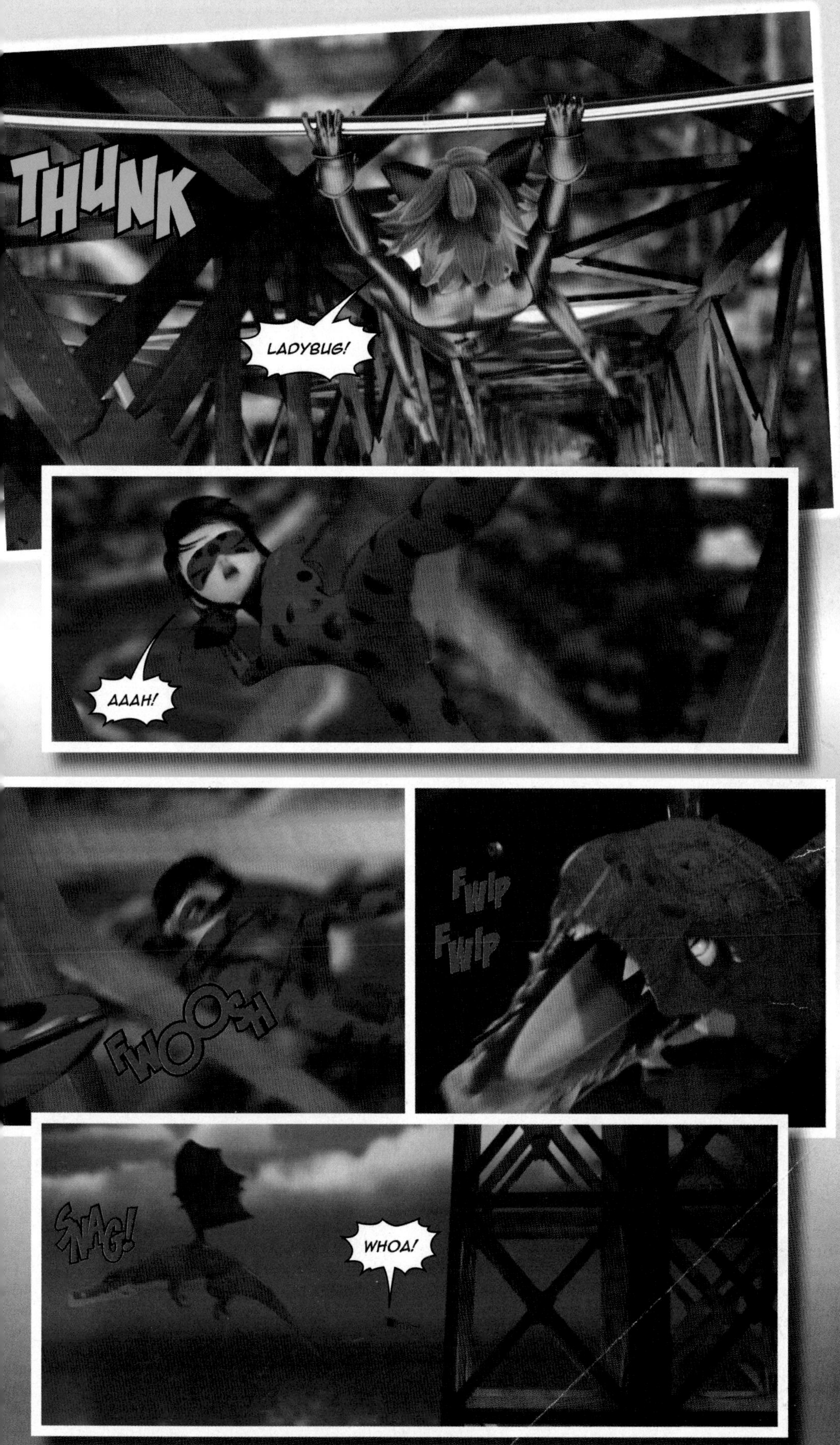
THUNK
LADYBUG!
AAAH!
FWOOSH
FWIP
FWIP
SNAG!
WHOA!

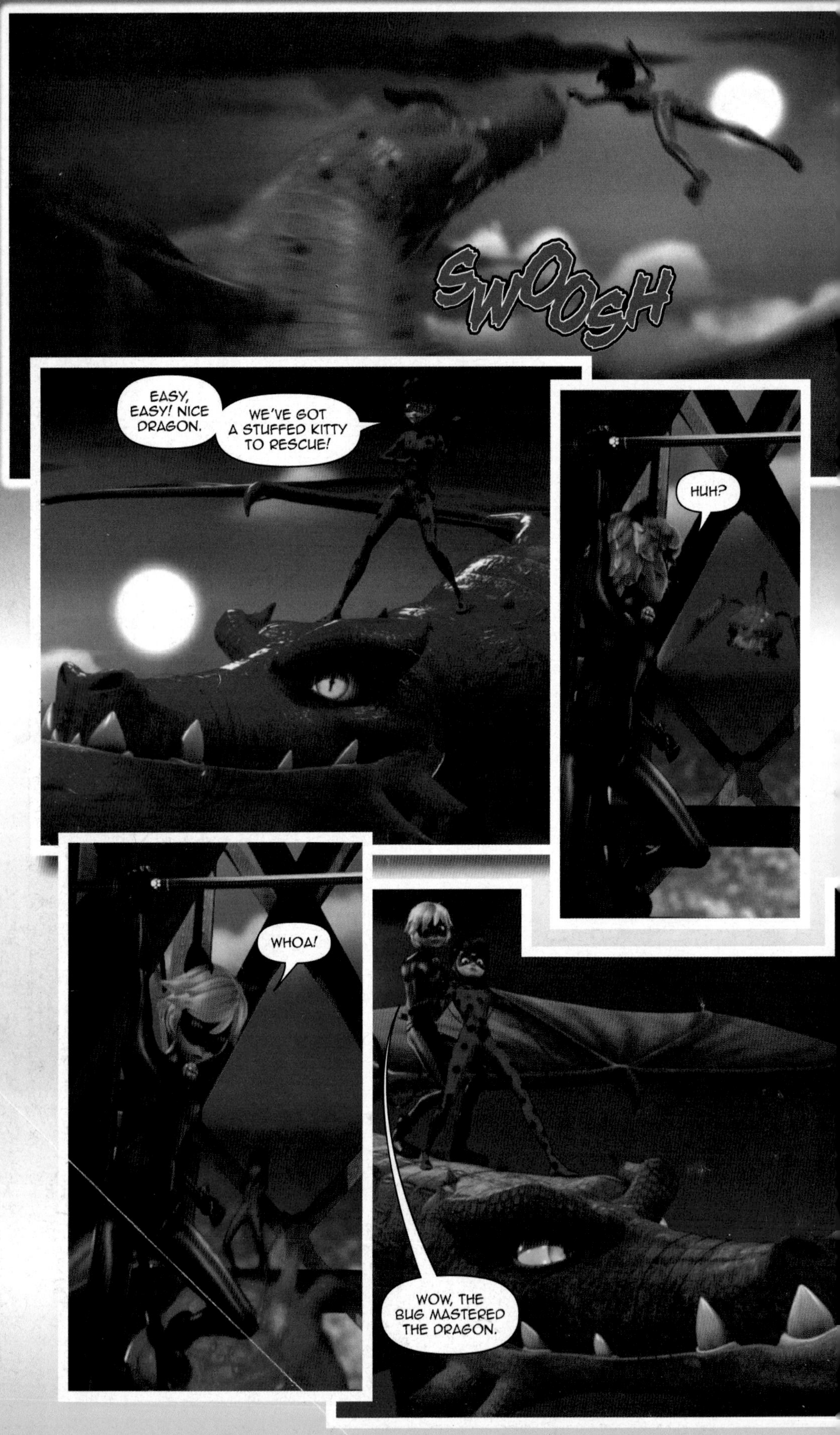
SWOOSH
EASY, EASY! NICE DRAGON.
WE'VE GOT A STUFFED KITTY TO RESCUE!
HUH?
WHOA!
WOW, THE BUG MASTERED THE DRAGON.

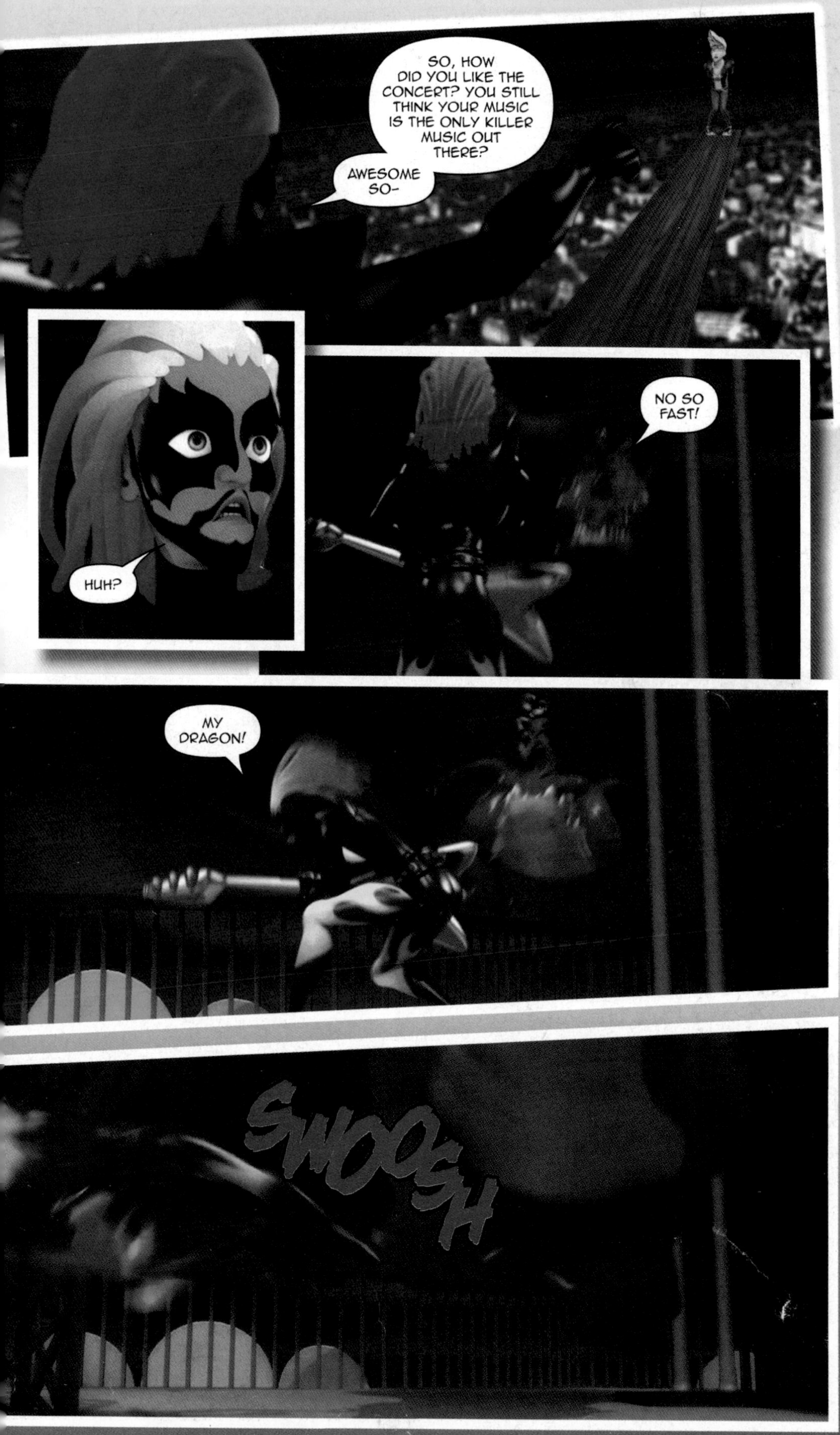
SO, HOW DID YOU LIKE THE CONCERT? YOU STILL THINK YOUR MUSIC IS THE ONLY KILLER MUSIC OUT THERE?
AWESOME SO-
HUH?
NO SO FAST!
MY DRAGON!
SWOOSH

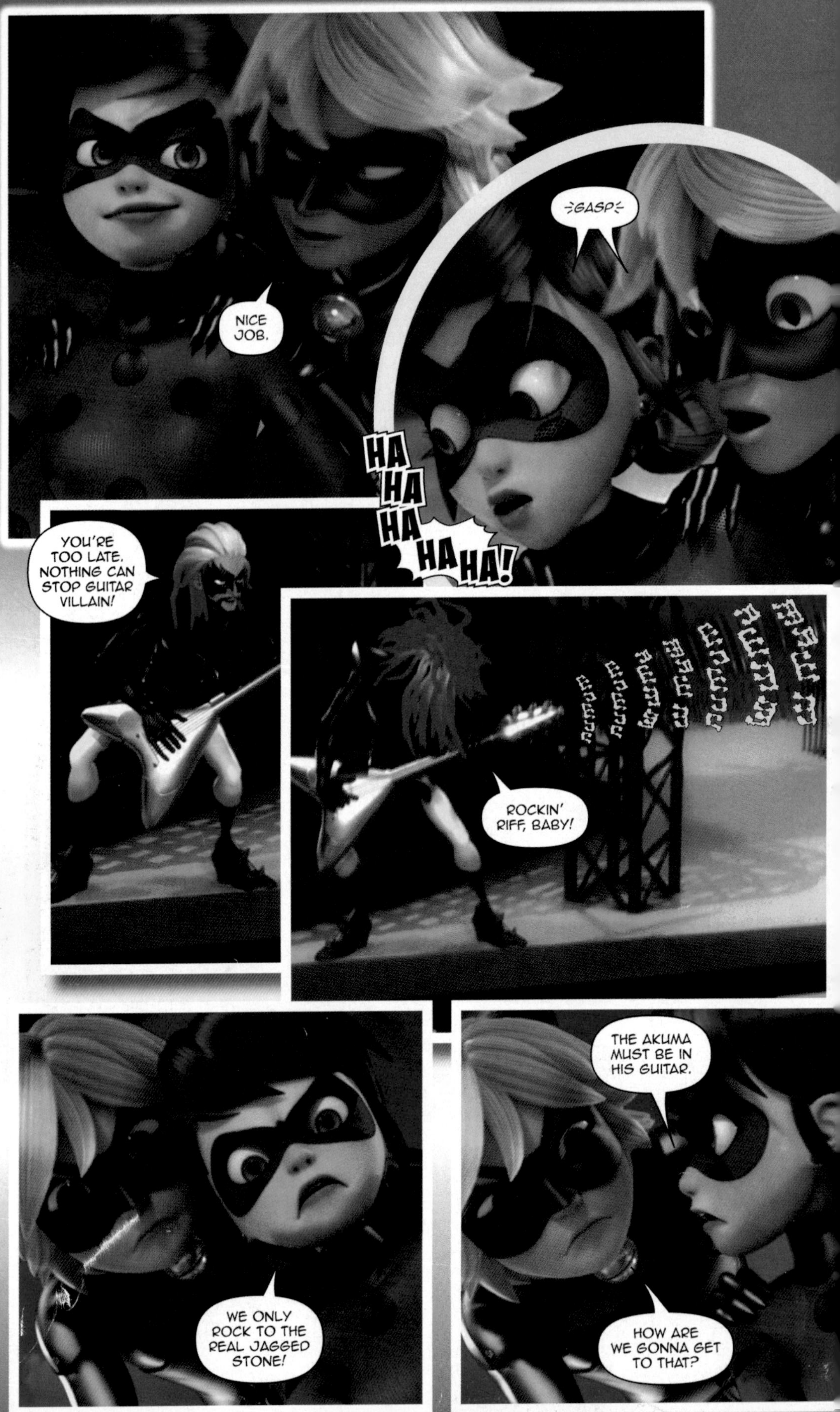
NICE JOB.
GASP
HA HA HA HA HA!
YOU'RE TOO LATE. NOTHING CAN STOP GUITAR VILLAIN!
ROCKIN' RIFF, BABY!
WE ONLY ROCK TO THE REAL JAGGED STONE!
THE AKUMA MUST BE IN HIS GUITAR.
HOW ARE WE GONNA GET TO THAT?

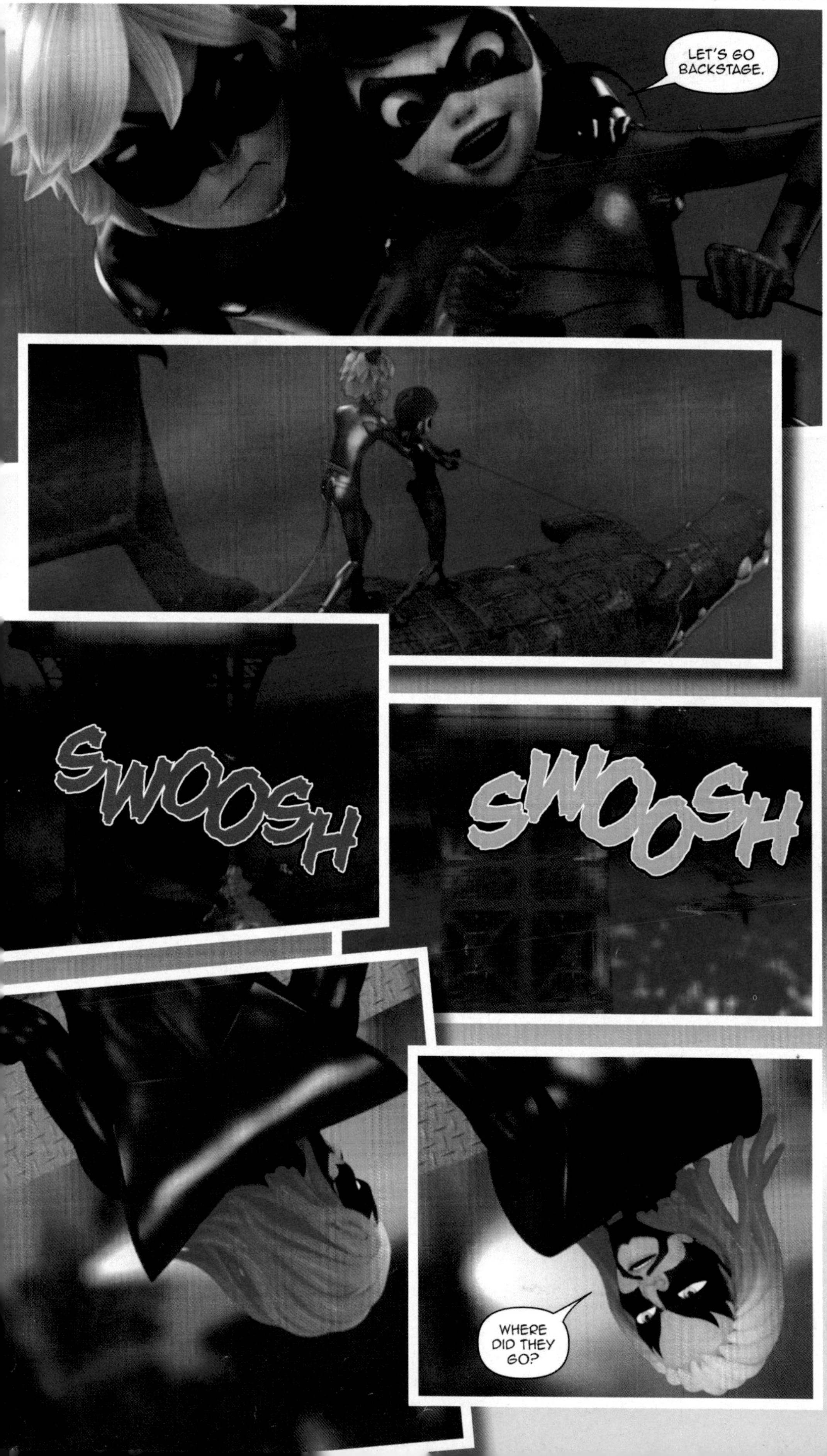
LET'S GO BACKSTAGE.
SWOOSH
SWOOSH
WHERE DID THEY GO?

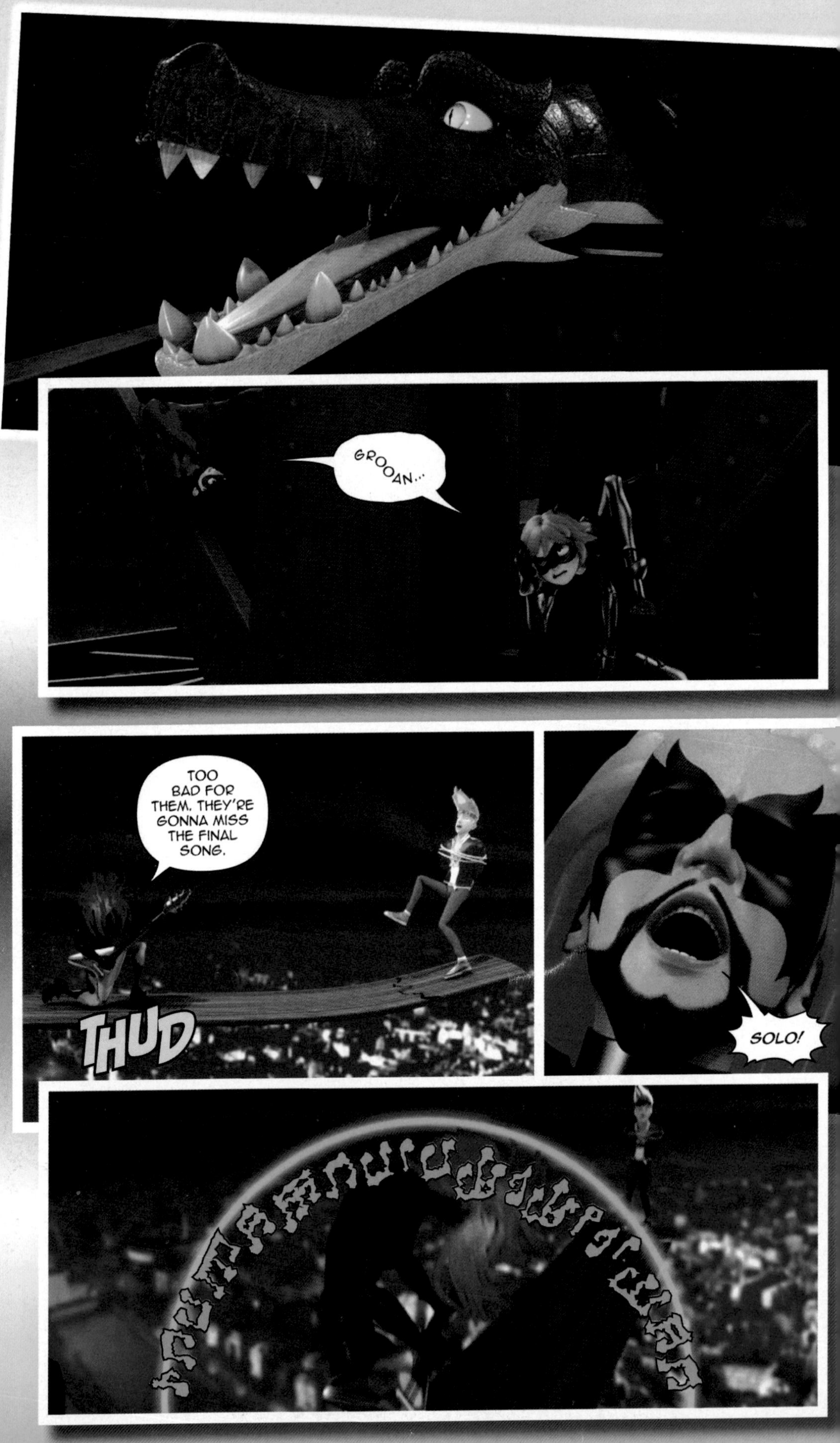
GROOAN...
TOO BAD FOR THEM. THEY'RE GONNA MISS THE FINAL SONG.
THUD
SOLO!

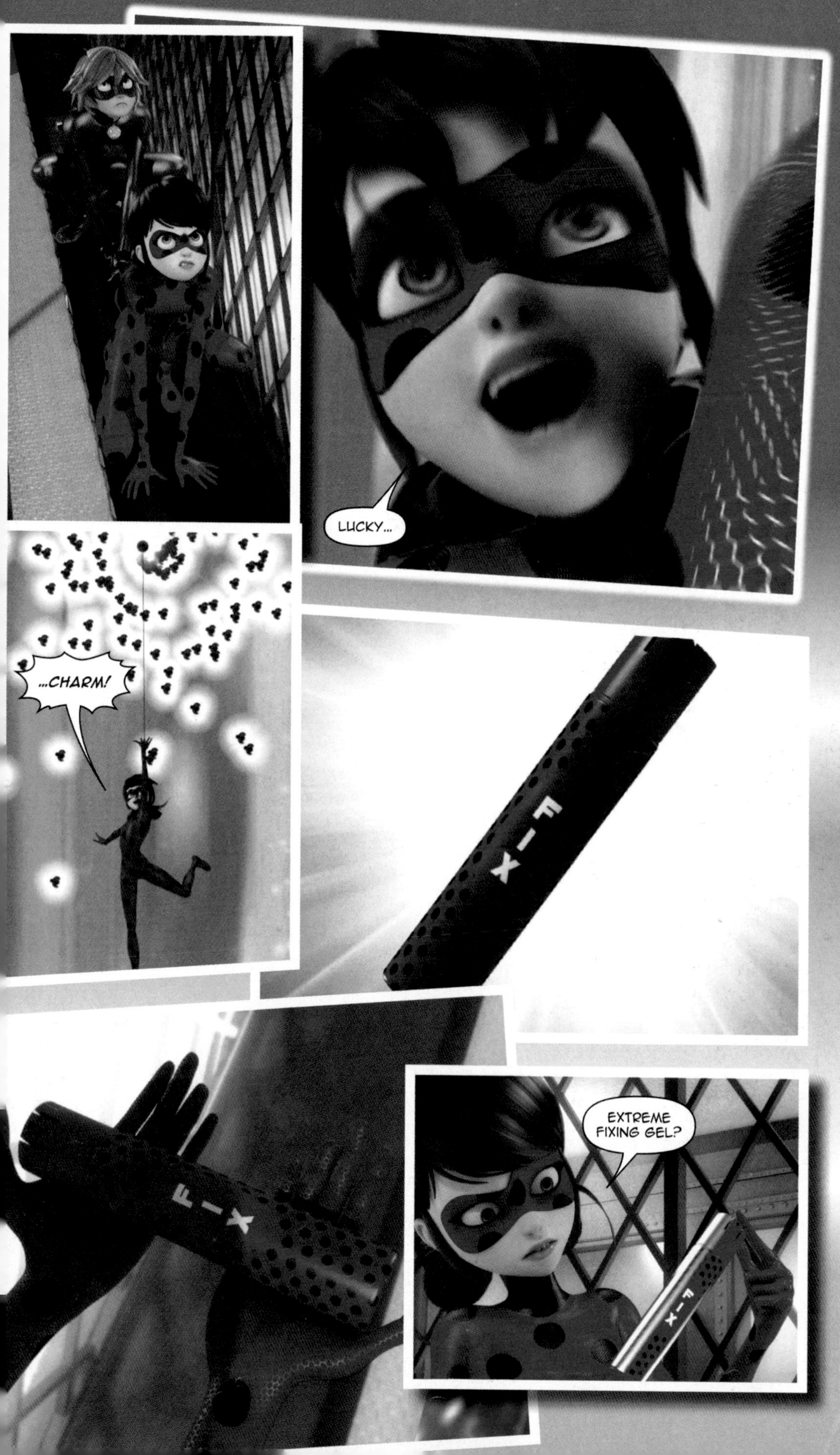
LUCKY...
...CHARM!
EXTREME FIXING GEL?

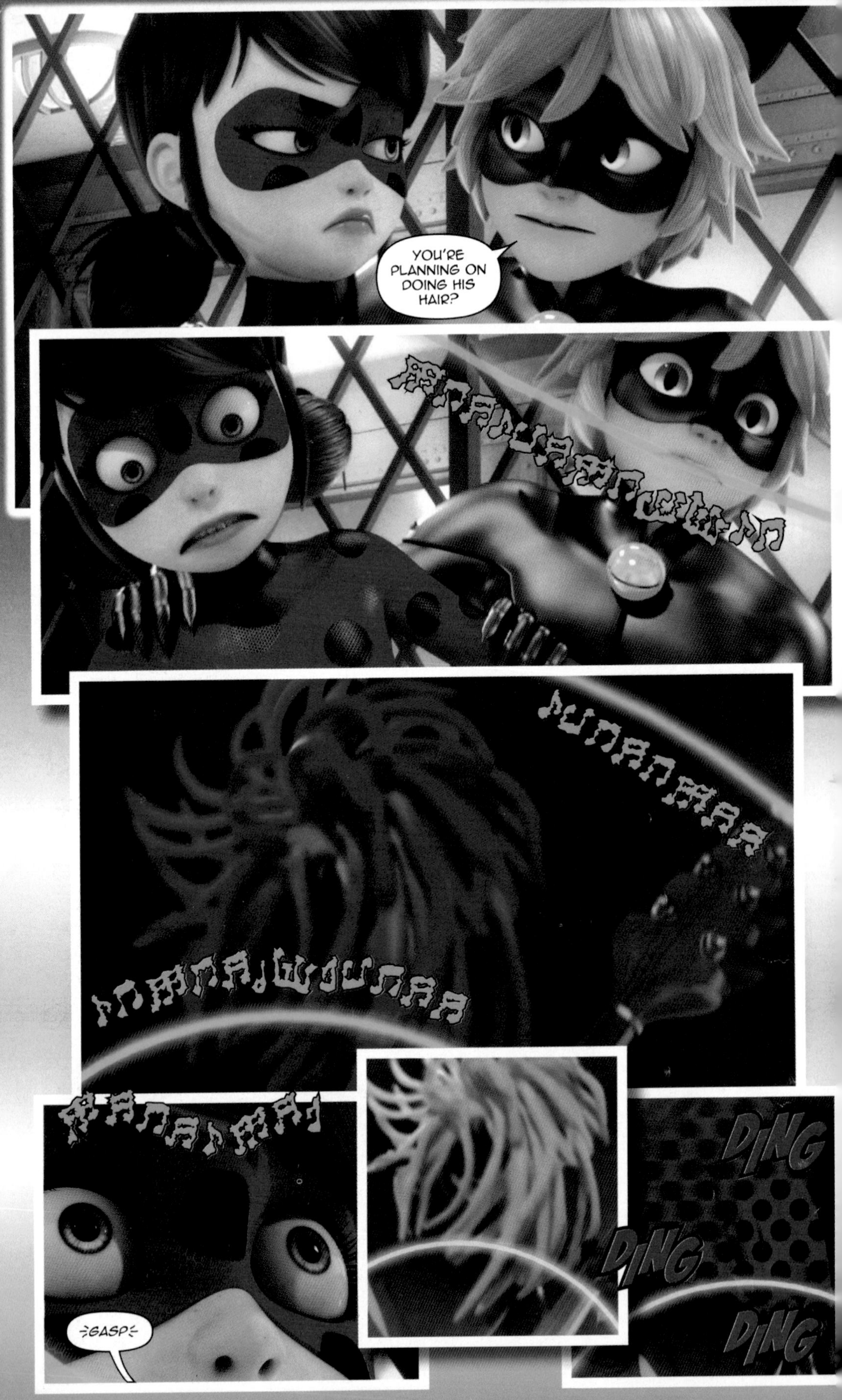
YOU'RE PLANNING ON DOING HIS HAIR?
GASP
DING
DING
DING

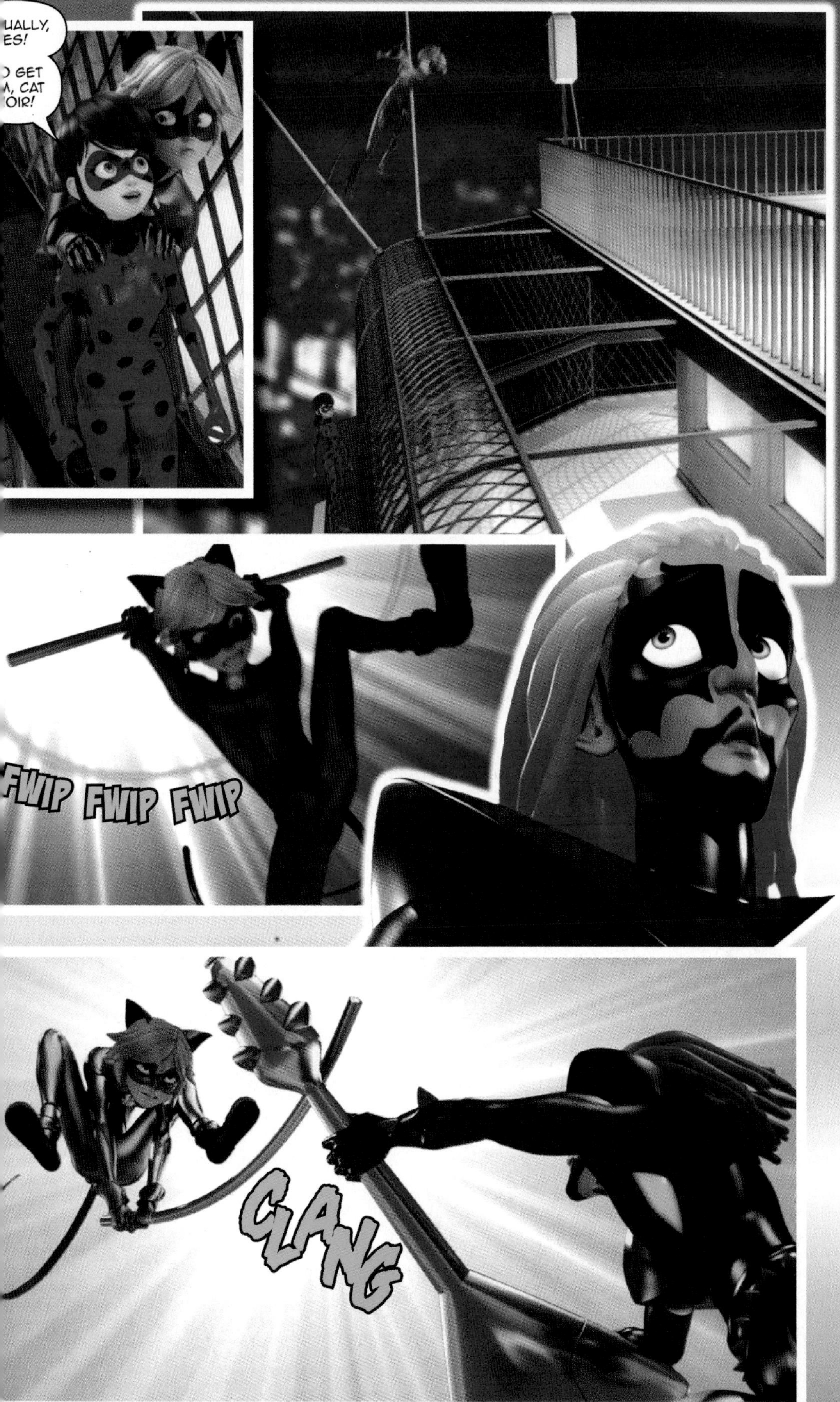
UALLY,
ES!
GET
, CAT
OIR!
FWIP FWIP FWIP
CLANG

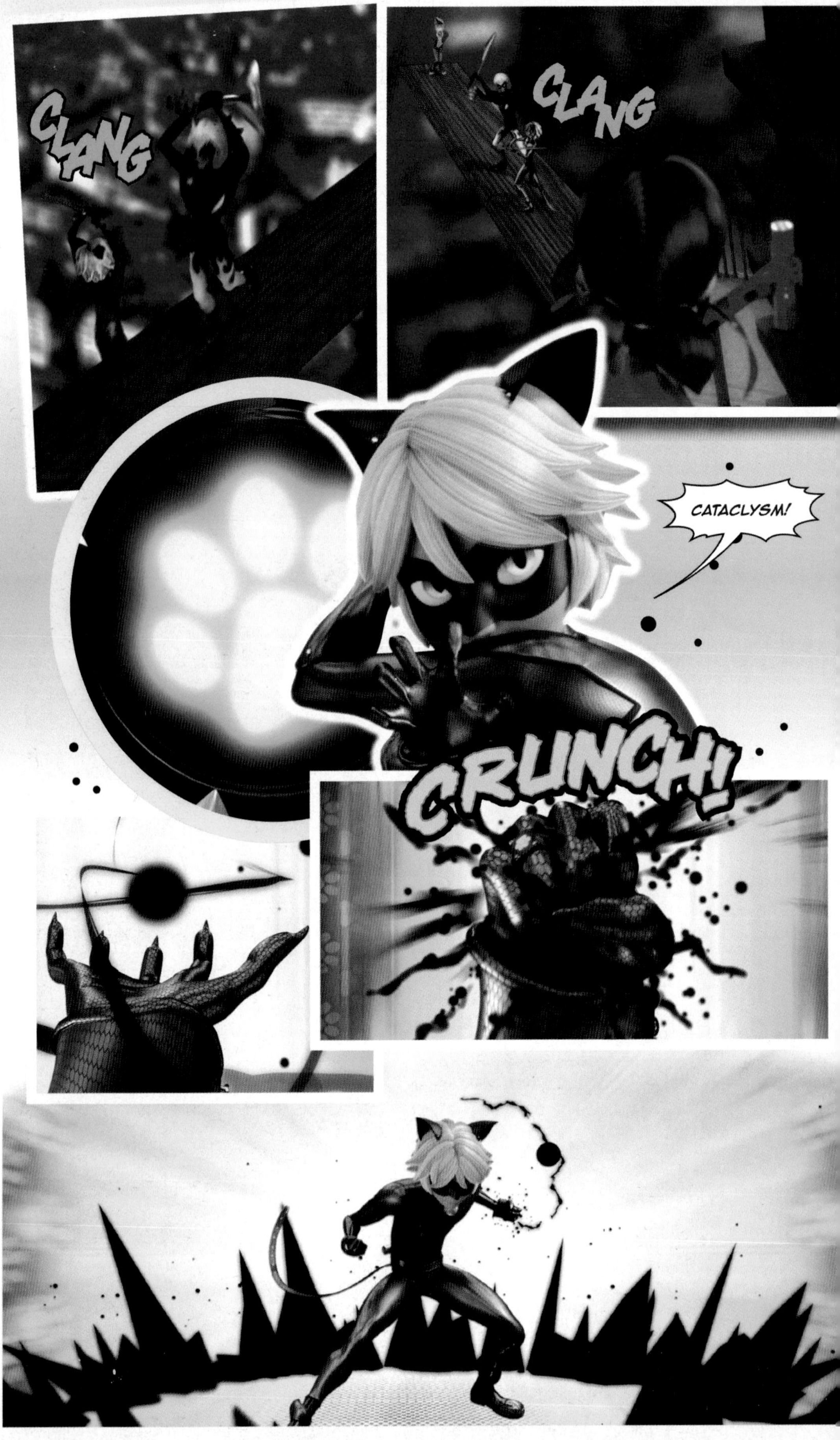
CLANG
CLANG
CATACLYSM!
CRUNCH!

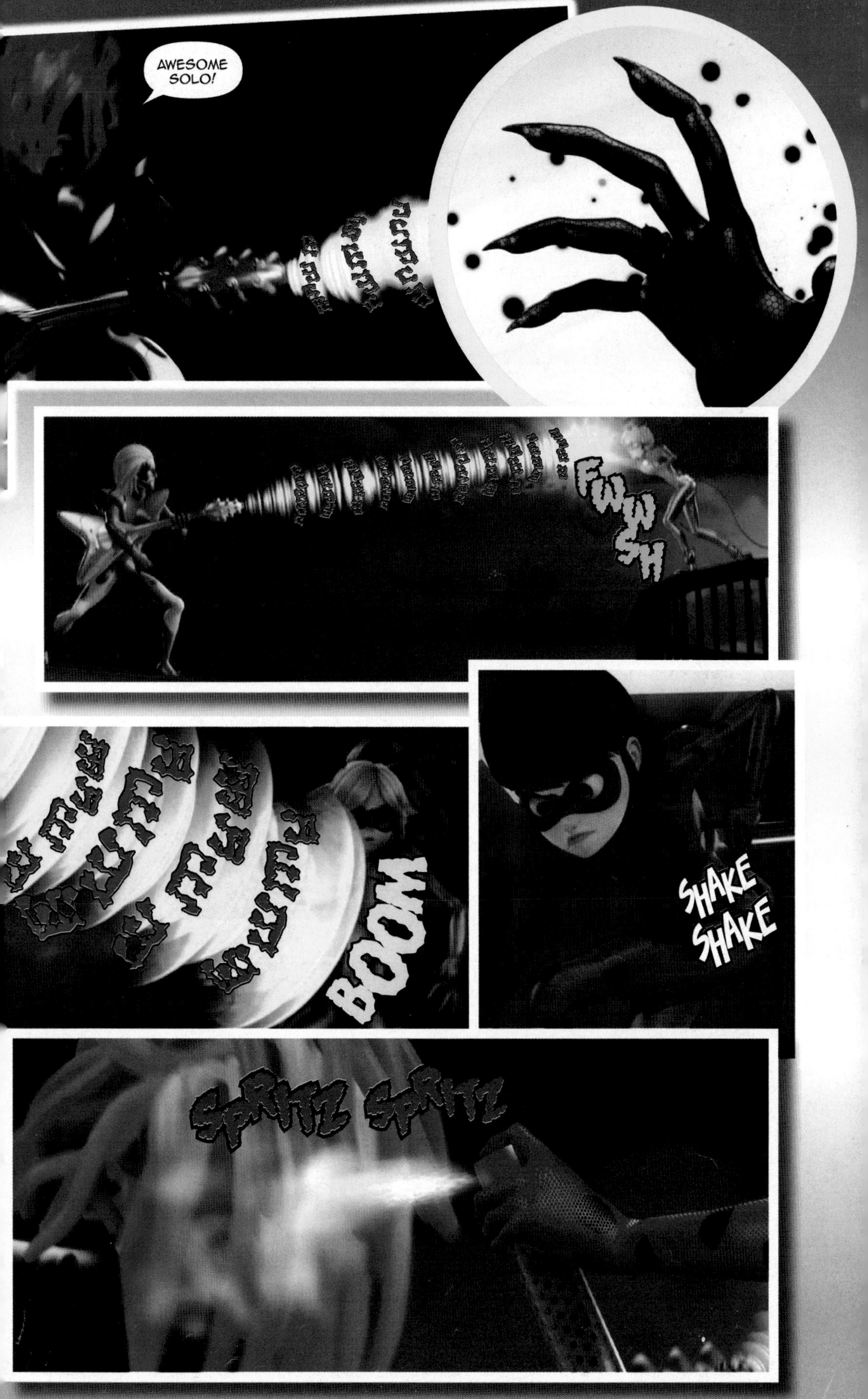
AWESOME SOLO!
FWWSH
BOOM
SHAKE SHAKE
SPRITZ SPRITZ

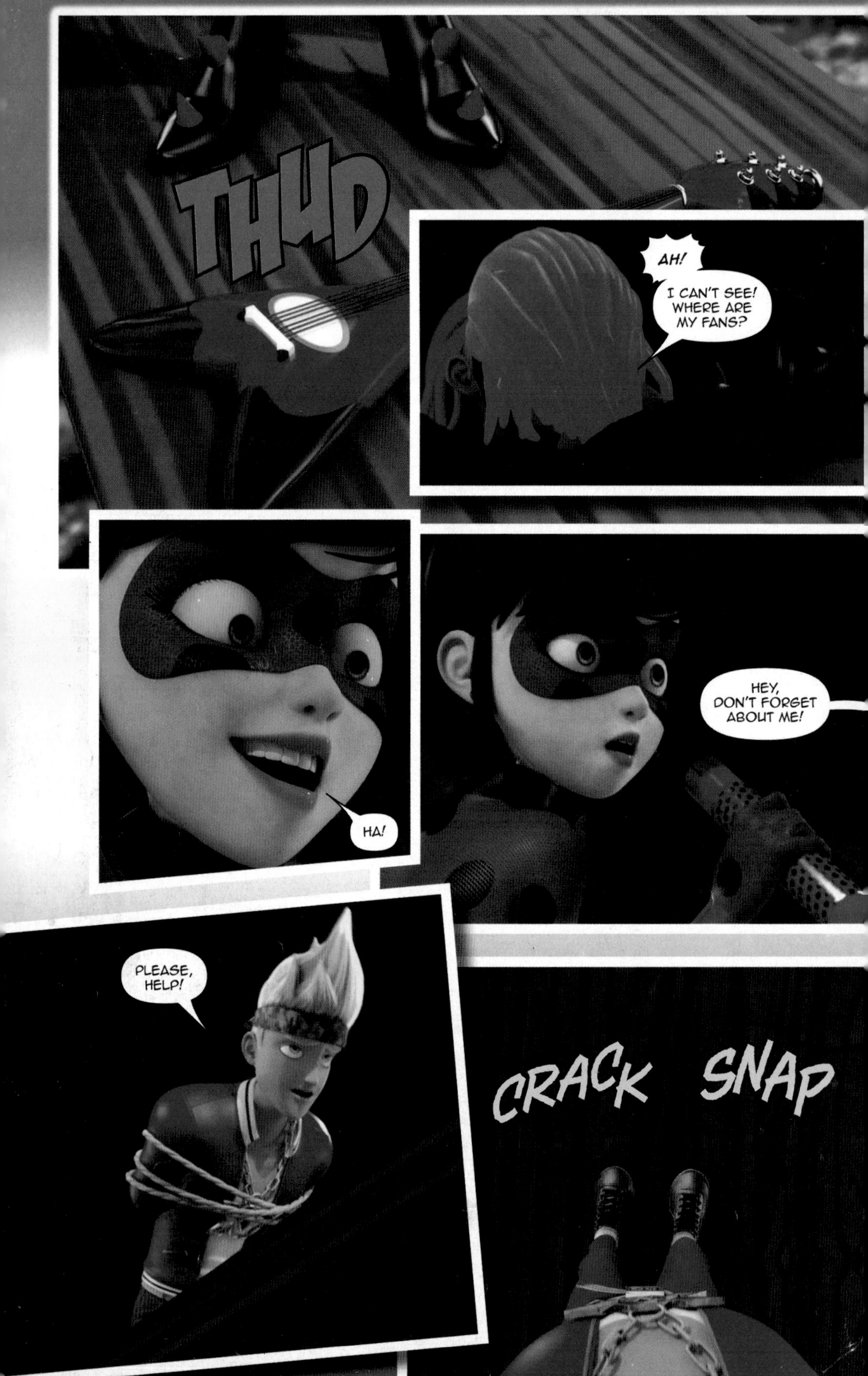
THUD
AH!
I CAN'T SEE! WHERE ARE MY FANS?
HA!
HEY, DON'T FORGET ABOUT ME!
PLEASE, HELP!
CRACK
SNAP

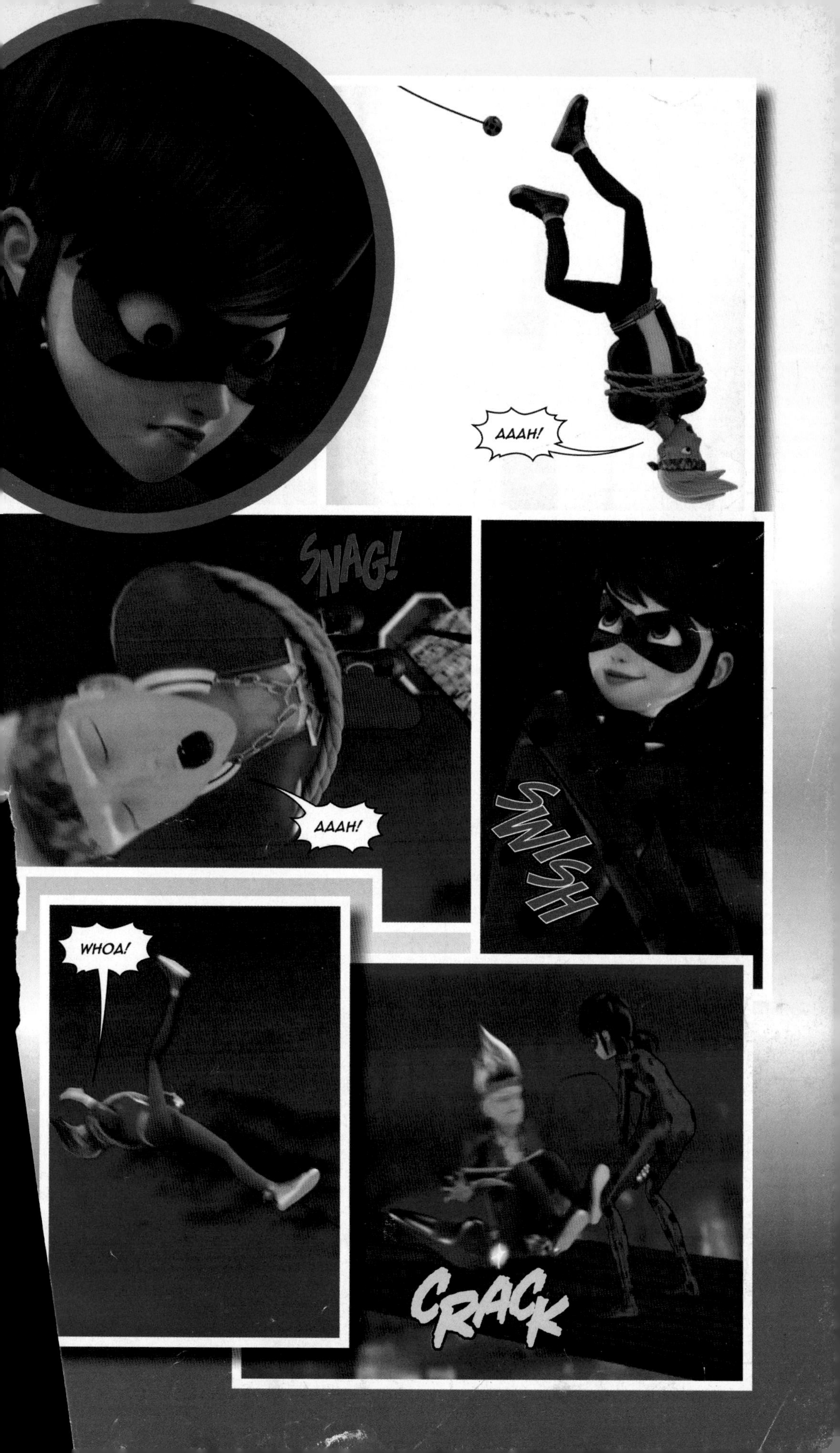
AAAH!
SNAG!
AAAH!
SWISH
WHOA!
CRACK

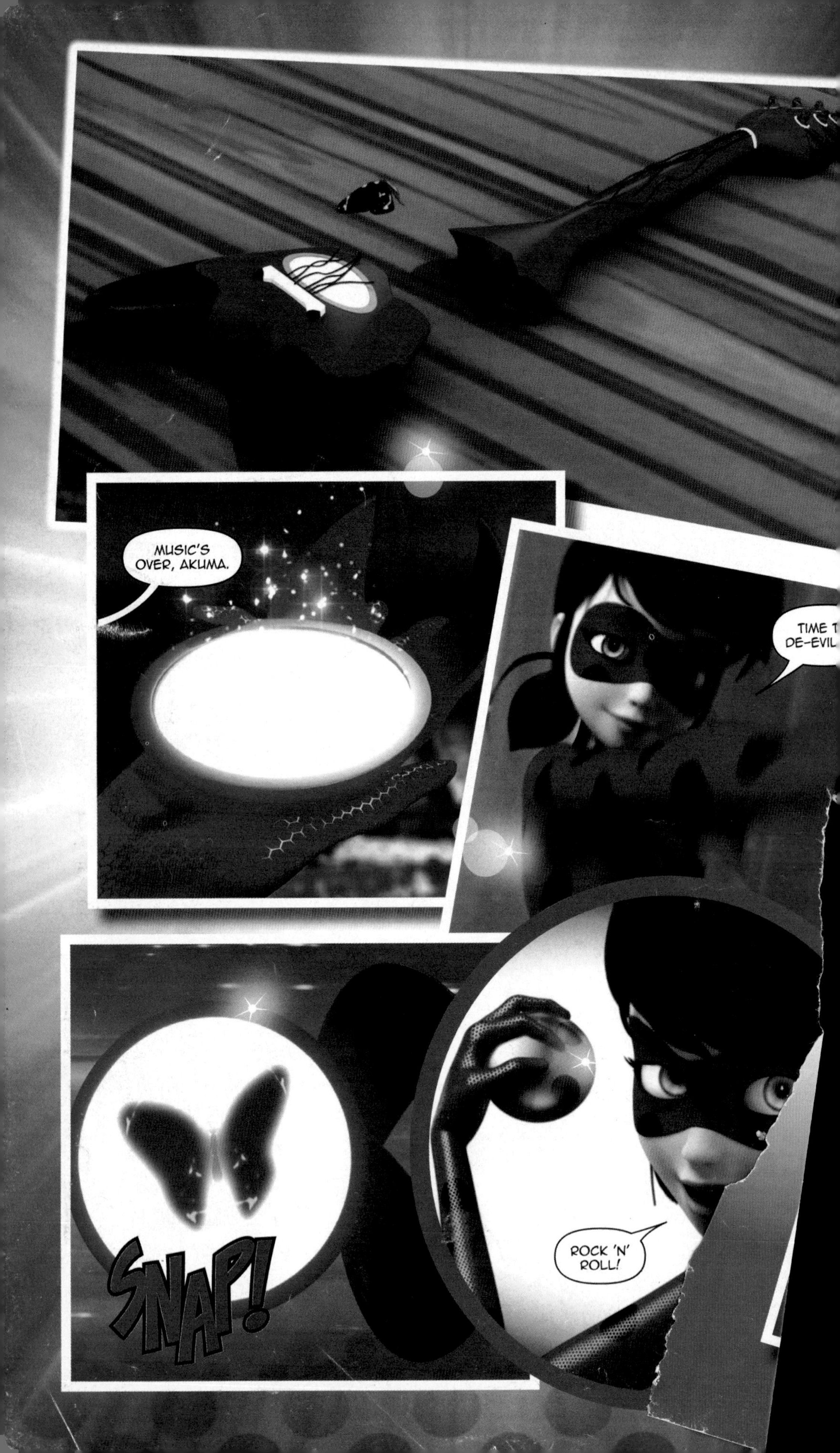
MUSIC'S OVER, AKUMA.
TIME T DE-EVIL
SNAP!
ROCK 'N' ROLL!

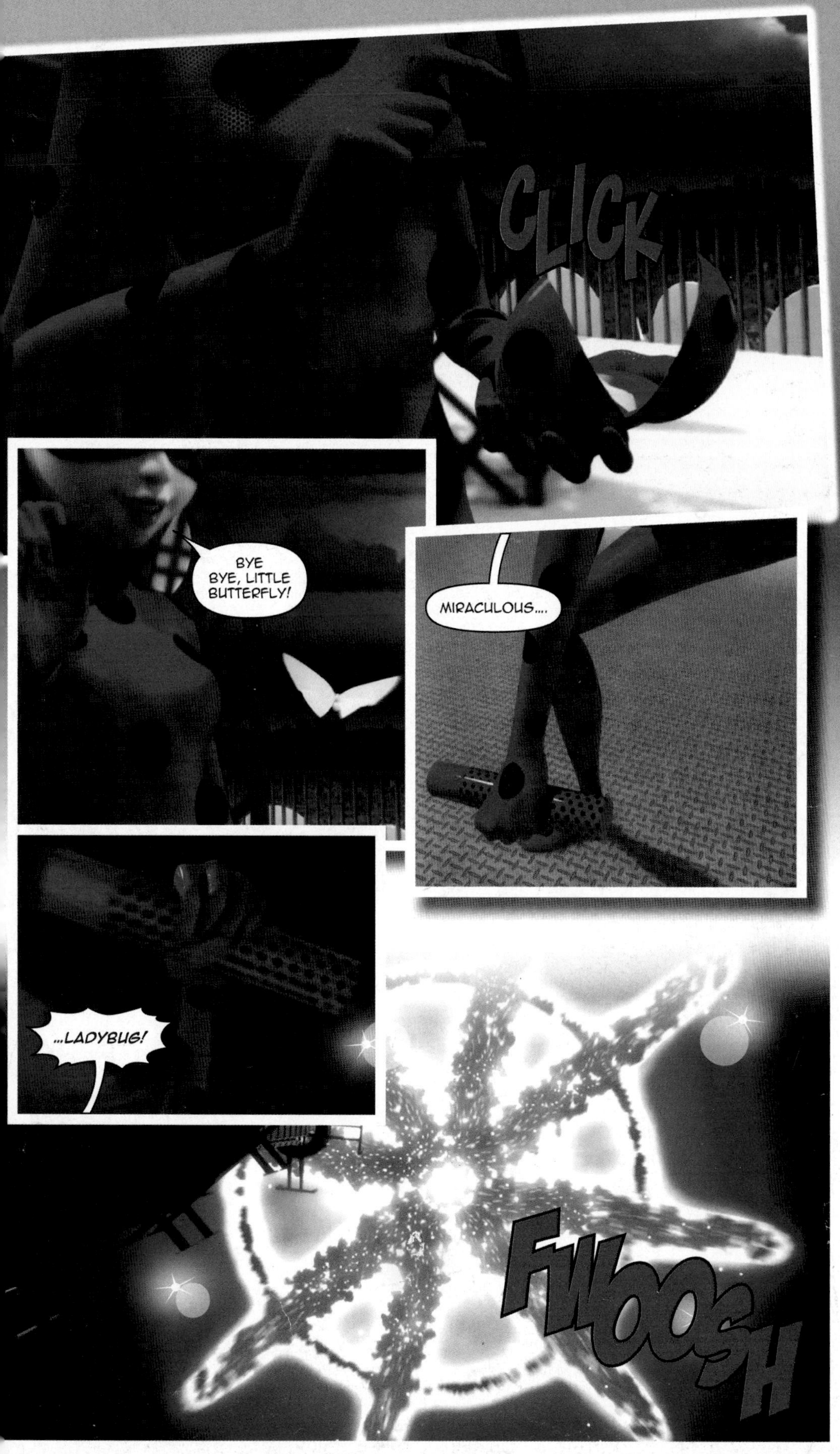
CLICK
BYE BYE, LITTLE BUTTERFLY!
MIRACULOUS....
...LADYBUG!
FWOOSH

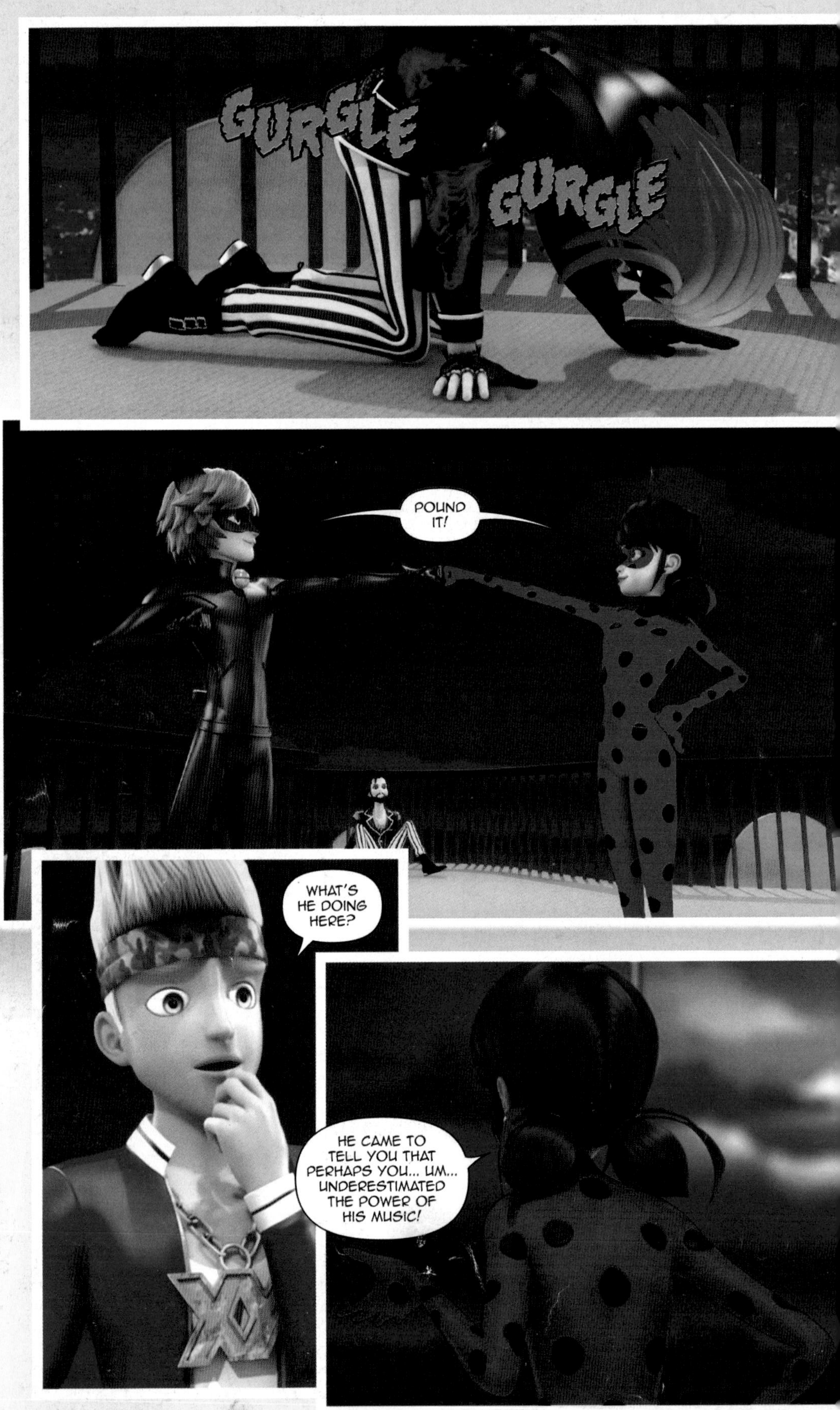
GURGLE
GURGLE
POUND IT!
WHAT'S HE DOING HERE?
HE CAME TO TELL YOU THAT PERHAPS YOU... UM... UNDERESTIMATED THE POWER OF HIS MUSIC!

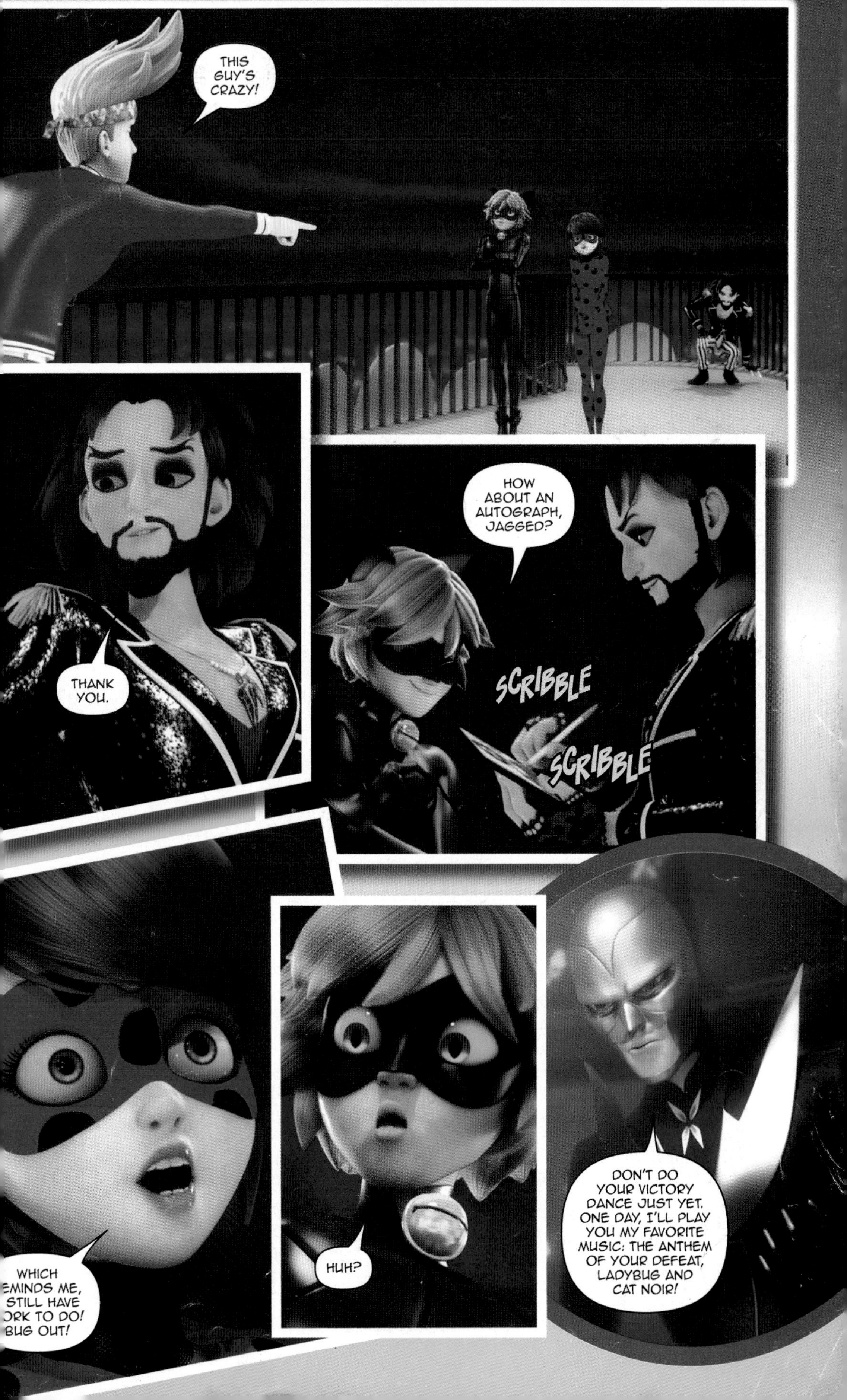
THIS GUY'S CRAZY!
THANK YOU.
HOW ABOUT AN AUTOGRAPH, JAGGED?
SCRIBBLE
SCRIBBLE
WHICH EMINDS ME, STILL HAVE ORK TO DO! BUG OUT!
HUH?
DON'T DO YOUR VICTORY DANCE JUST YET. ONE DAY, I'LL PLAY YOU MY FAVORITE MUSIC: THE ANTHEM OF YOUR DEFEAT, LADYBUG AND CAT NOIR!

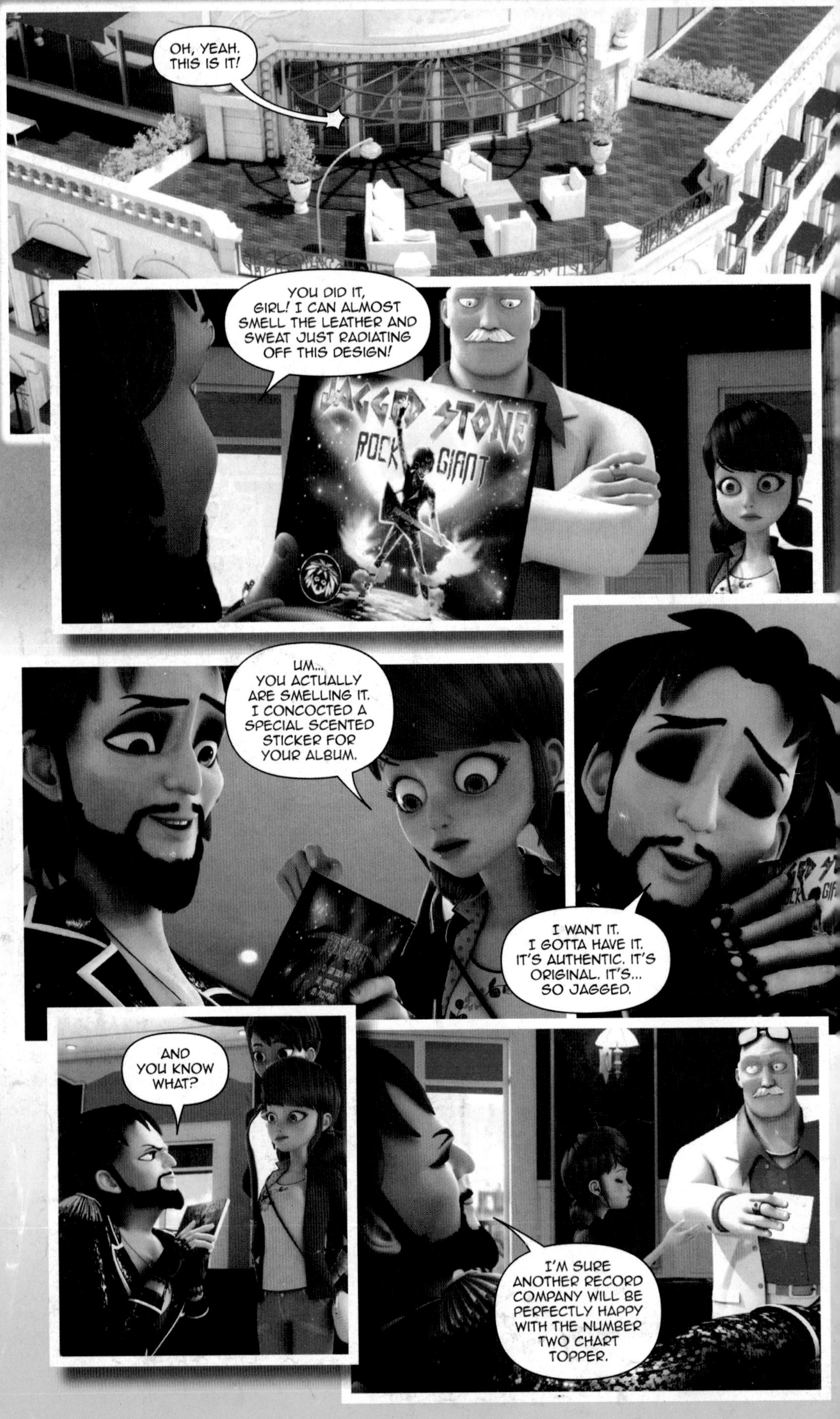
OH, YEAH. THIS IS IT!
YOU DID IT, GIRL! I CAN ALMOST SMELL THE LEATHER AND SWEAT JUST RADIATING OFF THIS DESIGN!
JAGGED STONE
ROCK GIANT
UM... YOU ACTUALLY ARE SMELLING IT. I CONCOCTED A SPECIAL SCENTED STICKER FOR YOUR ALBUM.
I WANT IT. I GOTTA HAVE IT. IT'S AUTHENTIC. IT'S ORIGINAL. IT'S... SO JAGGED.
AND YOU KNOW WHAT?
I'M SURE ANOTHER RECORD COMPANY WILL BE PERFECTLY HAPPY WITH THE NUMBER TWO CHART TOPPER.

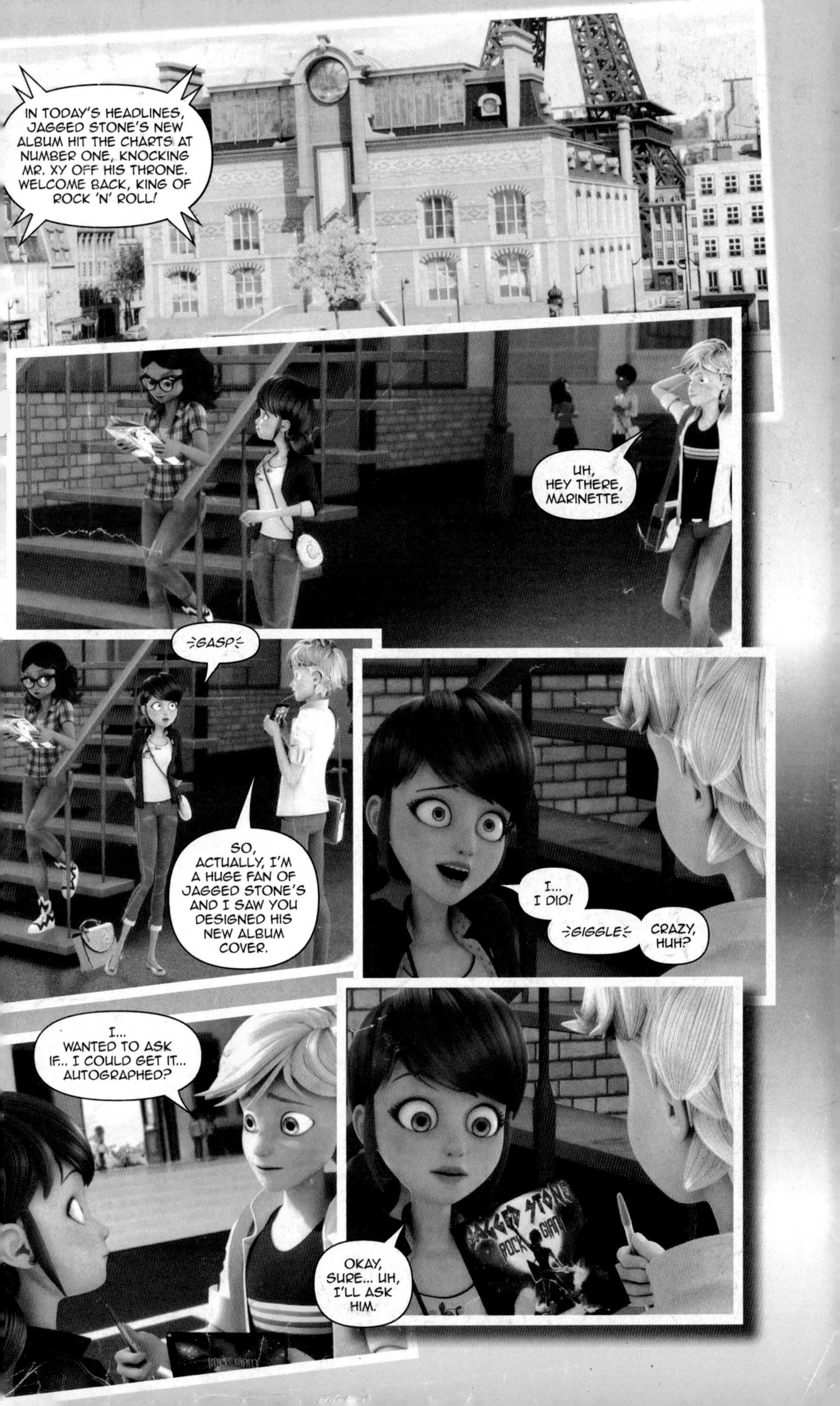
IN TODAY'S HEADLINES, JAGGED STONE'S NEW ALBUM HIT THE CHARTS AT NUMBER ONE, KNOCKING MR. XY OFF HIS THRONE. WELCOME BACK, KING OF ROCK 'N' ROLL!
UH, HEY THERE, MARINETTE.
GASP
SO, ACTUALLY, I'M A HUGE FAN OF JAGGED STONE'S AND I SAW YOU DESIGNED HIS NEW ALBUM COVER.
I... I DID!
GIGGLE
CRAZY, HUH?
I... WANTED TO ASK IF... I COULD GET IT... AUTOGRAPHED?
OKAY, SURE... UH, I'LL ASK HIM.

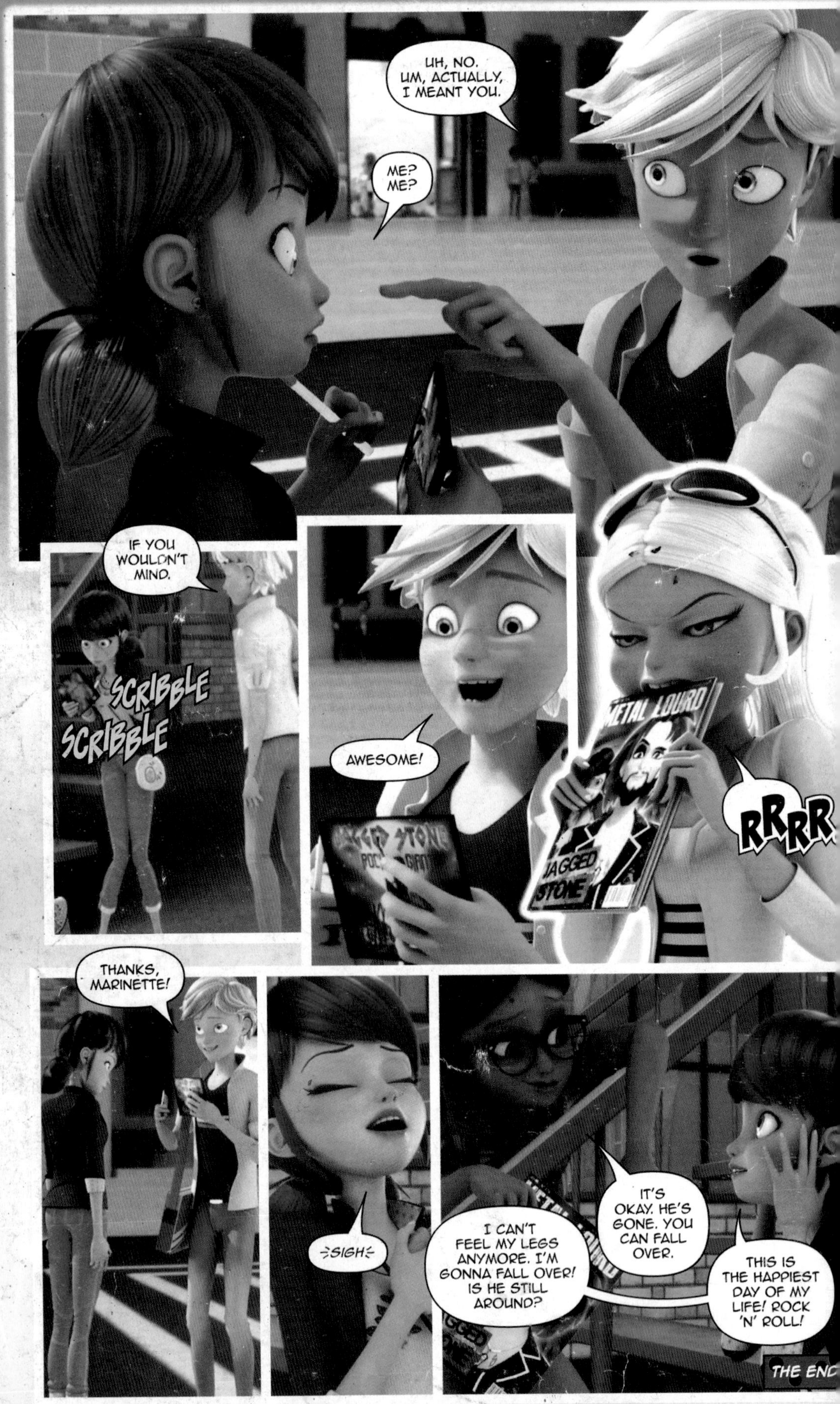
UH, NO. UM, ACTUALLY, I MEANT YOU.
ME? ME?
IF YOU WOULDN'T MIND.
SCRIBBLE SCRIBBLE
AWESOME!
METAL LOURD
JAGGED STONE
RRRR
THANKS, MARINETTE!
SIGH
I CAN'T FEEL MY LEGS ANYMORE. I'M GONNA FALL OVER! IS HE STILL AROUND?
IT'S OKAY. HE'S GONE. YOU CAN FALL OVER.
THIS IS THE HAPPIEST DAY OF MY LIFE! ROCK 'N' ROLL!
THE END